Praise for *New York Times* bestselling author RaeAnne Thayne

"RaeAnne has a knack for capturing those emotions that come from the heart."
—*RT Book Reviews*

"Thayne knows how to write the perfect romance."
—*Frolic* on *The Path to Sunshine Cove*

"RaeAnne Thayne gets better with every book."
—Robyn Carr, #1 *New York Times* bestselling author

Praise for *USA TODAY* bestselling author Michelle Major

"A sheer delight...I loved everything about [*The Magnolia Sisters*]."
—RaeAnne Thayne, *New York Times* bestselling author

"Major spins her storytelling web with a visual narrative that enlivens the majestic beauty of Colorado while telling her heartbreaking tale."
—*RT Book Reviews* on *A Second Chance at Crimson Ranch*

RaeAnne Thayne finds inspiration in the beautiful northern Utah mountains, where the *New York Times* and *USA TODAY* bestselling author lives with her husband and three children. Her books have won numerous honors, including RITA® Award nominations from Romance Writers of America and a Career Achievement Award from *RT Book Reviews*. RaeAnne loves to hear from readers and can be contacted through her website, www.raeannethayne.com.

Michelle Major grew up in Ohio but dreamed of living in the mountains. Soon after graduating with a degree in journalism, she pointed her car west and settled in Colorado. Her life and house are filled with one great husband, two beautiful kids, a few furry pets and several well-behaved reptiles. She's grateful to have found her passion writing stories with happy endings. Michelle loves to hear from her readers at www.michellemajor.com.

New York Times **Bestselling Author**

RAEANNE THAYNE

SNOWFALL IN COLD CREEK

Previously published as *Dalton's Undoing*

HARLEQUIN
BESTSELLING
AUTHOR
COLLECTION

If you purchased this book without a cover you should be aware
that this book is stolen property. It was reported as "unsold and
destroyed" to the publisher, and neither the author nor the
publisher has received any payment for this "stripped book."

**HARLEQUIN®
BESTSELLING
AUTHOR
COLLECTION**

Recycling programs
for this product may
not exist in your area.

ISBN-13: 978-1-335-97994-0

Snowfall in Cold Creek
First published as Dalton's Undoing in 2006. This edition published in 2021.
Copyright © 2006 by RaeAnne Thayne

A Deal Made in Texas
First published in 2018. This edition published in 2021.
Copyright © 2018 by Harlequin Books S.A.

All rights reserved. No part of this book may be used or reproduced in
any manner whatsoever without written permission except in the case of
brief quotations embodied in critical articles and reviews.

This is a work of fiction. Names, characters, places and incidents are
either the product of the author's imagination or are used fictitiously.
Any resemblance to actual persons, living or dead, businesses, companies,
events or locales is entirely coincidental.

This edition published by arrangement with Harlequin Books S.A.

For questions and comments about the quality of this book, please contact
us at CustomerService@Harlequin.com.

Harlequin Enterprises ULC
22 Adelaide St. West, 40th Floor
Toronto, Ontario M5H 4E3, Canada
www.Harlequin.com

Printed in Lithuania

MIX
Paper from
responsible sources
FSC® C021394

CONTENTS

Also available from RaeAnne Thayne

HQN

The Cliff House
The Sea Glass Cottage
Christmas at Holiday House
The Path to Sunshine Cove

Harlequin Special Edition

The Cowboys of Cold Creek

Starstruck
Light the Stars
Dancing in the Moonlight
Dalton's Undoing
The Cowboy's Christmas Miracle
A Cold Creek Homecoming
A Cold Creek Holiday
A Cold Creek Secret
A Cold Creek Baby
Christmas in Cold Creek
A Cold Creek Reunion
A Cold Creek Noel
A Cold Creek Christmas Surprise
A Cold Creek Christmas Story
The Christmas Ranch
The Holiday Gift
The Rancher's Christmas Song

Visit her Author Profile page at Harlequin.com,
or raeannethayne.com, for more titles!

SNOWFALL
IN COLD CREEK

RaeAnne Thayne

To Jared, for twenty-six wonderful years filled with joy and laughter and midnight trips to the store when I run out of printer ink. I love you dearly!

Chapter 1

Some little punk was stealing his car.

Seth Dalton stood on the sidewalk in front of his mother's house, the puppy leashes in his hand forgotten, and watched three years of sweat, passion and hard work take off down the road with a flash of tail lights and the squeal of rubber.

Son of a bitch.

He stood looking after it for maybe fifteen seconds, trying to comprehend how anybody in Podunk Pine Gulch would have the stones to steal his 1969 Matador red GTO convertible.

Who in town could possibly be stupid enough to dream he could get more than a block or two without somebody sitting up and taking notice that Seth wasn't the one behind the wheel and raising the alarm?

Just how far did the bastard think he would get? Not very, if Seth had anything to say about it. He'd worked too hard on his baby to let some sleazebag drive her away.

"Come on, kids. Fun's over." He jerked the leashes, grateful the dogs weren't in midpee, and dragged the two brindle Australian herder pups up the sidewalk and back into the house.

Inside, the members of his family were crowded around his mother's dining-room table playing one of their cutthroat games of Risk.

Looked like Jake and Maggie were kicking butt. No surprise there, with his middle brother's conniving brain and his wife's military experience. The Dalton clan was in its usual teams, Jake and Maggie against his mother and stepfather, with his oldest brother, Wade, and wife, Caroline, making up the third team.

That was the very reason he'd volunteered to take the puppies out for their business in the first place. It was a little lonely being the solitary player on his side of the table. Usually he teamed up with Natalie—but it was a little disheartening to find his nine-year-old niece made a more cutthroat general than he. She was in the family room watching a DVD with her brothers, anyway.

The only one who looked up from strategizing was his mother.

"Back so soon? That was fast!" Marjorie crooned the words, not to him but to the puppies—or her half of the dynamic duo anyway. She picked up the birthday gift he'd given her and nuzzled the little male pup.

"You're so good. Aren't you so good? Yes, you are. Come give Mommy a birthday kiss."

"Don't have time, sorry," Seth said drily.

He ignored the face she made at him and reached for the keys to Wade's pickup from the breakfast bar.

"I'm taking your truck," he called on his way out the door.

Wade looked up, a frown of concentration on his tough features. "You're what?"

He paused at the door. "Don't have time to explain, but I need your truck. I'll be back. Mom, keep an eye on Lucy for me."

"I just washed that truck," his brother growled. "Don't bring it back all muddy and skanky."

He wasn't even going to dignify that with a response, he decided, as he headed down the stairs. He didn't have the time, even if he could have come up with a sharp response.

Wade's truck rumbled to life, smooth and well-tuned like everything in Seth's oldest brother's life. He threw it in gear and roared off in the direction the punk had taken his car.

If he were stealing a car, which road would he take? Pine Gulch didn't offer a lot of escape routes. Turning south would lead him through the houses and small business district of Pine Gulch. To the east was the rugged western slope of the Teton Mountains, which left him north and west.

He took a chance and opted to head north, where the quiet road stretched past ranches and farms with little traffic to notice someone in a red muscle car.

He ought to just call the police and report the theft. Chasing after a car thief on his own like this was probably crazy, but he wasn't in the mood to be sensible, not with thirty thousand dollars' worth of sheer horsepower disappearing before his eyes.

He pushed Wade's truck to sixty-five, keeping his eye out in the gathering twilight for any sign of another vehicle.

His efforts were rewarded just a moment later when he followed the curve of the road past Sam Purdy's pond and saw a flash of red up ahead.

His brother's one-ton pickup rumbled as he poured on the juice and accelerated to catch the little bugger.

With its 400-cubic-inch V8 and the three hundred and fifty horses straining under the hood, the GTO could go a hundred and thirty without breaking a sweat. Oddly enough, whoever had boosted it wasn't pushing her harder than maybe forty.

His baby puttered along fifteen miles below the speed limit and Seth had no problem catching up with her, wondering as he did if there was some kind of roving gang of senior-citizen car thieves on the loose he hadn't heard about.

He kept a respectable two-car length between them as the road twisted again. He knew this road and knew that just ahead was a straightaway that ran a couple of miles past farmland with no houses.

He couldn't see any oncoming traffic so he pulled into the other lane as if to pass and drew up alongside his baby, intent on getting a look at the thief.

He *was* a punk, nothing more. The kid behind the wheel was skinny, dark-haired, maybe fifteen, sixteen. He looked over at the big rumbling pickup beside him and he looked scared to death, eyes huge and wild in a narrow face.

Good. He should be, the little dickhead. Seth rolled the window down, wishing he could reach across, pluck the kid out of the car and wring his scrawny little neck.

"Pull over," he shouted through the window, even though he knew the kid wouldn't be able to hear him.

He must have looked like the Grim Reaper, Freddy Kruger and the guy from *The Texas Chainsaw Massacre* all rolled up into one, he realized later, and he should have predicted what happened next. If he'd been thinking straight, he would have handled the whole thing differently and saved himself a hell of a lot of trouble.

Even if the car thief couldn't hear Seth's words, obviously

the message got through loud and clear. The kid sent him another wild, scared look and yanked the wheel to the right.

Seth growled out a raw epithet at the hideous sound of metal grinding against metal as the GTO scraped a mile marker post on the right. In reaction, the kid panicked and swerved too hard to the left and Seth groaned as his baby nosedived across the road and landed in an irrigation ditch.

At least it was blessedly empty this time of year.

The sun was just a sliver above the horizon and the November air was cold as Seth hurriedly parked the pickup and rushed to his car to make sure the kid was okay.

He jerked open the door and was petty enough for just a moment to enjoy the way the kid cringed against the seat like he thought Seth was ready to break his neck with his bare hands.

He felt like it, he had to admit. He had no doubt the GTO's paint was scraped all to hell from the run-in with the mile marker post and the left fender looked to be crumpled where she'd hit a concrete gate structure in the ditch.

He held on to his anger while he checked the thief for any sign of injury.

"You okay?" he asked.

"Yeah. I...think so." The boy's voice shook a little but he warily took Seth's hand and climbed out of the car.

Seth revised downward his estimate of the boy's age, figuring him to be no older than thirteen or fourteen. Just old enough to start shaving more than once a month, by the look of it.

He had choppy dark hair worn longer than Hank Dalton would ever have let *his* sons get away with and he was dressed in jeans and a gray hooded sweatshirt about four sizes too big with some logo of a wild-looking music group Seth didn't recognize.

The kid seemed familiar but Seth couldn't immediately place him—odd, since he knew just about every kid in the small community. Maybe he was the son of one of the dozen or so Hollywood types buying up good grazing land for their faux ranches. They tended to stay away from the general population, maybe afraid the down-home friendliness and family-centered values would rub off.

"My mom is gonna kill me," the kid moaned, burying his head in his hands.

"She can stand in line," Seth growled. "You have any idea how much work I've put into this car?"

The kid dropped his hands. Though he still looked terrified, he managed to cover it with a thin veneer of bravado. "You'll be sorry if you mess with me. My grandpa's a lawyer and he'll fry your ass if you try to lay a single hand on me."

Seth couldn't help a short, appreciative laugh even as the pieces clicked into place and he registered who the kid must be and why he had looked familiar.

With a grandfather who was a lawyer, he had to be the son of the new elementary school principal. Boylan. Boyer. Something like that.

He didn't exactly hang around with the elementary-school crowd but Natalie had pointed out her new principal and the woman's two kids one night shortly after school started when he'd taken his niece and nephews out to Stoney's, the pizza place in town.

His grandfather would be Jason Chambers, an attorney who had retired to Pine Gulch for the fishing five or six years back. His daughter had moved out to join him with her kids—no husband that Seth had heard about—when the principal position opened up at the elementary school.

"That lawyer in the family will probably come in handy, kid," he said now.

The punk groaned and his head sagged into his hands once more. "I am so dead."

He wasn't quite sure why but Seth was surprised to feel a few little pangs of sympathy for the kid. He remembered all too well the purgatory of this age. Hormones firing, emotions jerking around wildly. Too much juice and nothing to do with it.

"Am I going to jail?"

"You boosted a car. That's a pretty serious crime. And you're a lousy driver, which is worse, in my book."

"I wasn't going to take her far. You've got to believe me. Just to the reservoir and back, I swear. That's all. When I saw the keys inside, I couldn't resist."

Damn. Had he really left the keys in the ignition? He looked inside and, sure enough, there they were, dangling from the steering column.

How had that happened? He remembered pulling up to his mother's house for her birthday dinner, then rushing out to take care of business when Lucy started to squat on the floor mats. Maybe in all the confusion, he had been in such a hurry to find a patch of grass before his puppy busted her bladder that he'd forgotten his keys.

What kind of idiot left his keys in a ride like this, just begging for the first testosterone-crazed teenager to lift her?

Him. He mentally groaned, grateful at least that the boy hadn't been hurt by their combined stupidity.

"What's your name, kid?"

The boy clamped his teeth together and Seth sighed. "You might as well tell me. I know your last name is Boyer and Jason Chambers is your grandpa. I'll figure out the rest."

"Cole," he muttered after a long pause.

"Come on, Cole. I'll give you a lift to your grandpa's house, then I'll come back and pull her out with one of my brothers."

"I can walk." He hunched his shoulders and shoved his hands in the pocket of his hooded sweatshirt.

"You think I'm going to leave you and your sticky fingers running free out here? What if you happen to find another idiot who's left his keys in his ride? Get in."

Though Cole still looked belligerent, he climbed into the passenger side of the pickup.

Seth had just started to walk around the truck to get in the driver's side when he saw flashing lights behind him.

Instead of driving past, the sheriff's deputy slowed and pulled up behind the GTO. Seth glanced at the boy and saw he'd turned deathly white and his breathing was coming fast enough Seth worried about him hyperventilating.

"Relax, kid," he muttered.

"I am relaxed." He lifted his chin and tried for a cool look that came out looking more like a constipated rabbit.

Seth sighed and closed his door again as he watched the deputy climb out of the vehicle. Before he even saw her face, he knew by the curvy shape that the officer had to be Polly Jardine, the only female deputy in the small sheriff's department.

She dimpled at him, looking not much different than she had in high school—cute and perky and worlds away from his idea of an officer of the law. Though she still looked like she should be shaking her pom-poms at a Friday night football game, he knew she was a tough and dedicated cop.

He imagined she inspired more than a few naughty fantasies around town involving those handcuffs dangling from her belt. But since her husband was linebacker-huge and also on the sheriff's department—and they were crazy about each other—those fantasies would only ever be that.

"Hey Seth. I thought that was your car. Man! What happened? You take the turn a little too fast?"

His gaze shifted quickly to the boy inside the truck then quickly back to Polly, hoping she hadn't noticed. He found himself strangely reluctant to throw Cole Boyer into the system.

"Something like that," he murmured.

She followed his gaze to the boy and speculation suddenly narrowed her eyes. "You sure that's the whole story?"

He leaned a hip against the truck, tilted his head and gave her a slow smile. "Would I lie to an officer of the law, darlin'?"

"Six ways from Sunday, *darlin'*." Though her words were tart, she smiled in a way that told him she remembered with fondness the few times they'd fooled around under the bleachers before Mitch Jardine moved into town and she had eyes for no one else. "But it's your car. If that's the way you want to play this, I won't argue with you."

"Thanks, Pol. I owe you."

"That's the new principal's kid, isn't it?"

He nodded.

"We've had a few run-ins with him in the few months they've been in town," she said. "Nothing big, breaking curfew, that kind of thing. You sure letting him off is the right thing to do for him? Today a joyride, tomorrow a bank robbery."

He didn't know anything except he couldn't bring himself to turn him in.

"For now."

"Let me know if you change your mind. I'm supposed

to file an accident report but I'll just pretend I didn't see anything."

He nodded and waved goodbye then climbed into the truck. Cole Boyer watched him, his green eyes wary. "Am I going to jail?"

"No. Not today, anyway."

"Friggin' A!"

"Don't be so quick with the celebration there," he warned. "A week or two in juvie is probably going to look pretty damn good by the time your mother and grandfather get through with you. And that doesn't even take into account what you'll have to do to even the score with me."

She was late. As usual.

In one motion, Jenny Boyer shoved on slingbacks and shrugged into her favorite brocade jacket.

"Listen to Grandpa while I'm gone, okay?" she said, head tilted while she thrust a pair of conservative gold hoops into her ears.

"I always do." Morgan, her nine-year-old, going on fifty, sniffed just like a society matron finding something undesirable in her tea. "Cole is the one who doesn't like authority figures."

Didn't she just know it? Jenny sighed. "Well, make sure he listens to Grandpa, too."

Morgan folded her arms and raised an eyebrow. "I'll try, but I don't think he'll pay attention to either me or Grandpa."

Probably not, she conceded. Nobody seemed to be able to get through to Cole. She'd thought moving to Idaho to live with her father would help stabilize her son, at least get him away from the undesirable elements in Seattle who were leading him into all kinds of trouble.

She had hoped his grandfather would give the boy the male role model he had lost with his own father's desertion. So much for that. Though Jason tried, Cole was so angry and bitter at the world—more furious with her now for uprooting him from his friends and moving him to this backwater than he was with his father for moving to another continent.

She glanced at her watch and groaned. The school board meeting started in ten minutes and she was scheduled to give a PowerPoint presentation outlining her efforts to raise the elementary school's performance on standardized testing. This was her first big meeting with the school board and she couldn't afford to blow it.

The therapist she'd gone to after the divorce suggested Jenny's chronic tardiness indicated some form of passive aggression, her way of governing a life that often felt beyond her control.

Jenny just figured she was too busy chasing after her hundreds of constantly spinning plates.

"I've got to run, baby. I'll be home before you go to sleep, I promise." She kissed her on the forehead, wondering as she headed out of her room if she had time to hurry down to the basement to say goodbye to Cole. No, she decided. Besides her time crunch, any conversation between them these days ended in a fight and she wasn't sure she was up for another one tonight.

"Bye, Dad," she called down the hall as she grabbed her laptop case and her purse. "Thanks for watching them!"

"Don't worry about a thing." Jason Chambers appeared in the doorway, wearing his favorite Ducks Unlimited sweater and jeans that made him look far younger than his sixty-five years. "Give 'em hell."

She mustered a distracted smile, grateful all over again that they'd been able to move past their complicated, stiff relationship of the past and find some measure of peace when she moved to Pine Gulch.

Juggling her bags and her keys, she yanked open the door and rushed out, then gave a shriek when she collided with a solid, warm male.

With a little gasp, Jenny righted herself, registering the muscles in that hard frame that seemed as immovable as the Tetons. "I'm sorry! I didn't see you."

She knew who he was, of course. What woman in Pine Gulch didn't? With that slow, sexy smile and those brilliant blue eyes that seemed to see right into a woman's psyche to all her deepest desires, Seth Dalton was a difficult man to overlook.

Not that she didn't try her best. The youngest Dalton was exactly the kind of man she tried to avoid at all cost. She'd had more than enough, thank you very much, of smooth charmers who swept a woman off her feet with flowers and champagne only to leave her dangling there, hanging by her fingernails when they decide young French pastries are more to their taste.

What earthly reason would Dalton have for showing up at her doorstep? He had no children at her school, he was years past his own education and somehow she couldn't picture him as the type to bake cookies for the PTA fundraiser.

She couldn't think of anything else that would bring him to her door and the clock was ticking.

"May I help you, Mr. Dalton?"

Surprise flickered in those eyes for just a moment, as if he hadn't expected her to know his name. "Just making a delivery."

She frowned, impatient and confused, as he reached around the door out of her view, tugging something forward. No something, someone—someone with a sullen scowl, a baggy sweatshirt and a chip the size of Idaho on his narrow shoulders.

"Cole!"

Beneath her son's customary sulky defiance, she thought she saw something else beneath the attitude, something nervous and on edge.

"What's going on? You're supposed to be down in your room working on geometry!" she exclaimed.

"Geometry blows. I went out."

"You went out," she repeated, frustration and bewilderment and a terrible sense of failure rising in her chest. How could she possibly reach the students at her school when she couldn't manage to find even the tiniest connection to her own son? "Out where? I didn't hear you leave."

"Ever hear of a window?" he sneered. Nothing new there. He had been derisive and mean to her before they ever came to Pine Gulch. He blamed her for everything wrong in his life, from his short stature to Richard's affair and subsequent abandonment.

She was mortified that a stranger had to witness it. She was even more mortified when Seth Dalton raised one of those sexy dark eyebrows and placed a firm hand on Cole's shoulder. "Now, do you really think that's the proper way to address your mother?"

Jenny gave the man a polite smile, wishing him to Hades. "Thank you, Mr. Dalton, for bringing him home, but I believe I can handle things from here."

For some reason, either her words or her tone seemed to amuse him. His mouth quirked up and a masculine dimple appeared in his cheek briefly. "Can you, now? I'm afraid we still have a few matters of business to discuss. May I come in?"

"This isn't a good time. I'm late for a meeting."

"Sorry about that," he drawled, "but I'm afraid you'll have to make time for this."

He didn't wait for permission, just walked through her father's entry into the living room. She had no choice but to follow, noting as she went that Jason and Morgan were nowhere to be seen.

"Cole, you want to tell her what you've been up to?"

Her son crossed his arms, his expression even more belligerent, but again she caught a faint whiff of fear beneath it. Her stomach suddenly twisted with foreboding.

"What's going on? Cole, what is this about?"

He clamped his mouth shut, freezing her out again, but once more Seth Dalton placed a firm hand on his shoulder.

Cole suddenly seemed to find the carpet endlessly fascinating.

"Istolehisride," he mumbled in one breath and Jenny's heart stopped, hoping she'd heard wrong.

"You *what?*"

Cole finally lifted his gaze to hers. "I took his car, okay? What did he expect? He left the frigging keys in it. I was only going to take it for a mile or two. I figured I'd have it back before he even knew it was gone. But then I crashed..."

"You *what!* Are you hurt? Did you hurt anyone else?"

Cole shook his head. At least he had enough guilty conscience to look slightly ashamed.

"He scraped a mile marker post and front-ended into an irrigation ditch. The only thing damaged was my car."

She sagged into the nearest chair as her career suddenly flashed in front of her eyes. She could almost hear the echo of gossip across shopping carts at DeLoy's, under the hair dryers at the Hairport and over beer at the Bandito.

Did you hear about that new principal's wild boy? She can't control him a lick. That little delinquent stole a car.

Crashed it right into a ditch! Seems to me a woman who can't control her own son sure don't belong in that nice office down at the elementary school.

She screwed her eyes shut, wishing this was all some terrible dream, but when she opened them, Seth Dalton was still standing in front of her, as dangerous and sexy as ever.

"I am so sorry, Mr. Dalton. I…don't know what to say. Are you pressing charges?"

She thought she heard Cole make a small sound, but when she glanced at him, he looked as prickly and angry as ever.

"It's going to take me considerable work to fix it."

"We will, of course, cover any damages."

He suddenly sat down on the sofa across from her, crossing his boots at the ankle. "I had something else in mind."

She stiffened. "I'm an elementary school principal, Mr. Dalton. If you're looking for some kind of huge financial settlement, I'm afraid you're off the mark."

"I'm not looking for money." He glanced at Seth. "But I will need another set of hands while I'm doing the repair work. I figured the kid could work off the damages by helping me out with the repair work and around my ranch with my horses until the bodywork is done."

Cole straightened. "I'm no stupid-ass cowboy."

Seth Dalton gave him a measuring look. "No, from here you look like a stupid-ass punk who thinks he's living out some kind of video game. This isn't Grand Theft Auto, kid, where you can always hit the restart button. You broke it, now you're going to help me fix it. Unless you'd rather serve the time, of course."

Cole subsided back into his customary slouch as Jenny considered his proposal. Her gut wanted her to tell him to forget it. She didn't want her son to have anything to do with Pine Gulch's busiest bachelor.

Cole had had enough lousy male role models in his life—he didn't need a player like Seth teaching him all the wrong things about how to treat a woman.

On the other hand, her son stole the man's car—not only stole it, but wrecked the blasted thing. That he wasn't in police custody right now seemed nothing short of a miracle.

What choice did she have, really? Seth could easily have called the police. Perhaps he should have. Maybe a hard gut check with reality might be just what Cole needed to wake him up, as much as she hated the idea of her son in juvenile detention.

Seth Dalton was being surprisingly decent about this. From what little she knew about him—and she had to admit, most of her biased information came from overheard conversations and breathless comments in the teachers' lounge about his many flirtations—she would have expected him to be hot-tempered and petulant.

Instead, she found him rational, calm, accommodating.

And extremely attractive.

She let out a slow, nervous breath. Was that the reason for her instinctive opposition to the man's reasonable proposal? Because he was sinfully gorgeous, with that thick, dark hair, eyes a stunning, heartbreaking blue and chiseled, tanned features that made him look as though he should be starring in Western movies?

He made her edgy and ill at ease and that alone gave her enough reason to wish for a way to avoid any further acquaintance between them. She was here in Pine Gulch to help her little family find some peace and healing—not to engage in useless, potentially harmful fantasies about a charming, feckless cowboy with impossibly blue eyes and a smile that oozed sex.

"I'll know better after I tow the car out to the ranch and take a look at her but from my initial look, I'd estimate there was about fix or six hundred dollars' damage," he was saying. "The way I figure it, if he worked for me a couple afternoons a week after school and Saturday mornings, we should be clear in a few months. Is that okay with you?"

She looked at Dalton and then at Cole, his arms still crossed belligerently across his chest, as if everyone else in the room was responsible for his troubles but himself.

He disdained everything about Idaho and would probably consider being forced to work on a ranch every bit as much punishment as going to juvenile detention, she thought.

"Yes. That's more than fair. Wouldn't you agree, Cole?"

Her son glared at both of them—and while Jenny felt her own temper kindle in automatic response, Seth met his look with cool challenge and Cole quickly dropped his gaze.

"Whatever," he muttered.

"Thank you," Jenny said again, walking with him to the door. "As tomorrow is Saturday, I'll drive him out to the Cold Creek in the morning. What time?"

"How does eight work for you?"

"We'll be there. I'm very sorry again about this. I can't imagine what he was thinking."

His smile was slow and wide and made her insides feel as if she'd just done somersaults down a steep, grassy hill.

"He's a teenage boy, so I'd guess he probably wasn't thinking at all. See you in the morning."

Jenny nodded, wondering why that prospect filled her with an odd mix of trepidation and anticipation.

Chapter 2

"This is totally lame," her son muttered the next morning. "Why do I have to give up a whole Saturday?"

Jenny sighed and cast Cole an admonishing glance across the width of her little Toyota SUV. "You prefer the alternative? I can call Mr. Dalton right now and tell him to go ahead and file charges if that's what you'd rather see happen here."

Cole sliced her a glare that told her quite plainly he considered *her* totally lame, too, but he said nothing.

"I don't think it's fair, either," Morgan piped up from the backseat. "Why does Cole always get to do the fun stuff? I want to help with the horses, too. Natalie says the Cold Creek horses are the prettiest, smartest horses anywhere. They've won all kinds of rodeo awards and they sell for *tons* of money. She said her uncle Seth knows more about horses than anybody else in the whole wide *world*."

"Wow. The whole wide world?" Sarcasm dripped from Cole's voice.

Morgan either didn't pick up on it or decided to ignore it. Judging from past experience, Jenny was willing to bet on the latter. Her daughter tended to ignore anything that didn't fit into her vision of the way the world ought to operate.

Even during her frequent hospital stays after bad asthma attacks, she always managed to focus on some silver lining, like a new friend or a particularly kind nurse.

"Yep," she said eagerly now, with as much pride in Seth Dalton as she might have had if he were *her* uncle instead of her best friend's. "People bring their horses to the Cold Creek from all over the place for him to train because he's so good."

"If he knows more than anyone else in the world, why is he stuck here in Buttlick, Idaho?"

Morgan's enthusiasm faded into a frown. "Just because you don't like it here, you don't have to call it mean words."

"I thought that was the name," Cole said with a sneer. "Right next to Hairy Armpitville and across the holler from Cow's Rectum."

"That's enough." Jenny's hands tightened on the steering wheel and she felt familiar stress weigh like a half-ton hay bale on her shoulders. She wasn't at all sure she was going to survive her son's adolescence.

"I hope you treat Mr. Dalton with more respect than you show me or your sister."

"How can I not, since apparently the man knows more about horses than anybody in the whole wide world?" Cole muttered.

Who was this angry stranger in her son's body? she wondered. Whatever happened to her sweet little man who used to love cuddling up with her at bedtime for stories and hugs? Who used to let her blow raspberries on his neck and would run to her classroom after school bubbling over with news of his day?

That sweet boy had been slipping away from her since the year he turned eleven, when Richard had moved out. Through the three ugly years since, he'd pulled deeper and deeper into himself, until now he only emerged on rare occasions.

This obviously wasn't going to be one of them.

Somehow Cole had come to blame her for the separation and divorce. She wasn't sure how or why she had come to bear that burden but the unfairness of it made her want to scream.

She, at least, had been faithful to her marriage vows. Though she hadn't been perfect by any means and had long ago accepted her share of responsibility for the breakup of her marriage, in her heart she knew she had tried to be a good wife.

She had supported Richard through his last years of medical school, residency, internship. She had scrimped and saved throughout their twelve-year marriage to help pay off his student loans, had run the household virtually alone during that time as he worked to establish his career, had tried time and again to bridge the increasing chasm between them as he focused on his practice to the complete exclusion of his family.

She had tried. Not perfectly, she would admit, but she had wanted her marriage to work.

Richard had had other ideas, though. He went to Paris for a conference and met his Giselle and decided family and vows and twelve years of marriage didn't stack up well against a twenty-year-old Frenchwoman with a tight body and pouty lips.

Jenny had long ago come to terms with Richard Boyer's betrayal of her. But she would never forgive him for what his complete abandonment of his family had done to his children. Morgan had stopped crying herself to sleep some time ago and seemed to be adjusting, but Cole carried so much anger inside him he seethed with it.

Lucky her, she seemed to be the only outlet for his rage.

She tried to remember what the therapist she'd seen in Seattle had told her, that Cole only lashed out at her because she was a safe target. Her son knew she wouldn't abandon him like his father, so he focused all the force of his rage toward her.

She still wasn't sure she completely bought into that explanation. Even if she did, she wasn't sure it would make his rebelliousness and unhappiness any more palatable.

With each mile marker, he seemed to sink further into gloom on the seat beside her.

A large timber arch across a gravel side road proudly bore the name of the Cold Creek Land & Cattle Company in cast-iron letters. She slowed the SUV and turned in.

"It won't be so bad," she said, fighting the completely juvenile urge to cross her fingers. "Who knows? You might even enjoy it."

He rolled his eyes. "Cleaning up horse crap? Right. Can't wait."

She sighed, wondering if Seth Dalton had any clue what joy was in store for him today.

The ranch house was shielded from the main road by a long row of trees, which made the first sight of it all the more dramatic. It was perfect for the landscape here, a bold, impressive structure of rock and logs, with the massive peaks of the Tetons as a backdrop.

She'd always considered November a particularly lonely, unattractive month, without October's swirling colors or December's sparkling anticipation. In November, the trees were bleak and bare and everything seemed frost-dead and barren.

The Cold Creek seemed to be an exception. Oh, the gardens out front had been cut down, the beds prepared for winter, but the long rows of weathered fence line and the sheer impressiveness of the house and outbuildings gave a stark beauty to the scene.

Not sure quite where to go to find Seth Dalton, she slowed as she reached the house and then stopped altogether when she saw a figure emerge from an immense barn, carrying a bale of hay by the baling twine.

It wasn't Seth, she realized, but his brother Wade, Natalie's father.

The oldest Dalton brother had two children in her school—Natalie and her younger brother, Tanner. Natalie was a dear, though a little bossy, but Tanner had been in her office on more than one occasion for some mischief or other. He wasn't malicious, just highly energetic.

The few times she had met with Wade Dalton and his wife, Caroline, at various school functions and when having discussions about Tanner's behavior, she'd been struck by the deep vein of happiness she sensed running through the family.

She didn't like to admit she felt envy and regret when she saw two people so obviously in love.

Wade caught sight of them now and smiled, dropping the bale and tipping his hat in a way she still hadn't become accustomed to here in cowboy country.

He didn't look at all surprised to see them as he crossed the yard to her SUV. Seth must have told him the whole story about Cole stealing his brother's car. What must he think of her and her delinquent son? she wondered, her face warming.

He only smiled in welcome. "Ms. Boyer. Kids," he said in that slow drawl she'd noticed before. "Welcome to the Cold Creek."

She couldn't help but smile back. "Thank you. We were supposed to be meeting your brother Seth this morning."

"Right. He mentioned your boy would be coming by to help him. He's up at the horse barn. Just follow the gravel road there another half mile or so and you can't miss it."

"Thank you," she said, wondering how big the ranch must be if the horse barn was a half mile from the main ranch house. The road took them up a slight grade, through a heavy stand of spruce and pines and aspen and then the view opened up and she caught sight of the horse operation.

Two dozen horses grazed in the vast pasture, their coats gleaming in the cool morning sunlight.

Barn seemed a vast understatement for the imposing white-painted structure that dominated the view. It was massive, at least twice as large as the barn they had passed closer to the ranch house, and more horses were in individual corrals off it.

As she pulled up and parked, she caught sight of a small two-story log home behind it. Situated to face the Tetons, the house had one steep gable with a balcony protruding from a window in the center and a wide porch looking out over the view.

She wasn't sure how she knew—maybe the tiny saplings out front that looked like they hadn't been there long—but the house looked new. Everything did, she thought. From the corrals to the vast gleaming barn to the pickup truck parked outside, everything gleamed with prosperity.

She had barely turned off the engine when Seth Dalton walked out of the barn and she had to catch her breath at the picture he made. He was wearing a worn denim jacket and a black cowboy hat. As he moved with that unconscious grace she'd noticed the night before, she saw he also wore figure-hugging jeans that suddenly made her feel jittery and weak-kneed.

The man was entirely too good-looking. She wasn't sure why that observation made her so irritable, but she found herself fighting the urge to shut the SUV door with a little more force than necessary, especially when he aimed that killer grin in her direction.

"Morning. It's a gorgeous one, isn't it?"

She raised a skeptical eyebrow. Clouds hung low over the Tetons and the cold wind felt heavy with the promise of snow.

"If you say so."

He laughed, a low, throaty sound that made her insides flutter, then he turned his attention to Cole, who had climbed out the other side of the vehicle to slouch against the door.

"You ready to work?"

Cole glowered at his benefactor, much to Jenny's chagrin. "Do I have a choice?"

In answer, Dalton just gave him a long, slow look and Jenny was amazed to watch Cole be the first to back down, shifting his gaze to the work boots he'd borrowed from his grandfather.

Before she could say anything, Seth's attention shifted to Morgan, who had climbed out of the backseat to join them.

"And who are you?"

"I'm Morgan Jeanette Boyer." She spoke with formal precision and held out her hand exactly like a nine-year-old princess greeting her favorite courtier.

A muscle twitched in Seth's cheek but he hid any sign

of amusement as he took her hand and shook it. "Pleased to meet you, Miss Boyer. I'm Seth Dalton."

Morgan smiled. "I know. You're my friend Natalie's uncle. She says you have more girlfriends than Colin Farrell."

"Morgan!" Jenny exclaimed hotly, her cheeks fiery.

"What?" her daughter asked, all innocence.

Seth grinned, though Jenny thought she saw a hint of embarrassment behind it.

"Are all those horses your very own?" Morgan asked.

"Actually, most of them aren't. I have six or seven of my own but the rest I guess you could say I share with my family. Plus I'm training a few for other people."

He studied the avid interest in her eyes. "I don't suppose you'd want to have a look around, would you?"

Morgan gave a little jump of excitement. "Yeah! Can I, Mom?"

How could she say no? "I suppose. As long as you're sure we won't be in the way."

"Not at all. I have to show Cole around, anyway. No reason you two can't tag along."

They made a peculiar tour group, she thought as Seth led them inside the barn. It was more arena than stable, she realized. Though stalls ran around the perimeter, most of the space was taken up by a vast, open dirt floor. Handy for year-round training during the Idaho winters, she thought.

As he pointed out various features of the facility, Cole slouched along behind, Morgan asked a million questions and Jenny mainly focused on trying to keep her gaze away from Seth Dalton, difficult though it was.

"Everything looks so new," Jenny commented while Morgan was busy patting a horse and Cole slumped against the fence ringing the arena, looking as though he'd rather be anywhere else on the planet.

"The Cold Creek has been here for five generations, but the horse operation is pretty new. My brother and I decided a few years ago to diversify. We've always raised and trained our own horses on a limited scale and only for ourselves. We decided a few years ago to expand that part of our operations and try the open market."

"How has it been going?"

"I've got more work than I can handle right now."

"That's a good thing, isn't it?"

"Better than I ever dreamed." His smile was slow and sexy and seemed to suck all the oxygen molecules from the vast structure.

She didn't realize she was staring at it for several seconds, then she quickly shifted her gaze away from his mouth to find him watching her, an odd, glittery look in his blue eyes.

"What's that room?" Morgan asked, shattering the sudden painfully awkward silence.

Seth shifted his attention to her. "That's my office. Come on, I'll show you."

He opened the door to a small room several degrees warmer than the rest of the barn. When he opened the door, an oddly colored puppy blinked at them then jumped up from a blanket on the floor and started yipping a frantic greeting.

"You're finally waking up, sleepyhead?" Seth smiled at the pup. "Come and meet our company."

The puppy sniffed all their shoes in turn and made it as far as Morgan before the girl scooped him up and hugged him tightly. "He's so cute! What's his name?"

"He's a she and her name is Lucy."

"Oh, you are a pretty girl. Yes you are," Morgan cooed, rubbing noses with the puppy. Jenny felt a pang. Her daughter adored animals of all shapes and sizes and used to constantly beg for a dog or cat of her own, until her pulmonologist in Seattle recommended against it.

"What kind of dog is she?" Cole asked, his first words since they'd arrived at the ranch.

"Australian shepherd. I bought her and her brother at a horse auction in Boise last month. I only meant to buy one for a birthday present for my mother but I couldn't resist Lucy."

"You have sheep, too?" Morgan asked.

"Uh, no." He looked a little embarrassed. "But they work cattle, too, and I figured she can help me when I'm training a horse for cutting."

"Cutting what?" Morgan asked.

"Cutting cattle. That's a term for picking an individual cow or calf out of a herd. A well-trained cutting horse will do all the work for a cowboy. He just has to point out which cow he wants and the horse will separate him out of the rest of the cows."

"Wow! Can your horses do that?"

Instead of being put off my Morgan's relentless questions, Seth seemed charmed by her daughter. "Some of them," he said. "Sometime when you come out I'll give you a demonstration."

"Cool!"

He grinned at Morgan's enthusiasm and Jenny could swear she felt her blasted knees wobble. Oh, the man was dangerous. Entirely too sexy for his own good. She had to get out of there before she dissolved into a brainless puddle of hormones.

"Morgan, you and I had better go. Cole and Mr. Dalton have work to do."

She was pleasantly surprised when Morgan didn't kick up a fuss but followed her out of the barn into the cool November sunshine. Only as they approached the SUV did Jenny pick up on the reason for her daughter's unusual docility.

In just a few seconds, Morgan had turned pale, her breathing wheezy and labored.

She should have expected it from the combination of animal dander, hay and excitement, but the swiftness of the asthma flare-up took her by surprise.

Still, Jenny had learned from grim experience never to go anywhere unprepared. She yanked the door open and lunged for her purse on the floor by the driver's seat. Inside was Morgan's spare inhaler and she quickly, efficiently puffed the medicine into the chamber and handed it to Morgan, then set her on the passenger seat while she drew the medicine into her lungs.

Morgan had that familiar panicky look in her eyes and Jenny spoke softly to calm her, the same nonsense words she always used.

She forgot all about Seth Dalton until he leaned past her into the SUV, big and disconcertingly masculine.

"That's it, honey," Seth said, keeping his own voice low and soothing. "Concentrate on the breathing and all the good air going into your lungs. You're doing great."

After a moment, the rescue medication did its work and the color started to return to her features. The panic in her eyes slowly gave way to the beginnings of relief and Jenny's heart twisted with pain for her child's trials and the courage Morgan wielded against them.

"Better?" Seth asked after a moment.

The girl nodded and Seth was grateful to see the flare-up

seemed to be under control. "I'd tell you to go on back into the barn where it's warmer," he said to Jenny, "but I suspect the hay or the puppy triggered the attack, didn't they?"

Her eyes widened as if surprised he knew anything about asthma. He didn't tell her he could have written the damn book on it.

"That's what I thought," Jenny said. She was starting to lose her tight, in-control look, he saw, and now just looked like a worried mother. "I should have realized they might."

"Why don't we take her into the house over there for a minute until she feels better? This cold can't be the greatest for her lungs."

She looked as if she wanted to argue, but Morgan coughed just then and her mother nodded. "That's probably a good idea."

Seth scooped the girl into his arms easily, and headed for the house with Jenny and Cole following behind him. Morgan still breathed shallowly, her little chest rising and falling quickly as she tried to ease the horrible breathlessness he remembered all too well.

"I hate having asthma," she whispered, her voice far too bitter for a little girl.

He recognized the bitterness, too. He knew just what it felt like to be ten and trapped with a body that didn't work like he wanted it to. He had wanted to be a junior buckaroo rodeo champion, wanted to climb the Tetons by the time he was twelve, wanted to be the star pitcher on the Little League baseball team. Instead, he'd been small and weak and spent far too much time breathing into a lousy tube.

"Sucks, doesn't it?" he answered. "The worst is the one time you forget to take your inhaler somewhere and of course you suddenly you get hit by a flare-up."

She blinked at him and he was struck by how sweet it

was to have a child look at him with such trust. "You have it, too?"

He nodded. "I don't have attacks very often now, maybe once or twice a year and they're usually pretty mild. When I was your age, though, it was a different story."

He set her down on his leather sofa and grabbed a blanket for her.

She couldn't seem to get over the fact that he knew what she was going through. "But you're big! You ride horses and everything."

"You can ride horses, too. You just have to watch for your triggers, like I do, and do your best to manage things. When I was a kid, they didn't have some of the newer maintenance meds they have now and we had a tough time finding the best treatment for me but eventually we did. You probably know you never grow out of asthma, but lots of times the symptoms decrease a lot when you get older. That's what happened to me."

"You probably weren't afraid like I am when I have an attack. Cole says I'm a big wussy."

Jenny looked pained by the admission and Seth sent the boy a pointed look. At least Cole had the grace to look embarrassed.

"I was just kidding," the kid mumbled. He needed a serious attitude adjustment, Seth thought, wondering if he'd been such a punk when he'd gone through his rebellious teens.

"I can't think of anything scarier than not being able to breathe," Seth told Morgan. "People who haven't been through it don't quite understand what it's like, do they? Like you're trapped underwater and somebody's got two fists around your lungs and is squeezing them tight so you can only take a tiny breath at a time."

Morgan nodded her agreement. "I always feel like I'm trapped under a big heavy blanket."

"What's your peak flow?"

She told him and he nodded. "Mine was pretty close to that when I was about your age." He paused and saw the conversation was starting to tire her. "Can I get you a glass of water or some juice?"

She nodded, closing her eyes, and he rose and went into the kitchen to find a glass. Somehow he wasn't surprised when Jenny followed him.

"Thank you." She gave him a quiet smile and he felt an odd little tug in his chest.

"I didn't do anything," he said as he poured a glass of orange juice from the refrigerator.

"You were very kind to her and I appreciate your sharing your own condition with her. It's great for Morgan to talk to adults who have managed to move past their childhood asthma and go on to live successful lives. Thank you," she said again, following it up this time with another small, hesitant smile.

He studied that smile, the way it highlighted the lushness of a mouth that seemed incongruous with her buttoned-down appearance.

What was it about her? She wasn't gorgeous in a Miss Rodeo Idaho kind of way. Not tall and curvy with a brilliant smile and eyes that knew just how to reel a man in.

She was small and compact, probably no bigger than five foot three. He supposed he'd call her cute, with that red-gold hair and her green eyes and the little ski jump of a nose.

Seth couldn't say he had a particular favorite type of woman—he was willing to admit he loved them all—but he usually gravitated toward the kind of women who hung out at the Bandito. The kind in tight jeans and tighter shirts, with big breasts and hungry smiles.

Jenny Boyer was just about the polar opposite of that kind of woman. Cute or not, he probably wouldn't usually take a second look at a woman who looked like a suburban soccer mom, with her tailored tan slacks and her wool blazer. Jenny Boyer was the kind of settled, respectable woman men like him usually tended to avoid.

Yet here they were, and he couldn't seem to keep his eyes off her. She might not be his usual type but he sure liked looking at her.

He frowned a little at the unexpectedness of his attraction to her, then decided to shrug it off. He would never do anything about it. Not with a woman like Jenny Boyer, who had *Complication* written all over her.

Morgan's color was much better when they returned to the living room. She was sitting up bickering with her brother, something he figured was a good sign.

She took the juice from him with a shy smile.

"Cole and I have things to do but you two are welcome to hang out here until Morgan feels better."

"I think I'm all right now," the girl said.

"I should get her home for a nebulizer treatment and to check her peak flow."

"I can carry you back out to the car if you want."

Morgan shook her head. "I can walk. But thanks."

After her daughter was settled in the SUV, Jenny turned to him and to Cole.

"What time shall I come back?" she asked.

He thought of his schedule for the day. "Don't worry about it. I'll be running into town about four. We should be done by then so I'll bring him back and save you a trip. Just take care of Morgan."

"All right. Thank you." She looked at her son as if she wanted to say something more, but she only let out a long breath, slid into her vehicle and drove away.

"So are we going to work on the car or what?" Cole finally addressed him after the SUV pulled away.

If Seth hadn't noticed how concerned the boy had looked during those first few moments of the flare-up, he would probably find him more trouble than he was worth.

"Oh, eventually," he said with a smile that bordered on evil. "First, you've got some stalls to muck. I hope you brought good thick gloves because you're going to need 'em."

Chapter 3

Fourteen was a miserable bitch of an age.

Though more than half his life had passed since that notable year, it felt just as fresh and painful now as Seth watched Cole Boyer shovel manure out of a stall.

Though the kid wasn't tall by any stretch of the imagination, he was gangly and awkward, as if his muscles were still too short to keep up with his longer bones.

Seth remembered those days. He'd been small for his age, too, six inches shorter than most of the other guys in his class, and with asthma to boot. His father's death had been just a few years earlier. And while he hadn't been exactly paralyzed by grief over the bastard, he *had* struggled to figure out his place in the world now that he wasn't Hank Dalton's sickly, sissy-boy youngest son.

He'd been a little prick, too, full of anger and attitude. He had brothers to pound on to help vent some of it, but since fights usually ended with them beating the tar out of him, he tended to shy away from that activity. Eventually, he'd turned some of his excess energy to horses.

He trained his first horse that year, he remembered, a sweet little chestnut mare he'd ridden in the Idaho state high school rodeo finals a few years later.

Yeah, fourteen had been miserable, for the most part. But the next year everything started to come together. Between his fourteenth and fifteenth years, he hit a major growth spurt, the asthma all but disappeared and he gained six inches of height and thirty pounds of muscle, almost as if his body had just been biding its time.

Girls who'd ignored him all his life suddenly sat up and took notice—and he noticed them right back. After that, adolescence became a hell of a lot more fun, though he doubted Jenny Boyer would appreciate him sharing that particular walk down memory lane with her son, no matter how miserable he looked about life right now.

He *should* be miserable, Seth thought. Though he was tempted to turn soft and tell Cole he'd done enough for the day, he only had to think about the damage to his GTO to stiffen his resolve.

A little misery never hurt a kid.

"Can you hurry it up here?" Seth leaned indolently on the stall railing, mostly because he knew it would piss the kid off.

Sure enough, all he earned for his trouble was a heated glare.

"This isn't exactly easy."

"It's not supposed to be," Seth said.

After three hours, the kid had only mucked out four stalls, with two more to go. The more he shoveled, the grimmer his mood turned, until Seth was pretty sure he was ready to implode.

Tempted as he was to wait for the explosion, he finally took pity on him and reached for another shovel.

Cole gave him a surprised look when Seth joined him in the stall. "I thought I was supposed to be doing this."

"You are. But since I'd like to take a look at the car you trashed sometime today, I figure the only way that's going to happen is if I lend a hand."

"I'm going as fast as I can," Cole muttered.

"I know. If I thought you were slacking, you can bet I'd still be out there watching."

Surprise flickered in eyes the same green as his mother's, but he said nothing. They worked in silence for a few moments, the only sounds the scrape of shovels on concrete, the whickers of the horses around them and Lucy's curious yips as she followed them.

Only after they'd moved onto the last stall did the boy speak. "Why don't you have a real job or something?" he asked, his tone more baffled than hostile.

Seth raised an eyebrow. "You don't think this is real work?"

"Sure. But what kind of loser signs up to shovel horse crap all day?"

Seth laughed. "If this was the only thing I did around here all day, I'd have to agree with you. But I usually leave the grunt work to the hired help while I get to do the fun stuff."

"Like what?"

"Working with the horses. Breeding them, training them."

"Whatever."

"Not a real horse fan?"

"They're big and dumb. How hard could it be to train them?"

"You might be surprised." He scraped another shovel full of sunshine. "I can tell you there's nothing so satisfying as taking a green-broke horse—that means an untrained one—and working with him until he obeys anything you tell him to do without question."

"Whatever," Cole said again, his voice dripping with scorn.

To his surprise, Seth found he was more amused by the kid's attitude than he'd been by anything in a long time. "Come on. I'll show you. Drop your shovel."

Cole didn't need a second invitation. He dropped it with a clatter and followed Seth toward a stall at the end of the row, where his big buckskin Stella waited.

In moments, he had her saddled, then led her outside to one of the corrals where he kept a dozen or so cattle to help with the training.

"Okay, now pick a steer."

"Why?"

He had to laugh at the boy's horrified expression. "I'm not going to make you ride the thing, I promise. Remember how I was telling Morgan about cutting? Stella's going to cut whatever steer you pick out of the herd for you. Just tell me which one you want her to go after."

"How the hell should I know? They all look the same!"

"You've got a lot to learn, city boy. How about the one in the middle there, with the white face?"

At least the kid had lost his belligerence, though he was looking at Seth like he'd been kicked by a horse one too many times.

"Sure. Get that one."

He gave the commands to Stella then sat back in the saddle and let her do her thing. She was brilliant, as usual. In minutes, she had the white-faced Hereford just where

Seth wanted him, away from the herd and heading for the fence where Cole had perched to watch the demonstration.

"There you go. He's all yours," Seth called over the cattle's lowing.

The boy jumped down faster than a bullet at the sight of a half-ton animal heading toward him.

Seth pulled Stella off and let the steer return to the rest of the herd, then led the horse back through the gate.

"So what do you think? She's brilliant, isn't she?"

"You told her what to do."

"Sure. But she did it, didn't she? Without even hesitating. She's a great horse." He slid out of the saddle, then sent the kid a sidelong glance. "You do much riding?"

Cole snorted. "There aren't too many horses on Seattle street corners sitting around waiting to be ridden."

"You don't have that excuse here. Get on."

Before Cole could argue, Seth handed him the reins and hefted him into the saddle.

He looked even smaller than his age up on the big horse, though Seth gave him points for not sliding right back down. With one hand on the bridle, he led them back inside the training facility.

"You probably know the basics, even if you've never ridden before, just from watching TV. Keep a firm hand on the reins, pull them in the direction you want her to go. Above all, have fun."

He let go of the bridle, confident the horse was too well-trained to unseat her rider, no matter how inexperienced.

Sure enough, she started a slow walk around the arena. Cole looked terrified at first, then he gradually started to relax. By the second time around the arena, he even smiled a little, though he bounced in the saddle like a particularly hapless sack of flour.

"I suck, don't I?" he said ruefully as they passed Seth.

Sit up, boy. Or are you too tired *to learn to be a man? You'll never be able to ride the damn thing if you slouch in the saddle like that and gasp like a trout on the end of a frigging hook every time the horse takes a step.*

He pushed away the echo of his father's voice, wondering if he'd been four or five during that particular riding lesson. "You don't suck," he assured Seth. "You just have to learn to move with the rhythm of the horse. It takes a while to figure it out. For your first time, you're kickin' A."

For one shining instant, Cole looked thrilled at the praise. He must have felt himself smile, though, because he quickly retreated back into his brittle shell.

"Am I done here? My butt's starting to hurt."

Seth sighed as the momentary animation slipped away. He shrugged and held Stella again so Cole could slide down.

"We've got one more stall to finish. Work on that while I take off Stella's saddle."

Cole grimaced but headed back to his shovel.

He couldn't expect to change the kid's attitude with one horseback ride, Seth thought. But maybe the car would do the trick.

He caught his own thoughts and grimaced at himself. Since when was he the do-gooder of Pine Gulch? He had no business even trying to fix this troubled kid's problems. Better just to get his money's worth out of him in labor to compensate for the car damage and leave the attitude-adjusting to his mother.

Saturdays were usually one of her most productive days of the week, away from the office and all the distractions of running an elementary school with four hundred students.

She usually accomplished more in a few hours than she

could do in two days at school, between lunch duty and phone calls from concerned parents and dealing with state and federal education regulations.

Today, Jenny couldn't seem to focus on work at all while she waited for Seth Dalton to return with Cole.

After trying for an hour and a half to slog through some paperwork while Morgan rested on the couch next to her in the den watching television, she finally gave it up for a lost cause.

She wasn't worried about Cole. Not precisely. She was more concerned that her belligerent son would forget Seth was doing him a huge favor and instead would vent his unhappiness in all the usual ways.

She couldn't stress about that. Something told her a man like Dalton was more than capable of holding his own against a fourteen-year-old rebel.

He struck her as a man who could handle just about anything. She thought of those strong, capable shoulders and had to suppress a sigh. Why couldn't she seem to get the man off her mind?

She'd had an unwilling fascination for him since the first time she heard his name, long before her son's recklessness brought them into his orbit. It had been a month or so after school started and she'd been in her office after lunch when one of her brand-new teachers, just out of college and still half terrified of her students, stopped in during her prep hour to talk to Marcy, the school secretary.

It hadn't surprised her the two were friends. Marcy was only a few years older than Ashley Barnes, the new kindergarten teacher. Beyond that, she was warm and bubbly, the kind of person who drew everyone to her. Not only was she great at her job but the children adored her and Jenny had learned most of the other teachers did, too.

She hadn't meant to eavesdrop, but her door had been open and she'd been able to hear every word.

"He said he'd call me," Ashley complained. "How stupid was I to believe him?"

Marcy had only laughed. "You're human and you're female. There's not a woman in town who can resist Seth Dalton when he gives that smile of his. Heck, he even has all the old ladies in my grandma's quilting club batting their fake eyelashes at him."

"That night at the Bandito, you'd think I was the only woman in the world," Ashley said, the bitterness in her voice completely at odds with her usual sunny disposition. "He never left my side all night and we danced every single dance. I thought he really liked me."

"I'm sure he did like you that night. But that's the thing about Seth. He lives completely in the moment."

"He's a dog." Ashley sounded close to tears.

"No, he's not. Believe it or not, he's actually a pretty decent guy. He's the first one out on his tractor plowing his neighbors' driveways after a big snowstorm and he always stops to help somebody in trouble. But he was blessed—or cursed, however you want to look at it—with the kind of good looks that make women go a little crazy around him."

"You think I imagined that night?"

"No. Oh, honey, I'm sure you didn't," Marcy had replied in her patient, kind voice. "My friends and I have a theory. We call it Seth Dalton's School of Broncobustin'. If you're lucky to find him turning his attention to you, just climb on and hold on tight. It probably won't last too long, but it will be a hell of a ride."

"I'm not like that!" Ashley had exclaimed. "I never even go to bars. I don't drink. I probably wouldn't even have met him if my roommate hadn't dragged me along that night."

"Which is probably the reason he didn't call you," Marcy pointed out gently. "You're a kindergarten teacher with *Marriage Material* stamped on your forehead. You're sweet and innocent, and you probably have already got names picked out for the four kids you're going to have."

"Is that such a bad thing?"

"Oh, honey, absolutely not. I think it's wonderful, and somewhere out there is someone who is going to love those things about you. But that's not what Seth Dalton is about."

One of the third-graders had come in just then complaining of a stomach ache. Marcy had turned her attention to calling the girl's mother to come get her and Ashley had returned to her class, but not before Jenny had developed a strong dislike for the man under discussion.

It was one of those weird cases where, once she heard a name, she suddenly couldn't seem to escape it: Seth Dalton's kept popping up.

She heard another teacher just before the start of a faculty meeting talk about running into him in the grocery store and how she'd been so flustered just because he'd smiled and asked her how she was that she'd left without half the items on her list.

When they were brainstorming ways to raise money for new library books, someone suggested a bachelor auction and someone else said they'd have enough books to fill every shelf if only they could get Seth Dalton on the auction block.

Now that she'd met him, she certainly understood all the buzz about the man. A woman could forget her own name just from one look out of those blue eyes.

"Are you done with your work?" Morgan asked from her spot on the couch, distracting her from her completely unproductive train of thought.

She closed her laptop and gathered her papers, shoving them back into her briefcase. She had learned long ago how to recognize a lost cause. "For now. Want to watch a DVD or play a game?"

"Sure. You pick."

They were still discussing their options a moment later when she heard the back door open and a moment later her father came in, his cheeks red from the November chill and his arms full of wood to replenish the low supply in the firebox by the woodstove.

"You should let me do that," she chided, upset at herself for being too distracted by thoughts of Seth Dalton to pay attention to her father's activities.

"Why?" Jason looked genuinely surprised.

"I feel guilty sitting here where it's warm and comfortable while you're outside hauling wood."

"I need the exercise. Keeps my joints lubricated."

She had to laugh at that. At sixty-five, her father was more fit than most men half his age. He rode his mountain bike all over town, he fished every chance he got—winter or summer—and his new passion was cross-country skiing.

"Maybe I need the exercise, too."

"And maybe it does my heart good to know I'm still capable of seeing to the comfort of my daughter and granddaughter. You wouldn't want to take that away from an old man, would you?" Jason said, with a twinkle in his eyes and the incontrovertible logic that had made him such a formidable opponent in the courtroom.

She rolled her eyes and was amused to see Morgan copying her gesture.

"Grandpa, you're silly," her daughter said with fondness. "You're not old."

The two of them were kindred spirits and got along like

the proverbial house on fire. Coming to Pine Gulch had been the right decision, she thought again. Even if Cole still fought and bucked against it like one of Seth Dalton's horses with a burr under the saddle, the move had been good for all of them.

She couldn't be sorry for it. Morgan and Cole had come to know the grandfather they had been acquainted with only distantly, and in a lot of ways, Jenny felt the same. Jason had been a distant, distracted figure in her life, even before her parents had divorced when she was twelve. Coming here had led to a closer relationship than they'd ever had.

"We're going to watch a DVD. Are you interested? We're debating between a *Harry Potter* or one of the *Lord of the Rings* trilogy."

"Oh, Tolkien. By all means."

They settled on which of the three to see and were watching the opening credits when by some mother's intuition, she heard the low rumble of a truck out front.

"Go ahead and start the movie," she said. "Since I've seen it at least a dozen times, I'm sure I won't be too lost when I come back."

She reached the front door just as Cole hopped down from a big silver pickup truck. Through the storm door, she studied her son intently. Though he didn't appear to be exactly overflowing with joy, he didn't seem miserable, either, as he headed up the sidewalk to the house.

She wasn't really surprised when Seth climbed out the other side of the truck and followed the boy up to the house. She opened the door for her son, who would probably have walked right by without even a greeting if she hadn't stepped right in his way.

"How did it go?" she asked, fighting the yearning to

pull him into her arms for the kind of hug he used to give her all the time.

"My favorite Levi's smell like horse crap."

"I'm sure that will wash out."

"I doubt it," Cole grumbled. "They're probably ruined forever."

"Here's a tip for you," Seth spoke from the doorway with a lazy smile. "Next time you come to the ranch, maybe you shouldn't wear your favorite pair of Levi's."

"If you're going to suggest I buy a pair of Wranglers, I might just have to puke."

"I wouldn't dare," Seth drawled. "Then your favorite pair of Levi's would smell like horse crap and puke."

Cole's snort might have passed for a laugh, but Jenny could not be quite sure.

"Wear whatever you want. But if you take the school bus to the Cold Creek on Tuesday, we might be ready to get into the real work on the car now that we've taken a look at the damage. Bus Fifteen is the one you want to take. Ray Pullman is the driver."

"Right. I need to take a shower."

"Bring your jeans out when you're done so we can wash them," Jenny said.

Cole didn't answer her or even acknowledge her as he headed down the stairs to his bedroom, leaving her alone with Seth.

In part because of embarrassment over her son's rudeness and in part because Seth was so masculine and so blasted attractive, she was intensely aware of him. He seemed to fill up all the available space in the small foyer.

She gave a small huff of annoyance at herself and tried to ignore the scent of him that seemed to surround her, of warm male and sexy aftershave.

"Tell me the truth. How did it really go today? I doubt Cole will tell me much."

"Good. He worked hard at everything I asked him to do and some of it wasn't very appealing. I can't ask for more than that."

She relaxed the fingers she hadn't realized she'd clenched tightly in the pockets of her sweater. "Was he…" her voice trailed off and she couldn't figure out how to ask the question in a way that wouldn't make her sound like a terrible mother.

"Rude and obnoxious? Not much, surprisingly. He digs cars and we spent much of the afternoon working on mine, so everything was cool."

"I can't tell you how relieved that makes me."

"You should probably know I did throw him up on a horse for a few minutes. He actually seemed to enjoy it. Even smiled a few times."

She blinked, trying to imagine her rebellious city-boy "I-hate-everything-country" son on the back of a horse.

"You're sure we're talking about the same kid? He wasn't possessed by alien cowboy pod people?"

Seth laughed, his blue eyes crinkled at the corners, and she could swear she felt warm fingers trickling down her spine just looking at him.

"Not a UFO in sight, I swear."

She shouldn't be here, sharing laughter or anything else with Seth Dalton. With sharp efforts, she broke eye contact. "Thank you for all the trouble you've gone to," she said after an uncomfortable moment. "It would have been less work on your part if you had just turned him over to the authorities."

"I'm getting free labor with my horses and with my car. Not a bad deal. I'm no saint here."

"So they tell me."

Had she really said that aloud? She mentally cringed at her rudeness and Seth looked startled at first, then gave her one of those blasted slow smiles that ought to come with a warning label as long as her arm.

"Who's been talking about me, Ms. Boyer?"

Her nerve endings tingled at his low, amused voice, but she ignored it, turning her own voice prim. "Who hasn't? You're a favorite topic of conversation in Pine Gulch, Mr. Dalton."

He didn't seem bothered by town gossip—or maybe he was just used to it.

Looking for all the world as if he planned to make himself right at home, he leaned a hip against the door frame and crossed his arms across his chest. "That must tell you what a quiet town you've settled in, if nobody in Pine Gulch has anything more interesting to talk about than me. So what's the consensus?"

That you're a major-league player. That you flirt with anything female and have left a swath of broken hearts behind you. That half the women in Teton Valley are in love with you and the other half are in lust.

She *so* didn't want to be having this conversation with him. She thought longingly of the paperwork she'd been putting off all afternoon and would have given just about anything right then to be sitting at her desk filling out federal assessment forms. Anything but this.

"Nothing I'm sure you haven't already heard," she finally said. "You're apparently a busy man."

A purely masculine, absolutely enticing dimple appeared in his cheek briefly then disappeared again. "Yeah, starting a full-fledged horse ranch can take a lot of hours."

He had to know she wasn't talking about his equine

endeavors, but she decided she wasn't going to set him straight.

"I'm sure it does," she murmured drily. Dating a different woman every night probably tended to fill up the calendar, too. But not this woman, even if she wasn't four years older than him and the exact opposite of all the tight, perky young things he was probably used to.

She knew all about men like him. She'd been married to one, a man compelled to charm every woman in sight.

She had worked hard to rebuild her heart and her life and her family in the last three years. After a great deal of hard work and self-scrutiny, she had finally become someone she could respect again.

She was a strong, successful woman who loved her work and her family, and she wasn't about to let a man like Seth Dalton knock her on her butt again.

Even if he did make her hormones wake up and sing hallelujah.

"Thank you for taking the time away from your horses to bring Cole back," she said, in what she hoped was a polite but dismissive tone.

He either didn't pick on it or didn't care. "No problem. How's Morgan doing now?"

She didn't want him to be interested in her daughter or for the simple question to remind her just how kind and patient he had been during Morgan's flare-up.

That was the problem with charmers, she supposed. They seemed instinctively to know how to zero in on a woman's weak spot and use that to their advantage. He'd already slipped inside her defenses a little by being so decent about Cole crashing his car. She would have preferred if he ignored Morgan altogether.

How was she to pigeonhole him as a selfish womanizer

when he showed such genuine concern for her daughter's welfare?

"She's fine. By the time we returned home, her peak flow was about seventy percent. After we nebulized her, it went up to about eight-five percent."

"Good. I hope the flare-up doesn't discourage you from bringing her out to the ranch again. She's welcome to tag along with Cole anytime. You both are."

She smiled politely, though she had absolutely no intention of taking him up on the invitation. "Thank you. But I'm sure the very last thing you need underfoot—with you being so *busy* and all—is a wheezing nine-year-old girl."

"I'd like to have her back. Both of you. Pretty ladies are always welcome at the Cold Creek."

His smile was designed to reach right into a woman's soul and she felt it clear to her toes. Darn him. No, darn her for this ridiculous crush, the weakness she had for handsome charmers.

She couldn't endure his light flirtation, especially knowing he didn't mean any of it, it was all just a game to him.

He couldn't possibly be seriously interested in a stuffy, overstressed thirty-six-year-old elementary school principal with no chest to speak of and the tiniest bit of gray in her hair that she only managed to hide by the grace of God and a good stylist.

He wasn't interested in her, and he had no business smiling at her as if he were.

"Do you stay up nights thinking of lines or do you just come up with them on the fly?"

He raised an eyebrow, though amusement still lurked in his blue eyes, even in the face of her frontal attack. "Was that a line? I thought I was simply extending an invitation."

She sighed. "Look, you've been incredibly understanding about what Cole did to your car. If I had been in your shoes, I can't imagine I would be nearly so magnanimous. He's going to be working with you to make things right for at least a few months and I suppose we'll see a great deal of each other in that time, so let's get this out of the way."

"I'm all ears."

And sexy smiles and gorgeous eyes and broad shoulders that look like they could carry the weight of the world.

She frowned at herself. "I'm not interested in being charmed," she said bluntly.

"Is that what you think I was doing?"

"Weren't you?" She didn't give him a chance to answer. "I doubt you're even aware of it, it's so ingrained in your nature. The flirting, the slow bedroom smiles. Even if you're not attracted to a woman, something in your blood compels you to conquer her, to find her weaknesses and exploit them until she surrenders to your charm like every other woman."

He gazed at her, obviously taken aback by the sudden attack. She heard her own rudeness and was appalled but couldn't seem to stop the words from gushing out.

All she could think of was Ashley Barnes crying her eyes out when Seth never called her back and Richard murmuring lies and promises while he was already sleeping with another woman and planning to abandon his children.

"It's different if a man is genuinely interested in a woman," she went on. "If he truly wants to know about her, if he might feel some spark of attraction and want to follow up on it. That's one thing. But you're not interested in me. Men like you charm just because you can."

He straightened from the door jamb, a sudden fiery light in his eyes that had her stepping back a pace. "That's quite a scathing indictment, Ms. Boyer, especially since you've known me less than a day. I thought good teachers and principals weren't supposed to rush to snap judgments."

His words gave her pause and she had to wonder what in heaven's name seemed to possess her around him.

"You're right. Absolutely. I'm very sorry. That was completely uncalled-for. I'll make a deal with you. I won't rush to any snap judgments provided you refrain from trying to add me to your list of conquests."

Before he could answer, she held open the door in a pointed dismissal. Cold air rushed in, swirling around her like a malicious fog, but she knew it wouldn't be enough to take care of her hot embarrassment. "Thank you again for bringing Cole home. I'll be sure to send him out to your ranch on the bus Tuesday."

Seth gave her a long, hard look, as if he had much more he wanted to say, but he finally turned around and walked outside.

She closed the door and leaned against it, her hands clenched at her sides.

How had she let him get her so stirred up? He hadn't done anything. Not really. Sure, he'd flirted a little, but she had always been able to handle a mild flirtation. He seemed to push all her buttons—and several she hadn't realized were there.

How on earth was she supposed to face him again after she'd all but accused him of trying to seduce her?

She would simply have to be cool and polite. She would be gracious about what he was doing for her son but distant about everything else. She had no doubt she could keep him at arm's length, especially after she'd just slapped him down so firmly.

Keeping him out of her head was a different matter entirely.

Chapter 4

Seth stood on the porch of Jason Chambers's redbrick rambler, the November evening air sharp with fall, and tried to figure out what the heck had just happened in there.

He wasn't at all used to being on the receiving end of such a blunt dismissal, and he was fairly certain he didn't care for it much. He had only been talking to the woman, just trying to be friendly, and she was treating him like she'd just caught him looking up her skirt.

He wasn't quite sure how to react. He had certainly encountered his share of rejection. It never usually bothered him, not when there were so many other prospects out there.

He had to admit, he just wasn't used to rejection accompanied by such blatant hostility.

He ought to just march right back in there and ask Jenny Boyer what he had done in the course of their short acquaintance to warrant it. He lifted a hand to the doorbell then let it fall again.

No. What would that accomplish, besides making him look foolish? She had the right to her opinions, even if they were completely ridiculous.

Even if you're not attracted to a woman, something in your blood compels you to conquer her, to find her weaknesses and exploit them until she surrenders to your charm like every other woman.

That wasn't true. He didn't need to charm every female he came in contact with. He just happened to be a sociable kind of guy.

Where did she get off forming such a harsh opinion on him when they'd barely met?

More to the point, why did it bug him so much?

It was no big deal, he told himself as the cold wind slapped at him. Better to just forget about Ms. Uptight Jennifer Boyer and head over to the Bandito, where he could find any number of warm, willing women who didn't think he was so objectionable.

His boots thudded on the steps as he headed off the porch toward his truck. He climbed in and started the engine, but for some strange reason couldn't bring himself to drive away from the house just yet, too busy analyzing his own reaction to being flayed alive by a tongue sharper than his best Buck knife.

He ought to be seriously pissed off at the woman and not want anything more to do with her. He was, he told himself.

So why was he somehow even more attracted to her?

He liked curvy women who played up their assets, who wore low-cut blouses and short skirts and towering high heels that made their legs look long and sexy.

His brothers seemed to think that was just another sign that he needed to grow up and get serious about life. He had to wonder what Jake and Wade would say if they knew about this strange attraction for the new elementary school principal.

Yeah, he liked looking at her—the tilt of her chin and the flash of her green eyes and those lush lips that seemed at odds with her starchy appearance.

And she smelled good. He had definitely picked up on that. Her perfume had been soft and sweet, putting all kinds of crazy images in his head of wildflowers and spring mountain rain showers.

And her hair. A man could go a little crazy trying to figure out just how to describe it. It was red, yeah, but not just red. Instead, it was a hundred different shades, from gold to something that reminded him of the first soft brush of color on the maples in fall.

He let out a breath. Oh, he was attracted to her all right. Curiously more so now than he'd been even before he walked inside with Cole.

More than that, he was also intensely curious to know whether he could change her opinion of him.

The challenge of it seemed irresistible suddenly.

He shook his head at himself, wholly aware of the irony. He was sitting here pondering how to change the mind of a woman who thought he was nothing more than a womanizer. That was all fine, except for the reason he wanted to change her mind—because he wanted to seduce her, exactly like the womanizer she thought he was.

He ought to just drive away and leave her alone. But the thought of that was as unappealing as riding a steer. He had to try. Something about her prim, buttoned-down beauty appealed to him more than any woman in longer than he could remember.

He didn't even want to think what insight someone could get into his brain that the first woman to really intrigue him in a long time was the one woman who apparently wanted nothing to do with him.

Was she right, that it was all about the challenge to him? Maybe.

But what was life without a little challenge?

Jennifer Boyer was a tough nut to crack, Seth thought two weeks later outside the Cold Creek horse barn.

He'd seen her a handful of times since that first evening when he dropped Cole off. Though he'd been tempted to pour on the charm, he decided on a more low-key approach. She told him she wasn't interested in a flirtation and he had a strong feeling she would automatically reject any blatant overtures so instead he had tried to be warm and friendly, carefully suppressing any sign of his increasing attraction.

Whatever he was doing wasn't working. She wasn't interested. Worse, she seemed more distant each time they met than she had the time before. She responded politely enough, all the while looking at him out of those green eyes that he discovered could turn to ice chips in an instant.

He should have given it up for a lost cause a week ago, but the more she pushed him away, the harder he tried to find a foothold. He was determined to change her mind about him, but after two weeks he was beginning to fear it was a lost cause.

The only chink in her hard shell appeared to be Lucy, he had discovered. The stiff, distant principal seemed to melt around his puppy. Her whole demeanor relaxed and her face lit up in a smile that took his breath away.

Though it was no doubt ruthless of him, he had to admit, he flaunted his single advantage without scruple.

He wasn't a stupid man—he always made sure Lucy

was awake and nearby, looking her adorable self, whenever he knew Jenny was due to arrive at the ranch with Cole.

If nothing else, Lucy served the purpose of keeping his quarry around a little longer, when he was sure she would otherwise have rushed off in a second. She always seemed to be in a hurry to get somewhere, unless the puppy happened to be around.

He watched her and Morgan now tossing a ball for Lucy. The late-autumn sunlight glinted off that magnificent hair and she looked fresh and soft and beautiful.

He wanted her with a heat that continued to baffle him.

Morgan was the one throwing the ball, so by rights Lucy should have been returning it to her. But she couldn't seem to get the message and kept dropping it at Jennifer's feet, to the amusement of all of them.

"You silly girl. What are we going to do with you?" Jenny said after several repeats of the neat little trick he would have taught the puppy, if only he'd thought of it. She picked Lucy up and brushed noses with her and it was all he could do hide the naked longing he knew must be obvious on his face.

He turned his attention to Morgan instead. "You're really great with her. You ought to think about being a vet."

Morgan beamed at him with none of her mother's reserve. "That's just what I told my teacher I want to be! I wrote a paper about it in school. Me and Natalie both want to be veterinarians."

This was new. Last he heard, his niece wanted to be a rodeo queen, but then he figured Nat would probably change her mind a hundred more times before she even reached middle school.

He tugged at one of her ponytails. "Tell you what. The next time the vet is scheduled to come out to look at my horses for some reason on a weekend or holiday, I'll give you a call and you and Natalie can tag along and watch him. If it's all right with your mom, of course."

Morgan's face lit up, making him feel about a dozen feet tall. Now if only he could get her mother to look at him the same way....

"Oh, please, Mom!" she begged. "It would be so awesome to watch a vet work with real horses. We wouldn't get in the way, I swear."

Jenny didn't look thrilled to be put on the spot. "We'll have to see," she murmured in that cool, noncommittal tone every parent seemed to have perfected.

In his limited experience, a "We'll see" was just the same as a "No" but Morgan didn't seem to see it the same way. She looked ecstatic at the possibility. He wanted to tell her most of the time the vets just came out to give shots, not do anything exciting or dramatic, but he didn't want to spoil it for her.

The girl threw the ball for the puppy one more time just as Cole came out of the garage.

"Finished putting the tools away?" Seth asked.

The boy nodded. "You know, I bet she's looking better now than she ever has, even when she was new."

Seth laughed. "You might be right. I can't imagine the folks in Detroit took as much care building her as we've spent restoring her."

Cole grinned and held up his bandaged index finger, the result of a minor accident with a rough piece of metal. "And we've got the war wounds to prove it."

If Seth hadn't been watching Jenny, he might have missed the raw emotion on her face when she looked at her son.

"How's the work on the car coming?" she asked. Seth

opened his mouth to answer but saw her gaze was still trained on her son so he waited for the boy to answer.

"Okay," Cole said. Though he spoke only a single word, his tone wasn't at all his usual surly one.

"Better than okay," Seth corrected. "We've got the minor dings smoothed out and we're waiting for a new headlamp we had to order from a specialty shop back East. Cole here is kicking butt on smoothing out the scrape on the side."

The boy looked pleased. "It's nothing. I'm only doing what you tell me to do."

"That's just what you're supposed to be doing," he growled. "Now if only I can keep you from throwing in those crappy CDs you call music, we'll get along fine."

"Just because you drive an old car doesn't mean you have to listen to the same music my grandpa does."

"It's blues and classic rock. And good for your grandpa, if he listens to CCR and Bob Seger. Maybe between the two of us, we can teach you to appreciate fine music."

Cole made a gagging sound that sent his sister into the giggles. Seth had to admit, for all his belligerence at first, the kid had warmed to him far easier than his mother had.

Cole Boyer loved cars. No question about it. Every time he walked into the garage to work on the GTO, he became a different kid. It was a physical and emotional change that Seth found fascinating to watch. He lifted his shoulders and stopped the perpetual slouch, he made eye contact more, he climbed out of his attitude and talked and chattered as much as Seth's nephew Tanner.

He glowed while he was working on the GTO and it was one more vivid reminder to Seth of himself. It didn't matter how small he'd been until he was fifteen, that he was wheezy and raspy and weak. Behind the wheel of a hot car, everything was relative.

Cole even seemed to respond to the horses. Every time he came to the ranch, Seth saddled a horse for him to ride a little. At first he hadn't been very enthusiastic about it, but as he gained more confidence in the saddle, that seemed to be changing.

Today Cole had even spurred his horse to a slight lope around the arena and had looked as thrilled by it as a bronc rider the first time he hit eight seconds on the timer.

He had to admit, he liked the kid. He was smart and worked hard. Though he still adopted his tough-guy attitude from time to time, when he relaxed his guard enough to let it slip, he was funny and bright and full of interesting observations about the world around him.

His favorite days of the week were those when Cole came out and helped him around the place—and only part of that had to do with knowing he would probably see Jenny, since she usually drove out to the Cold Creek to pick him up.

"When we have her back to her full glory, we'll all have to take a celebratory drive somewhere," Seth said. "Maybe we can run over to Idaho Falls for dinner or something."

"Can we take Lucy?" Morgan asked.

"If she learns to behave herself and doesn't pee on my floor mats."

Morgan giggled. "She is so cute. I wish we could take her home."

"You should see her with her brother," Seth said. "The two of them are quite a pair."

"Is he bossy, too?" Morgan asked him, with a pointed look at her own brother.

"I think she's the bossy one, but it's hard to tell. They wrestle and play and get into all kinds of mischief when they're together."

"I bet they're funny," Morgan said.

"Come on, kids," Jenny finally broke in. "I have another school board meeting tonight and I don't want to dump all the chores and homework on Grandpa to supervise."

"Can I throw one more time?" Morgan asked. "I know she'll bring it back to me this time."

An idea sparked in his head as he watched the girl with the puppy—who finally seemed to get it right and dropped the ball at her feet instead of Jenny's.

He discarded it at first as completely out of the question, but it seemed to rattle around in his head as Cole and Morgan were climbing into her little SUV. He didn't want her to feel backed into a corner so he waited until they were settled inside the car, out of earshot, before he spoke.

"Do you have plans tomorrow?"

She looked at him warily. "Why?"

"I know it's still a week before Thanksgiving but my family is getting together tomorrow to go up on some land we've got up in the mountains to cut Christmas trees. We try to do it a little early before the real heavy snows hit. Why don't you all come along? My mother and brothers will be here. I'm sure Mom will bring Linus so Morgan can have the chance to play with both of the puppies."

She blinked, clearly not expecting that kind of invitation from him.

"It's a lot of fun," he pressed, warming to the idea more and more. "We usually take sleds up and make a big party out of it. The kids would have a great time."

She pursed her lips. "I don't think so. It sounds like a family outing. I wouldn't want to intrude."

"You wouldn't be, I swear. Wade has already invited our vet and his family along and there's always room for a few more. I was up there on our land a month or so ago during round-up and tagged more than a dozen little spruces that would be perfect for Christmas trees. You only have to pick out your favorite and there are plenty to go around. You won't find fresher trees anywhere."

She looked tempted as she gazed up at the mountains. Her eyes softened and her expression turned wistful. What would he have to do to have her turn that kind of expression in his direction?

Right then he would have crawled up that mountain on his knees and ripped a tree out with his bare hands if it would make her look at *him* with those soft green eyes.

"Just think what a great holiday memory that would be for your kids," he pushed, wondering when he'd become so ruthless.

Jenny let out a breath at his words. Blast him. Seth Dalton could sell sunshine in the desert. She had been right about him that day at her father's house. The man knew just the right buttons to push, somehow instinctively finding exactly a woman's weakness and using it against her. How could he possibly know that she dreamed of creating the perfect holiday for her children?

She had such hopes for this year, wishing she could make up for the awful holidays past. The last few had been anything but pleasant as both children had been angry and upset after their father had broken yet more promises to visit.

Even before he'd left for Europe and completely abdicated his responsibility to his family, she'd been on her own most holidays. Richard often chose to work extra shifts during the holidays and Cole and Morgan saw him only sporadically.

Like Chevy Chase in Cole's favorite Christmas movie, she had dreamed about making this year perfect. They were in a new home, with a clean, blank slate for creating family traditions. And wouldn't riding into the mountains for their own tree be a perfect start?

Oh, she was tempted by his offer. Her mind was already conjuring up some Currier & Ives images of sleigh rides and hot cocoa and jingle bells on stamping, snorting horses.

But this particular offer came with some serious strings—attached, unfortunately, to a man she was finding extremely difficult to withstand.

She could feel her resistance to him slipping away every time she was with him and she knew she couldn't just surrender it without a fight. She couldn't afford to fall for a handsome charmer, not now when things were finally starting to go right.

"I don't think so." She put on her most brisk tone, the one she used with recalcitrant students throwing food in the lunch room. "Thank you for the offer, but we couldn't possibly intrude on a family event."

For a long moment he studied her, his head canted to one side, then he finally sighed. "I know you dislike me, Ms. Boyer—"

"I don't!" she protested instinctively.

"Come on. The kids can't hear us so you don't have to pretend for politeness' sake," he said. "I'm not sure how it happened or why but I always seem to rub you the wrong way. Whatever I did, can't we somehow figure out a way to move past it for one day, just so you can allow Cole and Morgan to participate in something we both know they'll enjoy?"

Oh! How could he make her so angry and so guilty at the same time? He was right, blast him. She wanted so much to say yes. Morgan, at least, would have a wonderful time. Cole would probably say it was all lame, but she had a feeling he would secretly enjoy it, too, especially with Seth around.

The only reason she resisted the invitation was because she wasn't so sure she could resist *him*.

How could she deprive her children of this opportunity to create a lasting memory because of her own weakness?

For two weeks she had been doing her best to keep him out of her head, to pretend cool indifference to him. She tried to convince herself the little hitch in her chest every time she drove onto the Cold Creek was simply a little heartburn from eating school lunch with her students.

She knew it wasn't. Even though he was as polite and friendly and noncharming as she could have asked for, her attraction to him only seemed to blossom.

Somehow—without apparently making any effort at all—Seth seemed to be whittling away at her defenses. The prospect of having to pretend disinterest for an entire day was daunting.

She could do it, she thought. For her children's sake, she could be tough, couldn't she?

"What time?" she finally said.

He grinned with triumph, looking so gorgeous in the thin, fading sunlight that she had to remind herself she was supposed to be resisting him.

"We're probably heading up right after morning chores, maybe around eleven or so. Does that work?"

"It should. Yes."

"Bring your father along if you'd like. He can ride a sled up or my mother and stepfather usually stay behind to hang out."

"All right. Thank you."

"Make sure you dress warmly. It's supposed to snow tonight so we'll have plenty of fresh powder."

She nodded as she slid into her car, wondering as she started the engine if the temperatures would possibly cool enough overnight to keep her unruly hormones in the deep freeze she'd stored them in for the last three years.

Chapter 5

She was a bright, successful woman who was certainly mature enough to know her own mind, Jenny thought the next morning as she drove along freshly plowed roads toward the Cold Creek.

So how had she let Seth Dalton con her into this? Through the long, snowy night, she'd had plenty of time to think through the ramifications of what she'd committed herself and her children to by agreeing to come on this outing today.

An entire day in his company. What had she been thinking?

Easy. Thinking apparently wasn't an activity she excelled at when Seth Dalton was around. The man only had to look at her and her brain cells decided to head to the Bahamas.

However this excursion had come about, she didn't doubt Cole and Morgan—and Jason, when it came to that—would enjoy the day. She had to keep that uppermost in her mind.

It was a beautiful morning, at least. Seth had been right about the snow. Maybe some ranching instinct helped him predict the weather—or maybe he just watched the forecast more assiduously than she did.

He had said they would have fresh snow today. As predicted, three to four inches had dropped on the area during the night, something she learned from her father wasn't at all unusual for mid-to late-November in eastern Idaho.

Everything was gorgeous: fresh and white and lovely. This was the perfect kind of early storm, just enough to cover the ground but not enough to make driving a nightmare.

Not much of one, anyway. Her SUV hit a wet spot suddenly and her wheels lost traction a little but she turned into the skid and quickly regained control.

"That's my girl." Jason smiled. "Watch your mother, Cole. Before much longer, you're going to be driving in these kind of conditions. You should be sure you pay attention now and follow her example."

"Does that mean I have to scream like a girl every time I hit a slick patch?" Cole asked with a smirk.

"Hey! I didn't scream," she exclaimed hotly. "That was simply a loud gasp."

Her father and son shared a conspiratorial look. She didn't mind being the source of their amusement, as long as Cole wasn't brooding in the backseat.

The rest of the drive passed smoothly and she wanted to think it was a good omen when the sun peeked through the clouds just as they reached the Cold Creek, gleaming off the snow that covered everything from fence lines to barns.

The Daltons' gravel drive had been cleared and sanded and she tried not to imagine Seth out here on a tractor taking care of his family's and his neighbors' driveways.

Why she found that such an appealing image, she couldn't begin to guess. Better to focus on the picture the ranch made as the pale sunlight glittered off the new snow.

She parked behind a silver pickup. Almost as if he'd been standing at the window watching for them, Seth hurried out of the house an instant later to greet them, accompanied by two puppies dancing around his feet.

He made a stunning picture, she had to admit, the strong, masculine figure in a Stetson and ranch coat, surrounded by playful puppies. Her insides gave a quick little shiver that had nothing to do with the weather, and she worried that even the presence of her father and children wouldn't be enough to insulate her from his effect on her.

She let out a breath. She was tough: she could do this. How hard could it be to resist the man for one day?

She received some inkling of the answer to that question when he reached to open the door, his broad, delighted smile somehow outshining the sun.

"You made it! I was afraid the snow might deter you."

She made some murmured reply—she wasn't quite sure what—and was relieved when he turned his attention to the rest of the vehicle's occupants. "Hey, Morgan. Cole. Mr. Chambers."

"Call me Jason," her traitor of a father said.

"Jason, then. Welcome to the Cold Creek. I'm so pleased you're all coming along with us today."

"Is that Lucy's brother?" Morgan asked, climbing out to greet the cavorting dogs.

"Sure is. This is Linus."

"They're so cute!" she exclaimed, giggling as they licked her.

"We're just about ready to go," Seth said. "I was just giving the sleds one more look. Jason, you are more than welcome to come up the mountain with us. Or if you'd prefer, my mom and stepfather and our neighbors, Viv and Guillermo Cruz, are staying behind to sit by the fire and enjoy a fierce game of gin rummy while the rest of us are slaving out in the cold hunting Christmas trees for them."

Jason perked up. "Now that sounds like my idea of fun."

"Come on inside, everyone, and I'll introduce you around."

"Are we going to ride horses to find our Christmas tree?" Morgan asked eagerly.

Seth reached down and tugged the long tail of her fleece stocking cap and something sharp and sweet yanked at Jenny's heart.

"Sorry, sweetheart, but it would take all day to get up to where the trees are on horseback. We usually go after our trees on snowmobiles. It's faster that way. But you and Natalie can maybe ride around the arena later when we come back down the mountain if you'd like."

So much for her Currier & Ives fantasy, Jenny thought wryly. A reality slap was just what she deserved for jumping to romantic conclusions. Noisy, growly snowmobiles didn't quite fit her idea of a perfect holiday, but she supposed they would be more efficient.

She shook her head at own foolishness but followed Seth and the two wrestling puppies up the cleared sidewalk into the large log-and-stone ranch house.

Inside, she was assaulted by warmth and welcome. A fire snapped in a huge river-rock fireplace and the house smelled of apples and cinnamon and the sharp scent of wood smoke. For all its size—the soaring ceilings and the grand wall of windows overlooking the western slope of the Tetons—the house struck her as comfortable instead of pretentious.

"We're just waiting for Jake and Maggie," Seth said. "They had some kind of emergency at the clinic but called a few minutes ago and said they were on their way. They shouldn't be long. Take your coats off out here and come in and meet everyone else."

She complied and spent a moment gathering everyone's coats then handing them to Seth. For a moment their arms brushed and she felt hard strength beneath the heavy fabric of his coat.

She had to hope nobody else—especially Seth—noticed she sucked in her breath at the contact.

Seth gave no indication that he had seen anything amiss as he took their coats and set them over the arm of a big plump armchair.

The kitchen was just as welcoming as the great room but on a smaller scale. Painted a cheery yellow, it was airy and bright, with crisp white appliances and a huge pine table overflowing with people.

She was assaulted by noise as everyone seemed to have something to say at once to welcome the newcomers.

The instant they walked in, Natalie—Morgan's good friend and daughter to Seth's oldest brother, Wade—jumped up from her chair with a squeal and ran to Morgan.

They hugged as if they'd been separated for months instead of merely overnight, before quickly running off.

Jason slid right into Natalie's newly vacant chair and immediately struck up a conversation with a distinguished-looking gentleman and a woman Jenny recognized as Marjorie Montgomery, Seth's mother.

That left her and Cole as the odd ones out. For an awkward moment she and her son stood on the fringe of the crowd, and she experienced a rare moment of sympathy for him.

She had always been a little hesitant about meeting new people, though she had been forced to work hard to overcome it through nearly fifteen years as an educator.

Cole was a great deal like her in that respect, she realized suddenly. Perhaps he feigned indifference—and sometimes even contempt—to hide his own social discomfort. It was an astonishing revelation.

"Have you met everyone?" Seth asked from behind her, his breath warm in her ear.

"No. Not really."

He quickly performed introductions to his mother and stepfather, Quinn. Viviana and Guillermo Cruz both beamed at her in welcome. Seth introduced the man playing with the puppies Morgan had abandoned for her best friend as the best vet in town, Dave Summers, and his wife, Linda.

"My brother Wade is outside checking the snowmobiles and I told you Jake and Maggie are on their way. I'm not sure where Caroline is."

"Right here."

A voice spoke from behind her and Jenny turned and found Caroline Dalton walking into the kitchen, looking lovely and serene and extremely pregnant.

Jenny had met her at various school functions and knew she was married to Seth's oldest brother, Wade, and was stepmother to Wade's three children from a first marriage Marcy told her had ended with the tragic death of his wife just after the birth of their youngest child.

Caroline had always been friendly and kind, even when her stepson Tanner had been sent to Jenny's office for some mischief or other, and she had to admit she was grateful to see a familiar face.

"Cole, would you like a cookie?" she asked, and Jenny wanted to hug her for including him.

"Sure," he said, reaching for one.

He was just taking a big bite when they heard a commotion in the doorway. Jenny looked over to see a blond girl about Cole's age come into the kitchen holding hands with Tanner and Cody Dalton.

Cole hurried to swallow his cookie, straightening to his full height. He looked both surprised and pleased to see the girl.

"Uh, hey, Miranda," he said, his ears turning pink beneath his snowboarder toque.

She gave him a hesitant smile. "Hi, Cole," she said.

Jenny told herself she was glad her son had someone his own age to hang out with during this outing, though she wasn't sure she was ready to spend the day watching his painfully awkward adolescent interactions with a member of the opposite sex.

"This is Miranda Summers, Dave and Linda's daughter," Caroline said. "She's my lifesaver and watches the kids for me sometimes in the afternoon so I can get some work done."

Marcy—the eternally helpful fount of information that she was—had told her Caroline wrote motivational books and was also a very successful life coach.

Jenny wondered if Caroline Dalton might be able to offer any advice for a woman who seemed destined to be fascinated by the absolutely wrong sort of men.

"We were so thrilled when Seth said he had invited you and your family today," Caroline said with a warm smile that went a long way toward easing Jenny's worries about intruding.

"What a great idea and a wonderful chance for us to get to know you," Caroline went on. "I'm so glad you agreed to come."

"Your brother-in-law can be quite…" Annoying. Bossy. Manipulative. "…persuasive."

Caroline Dalton laughed. "That's an understatement."

"What can I say? It's a gift." Seth grinned, popping one of the cookies in his mouth. "I'm just full of them."

"You're certainly full of something," Caroline countered.

Seth only laughed and patted her abdomen with an easy familiarity that told Jenny they shared a close relationship.

"Don't listen to her, kid." He spoke in the general direction of Caroline's midsection. "A few more months and you can make up your own mind about who's your favorite uncle."

Caroline shook her head but with such affection Jenny wondered for an instant at their relationship.

Just then the outside door opened and Wade Dalton came into the increasingly crowded kitchen, stamping snow off his boots and hanging his Stetson on a hook by the door.

His gaze immediately went to his wife, and she smiled at him with such clear joy that Jenny felt foolish even wondering for an instant about Seth and Caroline.

The other woman was obviously crazy about her husband—and vice versa.

"What are we all waiting for here? The sleds are ready and the sun is shining. I say we get this done."

"Maggie and Jake aren't here yet," Caroline said. "They called a moment ago and said they were on their way."

"We can start suiting up anyway," he said. The veterinarian and his wife rose and started shrugging into heavy parkas.

She managed to wrench Cole's attention from Miranda long enough to drag him back to the ranch great room and their coats. For the next several minutes, they were all busy donning their winter gear—parkas, ski pants, thick gloves.

Jenny had just finished helping Morgan zip her coat when the front door opened, admitting two newcomers.

"You just made it," Seth said with a grin. "We were going to leave without you."

"I'm sure we would have survived the pain," his brother Jake said, his voice dry.

The woman with him—small, dark-haired and graceful as she maneuvered on forearm crutches—gave him a reproving look. "You can always stay here and play cards with the parents and I'll go up with the rest of them. I love cutting our own tree."

"We've got a nice Scotch pine in the backyard. Why couldn't we have saved ourselves the trouble and just cut that one so we could spend the day warm and dry by the fire?"

"Jenny, this complainer is my brother Jake and this beautiful creature is his wife, Maggie," Seth said, kissing the latter on the cheek. "This is Jennifer Boyer, the new principal at Pine Gulch Elementary."

She smiled. "I've met Dr. Dalton. Hello again. And nice to meet you," she added to Maggie, wondering about the crutches everyone else seemed to take in stride.

"Hi," Jake Dalton said. "And hello, Miss Morgan. How's the breathing today?"

"Good. Mom made me do a peak flow test before we left and it was ninety-five."

"Excellent!" He held out a hand for Morgan to high-five, which she did with a giggle.

Jenny had met Dr. Dalton soon after arriving in Pine Gulch when she had taken Morgan in for a refill of her asthma medication. Morgan had been to see him twice since then and each time, he struck Jenny as a very insightful, very compassionate physician, a combination that didn't always go together, in her experience.

"Maggie, sit down for a minute while you have the chance," he said to his wife.

"I'm fine," she said firmly.

"What's with the sticks?" Seth asked, a rude question, Jenny thought, but Maggie Dalton only made a face at him.

Before she could answer, the others came into the great room from the kitchen and Viviana Cruz caught sight of her daughter and hurried toward her.

The resemblance between them was startling, Jenny saw now they were together. The only significant difference was the hint of gray in Viviana's hair and some fine wrinkles in the corners of her eyes.

"Magdalena. What is this?" she asked, worry in her voice. "Why are you using the crutches today?"

"It is nothing, Mama. I promise. Just a little irritation, that's all. My personal physician insisted. I followed his advice since he tends to get pissy when I don't, but really, I'm fine."

"I don't get pissy," Jake growled. "I get even. Next time you put up a fuss, I'll just hide your prosthesis *and* your crutches and make you hop everywhere."

Jenny stared, stunned that the doctor she had come to respect so much would be so harsh with his wife. She was mortified when Maggie saw her shock and shook her head with a smile.

"He's teasing, Jenny, I promise. He wouldn't dare. I know all his hiding places anyway."

"What's a prosthesis?" Morgan asked, in one of those awkward moments all parents experience when they wish their children weren't so naturally curious.

Maggie Dalton didn't seem to mind. She pulled up her pant leg and Jenny saw her left leg ended just below her knee. "It's just a fancy word for a fake leg."

Morgan looked at the metal and plastic device with fascination. "Wow! Can you do cool stuff with it, like jump over cars and stuff?"

Maggie laughed. "Not yet, but I'm working on it."

Her mother still looked concerned. "If you are hurting, you should stay behind with us."

"No, Mama. I'm fine. I've been looking forward to this all week. I'll be sitting on the snowmobile the whole time, I promise."

Viviana bristled like she wanted to argue but her husband, a quiet, sturdy-looking man, put a hand on her arm and she subsided.

A short time later, everyone was ready and they walked outside in the cold air toward a row of gleaming machines.

Jenny gulped. Was she expected to drive one of these complicated-looking beasts? She knew absolutely nothing about snowmobiles. She wouldn't have the first idea how to even start the thing, forget about taking it up a mountain.

To her relief, Seth turned to Cole as soon as they reached the snowmobiles. "Cole, if I take your sister behind me, do you think you can handle driving one with your mom?"

A silly question to ask a fourteen-year-old obsessed with machines. His eyes lit up brighter than Jenny had seen in a long time.

"Oh, yeah," he said with a grin.

"Is it legal?" she asked warily.

"Absolutely or I wouldn't have suggested it," he assured her. "Let's show you how it works."

For the next few moments, he walked Cole through the steps for operating the snowmobile and even had him drive it twenty yards or so before coming back.

"You're all set," Seth assured him.

"Get on, Mom," Cole said gleefully.

She sent Seth a hesitant look but he gave her a reassuring smile. "He'll be great, I promise. I'll keep an eye on you the whole time."

She climbed on, grabbing tight, and realized everyone else was mounted and ready—even Morgan waited on the back of Seth's snowmobile for her driver.

Seth took a few more moments to give Cole some final instructions and she found herself impressed by both his patience and by his consideration. "We'll be climbing into the mountains but it's all pretty gentle and easy. I'll be right ahead of you and will keep an eye on you, and Dave and Linda will bring up the rear."

He paused and gave Cole a stern look. "No hotdogging, okay? Not with your mom on board."

Cole grimaced but nodded. Seth grinned at them both, then climbed onto his own sled and headed off after the others.

"You ready, Mom?" Cole asked.

She grabbed him tightly around his waist, wondering if Seth had arranged things this way so she could remember the joy and connection of being a team with her son.

"Let's go," she said.

With a little jerk, Cole pulled the snowmobile forward and they were off, following Morgan and Seth up the mountain.

Chapter 6

Seth pulled his snowmobile to a stop and turned around to watch Cole and Jenny's progress up the track through virgin snow Wade had cut with his bigger sled.

"Why are we stopping?" Morgan asked behind him, her voice pitched loud to be heard over the growling engines.

"Just checking on the slowpokes," he told her.

She laughed and lifted her face up to the sunshine. Morgan was a sweet kid, he thought, so appreciative of everything. She treated a simple snowmobile ride into the mountains like it was the grandest adventure of her young life.

He was a little surprised at how much he was enjoying this. When he was trying to figure out sled assignments earlier in the morning, he had instinctively wanted Jenny to ride with him. He was more than ready to ramp things up a level, to make her unable to avoid confronting the physical connection he sensed between them.

What better way than to have her holding tightly to him up and down the mountain? He had spent more than a few pleasant moments fantasizing about having her so close to him for the entire half-hour ride up and back down again.

On further reflection, he'd discarded the idea, appealing as it was. Crowding her physically would only push her away. This arrangement was better.

It was not only more safe to have Morgan with him rather than her inexperienced brother but it also provided the bonus of being able to watch Jenny enjoying a fun, peaceful moment with her son, something he'd figured out early wasn't a frequent occurrence between the two.

He hadn't expected to get such a kick out of Jenny's daughter, but he was discovering he enjoyed having her look at him as though he was some kind of hero.

In talking over the Christmas-tree excursion with Wade, they had decided to sandwich experienced drivers around the teens. Wade and his boy Tanner were riding point with Miranda driving a sled and Natalie riding behind her.

Dave and Linda were just ahead of Seth and Morgan, to keep an eye on the girls. Cole and Jenny were behind him, with Maggie and Jake bringing up the rear on another of the bigger snowmobiles. They also towed the sled that would be used to haul down the Christmas trees.

So far the arrangement seemed to be working. He couldn't remember the last time he'd enjoyed himself so much on the annual Dalton Christmas-Tree Trek. A big part of that came from the vicarious enjoyment he found watching Jenny and her kids.

"Are we almost there?" Morgan asked.

"Not much farther. See that small valley of pines up there about halfway up the mountain? That's where we're headed. It should take us about fifteen more minutes. How are the lungs up this high?"

She took a deep, noisy breath. "Great," she assured him.

He was going to tell her to make sure she let him know if she started having any trouble with her asthma, but just then Cole pulled up alongside him.

"What's the matter?" he called over the noise of the sleds.

"Just checking on you. Everything going okay?"

He nodded. "This is a kick!"

"Jenny? How about you?"

She smiled at him, her cheeks wind-chapped and her color high. She looked so bright and vibrant out in the cold sunshine that he had to fight a fierce desire to tug her off the sled and into his arms.

"It's wonderful! The view from up here is absolutely incredible!"

"It is," he agreed, though he was hard-pressed to drag his gaze away from her excitement.

With effort, he managed to do it and turn back to her son. "Cole, I wanted to show you where to go from here. We're heading for that stand of trees about halfway up there."

"Okay," the boy said. "Though I'm pretty sure I'm capable of following a trail made by four other snowmobiles."

"I'm sure you are, but sometimes it helps to have the bigger picture about where you're ultimately heading, instead of just following the exhaust of the machine in front of you."

"If I was stupid enough to veer off the trail, you'd all be on me like stink on cheese anyway."

He laughed. "Just so you know where you stand, kid."

Cole made a face at him. "Are we going to ride or are we going to sit around shooting the breeze all day?"

Jake and Maggie pulled up before he could answer. He

gave his sister-in-law a careful look but she didn't look to be in terrible pain, even though she had her crutches handy.

He knew Jake would never have let her come along if he worried she might overdo it, so Seth decided he would let his brother worry about his own wife.

"You're blocking the trail," Jake called.

"Yeah, yeah. We're going."

He started his sled again, feeling a curious warmth in his chest when Morgan gripped him tightly.

If he wasn't careful, he could seriously fall for Jenny Boyer's kids, he thought. That would be great if their mother came with them in a package deal but he was afraid things wouldn't work out that way.

This was a stupid idea.

An hour later, Seth wondered how in Hades he was going to make it through an entire day pretending this casual friendship with Jenny when he hungered for far more, especially since she seemed determined to push him away at every turn.

The more time he spent with her, the deeper his fascination for her seemed to run. It baffled and unnerved him. He didn't understand it—he just knew he couldn't seem to keep his eyes off her.

He was blowing all his plans to be cool and detached and to give her the time and space she needed until she was ready for him to kick things up a notch. Things weren't working out that way, mainly because he couldn't force himself to stay away from her.

Though he knew he should have let one of his brothers help her while he cut the trees for his mother and the Cruzes, he still found himself trailing after Jenny and her kids, his chain saw at the ready as they scoured the stand of evergreens for the perfect tree.

What he really wanted to do was drag her behind the closest trunk and steal any chance to explore that mouth, just so he could see if it could possibly taste as delicious as it looked.

With her two kids along, the possibility of that was fairly remote, he acknowledged. Still, a man could dream.

"This is way more fun than pulling our artificial tree out of storage like we've always done," a pink-cheeked Morgan exclaimed as they trudged through the snow toward the outer edge of the small forest.

He locked away his inappropriate lust and put on an exaggerated expression of horror. "Artificial. Please say it's not so."

Morgan giggled. "Yep."

"Don't tell me it's pink."

Jenny made a face at him. "Of course not. It was a perfectly lovely seven-and-a-half-foot spruce. Green, prelit and very convenient."

"That smells like the petroleum product that it is, no doubt. How can you stand here inhaling this delicious scent into your lungs and even consider having an artificial tree?"

"We gave it to Goodwill when we moved. And we're here now, aren't we, searching for the perfect tree? That has to count for something!"

"I don't know. Somebody who's always had an artificial monstrosity might not recognize the perfect tree even if it reached out a branch and tapped you on the head with it."

She stopped suddenly, so abruptly he almost plowed into her. Her gaze was glued to a blue spruce about eight feet high. Though a yellow ribbon tied to the trunk indicated he'd marked it for thinning, now he couldn't really see anything spectacular about it.

Jenny apparently did. She gave a happy sigh. "This one. I want this one."

He wasn't ready for the search to be over yet. Then they would have to go back and rejoin the rest of his family and he would lose any chance for privacy with her.

"There are still maybe a half dozen marked ones we haven't even looked at yet. Are you sure this is the one?"

"Positive. This one is perfect, don't you guys think?"

Morgan nodded with the same kind of glee as her mother but Cole only shrugged. "It looks like every other tree we've seen today," he said.

"What are you talking about?" Jenny exclaimed. "This tree has personality! It's wonderful! The color is a far richer green than all the rest and can't you see the way all the branches look so perfect except for that little one there in the back pointing in a different direction?"

"If you say so."

"It's just right. I only wish the school didn't have a fire-code policy against real trees or I'd put it out by the office."

She looked so thrilled, so bubbly and excited, Seth couldn't look away. Her eyes glowed and her nose was red and he couldn't seem to think about anything but tasting that bright smile.

He cleared his throat and made himself focus on the tree instead. "You want it, it's yours. Cole, you want to do the honors?"

The kid eyed the big machine in his hands with un-mistakable longing, then he looked away. "You can do it."

He probably didn't know the first thing about running a chainsaw, Seth realized. "It's easy. Come on. I'll walk you through it."

He showed Cole how to fire up the saw, then helped guide him to the right spot on the trunk. Between the two of them, they buzzed through the small trunk in seconds and the tree fell in a flurry of snow. It was a good choice, he thought, one of those he'd marked that were being crowded out by bigger trees.

"How are we going to carry our tree down the mountain now?" Morgan asked.

"Jake is pulling a sled behind his snowmobile. We'll tie them all together on that and he and Maggie will drag them down."

"Is that it?" Cole asked.

"I've got to cut one for my place now. Since you're so good at picking them out, you can help me find mine. With my vaulted ceilings, I've got room for a ten- or twelve-foot one. Think big."

They spent several moments walking through the heavy timber looking at possibilities until Jenny stopped in front of the one he'd actually had in mind for his place all along.

"Kids, your mother is a natural at Christmas-tree hunting. Just think what she must have been suppressing through all those years of artificial trees!"

Again he urged Cole to do the honors, though this time he let the boy handle the saw by himself, keeping a careful watch on him as he did.

"Why don't you go back to the one we cut for your house and carry it down to the snowmobiles while your mom helps me haul this one?" he suggested. "Can you find the way?"

"We can see it from here." Cole pointed down the hill to the sleds gleaming in the pale sunshine. He took off with Morgan following close behind, and finally Seth was alone with Jenny, just as he'd orchestrated.

He hadn't expected her to be looking at him with such a warm smile. "Thank you for this," she said. "You were right, it will be a wonderful memory for Cole and Morgan."

"What about for you?"

Her gaze flashed for just an instant then she looked away. He saw her swallow and would have given half his horses—and a cow or two, as well—to know what she was thinking.

"I've enjoyed it," she murmured.

"You don't relax enough. You should do it more often."

Her mouth opened, her expression indignant. Instead of the sharp retort he expected, after a moment she closed her mouth and sighed. "You're right. I know you're right but it's not always the easiest thing in the world for me to do with any success."

He dared take a step closer, keeping his hands carefully neutral at his sides. "Why is that, I wonder?"

Her gaze flitted back to his and stayed there a little longer, like a wild bird following a trail of sunflower seeds toward an outstretched hand. "I suppose because so much depends on me. It's hard work being a principal and even harder work being a single mother."

"You do both very well."

"And how would you know that? You don't have children in my school to judge my performance there and you don't have children of your own at home to comment on my mothering."

"You don't have to be a jockey to recognize a great racehorse."

She gave a short laugh. "I don't believe I've ever been compared to a horse before."

He debated backing off now, giving her a chance to regroup, then decided that would be foolish. Better to keep her off balance. He stepped forward again until only a foot or so separated them. From here, he could smell the fresh, flowery scent of her, an unlikely beacon of spring amid the wintry landscape.

She swallowed hard at his nearness but didn't step back. Instead, her chin lifted. "I don't like to be crowded, Seth."

For some strange reason, her defiance made him laugh. "Is that what I was doing?"

"Oh, I have no doubt you know exactly what you're doing. You're very good at what you do. I certainly won't deny that."

"What I do?"

"The whole seduction bit. The oh-so-casual touches, those sexy, intimate smiles. Stepping closer and closer until I can't focus on anything but you. I imagine most women probably melt in a big puddle at your feet."

The cynicism in her voice smarted. "But not you?"

"I'm sorry if this stings your pride but I'm just not interested. I believe I told you that."

"So you did," he agreed. "But are you so sure about that, Ms. Boyer?"

Against the howl of all his instincts, he stepped closer again. He watched a tiny pulse jump in her throat and her breathing seemed to accelerate. The hunger inside him to taste her threatened to consume him, to wipe out whatever remained of his self-control and his sanity.

"Ye-es," she said, though that single word came out breathy, hushed.

"I think we both know that's not precisely true," he murmured. He reached out and gripped the ends of her scarf in some halfhearted effort to keep her from fleeing, then leaned down slowly, carefully, anticipation thrumming powerfully inside him.

An instant before his mouth would have at last found

hers, some subconscious warning system picked up rustling in the underbrush. He dropped her scarf and stepped back just before Wade walked into their little clearing.

His brother surveyed the scene, his hard blue eyes missing nothing, but he only sent one swift, censorious look in Seth's direction. "Cole and Morgan said you cut a big one for your place. I came to see if you need help hauling it down so we can go back down the mountain. My boys are starting to get restless and I think Cody's ready for a nap."

"Yeah. We're on our way."

What the hell was he doing? Seth wondered as he and Wade hauled the big tree down the slope toward the waiting sleds. He had played that last hand like some damn greenhorn who'd never kissed a girl before. That's what was called jumping the gate before the starting pistol sounded.

She wanted him to back off. Hell, she'd practically *ordered* him to, and he'd ignored her. He had no doubt he would have had her pressed up against one of those trees in another ten seconds if Wade hadn't interrupted.

He didn't like the fact that he'd almost lost it back there, that he'd plunged ahead with something that all his instincts were telling him was a bad idea. It wasn't like him at all. He always, *always,* maintained some control over himself when it came to women.

Jenny Boyer somehow managed to shred that control to bits, like a chainsaw ripping through flimsy cardboard.

Where did he go from here? He didn't want to give up before he'd even enjoyed a tiny taste of that lush mouth, but he might just have to accept the grim reality that some things weren't meant to be.

She wanted him to leave her alone. Maybe that was what he ought to do. Forget about Jennifer Boyer, just as she had insisted, and move on. The thought filled him with an odd kind of restlessness but he didn't see any other choice. If she wasn't interested—or didn't *want* to be interested—he had to respect her boundaries.

He was subdued on the ride back down the mountain and everyone else seemed to be, too. A light snow started falling again and while it looked feathery and lovely when you were safe and dry inside watching it through the window, on a snowmobile, it pelted exposed skin like sharp pebbles. Everyone seemed glad when they reached the Cold Creek again.

At the house, they quickly unloaded the trees from the transport sled. Maggie was looking tired and the kids were cold, so Jake and Wade sent the women and children inside the ranch house to warm up.

While they tied the trees onto the respective vehicles for transport to their destination, Seth drove the Cold Creek snowmobiles into the storage garage and performed postride maintenance checks on them. He was the default mechanic on the ranch, and he liked to think he was the go-to guy when machines broke down.

He had just stowed the last one and was checking fluid levels on it when Jake showed up in the doorway of the garage.

"I'm about done here," Seth said. "Go ahead inside and check on Maggie."

"She'll be okay."

"What's her deal today, anyway? I haven't seen her use the canes for a long time. She said she was having some irritation. Is everything okay?"

"She's changing pain meds and we're trying to find a good safe combination."

His brother gave him a quiet smile that told wonders about how much he adored his wife. "Don't tell anybody, but we're talking about starting a family and Maggie wants to wean off some of her heavy-duty meds before we give it a serious try."

He felt another of those curious pangs in his chest. Both of his brothers were deliriously happy with their wives and their lives. He was glad for them, he told himself. He just couldn't quite figure out why the life he had always thought was perfect suddenly felt so empty in comparison.

"That's wonderful," he said. "I can't think of two people who would make better parents."

When Jake continued to stand in the doorway watching him, Seth sighed, screwed the oil cap back on the snowmobile and stood up to wait for the lecture he sensed was coming.

He knew that look in his brother's eyes all too well. Wade must have seen more of that encounter with Jenny on the mountain than he thought and sent Jake in to do his dirty work.

"Let's have it, then," he said.

"What?"

"You've got on your bossy-big-brother look. Wade was the one giving me the snake eye all the way down the mountain so how did you get to be the one roped into this?"

Jake leaned against the door frame. "We drew straws and I lost."

"Lucky you."

"Right. That means I get to be the one to ask you what the hell you think you're doing."

He really wasn't in the mood for this, Seth decided. He'd been on the receiving end of these little improving talks all his life from one or both of his brothers. He had to wonder if Wade and Jake would still feel inclined to tell him how to live his life when he was seventy.

Probably.

"I believe I'm putting the sleds away right now. You or Wade have a problem with that?"

"You know we don't. Do what you want with the snow-mobiles. But neither of us is too crazy about you tangling up a nice lady like Principal Boyer."

He arched an eyebrow. "Tangling up?"

"You know what I mean. What are you doing here, Seth? She's not your usual bar babe. She's a nice woman with a couple of kids and a retired father and a responsible job. She deserves better."

His brothers sure knew just how to twist the knife in his gut. "Thanks," he snapped. "It's always nice to get a vote of support from my family. Don't hold back, doc. Why don't you tell me what a selfish, irresponsible bastard I am, so we can all go in and have some lunch?"

Jake had always been slow to anger but he also never backed down from a fight. "Oh, screw the poor-me routine. That wasn't what I meant and you know it. I'm not talking about you as a person, I'm referring strictly to your usual playbook with women."

Seth yanked down the seat of the sled so hard he was pretty sure he broke something. "Memorized it, have you?"

"Since you've been sticking to the same game plan since before you were old enough to shave, it's not tough to guess where this is headed."

"And where is that?"

"You wine her, dine her, romance her, take what you want, then move on to the next lovely young thing to cross your path."

"Yeah, yeah. Selfish, irresponsible bastard. I got that part."

"I didn't say that. Most of the time the women you hook

up with know what to expect and probably are only after exactly what you're willing to give them. Fine. If you're both consenting adults, no harm no foul. But this is different. Jennifer Boyer isn't one of your Bandito bimbos. She's got kids, Seth, one of them a teenager who looks up to you. From what I hear, Cole has already been abandoned by his father. Don't you think you're only going to reinforce that lousy example of how a man should treat a woman when he watches you walk away from his mother, too?"

"I haven't even kissed the woman!"

"But you want to, don't you?"

"None of your business."

"It's not," Jake agreed. "But I have to point out those kids already care about you and if you take things where I think you want to, Cole and Morgan are likely to come out of this mighty damn hurt when you get bored and move on."

He hadn't given much thought to their feelings in all this, he realized, with no small amount of shame.

"There's a whole forest full of pretty young trees out there," Jake went on. "Find a different one to scratch your itch on. That's all I'm saying."

"What if I don't want a different one?"

He hadn't meant to say that, but somehow the words slipped out anyway. Jake gave him a long, hard look that made him feel like he was fifteen years old again.

"Maybe for once you ought to try thinking not so much about what *you* want but about what *she* wants, and see how that works out for you."

Before he could come up with some undoubtedly pithy reply, Jake left in that frustrating way of his.

Seth should have been relieved the lecture was over but he couldn't stop thinking about what his brother said. The hell of it was, he was absolutely right.

Jenny wanted nothing to do with him. Though he knew she was attracted to him despite her protests, he wasn't going to crowd her anymore, he decided.

He would still have to see her because of his arrangement with Cole. But after today, he would just be polite and friendly and forget about anything else.

No matter how impossible it suddenly seemed.

Chapter 7

She was going to have a tough time dragging everyone away.

Jenny surveyed her family crowded around the Daltons' big kitchen and tried to remember the last time she'd seen them all enjoying a meal so much. Yes, the food was fabulous—a half-dozen different kinds of soup, hot rolls and a salad bar that rivaled anything in a restaurant—but the company was the most appealing part of this meal.

Morgan and Natalie were giggling at the smaller table brought in for the children. At the breakfast bar, Cole and Miranda were deep in a debate over the best ska band of all time. Even Jason was in his element laughing at something Quinn Montgomery said, down at the other end of the big dining table.

It was noisy and crowded and warm but her family seemed to be thriving. In fact, everyone seemed to be having a wonderful time except for her.

She couldn't seem to relax and allow herself to have fun. The Daltons had been everything kind. She found them all warm and friendly—even Seth's oldest brother, Wade. At first he had seemed gruff and intimidating, but throughout the day he had treated her and the children with nothing but kindness.

Despite the jovial company, she couldn't seem to move past her own awkward discomfort.

She was also painfully aware that everyone at the big table had been divided by couple—so by default she sat next to Seth. She had a hard time focusing on anything else but his nearness throughout the meal, his strong hands and his seductive masculine scent and the heat that seemed to shimmer off him in waves.

She didn't want to be here. She would have preferred sitting at the children's table to enduring this close proximity, especially as Seth had been distant and distracted throughout the meal and seemed to become more so as the meal wore on.

He obviously had second thoughts about inviting her and her family and regretted their de facto pairing.

Despite the fabulous food, her stomach felt hollow and achy and she wanted to disappear. That, in turn, made her angry with herself and more determined to see this dinner through as quickly as possible. At least they were already having dessert so the torture would be over soon.

"This pie is delicious," Caroline Dalton exclaimed from across the table with her warm smile. "I love the crunchy caramel topping."

Jenny smiled politely as others at the table joined in the praise for the caramel apple pie she'd brought along, one of her very few specialties. But even as she smiled and thanked them all for the compliments, she was aware of

Seth next to her setting down his fork as if he were suddenly eating fried motor oil, leaving the rest of his pie uneaten on his plate.

A few moments later, he pushed back his chair and aimed his charming smile around the table at every single person but her.

"Thanks for a delicious meal, everybody, but I've got to run up to the barn."

"Can we go, Uncle Seth?" Natalie asked. "You said maybe we could ride later."

"You could go for a horseback ride, I guess." He paused then looked as if he regretted his words even as he spoke them. "Or Cole could grab one of the snowmobiles and pull you up the hill behind the barn so you can tube down. If it's all right with your mother, of course."

Natalie, Morgan and Tanner looked ecstatic at the possibility and even Cole and Miranda appeared thrilled.

"Oh, please, Mom!" Morgan begged.

How was she supposed to refuse with all those young eyes looking at her with identical entreaties?

"Thanks," she murmured under her breath to Seth.

He gave a smile that seemed only slightly repentant—but at least he wasn't completely ignoring her the way he'd done since that breathless moment on the mountain when he'd nearly kissed her.

"I suppose, if it's all right with the other parents."

"You all just warmed up," Caroline exclaimed. "Are you sure you want to go back out in the cold?"

The children gave a resounding answer in the affirmative and scrambled up from the chairs to climb back into their cold-weather gear.

Half an hour later, they were being pulled up the hill in

turns by Cole on the snowmobile, who appeared to be having the time of his life.

Caroline had volunteered to go with them to keep an eye on the children while the others stayed behind to watch a holiday movie. Though Jenny hadn't wanted to spend another minute with Seth, she had also hated thinking of the pregnant woman standing out in the snow.

"I'll do it," she insisted, so here she sat on a bench overlooking the sledding hill.

At least she didn't have to endure more stilted conversation with Seth. After dragging her into this whole thing, he had been astonishingly quick to disappear.

The minute Cole had the snowmobile tow rope figured out, Seth spent a few moments starting a small fire in a small cast-iron outdoor fireplace nearby, then claimed he had some things to do inside the horse barn that couldn't wait.

She hadn't minded sitting alone watching the children. It gave her a chance again to savor the magnificence of the setting. She found a raw grandeur in the snow-covered landscape with the backdrop of wild, rugged mountains.

Though sunset was still a few hours away, the afternoon sky was already beginning to turn lavender and it had started snowing again, big, fluffy flakes that made her want to catch one on her tongue like the children on her playground.

After a moment, she gave into the temptation and stuck out her tongue. Of course, it was at that instant that Seth walked out of the barn, apparently finished with what had been so urgent.

She jerked her tongue back into her mouth and kept it firmly planted there as he stood at the open doorway watching her. She had to hope he hadn't seen that completely childish impulse, though she had a feeling it was a vain hope.

After a moment he pulled the door closed behind him and approached her, looking solid and dark and almost predatory against the snowy white landscape.

She hated herself for the little flutter in her stomach but couldn't seem to control it.

He sat down beside her on the bench. "Looks like they're having a good time. This was always the perfect sledding hill when we were kids."

She couldn't quite manage to wrap her mind around the image of this wholly masculine man in front of her as a gleeful child sledding down the hillside.

"This is much more fun with deeper snow," he went on. "You'll have to bring Morgan and Cole back in a month or so when the conditions are a little better."

The chances of that were fairly slim, she thought. "I can't believe we're still a week away from Thanksgiving and your mountains have more than two feet of snow."

"Better get used to it. We probably won't see bare earth again until March or April at the earliest. The higher elevations might be two or three months after that."

She shuddered, earning a laugh from him. "Didn't your dad warn you about our winters before you moved down from Seattle?"

"He told me they were on the harsh side but he's promised me the summers make up for it."

He smiled a little, though she thought he was still distant. "That's true enough. My mother always says if you complain about the winter, you don't deserve the summer."

"I guess I should watch my mouth, then."

"Just find a winter sport you enjoy, like ice climbing or

cross-country skiing. That tends to give you a completely different perspective on the cold weather."

The idea of that wasn't very appealing, since she figured she was probably about the most unathletic person in town. "Does curling up by the woodstove with a good book count?" she asked.

He grinned. "Sure. And you get bonus points if it's at least a book about winter sports."

"I'll have to dig through Dad's library to see what I can find about hockey or ice fishing," she said with a laugh. "I'm all for coming up with anything to make the winter pass more quickly."

"If you're not much of a cold-weather lover, what brings you to Pine Gulch?" he asked. "I would think a school principal could find work just about anywhere."

"Maybe. But I couldn't find my dad anywhere but here. He loves Pine Gulch. After the divorce, he offered to come live with us in Seattle but I knew he would hate it there. All the friends he made after he retired are here and he's got a rich, fulfilling life. The fishing, the photography, his monthly poker game with his friends in Jackson. I couldn't drag him away from that."

Jenny paused, surprised by her compulsion to confide in him. She wouldn't have thought it possible but Seth could actually be a comfortable conversationalist, if she could put her hormones on hold.

"At the same time, I knew my children needed him. Especially Cole. A boy his age needs strong male role models. Since his father's not in the picture anymore, I had to do something. When the principal position opened up at the elementary school, it seemed like an opportunity I couldn't pass up."

Their situation wasn't perfect, but she couldn't regret moving here. She was trying to do the best she could.

"So that's why you took the job at the elementary school and moved to town?" he asked. "To be near your dad?"

"I had to do something. Cole was in trouble almost all the time in Seattle. I hoped moving him here would steady him a little. Of course, six weeks later, he managed to steal and wreck a classic car," she said wryly.

"He's doing a good job of making it right, though."

"You know, the first month or so after we moved here, I thought I'd made a terrible mistake. These last few weeks have been much better. Whatever you've been doing with Cole, thank you."

Seth raised an eyebrow at her words and she saw surprise flicker in the deep blue of his eyes. "I haven't done anything but put him to work," he answered.

"Maybe that's exactly what he needed. A project to focus on. Or perhaps simply someone taking an interest in him. I don't know what it is, I only know things have improved considerably since he started coming out here. He doesn't seem to hate either me or Idaho as much as he used to."

"I'm glad," he said simply.

They sat in silence for a moment, broken only by the distant shrieks of the children and the snap of the fire in the little stove.

This was nice, she thought. Too nice. She could feel herself slipping under his spell again—and this time she couldn't really blame the man, since he wasn't doing anything but sitting there.

She was relieved when Cole pulled up to them a few moments later, breaking the fragile mood.

"Your turn, Mom," her son said. "Hop on. You can use Morgan's inner tube."

Jenny shook her head vigorously. "No. That's okay. I like my legs unbroken, thanks."

Astride the snowmobile, Cole flapped his arms and made a clucking sound. "Come on. Morgan's gone down six or seven times and she's only nine. Is she tougher than you?"

"Oh, without question."

"Come on," Cole cajoled. "Everybody's having a great time. You can't sit down here the whole time."

"You'll have fun," Seth joined in. "You can count this as your first experiment in winter sports."

She gazed at the two males, so physically dissimilar but so surprisingly alike, then sighed and rose from the bench.

"I'm blaming you when this goes horribly wrong," she told Seth with a laugh as she climbed onto the snowmobile behind her son.

Her smile faded when she realized Seth was staring at her mouth. Awareness bloomed in her stomach and she was almost grateful when Cole gunned the engine and started up the mountainside.

He needed to get out of there.

Fast.

All his lofty intentions were being shot straight to hell the more time he spent with Jenny Boyer.

He watched her on the snowmobile behind her son as the boy climbed to the top of the hill.

Even from here, he could see the tension in her posture. She clearly didn't want to be up there but she was doing it anyway, refusing to let her fears hold her back. He admired that in a woman.

He admired a lot about her. He liked the way her eyes lit up when she talked about her children, he liked the way she seemed to sincerely listen to a person, he liked the way she was willing to laugh at herself.

He let out a heavy breath. What the hell good did it do to count down all the things he liked about her? The grim fact remained that Jake was absolutely right. She deserved somebody better than him, somebody who wasn't always looking around the next bend.

He'd been crazy to come out here again. He should have just holed up in the barn until she was gone, taking her big green eyes and her lush mouth and her sweet-as-sugar smile with her.

From here, he could see her arguing with her children, then a minute later she climbed onto the inner tube. She sat there for a long moment, then nodded to her kids, who gave her a push.

She shrieked then he heard her exclamation turn into a delighted laugh that seemed to reach right through him and tug at his insides.

He should make his escape while he had the chance, he thought. He even turned around and headed for the barn but he'd only made three steps when he heard the laughter cut off into an abrupt scream.

He jerked back around just in time to watch her spiral off the inner tube. The tube went one way and she went the other. To his horror she rolled three, possibly four times, then she lay horribly still about twenty yards from the bottom.

He was already racing up the slope before she came to a stop, his heart pumping like crazy. He reached her just seconds later, astonished by his protective impulses. He wanted to grab her close and hang on tight.

"Jen. Talk to me, sweetheart."

She didn't answer, though he could see her chest rising

and falling beneath her winter parka. He unzipped it just as Cole roared up on the snowmobile.

"Go down to the ranch house and get my brother Jake," he told the boy, whose face was as white as the landscape around them. "Hurry."

"Right. Okay."

He gunned the snowmobile and took off down the road and Seth turned his attention back to Jenny.

His brother might be the doctor in the family but years of ranch living and dealing with various mishaps had given Seth a basic knowledge of first aid. He ran his hands over her but couldn't find any broken bones.

By now Miranda, Tanner and the girls had gathered, watching him solemnly as he examined her. Tanner and the younger girls looked terrified and even the normally sensible Miranda seemed anxious.

The snow had kicked up in the last few moments and giant flakes drifted down to settle on her still features, alighting on her eyelashes, in her hair, on the curves of her cheek.

By his estimation, it would take Cole ten minutes or so to ride down to the house, grab Jake and drive back up here. He couldn't bear the idea of Jenny lying out here in the snow all that time.

Besides that, the children needed to be inside where they could get warm. All of them were going to be shocky soon if they didn't go inside.

Making a split-second decision, he scooped Jenny into his arms. Moving her some place warm and dry outweighed the first aid axiom about not moving her, he decided. Jake would probably yell at him, but he knew his brother would have done the same.

"Miranda, I'm taking Ms. Boyer inside. Come with me

and take the kids into the kitchen, okay? I've got some cookies and I think there's some hot cocoa mix somewhere in there. Morgan, Nat, I need you two to help Miranda with Tanner."

"What about my mom?" Morgan asked. Her features were pale with fright. He could only hope she didn't have an asthma attack just now since he wasn't sure he could cope with a second crisis.

He gave her what he hoped was a reassuring smile as he carried Jenny into his house. "She just bumped her head a little when she fell off the inner tube but I'm sure everything's going to be fine. Aren't we lucky to have a doctor so close? Jake will take care of her, I promise."

"Why are her eyes still closed?" she asked as he set her mother down carefully on the couch.

He'd been the one pushing her to go on that tube, he thought with guilt. "Have you ever fallen at the playground and had the wind knocked out of you? That's what happened to your mom."

He took time away from his worry over Jenny to give Morgan a quick, reassuring hug. She seemed to find comfort from it—and so did he. "Go on into the kitchen with the others and as soon as Dr. Jake takes a look at her, you can come back and talk to her, okay?"

"She always stays with me and holds my hand when I'm having a flare-up. Will you stay with her?"

"I'm not going anywhere, honey," he promised.

With one last anxious look, she went into the kitchen and he turned his attention back to Jenny.

She looked so frail against the dark maroon leather of his couch. A moment ago she had been laughing with him and complaining about the weather and now she was so terribly still.

He pulled her coat open and was running a hand over her again, looking more carefully this time for anything out of the ordinary when her eyes fluttered open.

She gazed at him for a long moment, her eyes hazy and baffled, then she blinked and seemed to become more alert by the second.

"Seems like a lot of trouble to go to just so you could cop a cheap feel," she mumbled, her voice hoarse.

Relief flooded through him and he closed his eyes for a moment and said a silent prayer of gratitude. She couldn't be at death's door if she could manage a tart comment like that.

He grinned, fighting the urge to pull her into his arms. "That was just a side benefit. And believe me, it wasn't cheap in the least."

To his surprise, she smiled back, then winced at the movement.

"What hurts, besides your head?"

"What doesn't?" She tried to pull herself to a sitting position.

He shook his head. "Take it easy. I'm not letting you go anywhere so you might as well relax for now."

She obeyed, though he thought her compliance stemmed more from her lack of strength than anything else.

"Nothing seems broken from what I could tell," he told her. "Any acute areas of pain?"

"Only my head. Most of me is just one big ache except my head, which I'm afraid might be ready to fall off."

"It wouldn't surprise me if you've got a concussion. You conked it pretty hard."

She winced. "Graceful, as usual."

Tenderness washed through him and he couldn't prevent himself from picking up her hand. Strictly to warm her cold fingers, he told himself, even as he savored the contact. "It was just your trajectory. You couldn't avoid that rock, no matter what you tried to do. Anybody would have crashed in the same situation."

"Thank you for trying to make me feel better," she murmured.

Her fingers curled in his and a terrifying tenderness seemed to soak through him. "Is it working?"

She made a face. "Not really."

They both shared a small laugh he found oddly intimate and again he had to fight the fierce desire to pull her into his arms.

"Where are my kids?" she asked.

"Morgan's in the kitchen with Miranda and the others and I sent Cole down to the house on the snowmobile for Jake. They should be here in a minute. Matter of fact, if I'm not mistaken, I hear an engine out there right now."

Seth barely had time to pull his hand away from hers before Jake and Cole both burst into the house.

Chapter 8

"**I**'m sorry about this," Jenny said five minutes later to Jake Dalton as he gave her a careful exam after banishing Seth and Cole from the room. "I feel like such an idiot."

He smiled with the calm competence she'd noticed during Morgan's asthma-related office visits. "Don't worry about it. You're not the first one to ever tumble down that hill. I think all of us have done our share. Seth even broke his collarbone on that hill when he was around Morgan's age. I don't suppose he told you that, did he?"

"No. He didn't mention it."

"He saw some snowboarders on TV and thought he'd like to try it."

"Oh, no," she murmured.

"Exactly. We didn't have any equipment, of course, so he improvised with a piece of plywood he found in the barn. He was lucky he only broke his collarbone."

She smiled, though she really didn't want to talk about

Seth Dalton. She couldn't seem to shake the memory of that moment she'd awakened and found him examining her.

In her dazed, half-conscious state, she had come dangerously close to wrapping her arms around him and holding on tight. A million sensations had poured through her as his hand touched her ribs, hungers she barely remembered from the early days of her marriage.

She sighed and Jake Dalton gave her a curious look and pressed harder on her shoulder. "Is that a touchy spot?"

"No. Sorry."

"Well, I can't find anything broken. You've got a nasty goose egg where you fell and I suspect a concussion but I'd like to keep a closer eye on that headache for the next hour or so. I'd like you to rest here for a while so I can monitor your head, okay?"

"I've been such a bother."

"You haven't, I promise. I don't want you driving today so your dad is going to take Morgan and Cole home. I'll come check on you in an hour. If you're feeling better at that point, Seth can drive you home."

"I'm fine now."

"I'm sure you are. But you'll have to humor me, okay? It's a doctor thing." He winked at her. "I wouldn't want you to go home too early and drag me out of my warm, cozy bed in the middle of the night if you have any complications. Just rest, okay?"

Her head threatened to throb right off her shoulders and she was exhausted suddenly. She nodded. Closing her eyes gave some relief from the pain anyway.

She awoke some time later to find the room dark except for the flickering fire and next to it a pool of light from a floor lamp of entwined elk antlers. That glow illuminated an entirely too attractive man sitting in an armchair near the fire, a magazine open across his lap and a puppy stretched out at his feet like a pair of fuzzy slippers.

He looked up suddenly as if sensing her gaze. When he saw her eyes open, he gave a slow, painfully sweet smile, and her heart seemed to skip a beat.

"How's the head?" he asked, his voice a low, seductive whisper in the dimly lit room.

As if she could concentrate on anything but him! She closed her eyes for a moment to gauge her pain level then opened to meet his gaze. "Better, I think. Still a bit sore but I'm sure I'll survive. I can tell you with a fairly high degree of certainty that I won't be in a big hurry to go sledding again anytime soon."

He smiled and she felt that same exhilarating, pulse-pounding, toe-curling sensation she'd experienced on the mountain just before she hit that boulder and ruined the ride.

She pulled herself to a sitting position, ignoring the dozens of little elves hammering wildly in her brain. "Has your brother been back?"

"No. He said he'd be here about six and it's only quarter to. You were only asleep for forty-five minutes or so."

"I really think I'm fine to leave now. I just want to go home. I'm sure my father and children are worried about me and I've imposed enough on you and your family."

He closed his magazine and set it on the table beside him, giving her a stern look as he did. "You have any older brothers?"

"No. I'm an only child."

"Ah. Then you have no idea the emotional and psychological torment I would endure if I dared ignore my brother's strict instructions and took you home before he had the chance to take a look at your head again. I'm on strict orders here."

"Do you always do what your older brothers tell you?" she asked.

He gave a snort of laughter. "Hardly ever. Just ask them."

His levity vanished as abruptly as it appeared. "But in this case, I'm not going to take any chances. If Jake thinks you should rest until he checks you out again, that's exactly what you're going to do."

"All this fuss for nothing."

"Nothing? You have no idea how awful it was watching you tumble through the air and hit the ground so hard. I've been having flashbacks about it all evening."

She winced. "It was probably quite a sight, wasn't it?"

"I'd give you an eight for form and a ten for creativity. I'm afraid your bumpy landing knocked down your over-all score."

She smiled at his teasing. "I suppose I shouldn't be surprised this happened to me. I faced the painful truth a long time ago. I'm hopelessly uncoordinated. I would have been valedictorian of my class except I never learned to serve a lousy volleyball and couldn't manage to bring my sophomore P.E. grade up past a B."

His laughter rang through the room.

"I'm serious. It's not funny. You have no idea how traumatic it can be for a fourteen-year-old girl who can't shoot a basketball or catch a baseball to save her life."

"I understand. Believe me. You're talking to the kid who was always chosen last for dodgeball teams—and always the first one out."

She studied his athletic build, his broad shoulders and muscled chest and pure masculinity. "Okay, now you're out-and-out lying."

"Ask my brothers! I was small for my age and had asthma. Nobody wanted a shrimp who couldn't breathe on their team."

"You're not a shrimp."

He shrugged. "I hit a growth spurt when I was about Cole's age. Before then I was scrawny."

"Let me guess," she said, with a considering look. "You also started lifting weights around that same time."

"I didn't need to. When you work on a cattle ranch, every day is a workout. Once my asthma was mostly under control, I could do more around the ranch. It's amazing how much a kid can bulk up hauling hay and herding cattle."

She tried to picture him a scrawny, sickly boy suddenly getting taller and bulkier. With those chiseled features and those intense blue eyes that seemed to see right into a woman's deepest desires, he had no doubt always been gorgeous. She imagined when he started to putting on muscle and height, every girl in the county probably sat up and took notice of the youngest Dalton brother.

And they'd been noticing him ever since.

She tilted her head to study him, wondering how much of that late development—coupled with his health issues as a child—had affected his psyche.

"Why are you looking at me like that?" he asked.

She would have liked to be the kind of woman who could instantly sling back some sort of witty repartee. She wanted to be quick and funny and self-assured.

With him gazing at her out of those impossibly blue eyes, with a smile hovering around that sinful mouth, with the lingering scent of leather and pine clinging to him, she couldn't seem to think of anything to say but the truth.

"I was just wondering if that was around the time you discovered you were irresistible to women."

As soon as the words escaped her mouth, she wanted to call them back—or at least pound her head against the coffee table three or four times at her own stupidity.

"Irresistible?" He gave a disbelieving laugh. "Not even close. You, for one, seem to be doing an excellent job of resisting me."

"Am I?"

An arrested look flickered across his features and the room suddenly thickened with tension. Her pulse seemed abnormally loud in her ear and every sense seemed exaggerated. As he continued to gaze at her, she became aware of a hundred different sensations she'd barely noticed before—the slick, cool leather of the couch, the nubby blanket he'd thrown over her, the shadows dancing on the wall from the fire's glow.

She was especially aware of Seth, of his hands strong and square-tipped and masculine, of the slight evening shadow along the curve of his jaw, of the sudden intense light in his eyes.

He seemed big and dangerous and ferociously attractive to her and she wanted to tell him she wasn't anywhere *close* to resisting him.

She couldn't say the words but he seemed to sense them anyway. "This is a mistake," he murmured.

"What is?" she asked, wondering why her lungs couldn't seem to hold a breath.

Before the two words were even out, he gave a low kind of groan that sounded as if he'd lost some kind of internal struggle, then he leaned forward and kissed her.

Oh, he was good at this, she thought as his warm mouth slid gently over hers. Any attempt at overt seduction, an intense or passionate embrace, probably would have sent her spiraling into panic and she would have pulled away.

But his kiss was slow, soft as the purest of silk and incredibly erotic. He touched her with nothing but his mouth, but she still felt surrounded by him, consumed by him.

She should stop this, she thought, for her sanity's sake, if nothing else. But his mouth was so warm and tasted of cinnamon and apples and she felt as if she'd been standing out in the cold forever.

How could he think for an instant she had the capacity to resist him? she wondered. With a sigh of surrender that somehow didn't seem at all like defeat, she returned the kiss, splaying one hand across the soft material of his shirt and winding the other around his neck to tangle her fingers in his thick hair.

He was right about this being a bad idea. She knew it, had done nothing but warn herself of the dangers since the day she met him, but she resolved to worry about that later.

She suddenly thought of her assistant Marcy's theory she'd shared with Ashley that day in the office—The Seth Dalton School of Broncbusting. *Just climb on and hold on tight. It probably won't last too long, but it will be a hell of a ride.*

For now, she would just savor the wild punch of adrenaline, she decided, and enjoy the moment.

Calling this a mistake was a bit like calling the Tetons outside his window a couple of pleasant little hills.

Seth tried to catch his breath, wondering how the hell a simple kiss had so quickly twisted out of his control. He'd only meant to steal one small taste of her, just enough so he wouldn't have to wonder anymore. But the moment his mouth met hers, he felt as if he was the one tumbling head over heels down the mountain out there, as if no matter how he tried he couldn't manage to find his footing in the slippery snow.

He supposed in the back of his mind, he'd thought perhaps they could just share a quick kiss and that would be the end of it. One kiss probably wouldn't have sated his curiosity, but at least it might have been temporarily appeased.

But she had been so soft, so warm and welcoming, and she had given just the tiniest of sighs when he kissed her, and shivered against his mouth.

How could a man resist that?

When she returned his kiss and pulled him closer, he had to use every ounce of strength to keep from pressing her back against the sofa cushions and devouring her. The only way he held himself back was remembering she'd just suffered a head injury and was in no condition for anything more strenuous than a kiss.

When he felt his control fray, he forced himself to pull away, feeling as breathless and lightheaded as he had when he climbed the Grand out there.

In the fire's flickering glow, she looked soft and lovely, like something in one of those watercolors hanging in the Jackson art galleries.

"Have dinner with me tomorrow," he said on impulse. "I know this great place in Idaho Falls."

She gazed at him for several seconds, then she seemed to close up like his mom's flowers at the end of day. She shuttered away all the soft sweetness of her kiss as if it had never been.

"No."

He raised an eyebrow. "Just like that?"

"What else do you need? I know it's probably not a word you're well acquainted with, but I won't have dinner with you. Thank you for asking, though."

He shouldn't have been surprised by the rejection, but after her response to his kiss, he had hoped perhaps she might have changed her mind about him. Obviously, one kiss was not enough to do the trick.

Perhaps he also should have expected the bitter disappointment, but all this seemed uncomfortably foreign.

The silence stretched between them, awkward and uneasy, until finally he spoke, doing his best to keep his voice cool and unaffected.

"Is that a no because you genuinely don't want to, or a no for some other reason?"

She pulled the blanket around her more tightly. "Does it matter?"

"Yeah." More than it should, he admitted to himself. "Humor me. I'd like to know."

She let out a breath. "All right. I'm attracted to you, Seth. I would be lying if I said otherwise."

He frowned. "And yet you say that like it's a bad thing."

"It *is* a bad thing, at least from my perspective. Or if not a bad thing, precisely, at least an impossibility."

"Why?"

She seemed suddenly fascinated by the flickering of the flames. "I'm in a precarious position here. Surely you can see that."

He tried to make sense of what she was talking about but came up empty. "I guess I'm just a big, stupid cowboy," he said. "Why don't you explain it to me?"

"Pine Gulch is a small town. If we—if *I*—gave in to that attraction, people would know. They would talk."

"You're exaggerating a little, don't you think? Who would know or care what you might do in your personal life?"

She shook her head. "You're either incredibly naive—

which I find rather hard to believe—or you're being disingenuous. Of course people will care! I'm in a position of trust and responsibility, charged with educating their children! And you are…"

Her voice trailed off but not before he felt his defensive hackles rise. Suddenly he felt ten years old again, on the receiving end of one of Hank's more vicious diatribes. "I'm what?"

She shifted on the couch and refused to meet his gaze. "A favorite topic of conversation around here, for one thing."

"I can't help what people say about me."

"Can't you?"

"What's that supposed to mean?"

She closed her eyes for a moment but when she opened them, they seemed more determined than ever to push him away. "You're a player. You never date a woman more than a few times and you've left a trail of broken hearts strewn across the county. By all accounts, your conquests are the stuff of legend and frankly, I'm not interested in becoming one of them."

She was even better than Jake and Wade at twisting the knife. He wondered if his guts were spilling all over the carpet from that particular jab because it sure as hell felt like it.

"I suppose that's clear enough," he said quietly.

Her eyes darkened and he thought he saw regret there, but he couldn't swear to anything. "I can't afford a complication like this, Seth. Not now. It would be career suicide."

He forced a laugh he was far from feeling. "A little dramatic, don't you think? I only invited you to dinner, not to have wild monkey sex on the front lawn of the school during recess."

She flushed but held her ground. "I can't afford it," she repeated. "Surely you can see that. I am perfectly aware that when the school board hired me, some people protested hiring an outsider—and a divorced woman at that. I haven't had time to prove myself yet. If I were to jump into something with you, it will forever define me in the eyes of my faculty and the parents at my school. Those voices who spoke out against hiring me will become a cacophony of protest. I'm trying to build a new life here for me and for my children. I can't risk anything that might threaten that."

He wanted to argue, to find some way around her refusal, but before he could form the torrent of words in his head into anything coherent, the doorbell rang and an instant later, Jake walked into the room without waiting for him to answer it.

Lucy woke up with a start and yipped a welcome.

"Sorry I took a little longer than I'd planned," Jake said, shrugging out of his coat and picking up the puppy. He seemed oblivious to the thick tension in the room, a fact that Seth could only view with gratitude. He was *not* in the mood for another lecture.

On the other hand, he wouldn't mind pounding on something right about now and Jake seemed a convenient target. The only downside to that he could see would be facing the wrath of Magdalena Cruz Dalton, who scared him a whole lot more than her husband.

"Caroline decided she couldn't wait to put her tree up so we were all helping her decorate it and I lost track of time," Jake went on.

"You didn't need to return at all," Jenny said briskly in that prim schoolmarm voice Seth was finding increasingly adorable. "I'm perfectly fine, I promise, and more than ready to go home."

Jake studied her carefully and something in her tone or her features had him shifting his gaze back to Seth, his eyes suddenly hard. Seth stared back, hating that his brother could make him feel as though he was sixteen years old again.

"She slept most of the time and has only been awake for the past fifteen minutes or so." He hadn't meant to sound defensive but he was very afraid that was how his words came out.

Jake met his gaze for a long moment then turned back to Jenny. "Good. Rest is just what I would prescribe for you. I'm going to recommend taking it easy for the next few days. You're going to feel like you've been hit by a bus at first, but that should only last a day or two."

"All right. Something to look forward to, then," she said, making Jake smile.

"Maggie and I will give you a ride home. We're ready to go back into town and can drop you off with no problem."

Seth started to protest that he wanted to stick to the original plan and be the one to take her home. He would sound ridiculous if he did, he realized, so he opted to keep his mouth shut.

"Thank you," she said without looking at Seth. She managed to avoid his gaze the entire time Jake helped her into her parka and led her toward the door.

He thought she might leave without a word but just before she left, she turned around, her eyes shuttered. "Thank you for inviting us today. My children had a wonderful time."

Her children. Not her.

"I'm sorry it had to end on a sour note," he said.

"So am I," she said, her voice low, and they both knew they weren't talking about her tumble down the mountain. "Goodbye."

He stood on the porch, the icy air cutting through his

clothes, as Jake led her down the steps to his waiting Durango. For a long time after their taillights disappeared down the hill, he stood in the cold, watching after them and wondering why *he* was the one who felt as though he'd been hit by a bus.

Chapter 9

He hadn't missed her. Not a bit.

That was what he tried to tell himself, anyway.

For two weeks, he and Jenny Boyer had successfully managed to avoid each other. Not exactly an easy task in a community as small as Pine Gulch, Idaho.

Now, as Seth drove Cole home after a Saturday spent in the garage working on the GTO, he wondered if this would be the one time he might catch a glimpse of her—or if she would remain frustratingly elusive.

He might not have physically seen her since the day they went hunting Christmas trees on the Cold Creek, but she had never been far from his thoughts.

It was just because she had rejected him, he told himself. She represented the unattainable, the impossible. So naturally, he couldn't focus on anything but her.

For all that he hadn't been able to stop thinking about her, he wasn't completely sure he was all that eager to see her again, not when he was still nursing his wounds from their last encounter. He tended to veer between anger and hurt at the brutal way she had shoved him away after a kiss that to him had been sweetly magical.

She was definitely avoiding him—that much was obvious. The handful of times Cole had come out to the Cold Creek to work on the car or the horses, he had taken the school bus out and his grandfather had picked him up.

She couldn't run from him forever—and she didn't need to. Her message came through loud and clear. He certainly understood rejection when it reached out and slapped him across the face, though that didn't make it any easier to accept.

Cole wound down his monologue about the work they had done on the GTO when they reached the outskirts of town. "Thanks again for giving me a ride," he said.

"No problem. I needed to pick up some things at the store in town anyway."

The only thing in his house was a bottle of Caroline's strawberry jam and a solitary egg and he was out of laundry soap. But he supposed it was safe to admit deep in the recesses of his heart that he'd offered Cole a ride half hoping he might see the boy's mother.

He was pathetic, he thought. What *was* this obsession with her?

This was a pretty miserable way to spend a Saturday night, listening to a teenage boy talk about cars and thinking about his grocery list—and a woman he couldn't have.

So much for her theory that he was some kind of wild-ass cowboy with nothing on his mind but whiskey and women.

Maybe he ought to drop by the Bandito to shake things up a little before he went grocery shopping. He tried to summon up a little enthusiasm for the idea but the prospect was about as appealing as walking through the grocery store wearing only his Tony Lamas.

Something was seriously wrong with him.

He hadn't avoided the place in the past two weeks, he reminded himself. He had stopped at least two or three times to shoot a little pool, have a couple beers, flirt a little with some pretty girls. But he hadn't enjoyed it much.

Maybe if he tried to enjoy it a little more, expended a little energy and took one of those nice ladies up on their subtle offers, he might not be so edgy and restless, he thought as he drove through the thickening snow. Even as he thought it, he knew he wouldn't.

None of them had soft hair of a hundred different shades and a lush mouth that kept a man up at night.

None of them was Jenny Boyer.

"How much longer before the custom touch-up paint you ordered comes in?" the boy asked.

Seth dragged his mind away from his current dry spell in the romance department and turned his attention to the kid. "They said a week or two. Then all we have to do is give her a couple of coats and we'll be done. Maybe during Christmas break we can take her for a ride, if the weather's not too snowy."

"Yeah. Okay." For all his enthusiasm about working on the GTO, Cole didn't look too thrilled by the idea.

"You've worked hard to pay your debt. I figured when we're done with the touch-up paint, we'll be square. You'll be glad to lift your last shovelful of horse manure, I'm sure."

"I guess." Cole slumped in the seat and gazed out at the wintry landscape.

He frowned at the almost sullen note of dejection in the boy's voice. Was Cole upset not to be working on the Cold Creek anymore?

He would be sorry to see the last of him. Tinkering with cars had always been a solitary escape for him, but he'd enjoyed having company the last month and Cole had been a different kid when he was working on the GTO, curious and talkative and enthusiastic.

He studied him across the dimly lit truck. "Of course, I wouldn't turn away a hard worker if he wanted to earn a little extra money working with the horses and helping out with the occasional mechanical repair," he said on impulse. "The pay's not the greatest, but you could ride the horses all you want. And in the summer after school gets out, I could probably give you all the hours you wanted to work, provided you would be willing to drive a tractor."

Cole straightened, his features suddenly animated, though he was obviously trying not to show too much excitement. The kid reminded him so much of himself sometimes, watching him was almost painful.

"We'll have to talk to your mom about it," Seth cautioned as he pulled up in front of Jason Chambers's house. "She might prefer you to find an after-school job closer to home."

Cole's enthusiasm wavered a bit but not completely. "We could talk to her now," he suggested. "If you wanted, anyway. I know she must be home since my grandpa went to Jackson Hole yesterday and won't be back until Monday."

Oh, Jenny would love having him show up on her doorstep with an offer like this out of the blue, he thought. But Cole was so eager, he didn't have the heart to refuse.

"Okay," he agreed, anticipation churning through him at knowing he would see her in just a few moments.

He parked his truck in front of the house, noting as he did that the sidewalk and driveway needed shoveling. Three or four inches had fallen since noon and several more were forecast before morning.

"I'll talk to your mother with you, on the condition you help me shovel this snow after we're done."

Cole made a face. "What's the good of shoveling while it's still snowing? Seems a whole lot smarter to wait until it stops and then you only have to do it once."

"Here's a little life lesson for you, kid. I know this is probably your first big storm so you might not have learned this yet. Most jobs are easier to swallow if you take them in small bites. Shoveling four inches of snow three separate times in one storm might seem like a pain in the neck. But trust me on this, it's a whole lot easier than waiting until it's all over and having to work a shovel through two-foot deep drifts."

"Or we could all move somewhere warm so we wouldn't have to worry about shoveling snow."

"What? And miss all this?" Seth opened the door and snow swirled inside, icy and cold. The kid rolled his eyes but climbed out of the passenger side.

Their boots left prints in the snow as they trudged up the sidewalk through the dark night. He could see the dark shape of the Christmas tree they'd cut in the window but the lights hadn't been turned on and neither were the porch lights.

Odd, he thought.

Cole pushed open the front door. "Mom, I'm home," he called. He hit a switch and instantly the tree lit up with hundreds of colorful lights. It was beautiful, decorated with a hodgepodge of ornaments, most of which looked home-made. His favorite kind of tree, Seth thought with satisfaction.

"Mom?" Cole called again.

An instant later, Jenny burst into the room wearing a

half-buttoned coat and one glove and holding her car keys in the other hand. She looked frazzled and close to tears.

Her gaze locked on Seth. "Oh, thank heavens! I can't tell you how glad I am to see you."

Seth raised an eyebrow. It wasn't quite the reception he'd expected. He might have made some crack about absence making the heart grow fonder, if she hadn't looked out of her head with worry.

"What's going on?"

"Morgan. She's having a bad flare-up. It's been going on for nearly half an hour and nothing we've tried is helping. I called your brother and he's meeting us at the clinic but I can't get my car started."

"I'll drive you," he said instantly, already moving. "Of course I'll take you! Where is she?"

"In the kitchen."

She led the way and his heart broke when he found Morgan looking terrified and breathing into a nebulizer.

For a moment as he took in her pale features and labored respirations, he was ten years old again, frightened and unable to breathe. He pushed away the ghosts of the past.

"Okay, sweetheart. Asthma-slayers to the rescue here. We're going to get you to Dr. Jake and he'll make everything okay."

He was completely humbled by the absolute and unequivocal trust in her eyes as she nodded.

He scooped her up, blanket and all, and headed back through the house toward the front door and his waiting truck.

After he set Morgan on the seat and fastened her belt, he helped Jenny in after her.

"I've only got three seat belts in my pickup, and I don't

dare drive without everyone belted in these road conditions," he said to Cole. "Do you mind staying here?"

"No," he said, looking worried. For all his attitude sometimes, he was just a kid, Seth reminded himself. A boy
worried for his sister.

"Don't worry," he said as he went around the truck.
"She's tough. Jake will take care of her and she'll be just
fine. Meanwhile, your mother and sister would probably
appreciate it if they didn't have to trudge through snow to
get into the door when we get back."

Cole nodded with a man-to-man kind of look and Seth
was pleased to see him already reaching for the snow shovel
on the porch.

"I'm very sorry about this," Jenny said as he drove toward the clinic. "I was just about ready to call the ambu-
lance."

"Forget it. We can get her there faster this way, rather
than wait for the volunteer paramedics to try to come in to
the fire station through the snow."

He had to concentrate on driving for the next few moments as the storm's intensity seemed to increase by the
minute. With each passing second, he was aware of Morgan's wheezy struggle to breathe and the huge weight of
responsibility pressing down his shoulders.

It gave him some tiny inkling of what parents must go
through, this fragile terror at knowing they can sometimes
literally hold a child's life in their hands.

When he finally pulled up in front of the clinic, he was
sweating through the heavy layers of his coat. He gave a
silent prayer of gratitude when he saw Jake's Durango already in the parking lot and all the lights blazing inside.

He scooped Morgan into his arms and headed for the
door, shielding her from the snow with his body. His sister-

in-law Maggie was the first one to greet them inside, ready with oxygen and a wheelchair. Jake was right behind her, bustling with the calm competence that made everybody in town trust him with their health.

They both looked surprised to see him there but he didn't waste time in explanations as he set Morgan into the wheelchair then stepped back to let them do their thing.

There was no one on earth he'd rather entrust this sweet little girl to than Jake and Maggie, he thought as he watched them work.

An hour later, Jenny sat beside her daughter's bed in one of the small treatment rooms of the clinic holding Morgan's hand and reading to her from an *American Girl* magazine Seth had found for them in the waiting room while Jake Dalton checked her vitals.

"We seem to be through the worst of it," Jake said now, pulling his stethoscope away from his ears.

"So you think it was her cold that triggered it?" she asked.

"There's a trace of bronchitis there and I'm sure that didn't help anything. My gut tells me it's viral but I'm going to give you some antibiotics anyway, just in case I'm wrong."

"Okay."

"And we'll need to continue the steroid nebulizer treatments every four hours."

"Check."

Jake leaned back against the sink. "Now we have a decision to make and I'm going to leave it up to you. I can ship you to the hospital in Idaho Falls if you would feel better spending the night there."

"Or?"

"I can send you home with a monitor and you can keep an eye on her oxygen levels throughout the night and run the nebulizer treatments on your own. Either way you're probably not going to get any sleep but she might do better in her own bed. If you have problems, I can be at your house in five minutes."

Oh, Jenny absolutely *hated* having to make these decisions on her own. These were the moments she missed having a partner she could count on, someone to lean on during hard times and to help her with these terribly tough calls.

"Are you sure that's wise?" Seth said from the corner. She'd thought he would retreat to the waiting room, but he had stuck around for the whole proceedings, teasing Morgan and asking questions of Maggie and Jake and offering quiet support to Jenny.

She wasn't sure what she would have done without him.

Jake didn't seem upset at the question. "I wouldn't have suggested it as an option if I didn't think she would be fine at home. Since the flare-up is under control, it's probably safer having her in her own bed than trying to transport her through the storm just for observation."

"I want to go home," Morgan said, her voice frail and small. Jenny squeezed her hand, knowing how much her daughter hated hospitals.

"I guess we'll take door number two," she finally said. "I have to think the worst of it has passed."

"I agree. But the only way I'm going to let you take her home is if you promise to call if you have any concerns at all in the night."

Jenny nodded and gave him and Maggie a tired but grateful smile. "Thank you both for meeting us here. I have to confess, one of my biggest worries of moving to a small town so far from a major medical center was finding good care for Morgan's asthma. I never expected to find such wonderful providers in tiny Pine Gulch. I can't tell you what a comfort it is to have you close by."

"You won't find better medical care anywhere," Seth spoke up, his voice gruff. "Pine Gulch is just lucky Jake decided to come home instead of taking one of the big-city offers that came down the pike when he finished medical school. Having an experienced nurse-practitioner like Mag is icing."

His brother looked surprised and touched at the praise, though she thought Seth seemed a little embarrassed after he spoke.

"Well, I'm sorry I had to drag you both out on a night like this."

"It's all part of the job description," Maggie assured her. "Don't give it a thought."

After Jake rounded up an oxygen-saturation monitor, Maggie brought a wheelchair for them to use to transport Morgan out to the truck, but Seth shook his head.

"I've got it," he said, wrapping the little girl in a blanket and lifting her into his arms again.

He had pulled his truck right up to the door so only had to take a few steps through the blowing snow to set her inside carefully.

Jenny's heart seemed to shift and settle as she watched this big, overwhelmingly masculine man take such gentle care with her child. Morgan gave him a sleepy smile as he fastened her seat belt and Jenny had to swallow her sigh.

Her daughter was already crazy about Seth. This little episode wasn't going to do anything to diminish her hero worship. She desperately hoped her daughter wouldn't have her heart broken by another male in her life.

Exhausted by her ordeal, Morgan fell asleep before they even made it out of the parking lot.

Seth drove with native confidence through the miserable conditions. At least a foot had fallen since the storm had started earlier in the evening and most of it was still on the roads, but he hardly seemed to notice it.

At her father's house, she was surprised to see all but a skiff of snow had been cleared from the driveway. She frowned. Who could have done it? She could only hope Jason hadn't driven home in these conditions from Jackson Hole.

Maybe a neighbor, she thought as she followed Seth and Morgan inside. She was discovering people in Pine Gulch took care of each other. It was another reason she desperately wanted to make things work out for them here. She loved being part of a community, a small part of the greater whole.

"Where am I heading?" Seth whispered inside the welcome warmth of the house. Morgan was still sleeping, she saw.

"Her room," she whispered back. "I'll show you."

She led the way to Morgan's room, across the hall from her own and he set her carefully down on the bed.

"Thank you," she murmured, aware of him watching her intently as she hooked up the monitor then drew the quilt up over Morgan's sleeping form.

In the living room, they found Cole waiting for them, trying hard not to look worried.

"How is she?" he asked.

"Better. Good enough that Dr. Dalton seemed to think she'd be all right at home tonight," Jenny said.

She was suddenly exhausted after the last two hours of stress and she could feel an adrenaline crash coming on.

"Good job clearing the walks and the driveway," Seth said.

She stared at her son. "You did that?"

He stuck out his jaw. "Yeah. So?"

She sighed, wondering how she always seemed to say exactly the wrong thing to him. She decided to use actions instead of words and pulled him into a hug. "Thank you."

In a rare and precious gift, he let her hug him for a long moment before he stepped away.

"You're supposed to call Grandpa. He said he can come home if you need him."

"I don't want him driving in this mess. But I also don't want to be stuck here without transportation if Morgan has a relapse."

"You won't be without transportation," Seth put in. "You'll have my truck."

She frowned. "If you leave your truck, what will you use to get back to the Cold Creek?"

"Nothing. Not tonight, anyway. I'm bunking on your couch."

Chapter 10

As he might have expected, Jenny was less than enthusiastic about his declaration.

Sparks seemed to shoot out of her suddenly narrowed eyes and the look she gave him plainly did not bode well for him. She opened her mouth—to flay him alive, no doubt—then cast a look at Cole and closed it again. He had never been so grateful for her son's presence.

"I appreciate the offer," she said tightly, "but that's really not necessary. I'm sure you have plenty of other places you would rather be on a stormy night like tonight."

"Nope," he said, and was astonished to realize it was true.

Something was definitely wrong with him. This was usually his favorite kind of night, stormy and cold, the kind of night designed for cuddling up under a warm quilt with a sweet young thing, putting his mind to work coming up with imaginative ways to keep warm.

Why did that seem so totally unappealing to him right

now? He would far rather be here in Jason Chambers's house with a woman who wanted nothing to do with him, sleeping alone on a cold couch.

"Jenny, there's no way under the sun I'm going to leave you alone here tonight and that's the end of it. I would never sleep worrying about Morgan and about you stuck here without wheels in this weather. I don't mind the couch."

The phone rang suddenly in the kitchen and though he looked loath to leave this interesting battlefield, Cole went to answer it.

Jenny cast a quick look through the doorway to make sure her son couldn't overhear, then she spoke in a low voice. "You can't stay here. It's impossible. What would people think if your truck were parked out front all night?"

For one near-disastrous second, he almost laughed, but she seemed so serious, so genuinely distressed, the impulse died, leaving a hollow feeling in his gut.

She wasn't joking. She was so concerned about her reputation, she thought just the sight of his truck parked out front of her house all night would destroy it.

He had no idea what it was like to be a pillar of society—and he wasn't sure he wanted to know, especially if it meant worrying about something that seemed so inconsequential to him.

Did she really think anybody would believe the elementary school principal would invite the town's bad boy over for a night of wild sex while her children were in the house?

He had to admit, the thought of that soft body of hers all warm and cuddly was far too appealing under the circumstances, but he managed to rein in his overactive imagination.

"Nobody's going to be out in this weather to be snooping on the neighbors," he assured her. "All the town busybodies are tucked up in their beds dreaming of catching the mayor's wife shoplifting or something. And if anybody's rude enough to ask, we can just tell them the truth. Or if you don't think that's good enough, we can always tell them I loaned my truck to you when your car broke down."

She didn't look convinced. "It's the ones who *won't* say anything who worry me most. Those are the kinds of whispers that can destroy a reputation in an instant."

He couldn't have said why it bothered him so much that she was so concerned about her precious reputation—or that she seemed so convinced he held the power to completely destroy it.

"You really care about the opinions of some old biddies with nothing better to do than bad-mouth a woman whose only crime is worrying about her sick child?"

"It's not that simple."

"What's your alternative? Dragging your father home from Jackson Hole in this weather? I know you don't want to do that."

"No. There must be some other solution."

"Not that I can see. I'm staying, Jen. You don't know stubborn until you've taken on a Dalton."

She opened her mouth to answer but Cole appeared in the doorway, looking from one of them to the other out of curious eyes. He held out a black cordless phone. "Grandpa's on the phone again, Mom."

She took it from him and Cole disappeared. A moment later, Seth heard his tread on the stairs and assumed the boy had retreated to his room.

While Jenny was on the phone, Seth took off his coat and hung it on a hall tree in the entryway, then returned to the living room. Jenny'd had the same idea—she'd taken off her hat and scarf and her coat and tossed them over a chair.

"No, Dad. I don't want you to come home," she said, unbuttoning her cardigan to reveal a formfitting forest green turtleneck underneath. She slipped out of the sweater, and Seth slid onto the couch and stretched his legs out in front of him, enjoying himself immensely.

She narrowed her eyes at his comfortable pose. "There's nothing you can do. Nothing *anyone* can do," she added with a pointed look at Seth.

He smiled benignly, wondering how much more she might be planning to take off.

"All right. I'll call you if there's any change, I promise. Yes. Okay. Stay safe. Have fun with your friends and don't lose too much money. I know. You always win. That's why you go. All right. I love you, too, Dad."

She hung up from her father, set the phone on the coffee table and stood gazing at her bright Christmas tree, looking so dejected Seth almost offered to go find a nice, respectable widow with her own snowplow if it would make Jenny feel better about the situation.

After a moment, she straightened her shoulders and faced him. He suddenly wanted more than anything to take that grim look out of her eyes, to make everything okay.

"Your dad is obviously a cardsharp, but how are *you* at poker?" he asked.

She blinked, looking a little disoriented. "Sorry?"

"We're going to be up all night worrying about Morgan and giving her treatments every four hours, but we don't have to be bored. Let's call Cole up to play some cards. What do you say? We can play for pennies or toothpicks or matchsticks or whatever you've got. Unless you think we'd be corrupting the morals of a minor."

Her laugh was abrupt, but he took comfort that it was still a laugh. "Are you kidding? My dad taught him to play blackjack the minute he was old enough to count. He'll wipe the floor with both of us."

"Speak for yourself, ma'am. You've never played cards with me. I don't like to lose."

She sniffed. "I believe I've figured that out by now."

He laughed, glad that he'd been able to distract her, if only for a moment.

Where was her child?

Jenny raced through the halls of an unfamiliar hospital, her way strewn with gurneys and hospital equipment and hallways that led nowhere.

She opened every door but couldn't find Morgan anywhere. Somewhere in this labyrinthian hell was her child, ill and wheezy, but Jenny had no idea where to look. Her baby needed her and she wasn't there for her.

She begged everyone she passed to please help her, but no one answered. No one at all. Finally, when she was nearly wailing with defeat, she headed down one last, crowded hallway, devoid of doors except for one at the very end, lit by a strange orange glow from within.

Her child had to be there, she thought, trying to shove her way past uncaring people who blocked her at every turn. She felt so alone, so utterly forsaken. She was so tired of fighting this battle by herself. All she wanted was to curl up and weep out all her pain and frustration, but she had to find her child.

Suddenly—like a miracle, like the parting of the Red Sea—a path opened up for her through the crowd of people. Someone stood in front of her, someone with shoulders broad enough to carry the weight of all her fears. She couldn't see his face, but her salvation blazed a trail for her and she rushed toward the door. When she reached it, she extended a hand to thank the only person who had helped her.

He turned and gave her a slow, painfully sweet smile and opened the door for her. Somehow she had known it was Seth, she thought, even as she rushed inside to her child, sobbing with relief to find her healthy and whole, her breathing slow and even.

She awoke with a start, disoriented by the strange dream.

She wasn't sure where she was at first, then she realized the orange glow she had dreamed about must have been from the woodstove, where a fire still flickered softly.

She was in her father's den, curled up on the couch. She frowned, trying to remember why she'd fallen asleep there, then the lingering tendrils of her dream wrapped around her again and she drew in a quick breath.

Morgan!

Jenny yanked off the soft knitted afghan she couldn't remember pulling around herself and rose so quickly the room whirled for a moment. She barely waited for the walls to steady before rushing down the hall to her daughter's room, her heart pounding.

All was quiet there. The alarm clock by the bed told Jenny she'd slept longer than she thought—it was nearly quarter after four. How could she have fallen asleep when her daughter needed her?

But no. A quick check told her Morgan was sleeping soundly. The oxygen monitor on her bedside table registered a respectable ninety-four. Not fabulous but not terrible, either.

She let out a low sigh of relief and lifted a trio of stuffed animals from the glider rocker by Morgan's bed so she could take their place.

Her daughter was due for another nebulizer treatment

and though Jenny hated to wake her, she knew it was something neither of them could avoid.

Poor little thing, to have to endure so much, she thought, as she poured the medicine into the nebulizer then shook her awake.

"I'm sorry, sweetheart, but you need a treatment."

Morgan groaned but blinked her eyes open blearily, just long enough for Jenny to fit the mask over her nose and mouth and turn on the machine. Medicated air blew into the mask, forcing its way into her daughter's lungs. Morgan hated that part, she knew.

"Do you want me to hold you?" she asked.

Morgan nodded, so Jenny slid into bed with her, cuddling her tight and singing softly to her until the medicine was finished.

She settled Morgan back into bed and was grateful when she closed her eyes and slipped easily back to sleep.

Perhaps because of the silly dream and the remembered terror of not being able to find her, Jenny stood for a long time by her daughter's bed, thinking how very much she loved her. Despite what she sometimes had to endure, Morgan was warm and good-natured. An uncommonly kind child, she often thought.

She couldn't imagine how cold and lonely her life would have been without either of her children.

Cole might be struggling through his teenage years but she wouldn't trade him for anything. As she finally left Morgan's room, she couldn't help thinking of the evening she, Seth and Cole had spent together and she had to smile.

She didn't know how Seth had done it, but somehow in the course of the night while they played Five-Card Stud and Acey-Deucy and Texas Hold 'em, he had returned her funny, sweet son to her.

She knew it was probably fleeting, that in the morning Cole would likely revert to his normal sullen, unhappy self. But for a few hours he had laughed and joked and teased with her and—miracle of miracles—had even seemed to enjoy her company.

Around midnight, Cole had been drooping over his cards so Jenny sent him to bed. She had been loath to say goodnight to him, both because she had so enjoyed her time with him and because she desperately needed the buffer he provided between her and Seth.

She needn't have worried. While she woke Morgan for her midnight treatment, Seth apparently had thumbed through her father's DVD collection until he found an old Alfred Hitchcock movie, one of her favorites.

"I haven't seen this in years," he exclaimed when she returned to the den after that treatment earlier. "What do you think? Are you up to watching a movie?"

She had agreed and had tried to stay awake, but the long, arduous evening of worry and caregiving took its toll. She didn't think she had made it very far through the movie.

Now the TV was dark and her unwanted houseguest was nowhere in sight. Had he gone home? She hurried to the window but there was his big black pickup truck, looking dark and menacing and incriminating against the snow.

He must have decided to go to bed. It couldn't have been too long before she woke up, as the log in the woodstove still looked fresh and barely burned through.

How long had she been out of it while he sat watching the movie? she wondered. She felt curiously vulnerable knowing she must have slept in front of him. It was a disconcerting thing to realize another person might have watched her sleep—especially when that person was a man she found enormously attractive.

Where was he now? Some hostess she was, whether or not her guest was an invited one. Perhaps he had found an empty bed to stretch out on, either in her room or her father's.

She should at least check to see if he had found somewhere to rest. If her guest was awake, a good hostess should at least ascertain if he needed anything.

Her pulse kicked up as a heated image jumped into her mind of wild kisses and tangled limbs.

No! She only meant a clean towel or a spare toothbrush.

She did her best to push the fiery images away but they haunted her as she paused outside her father's bedroom. No light shone underneath the door but she was still cautious as she pushed it open, only to release a heavy breath when she found an empty bed.

He must have gone to her room, then. Her stomach fluttered as she pictured that long, powerful body stretched out on her bed. Her pillow would smell like him, she thought. Leathery and masculine and delicious.

She stood outside the door, her stomach twisting with nerves. She rolled her eyes at her reaction. This was ridiculous. He was only a man, for heaven's sake. Just a man who was probably snoring up a storm right now.

Still, she felt a little like Pandora lifting the lid of her box as she pushed open her bedroom, then slumped against the door.

He wasn't there, either. Her bed was just as she had left it that morning, the corners neat and the pillow shams aligned.

Completely baffled now, she returned to the kitchen. He had to be *somewhere* in the house. She was about to check if he had somehow managed to find her father's guest room in the basement when she heard a clatter on the other side of the door leading to the garage, then a muffled curse.

For the first time, she noticed a narrow slice of light under the door. She frowned. The garage? What on earth would Seth be doing in the *garage* at four-thirty in the morning?

Shaking her head in confusion, she pushed open the door and shivered as a blast of cold air slapped at her.

She heard whistling first, some tune she couldn't name but that she suspected was on the bawdy side. She followed the sound and nearly tumbled down the two small steps leading into the garage at what she saw.

The hood of her little SUV was open and Seth was bent over fiddling with something under it.

She couldn't seem to take her eyes off him as she tried to process what he was doing. It was hours before dawn and he was out in below-freezing weather in the middle of a blizzard working on her car.

This was the man she thought was an immature womanizer interested in only one thing, the man she wouldn't go to dinner with for fear someone might see them and her job might be threatened, the man she had rejected a dozen different ways.

Why would he do such a thing?

Something seemed to break loose inside of her, something precious and tender and terrifying, and she pressed a hand to her mouth, shaken to her soul.

She must have made some sound because the whistling broke off in midnote and he peered his head around the side of her hood. When he saw her, he gave her one of those heartbreaking smiles of his.

"Hi!" he said cheerfully.

She couldn't think of anything to say, lost in the tumult of emotions washing through her.

At her continued silence, his smile slipped away. "Is everything okay with Morgan? I checked on her a while ago and everything seemed fine, I swear, or I would have woken you."

She had to force herself to speak, if only to allay his worry. "She is. Her oxygen levels are still within normal range and I just gave her another nebulizer treatment. As soon as she finished the last of it, she went right back to sleep, just like she did at midnight."

She didn't trust herself to say anything more just now, too stunned by his actions.

"That's wonderful," he said fervently.

She walked down the steps until she stood only a few feet away from him. "Seth, what are you doing here?"

He gave a little laugh that seemed to run down her spine like a warm caress. "A little self-evident, don't you think?"

"It's four-thirty in the morning! You should be home in bed, not standing in my ice-cold garage monkeying under my hood."

He raised an eyebrow and by the sudden amusement in his eyes, she realized how her words could be taken as a euphemism.

Why did men have to turn so much having to do with automobiles and their maintenance into sexual double entendres? *Lube her chassis, rotate her tires, give the old engine a tune-up.* And of course, all engines were female, the better for them to work their wiles.

To her relief, Seth didn't make any smart remark, though—he just smiled. "It was no big deal. I just didn't want you being stuck here tomorrow if your father doesn't make it back from Jackson because of the weather. Anyway, I'm just about done. Let's see if my monkeying did the trick."

He slid behind the wheel and turned the key he must have found on her key ring in the kitchen. The engine started up instantly, practically purring in the cold garage.

"Of course," she muttered to herself. Just like everything else female the man touched.

Seth slid out with a satisfied smile. "There you go. She's all ready to rock."

Oh, she was in serious trouble.

"What was my problem?" she managed to ask. *Besides this foolish, foolish heart?*

"Corrosion around the battery cables. I only cleaned her up a little with some baking soda and water. But then I saw by the sticker on your windshield you were past due for an oil change and discovered your dad happened to have five quarts of the right grade oil, so I decided to take care of that, too. No big deal."

"It's a very big deal to me," she murmured. She couldn't remember the last time anyone had performed such a gesture for her. Against her will, she thought of the nightmare she'd had just before she awoke, of feeling helpless and alone and terribly frightened. And then he was there, lending her his strength when she had none of her own left.

"I'm just glad you won't be left without a car now," he said, wiping his hands on one of the rags from a box her father kept in the corner.

She leaned closer. "You've got a smudge on your face."

"Yeah, I always make a mess when I'm working on a car."

He scrubbed it without success. Without thinking, she took the rag from him and stepped forward, carefully wiping at the small spot of grease just above his jawline.

An instant later, she realized what she was doing and she stopped, mortified. Her gaze slid to his and the sudden heat there seemed to burn through her, setting every nerve ending ablaze.

She swallowed hard and thought she might have whispered his name, but it was lost in the wild firestorm of his kiss.

Chapter 11

His arms wrapped around her, tangling her up in a heat and strength that smelled vaguely of motor oil and sexy male.

She clung tightly to his shirt and slid into the wonder of his kiss. He was so good at it, his mouth teasing and tasting until she couldn't seem to grab hold of a single coherent thought.

A corner of her mind protested that she played a risky game. This was crazy, foolish. A smart woman should be running for all she was worth from the heartbreak he would inevitably leave behind, not reaching out to grab it with both hands.

She knew it, but she couldn't let herself think about that now, when his mouth was so warm and exhilarating, with his hard strength beneath her fingertips, with her heart still reeling from the magnitude of what he had just done for her.

The cold and rather drab garage seemed to disappear. Her SUV, her father's power tools, the snow still whirling outside the window. Nothing existed but the two of them, this man who seemed to know her so well, who somehow reached into her deepest dreams and gave her a reality far more magical than anything she could have imagined.

She felt safe in his arms. It was an odd thought—one she didn't quite understand, considering he was the most dangerous man she'd ever met. At least to her emotions.

At this moment, though, as his mouth explored hers and his arms held her tightly, she felt protected from the cold and storms of life, as if he would safeguard her from any threat.

She didn't know how long the kiss lasted. Time seemed to have no meaning, elastic and malleable. Einstein's theory of relativity held new meaning when a woman found herself in Seth Dalton's arms.

When at last she came up for air, they were both breathing hard and she wondered if she looked as dazed as he did.

"Wow," he said, his voice ragged. "That's one hell of a tip just for cleaning off a little battery corrosion."

She flushed and tried to retreat, but he wouldn't let her, pulling her close until she fitted snugly against him. His heat surrounded her, taking away the chill from the cold garage.

"I should *not* have done that," she murmured, though with him so close, crowding out all her good sense, it wasn't easy to hang on to all the reasons why.

"If you're looking for me to agree with you on that particular point, I'm afraid you're going to be doomed to disappointment."

What must he think of her? She had been an idiot around him, weak and mercurial, since the day they met. Like now, for instance. She knew she shouldn't be so content in the circle of his arms but she couldn't manage the strength to pull away.

"I have no willpower where you're concerned. I'm sorry."

His arms tightened around her. "Sweetheart, you have nothing to apologize about."

She drew in a deep breath and summoned all her strength so she could force herself to step out of that warm haven. "Yes, I do. I've done nothing but give you mixed signals about what I want since that first day you came to the house with Cole. I tell you I'm not interested, then I attack you like some kind of…of sex-starved divorcée."

That masculine dimple appeared briefly. "Are you?"

Yes. *Oh, yes,* at least where this man was concerned. A few weeks ago she would have laughed at the notion that she could be so hungry. She hadn't had a physical relationship since her divorce, hadn't even considered one until Seth—and hadn't noticed the lack of it.

She had devoted all her energy and time to her children and her career. No man had even tempted her until Seth blew into her life with his sexy smile and his broad shoulders and those eyes that seemed to see right into her deepest desires.

Oh, yes. She was starving and he was like a big, gluttonous, delectable feast.

"You're blushing," he observed.

She felt herself flush even hotter and didn't know how to respond to his teasing.

"I'm trying to apologize for the mixed signals. I'm just… I'm not very good at all of this."

"This?"

"We have this…thing between us. I don't know what to do with it. I thought keeping a safe distance was the answer, but that obviously isn't working."

"No?"

"Even though I know perfectly well you're so bad for me, I can't seem to stop thinking about you."

At her words, something hot and intense sparked in his eyes. Perhaps she ought not have mentioned that last part, she thought nervously.

"Why am I so terrible?" he asked. "Because you think the whole town will start a riot if they should find out the elementary school principal might actually want a life?"

A life was one thing. A torrid affair with the town's hottest bachelor was something else entirely.

"You're out of my league, Seth. Way, way out of my league. I'm like the water boy on a Pop Warner football team and you're the starting quarterback in the Superbowl."

"Sorry, but baseball was my game."

"You know what I mean. I don't even know why you're here. You're a…a *player.* You're sexy and exciting and gorgeous. And I'm just a boring, dumpy thirty-six-year-old elementary school principal who has slept with exactly one man in my entire life."

Oh, she shouldn't have said that, either. His gaze sharpened and she could swear he saw right into her soul.

"Really?" he asked in an interested voice.

She flushed. "That's beside the point. What I'm trying to say is I can't figure any of this out. What do you want from me, Seth? I know perfectly well I'm not your usual type. I'm not beautiful or sexy or exciting. I've never been the kind of person who's always the life of the party. I'm just an ordinary woman, someone a man like you shouldn't even look twice at."

He looked astonished at her blunt self-assessment. "How can you say that with a straight face?"

"Because it's true!"

"I don't think you know yourself very well," he murmured. "And I'm certain you don't know me."

She couldn't argue with that. If she knew him, perhaps he wouldn't baffle her so completely.

"You seem to think I'm some rowdy cowboy with nothing on my mind but carving notches on some imaginary bedpost," he went on. "I'll admit, I have a bit of a reputation. Some of it earned, I'm sorry to say, but most of it exaggerated."

He was quiet for a moment, and then he gave her a solemn look, more serious than she'd ever seen from him. "But you know, there's more to me than whatever reputation I might have."

She wrapped her arms around herself, struck by his words. He was right. How unfair had she been to him, to hang everything on some whispered gossip overheard in her office?

He was more than what people said about him. She only had to look at what he had done for her little family in the last month to see the truth of that.

He had been wonderful to Cole, patient and kind and understanding when most other men would have ranted and raved and pressed charges, more concerned about the damages to their prize automobile than about a troubled boy.

And Morgan adored him. He had shown extraordinary gentleness and rare perception to her daughter, and for that she would never be able to thank him enough. If nothing else, he'd shown her daughter it was possible to move past the frustrating limitations of asthma to have a successful, rewarding life as an adult.

She thought of his steady strength during Morgan's flare-up. They had all been so frightened, but Seth hadn't hesitated for an instant, had stepped into the breach and helped them all find their way through it.

If she needed further confirmation there were deeper

levels to him than the world might see, she only had to look at his relationship with his family. The Daltons were a close and loving group and he seemed crazy about them all.

He had no problems hugging his mother in public, he plainly adored his niece and nephews, he was passionate about his horses.

And he had been willing to come out to a cold garage in the middle of a stormy winter night to fix her car so she wouldn't be stranded.

She hadn't wanted to see all those good things about him, she realized. It was far easier to use his wild reputation as a shield to keep him away—and to keep her heart safe.

Continuing to focus on that one aspect of him was doing both of them an injustice.

"I know there's more to you," she finally admitted. "Perhaps that's why I can't stop thinking about you."

At her low words, a soft and tender warmth stole through him and he couldn't seem to stop looking at her in the dim light of the garage.

How could she actually say she wasn't beautiful? Just now, with her mouth swollen and her eyes still heavy-lidded from their kiss, he had never seen such a stunning sight. She looked rumpled and warm and he wanted her with a ferocity that astonished him.

For now, he contented himself with simply reaching for her hand. "I don't know if this helps anything," he finally said, "but I can't stop thinking about you, either. This sounds crazy, I know, but somehow I missed you these last few weeks. You told me to back off and I've tried to respect that. But I couldn't get you out of my head."

Her hand trembled in his. "How could you miss me? You don't even know me. Not really."

"I don't know the answer to that, I just know it's true. I'd like to know you, Jenny. Just as I'm more than my wild reputation, you're more than the boring, ordinary educator you see in the mirror. I know you are. You're beautiful and smart and funny."

She looked as if she wanted to protest but he didn't give her the chance. "I think we owe each other the chance to see beyond the surface."

"Seth—"

"Have dinner with me. Just one date. That's all I'm asking," he pressed. "One evening without all this tension and conflict that doesn't have to be there. There's this great restaurant I know in Jackson Hole. Neutral territory. We won't see anybody we know and we can talk and laugh and enjoy each other's company. I'll even promise to keep my hands to myself, if that's what it will take."

It just might be the toughest promise he ever had to keep, he thought, but he could handle it if it offered him the chance to bust through all her roadblocks.

She slipped her hand from his and wrapped her arms around herself. His heart sank and he braced himself for one more rejection from her, knowing somehow this one would hurt worse than all the others combined after that tender kiss they had just shared.

He saw the indecision in her eyes, then her gaze shifted from him to her car for just a moment. He had no idea what she saw there, but when she looked back, he was stunned to see the uncertainty replaced by something soft and warm, something that left him breathless.

"All right. Yes. I'll go to dinner with you."

He wasn't at all prepared for the raw emotion that coursed through him at her words—a tangle of joy and relief and elation. It left him more than a little uneasy, but he resolved not to worry about that now.

How had things come to this?

Ten days later, just a week before Christmas, Jenny pulled out the roast chicken to check it one final time. The skin looked perfect, crisp and golden, and the whole kitchen was redolent with delicious smells—fresh rolls, creamy mashed potatoes and the succulent chicken.

"Does this look right?" Morgan asked from the kitchen island where she was drizzling chocolate syrup across the cheesecake she'd made earlier in the day.

"Delicious," she assured her daughter, who unfortunately had inherited her somewhat less-than-gourmet skills in the kitchen.

"Do you think Seth will like it?"

"Will like what?" the man in question asked from the doorway and her heart gave its customary foolish little leap.

She really needed to have a talk with her father about letting Seth into the house without giving her some kind of warning so she could brace herself for his impact on her.

How was it possible he was more gorgeous every time she saw him? she wondered. Tonight he wore faded jeans, worn boots and a burgundy fisherman's sweater that made her mouth water. Throw in that heartbreaking smile and the sweet little puppy cavorting around his legs and it was no wonder she had no defenses against him.

She cleared her throat. "Hi," she said.

His smile widened and she wondered how he could consume every oxygen particle just by walking into a room.

"Hi." His greeting encompassed both of them, but the light in his eyes was entirely for her, she knew, though she didn't understand it and couldn't quite believe it.

"What will I like?"

"Morgan made you a dessert," Jenny said. "She's a little worried you won't like it."

"You made that?"

He walked closer, bringing with him the clean, masculine scent of his aftershave. He smelled far better than anything she'd fixed for dinner and all she wanted to do was devour him.

She forced herself to take several deep, cleansing breaths to calm down as Morgan nodded with a grimace.

"It's kind of uneven," her daughter admitted. "I was hoping the chocolate syrup would hide it."

"Are you kidding? It looks like something out of a magazine. I hope nobody else is hungry because I just might have to eat that whole thing all by myself."

Morgan giggled, her eyes glowing. Jenny knew she must look the same.

How had things come to this? She had no willpower where the man was concerned.

What had started out as one simple dinner invitation to one of the more exclusive Jackson Hole restaurants had somehow slid into a regular event in the last ten days.

She had seen him nearly every day since the night he'd helped with Morgan's flare-up and fixed her car. They had gone to dinner twice in Jackson Hole, had taken the kids to a movie in Idaho Falls one day, had taken a drive to Mesa Falls to watch the spectacular show of water thrusting through ice.

They'd even gone for a snowy moonlit horseback ride on the ranch—which might have been romantic if they hadn't had both Natalie and Morgan along, chattering all the way.

It was after that horseback ride two nights before when

they'd been sipping hot cocoa by his soaring Christmas tree that she'd taken the huge step of asking him to dinner.

She hadn't meant to—had actually been working up to telling him she couldn't see him anymore. But the invitation had slipped from her subconscious to her tongue before she knew it.

She couldn't take it back, especially when he had looked so delighted. It was the first time she had initiated a social encounter between them and she knew he must have realized that fact as well as she did.

As wonderful as she had to admit these ten days had been, she wasn't quite sure where things stood between them. Despite the wild heat of that night in the garage, they hadn't shared anything like that since. He was true to his word, she had discovered. When he said he would keep his hands to himself, he meant exactly that.

Though he was attentive and courteous, any physical contact between them was casual—a hand on her arm to help her over an icy patch, fingers casually laced through hers in a darkened theater as they watched a movie, a barely-there good-night kiss when he dropped her off after dinner.

If he meant to drive her crazy with lust, he was certainly succeeding. She was a quivering mass of hormones when he was around.

They couldn't keep on like this.

The thought crawled through her mind again, stark and depressing. Seeing him was accomplishing nothing except giving her this wild hunger for something she knew she couldn't have.

"Anything I can do?" Seth asked.

She pushed away the thought for now and mustered a smile. "I think we're there, aren't we, Morgan?"

Her daughter nodded.

"We only have to take the food into the dining room."

"I can't even begin to tell you how delicious everything looks," he murmured, and her whole body seemed to shiver and sigh. He was looking at *her* and not the dinner she'd spent so much time preparing.

"Here," she said abruptly, thrusting a dish to him. "You can carry in the bird."

He grinned as if he knew exactly his effect on her, but took the tray from her and headed out of the kitchen.

After he left, Jenny turned to find Morgan watching, a curious light in her eyes. Her daughter waited about ten seconds before she spoke in a voice pitched low. "Are you going to marry Seth?"

The bowl of mashed potatoes slipped from Jenny's suddenly nerveless fingers and she had to scramble to keep them from splattering all over the kitchen floor.

"No! Wherever did you get that idea?"

"You like him though, don't you?"

Heaven spare her from nine-year-old girls who saw entirely too much. "I...yes. Of course I do. But that's a far cry from marrying him, honey. We're only friends."

Morgan digested that, looking a little disappointed. "I just wanted you to know I wouldn't mind. I don't think Cole would, either. He's a lot nicer when Seth is around."

"Okay. Um, good to know." This wasn't a conversation she wanted to have right now, with Seth just on the other side of that wall. She could only pray he didn't come back in.

"Natalie says it's pretty cool having a stepparent. Mrs. Dalton is way nice to her and fixes her hair and everything."

"You already have someone to fix your hair," she pointed out, hoping to distract her. "Me!"

"I know. But I don't have someone to teach me how to ride horses or who knows what I feel like when my asthma flares." Morgan was quiet for a moment. "You laugh a lot more when Seth is here. So if you want to marry him, I wouldn't mind."

Her daughter picked up the cheesecake she put such effort into and carried it out of the kitchen.

When she left, Jenny pressed a hand to her mouth. Oh, she needed to put a stop to this. She should have realized how Morgan would construe the fragile beginnings of whatever this was with Seth. He was the only man she had spent any time with socially since the divorce, so it was logical for Morgan to jump to the wrong conclusion.

Shaking him loose was going to hurt.

The knowledge left a cold knot in her stomach. It would hurt, but not as much as they would all hurt if she let things continue as they were.

He wasn't serious about her. She still didn't know why exactly he seemed to want to spend so much time with her, but she knew he couldn't possibly have anything lasting in mind.

"Are we eating or are we going to sit here looking at all this pretty food all night?" her father called from the dining room.

"I'm coming. Sorry."

She let out a breath, then grabbed the rolls and the salad. Tonight. She had to find some way to tell him this had to be the end of it.

No matter how much she loved being with him, how the whole world seemed more vivid and wonderful whenever he was near, she had to stop indulging herself before her children opened their hearts and their lives to him any further.

And before she did the same.

Chapter 12

Forty-five minutes later, she was no closer to figuring out how she was going to force herself to end something that seemed so perfect—though with each passing moment, she knew she had no choice.

Seth set down his fork with a sigh of satisfaction. "Ladies, that was just about the best dinner I've had in longer than I can remember. Especially the cheesecake."

Morgan beamed, clearly smitten. "It's my mom's recipe. I just followed the directions."

"Even though you had a great recipe to start with, you were the one who did such a good job following it. But kudos to your mom, too."

"I can't really take credit," Jenny protested. "I always just use the recipe that comes on the cream cheese package—nothing very original, I'm afraid."

He laughed. "Enough of this humility! Will somebody please accept the compliment?"

"I will," Cole offered with a grin.

Everyone laughed, since Cole had had absolutely nothing to do with the cheesecake except eating a hefty slice.

As the laughter faded, Jenny looked around the table, a bittersweet pang in her chest. Her children would be hurt when Seth stopped coming around. Would Cole and Morgan understand why she had to send him packing? Or would they blame her for it?

"I need to move after that big meal," Seth said with a smile. "Anybody feel like taking a walk? I figured we could walk the few blocks to downtown and judge for ourselves which house ought to win the town's holiday lighting contest."

"I want to!" Morgan exclaimed.

Cole shrugged but didn't seem opposed to the idea. Or if he was, at least he didn't roll his eyes or say it blew.

"Jen? Jason? What about you two?"

"I have to finish the dishes," Jenny stalled, despising herself for her cowardice.

She had yet to go anywhere in town with Seth where others might see them together.

Though she knew they always stood the chance of running into someone from Pine Gulch in Jackson or Idaho Falls, she'd convinced herself the likelihood of that was slim.

On the other hand, even if someone *did* see them tonight as they walked through town, what would be the harm in enjoying the holiday sights with him accompanied by the rest of her family?

Her father slid his chair back from the table and started to clear away dishes. "You all go have some fun. I'll clean up."

"The kitchen's a disaster," she said. "You know what a mess I make when I cook."

Her dad only smiled. "Well, you *are* the only person I

know who can dirty three or four pans just boiling water for pasta. But I think I'm up to the task. Go on."

He used that implacable "don't argue" voice and she sighed. She could have used a little backup, but she didn't think she would find it from her father. At least not in this instance.

Though she wouldn't have expected it, Seth had managed to charm even Jason, quite a feat, since her father had disliked Richard from the start.

The two of them talked about fishing, cars, even politics. After one of their trips to Jackson for dinner, her father had let her know in a subtle way that he thought Seth was a good man.

She didn't have the kind of relationship with her father where she could spill all her own angst to him—all the reasons she knew Seth was bad for her—so after a stunned moment, she had just thanked him for watching Morgan and Cole for her and gone to bed.

No, she couldn't expect any aid from that quarter.

"All right," she said now. "Thanks. I just need to grab my coat."

It wouldn't be so bad, she decided. If she could find a quiet moment while Morgan and Cole were distracted, perhaps on this snowy, moonlit walk, she might be able somehow to find the opportunity—and the strength—to talk to Seth.

Fifteen minutes later, bundled against the cold wind blowing down off the mountains, they walked out into the night, Lucy in the lead, scampering a short way ahead of them.

People in Pine Gulch took their holiday lighting seriously, she had learned the last few weeks. Nearly every house had some kind of holiday decoration, from a string of basic colored lights framing a window to more elaborate displays of reindeer and Santas and full-size nativities.

All the holiday spirit gave the little town a quiet, magical air on a winter evening. They seemed to be the only ones outside and their boots left tracks in the skiff of new snow covering the quiet streets as they walked toward the small downtown.

Seth walked at Morgan's side, easily matching his long-legged stride to her much shorter one, while Jenny walked beside Cole, grateful her son had come along.

The town had its own light display at the small park next to her elementary school and that was their ultimate destination.

Here, the trees were lit with what seemed like millions of tiny multicolored twinkling lights. They were lovely, Jenny thought, though the rest of the display looked as if had been added to piece by piece over the years. A trio of illuminated carolers stood next to a plastic snowman of a different style and size and across the sidewalk from a couple of giant nutcrackers.

Lucy's leash suddenly slipped out of Morgan's hand and the puppy took advantage of the unexpected freedom to race across the park toward the play equipment, her leash dragging through the snow.

"Oh, no!" Morgan exclaimed.

"Don't just stand there like an idiot," Cole snapped. "Go get her."

Seth didn't even say anything, he just raised an eyebrow at the teen. That always seemed to be enough to remind Cole to stow the attitude. This time was no different. After a second, Cole huffed out a breath and went after his sister and the recalcitrant puppy.

As soon as they were out of earshot, Jenny was painfully

aware this was the private moment she'd been seeking. She was trying to figure out the right words when Seth spoke.

"What's wrong?" he asked.

She opened her mouth to tell him the truth but the words seemed to catch in her throat. "What makes you think something's wrong?" she stalled.

"You haven't said more than a few words at a time all night. Is something on your mind?"

It was exactly the kind of opening she needed and she knew couldn't put this off anymore, no matter how hard it was. She might not have a better opportunity all night. A careful glance at her children told her they had caught the puppy and were busy watching her scamper through snow-drifts as tall as she was.

Between the three of them, they were making enough racket that anything she might say to Seth wouldn't be overheard.

She released a puff of condensation on a heavy breath. "Yes, actually. Something is on my mind. Seth, I…we can't do this again."

In the colored glow from the lights, she thought she saw some strange emotion leap into his eyes, almost like panic, but it was gone so quickly she thought she must have been mistaken.

"Yeah, you're right," he said after a moment. "We can see the Christmas lights better this way, up close and personal, but it's just too darn cold. Next time we'll take a car so we can cover more ground."

"You know that's not what I mean." She sighed. "This has been wonderful. It has. But—"

Her words ended in a shriek as something cold and wet suddenly exploded in her face.

She brushed snow off and scowled at her offspring, who

both surveyed her with expressions so innocent they could have belonged to the angels in the town's crèche.

Even Lucy gazed at her, her little head cocked and her eyes soft and limpid as if butter wouldn't melt in her mouth. Morgan and Cole's innocent looks lasted only seconds before they busted out laughing.

"Oh! That was so not funny!" she exclaimed.

"Don't worry, Jen." Seth bent down for a handful of snow. "I've got your back."

He lobbed the snowball—but instead of aiming it toward her kids, the man she knew perfectly well had been a star baseball pitcher miscalculated by a mile and threw it at her instead, where it thudded against the back of her coat.

Of course, this set Morgan and Cole into more hysterics.

She rounded on him, her glare promising retribution. "I think you are missing the intent of that particular phrase."

Any response he might have made was lost by another snowball, this one launched by Cole, that landed exactly in the center of his chest.

"Kid, that was a big mistake," Seth said, though she didn't miss the glee in his eyes.

From then on, it was full-out war. She took cover behind the plastic snowman and had the satisfaction of hitting both Cole and Seth with solid lobs.

With maternal consideration, she took pity on Morgan, but her daughter repaid her kindness with a sneak attack to her flank. While Jenny was busy evading a concerted attack from the males, Morgan must have skulked along the shrubs until she was just behind her mother, where she had an unobstructed shot. She took full advantage of it, then raced back for cover.

After fifteen minutes or so, Seth finally raised the white flag—or in this case a tan flag, one of his gloves.

"Okay. Enough. Enough!" He stood up. "We're all going to freeze out here if we keep this up. I say we call it a draw and head back to your house for hot chocolate."

As if they had all perfectly choreographed it, she, Morgan and Cole each launched snowballs at him simultaneously, hitting him from every direction while Lucy barked with delight and danced around his feet.

Seth looked down at the dripping mess on his coat and shook his head with a rueful grin. "Remind me not to take on the Boyer clan again unless I have better reinforcements than an Australian shepherd pup."

His laughing gaze met Jenny's, the colored lights gleaming in his eyes. She stared at him and suddenly felt as if an entire truckload of snow had just been dumped on her head.

There in the city park on a cold December night, the truth washed over her stronger than an avalanche, and she had to grab the plastic snowman just to keep upright.

This wasn't just a casual attraction, something she could walk away from without any lasting ramifications.

She was in love with him.

She shivered, chilled right down to her bones, and she couldn't seem to catch her breath.

Oh, how could she have let this happen? She knew he wasn't good for her. From the very beginning, she had told herself he would break her heart but these last few weeks had been so wonderful, she had completely ignored all the warning signs and plunged straight ahead anyway.

And now look what a mess she'd created!

She was in love with a completely inappropriate man, a man who had probably never had a serious relationship in his life.

The gaping maw of heartache beckoned her. She could see it as clearly as if it were in front of her outlined in bright, blinking Christmas lights. Of what use was it to know just what was in store for her, she wondered, since she was suddenly terrified it was far too late to do anything about it?

"I'm cold, Mom. Can we go home?" Morgan's voice jerked her out of her stupor and she somehow managed to catch her breath again.

"Of course, honey. Let's go," she said, forcing a smile that felt like it was made of thin, crackly ice.

They covered the few blocks toward her father's house quickly as the cold wind cut through their snow-dampened clothes like a chainsaw.

When they reached the house, both kids rushed to their respective rooms to change into dry clothes.

Jason was probably in his den—she could hear the TV going—but he didn't come out to greet her and for the first time in a long time, the silence between her and Seth seemed awkward.

He cast a look at the door, looking suddenly anxious to leave. Why? she wondered nervously. He couldn't suspect her feelings, could he?

She cleared her throat. "Would you like to put on something dry from my father's closet?"

"No. I'll just run the truck's heater full-blast on my way home and I'll be dry soon enough."

"Are you sure?"

"Yeah. I'll be fine."

Again they slipped into that awkward silence. Here was where she should tell him she couldn't see him again, she thought. She opened her mouth but he cut her off so abruptly she almost wondered if it was deliberate.

"Thanks again for dinner. It was really delicious," he said.

"Um, you're welcome. Seth—"

"What are you doing tomorrow?"

She blinked, wondering at his apparent urgency. "I don't know. I have a faculty thing Sunday, but tomorrow I just need to take care of some last-minute shopping for the kids. The last Saturday before Christmas is the biggest shopping day of the year, did you know that? A lot of people think it's the day after Thanksgiving but it's not."

She was babbling, she realized, but she couldn't seem to rein in her unruly tongue. Filling up the space with the inconsequential and mundane only delayed the inevitable, she told herself.

"Shopping is on my agenda, too," Seth said, then smiled suddenly, though she thought it looked a little strained. "You know, I could sure use your help."

"My help?"

"I'm not having much luck this year shopping for my brothers' wives or for Natalie and I'm running out of time. I could use a woman's perspective, you know?"

This from the man who seemed to know far more than most women about what they wanted?

"I was planning to head into Jackson Hole," he went on. "Maybe check out some of the galleries. We ought to save gas and go together. What do you think?"

She didn't think he really wanted to know the grim thoughts running through her mind—that she should run far away from him, that she should make this their last good-bye, that her heart was already bracing itself for the pain.

But, oh, she wanted to say yes. One more time. That was all she craved. A few more hours to spend with him. She would go shopping with him in Jackson and store up one last day of priceless memories and then she would have to break things off.

"All right," she said before she changed her mind.

Again he had an odd reaction. Something like relief flickered in his blue eyes.

"I'll pick you up at nine. Does that work?"

At her nod, he stepped forward for the kind of hurried kiss she'd come to expect from him at the end of the night.

She wanted to curl her hands into his parka and hold him tight for a real kiss, the kind they'd shared that night in the garage, the kind she dreamed about at night. But she knew she couldn't, not in her father's entryway with Jason just down the hall, where her children could come running in at any moment.

"Good night," he said, giving her that slow, sexy smile that curled her toes, then he walked out into the night.

She closed the door behind him and leaned against it. She was weak. Weak and stupid and doomed.

The next morning, Seth climbed back into his pickup after dropping Lucy off with Quinn and Marjorie for a play day with her brother.

Her delight at the prospect of a full day of cavorting with another puppy hadn't quite been enough to prevent her from giving him a reproachful look when he headed for the door without her.

He had withstood her canine wiles, though, not wanting anything—not even his adorable but energetic puppy—to get in the way of what he was hoping would be a perfect day.

Even the weather was cooperating. It was a gorgeous Teton Valley day, the kind they ought to put on travel brochures. The inch or two of new snow from the night before sparkled in the brilliant sunshine and the sky was a bright, stunning blue.

He drove the few blocks from his mom's house to Jenny's, his stomach jumping with anticipation. He wasn't sure he liked the jittery feeling in his gut. It was just a date, after all. Nothing to get so worked up about.

He had been telling himself that all morning while he fed and watered the horses and hurried through the rest of his chores, but he couldn't seem to escape the conclusion that he had to make everything about their time together unforgettable, so incredible she wouldn't be able to bring herself to end things.

He wasn't an idiot. He knew damn well she'd been about to break things off with him the night before while they'd been walking through the town square.

He had seen it in her expressive green eyes, that moment of resignation and resolve, and he'd known a moment of sheer, blind panic before the kids had unknowingly bailed him out by starting their snowball war.

She had agreed to go with him today, though. The way he saw it, he had one last chance to change her mind.

He had to. He didn't even want to think about the alternative. He didn't understand any of this, he just knew he couldn't bear imagining his world without her and the kids in it.

These last few weeks with her had been incredible. He'd never been so fascinated with a woman before. Obsessed, even. He thought about her all the time and he couldn't wait until the next time he would see her.

If she asked him why, he had to admit he wasn't sure he could put a finger on it. It was a hundred different things— the way she pursed her lips when she was concentrating on something, the tenderness in her eyes when she looked at her kids, the little tremble she tried to hide whenever he happened to touch her, even in the most casual way.

She was smart and funny and beautiful, and she had

this quiet strength about her he found soothing and incredibly addictive.

He was also amazed how she seemed to bring out the best in everybody around her—even him. When he was with her, he felt like a better man, somebody kind and good and decent.

He wasn't ready to lose all that. Not yet. Maybe after the holidays, though even the thought of that left him with a cold knot in his chest.

He pushed away his nerves as pulled into her driveway. Today he wouldn't think about goodbyes. The sun was shining, the day was perfect, and he would spend the rest of their time together showing her all the reasons she needed him.

"Please! I just want to go home," Jenny practically wailed ten hours later. The bruise around her eye looked dark and ugly—almost as miserable as the blizzard that swirled around his pickup.

"I'm real sorry, ma'am," the highway patrolman at the roadblock to the canyon between Jackson and Pine Gulch leaned across Seth in the driver's seat to say to Jenny in a patient voice, "but I'm afraid nobody's getting through this canyon right now. Between the storm and that jackknifed big rig, the canyon's going to be closed anywhere from three to four more hours. Maybe longer. This is one heck of a nasty storm, coming out of nowhere like it did. It's shut down this whole region and we're recommending that people who don't have to travel stay put until it lets up."

She let out a little sound that sounded suspiciously like a sob. The frazzled highway patrolman gave Seth a dark look before turning back to Jenny.

"I wish I could give you a better option but right now I'm

afraid you folks are going to have to turn around and head back into town and find a place to wait out the storm until we open the canyon again. The Aspen is a pretty nice place."

"No!" Jenny and Seth both said sharply.

The patrolman looked a bit taken aback by their vehemence, but there was a long line of cars behind them at the roadblock trying to get through the canyon and Seth knew the man had other frustrated motorists to deal with.

"There are other restaurants in town. You can try to find a hotel room, too. That might be your best bet."

"Thank you for your help," Seth said grimly. "We'll figure something out."

The man waved them on and Seth rolled up his window and turned his truck around to head back into Jackson Hole.

Jenny stared out the windshield, her features stony, and his hands tightened on the steering wheel.

He had screwed up everything. The way things were going, he would be lucky if she ever talked to him again.

He should have paid more attention to the weather, but he had been working so hard to make sure she had an unforgettable time, he hadn't given the gathering clouds much thought.

If he had just paid a little attention to the warning signs, he would have left two hours ago before the storm that forecasters had said would be just a little skiff decided to hit with a vengeance.

They would have made it through the canyon before the semi jackknifed and they would have been home by now. Maybe Jenny would have been basking in the glow of a wonderful day instead of sitting beside him, her features stiff as if she'd been turned to ice by the storm.

How had things taken such a wrong turn? he wondered. He still couldn't quite figure it out.

For much of the day, everything had gone so well, just as he'd planned. Jackson at Christmas was an exciting, dynamic town, bustling with skiers and shoppers and tourists. He and Jenny had had a great time combing through the trendy little stores and galleries to find last-minute gifts for the rest of the people on their respective lists.

With Jenny's help, he had found the perfect gifts for the important women in his life. He'd already bought his mother and Quinn a gift so he didn't need to worry about them.

For Maggie, he bought a matted and framed photograph of a field of mountain wildflowers in the middle of a rainstorm, their hues rich and dramatic. Caroline's gift was some whimsical handmade wind chimes to go with her collection on the Cold Creek patio, and for Natalie, Jenny had steered him to a set of earrings shaped like horses.

Jenny had already bought most of the gifts for her children and just needed some last-minute things. He helped her pick out a wool sweater for her father that would definitely turn some sweet older lady's head.

For Morgan she bought a whole basket full of books and a pair of earrings just like the set he'd bought for Nat and she finally gave in and bought Cole the snowboard he'd been hinting not so subtly about.

Just as Seth had dreamed, Jenny had glowed through most of the day. She had laughed more than he ever remembered and she had touched him often, taking his arm while they walked, touching him to make a point, even slipping her hand through his as they stood looking at some of the gallery offerings.

And then Cherry Mendenhall had ruined everything.

No. Though it would be easier to blame the other woman, he knew the responsibility for the disaster of the rest of the day rested squarely on his own shoulders.

If only he had paid attention to the weather and left two hours earlier. If only he had picked a different restaurant for their early dinner. Beyond that, if only he'd walked away a few years ago when Cherry had come over to his table at the Cowboy Bar after a business meeting, all tight jeans and pouty lips.

But he hadn't walked away. In fact, idiot that he was, he had invited trouble to sit right down and have herself a drink.

He hadn't really been looking to start anything that night two years ago, but Cherry had been more than enthusiastic, five feet nine inches of warm, curvy, willing woman.

They'd both been a little tipsy—only he hadn't realized until much later that was more the norm than the exception for her. They'd danced, they'd flirted, and to his everlasting regret now, they'd ended up taking the party back to his hotel room.

He'd thought she just wanted a good time and he'd looked her up a few more times when he was in Jackson, but he quickly discovered he'd badly misjudged her.

Suddenly the fun-loving party girl turned clingy and emotional and started calling him all the time, so much so he finally had to change his cell phone number.

He should have handled things far differently. The decent thing would have been to sit her down and try to explain that they were obviously after different things. But he'd been right in the middle of building the training arena, up to his ears in details, and hadn't had time for that kind of complication. It had seemed easier just to ignore her and hope she would just go away.

The whole situation with her hadn't been one of his better moments and he was ashamed of himself for it all over again.

When he and Jenny walked into the Aspen for a late

lunch and he'd seen Cherry sitting at the bar, he'd just about turned around and walked back out again.

He should have, even at the risk of Jenny thinking he was crazy, but he had figured nearly two years had passed since he'd even spoken to the woman. She couldn't hold a grudge that long, no matter how stupid he'd been over the whole thing. And besides, she probably wouldn't even remember him.

That had been mistake number 421 in this whole thing.

They'd been seated immediately, at a secluded booth near the fireplace with a spectacular view overlooking the ski resort. Everything had been going so well—they ordered and sat talking about their holiday plans and watching the skiers. When he'd stretched a casual arm across the top of the booth, Jenny had cuddled closer and he couldn't remember ever feeling so happy.

And then Cherry had passed their table on the way to the ladies' room.

From there, their whole magical day went straight to hell.

She'd caught sight of him snuggling there with Jenny and instead of making a polite retreat as he might have hoped, she marched right over to their table and started spewing all kinds of ugliness at him. He couldn't remember most of it, but he was pretty sure *rat bastard* had been about the mildest thing she'd called him.

He had done his best to calm her down, aware of the increasing attention they were drawing from others in the restaurant and of Jenny sitting horrified beside him.

When she turned on Jenny, though, calling her his latest stupid bitch, Seth's patience wore out. He stood up, thinking he would lead Cherry somewhere more private where he could try to calm her down and at least apologize to her for the lousy way he'd treated her. But when he reached for her arm, she went berserk and swung at him.

Unfortunately, she missed—and somehow hit Jenny instead.

From there, the whole episode turned into a farce. Cherry had instantly burst into hysterical sobs—and Jenny had been the one to sit her down at their booth, have the waiter bring her coffee and comfort her while Seth had stood there feeling like the world's biggest idiot.

"I just loved him so much!" Cherry had sobbed and Jenny had hugged her.

"I know, honey. I know," she murmured, giving him a censorious look out of her good eye across the table.

It turned out Cherry had only been at the restaurant waiting for her roommate's shift in the kitchen to be over so she could get a ride home. After a few more painfully miserable moments while they both commiserated about men in general and him in particular, the other woman came out, gave Seth another dirty look and led Cherry away, along with any chance he had of convincing Jenny he was more than his reputation.

Neither of them touched their food. He tried to explain but Jenny hadn't been in any kind of mood to listen as he tried to convince her he wasn't the jackass he appeared— though right about now, even *he* wasn't so sure about that.

He'd finally given up, paid their check and walked outside, only to discover that while they'd been preoccupied inside the Aspen, a blizzard had hit with a vengeance rivaling only the proverbial scorned woman.

He sighed now as they reached the outskirts of town, wondering at what point he might have been able to salvage the disaster.

He was all those things Cherry had called him and more and he didn't deserve a woman like Jenny.

He pulled into the snow-covered parking lot of the grocery store. "So what do you want to do? We can find somewhere to wait around for the pass to open in three or four hours or we can take our chances and drive down through Kemmerer and back up through Star Valley."

"How long would that take us?" she asked, still without looking at him.

"In this weather, about six hours."

She looked close to tears but didn't say anything.

"Or, like the trooper suggested, we could try to find a hotel room somewhere for the night and head home in the morning. That's probably our safest alternative."

She looked miserable at the idea of spending even another second in his company. Her eye had swollen almost shut and around all that color, her face was pale and withdrawn.

"All right," she finally said.

"We probably won't have an easy time finding a room," he was compelled to warn her. "Between the holidays and the ski season, Jackson hotels are usually pretty full this time of year. I'll give it my best shot but it might take me a while."

"We have all night, don't we?" she said.

Two hours ago, the prospect of a night with her would have had his imagination overheating with all the sensual possibilities.

Now he thought he'd almost rather walk barefoot over the pass in this blizzard than have to sit by all night and watch her slip further away from him.

Chapter 13

Barely an hour later, Jenny sat ensconced in a plump armchair pulled up to a crackling fire.

"I'm sorry to do this to you, Dad," she said into her cell phone, "but the storm came up out of nowhere. How is it there?"

"We've got a couple inches but it looks like more is on the way. If this keeps up, you're going to think it never stops snowing around here."

"Does it?" she asked.

"Sure. Round about June." Her dad laughed and Jenny wished she had the capacity to find anything amusing right about now. Her sense of humor seemed to have deserted her.

"Seth talked about trying to push our way through as soon as they open the pass again but even under the best-case scenario, we probably wouldn't make it home until two or three in the morning."

"There's no sense in that. Just stay put. We'll be fine.

Morgan and I are watching a great kung fu movie and Cole is on the computer instant-messaging his friends back in Seattle. Are you sure you're okay?"

With a sigh, Jenny looked around the beautiful three-room suite with its massive king-size canopy bed, the matching robes hanging on a hook by the bathroom, the soft rug in front of the fireplace.

Trust Seth to come up with the only room left in town—the honeymoon suite of an elegant bed-and-breakfast she had heard touted as one of the ten most romantic small inns in the West.

She couldn't speak for the rest of the place but the honeymoon suite just screamed romance. Everything about it—from the matching armchairs to the huge whirlpool tub—was designed with lovers in mind.

How on earth was she supposed to be able to resist Seth Dalton under these circumstances?

"I'm fine," she finally lied to her father. Black eye notwithstanding, she reminded herself firmly.

If she had trouble remembering why she needed to keep her distance from Seth, she only needed to find a mirror. That vivid, iridescent shiner ought to do the trick.

"Don't let Cole I.M. all night. He should be off by ten. If he gives you any trouble about it, call me and I'll set him straight."

"We'll be fine. You just stay warm."

At that moment, she heard the key turn in the lock and Seth came in carrying the ice bucket. His reflection in the window looked big and male and gorgeous, and she knew without a doubt keeping warm was definitely not going to be the problem.

"Thanks again," she said to her father. "I'll see you in the morning."

"Don't forget your faculty party."

She winced, wondering if she could find enough makeup in all of Pine Gulch to camouflage her black eye to all her teachers.

"That doesn't even start until six tomorrow night so we should have plenty of time to make it back."

She said her goodbyes to her father and hung up as Seth set the ice bucket down on the dresser.

"Everything okay at home?" he asked.

"Fine. Dad's got everything under control. I shouldn't worry."

His smile didn't quite reach his eyes. "But you're a mother and that's what you do."

"I suppose."

He sat down in the armchair next to her and she wondered how the elegant romance of the room only seemed to make him that much more dangerously male.

"You're lucky you've got your father to help you with Cole and Morgan," he said.

"Moving here has worked out well in that regard."

"But not in others?"

If she had stayed in Seattle, she would have been safe. She wouldn't be trapped here in a romantic inn trying to fight her attraction to a man who would dump a woman without even telling her.

"This is a nice room your friend was able to find for us," she said instead. "I guess it helps to know the manager."

She hadn't missed the familiarity between the two when they checked in and she had to wonder if there were any females in the three-state region Seth *didn't* know.

"Yeah, Sierra's great. She grew up in Pine Gulch before she moved to the big time here in Jackson. We've been friends forever."

More than friends at some point, unless Jenny missed her guess, but she decided not to press it. She really didn't want to know anyway.

"Are you hungry?" he asked. "You didn't eat much at dinner."

"I'm fine," she said.

He lapsed into silence and she was acutely aware of him and the long evening stretching out ahead of them.

"Oh, I almost forgot. Along with spare toiletries, Sierra gave me a couple of cold packs from the hotel first aid kit for your eye."

He grabbed one from the dresser, popped it to activate the chemicals, then held it out to her.

Their hands brushed as she took it from him and despite everything, her whole body seemed to sigh a welcome at his nearness.

"Thank you," Jenny murmured, grateful for the slap of cold as she held it to her eye. "I'm sure she must have wondered why I look as though I just went ten rounds with a prizefighter."

He lifted a shoulder in a shrug. "I told her the truth. That you stepped in the way of a punch aimed at me. She didn't seem to find that hard to believe at all."

"You mentioned the vengeful ex-lover, I assume."

He winced. "I did. For some reason, she *really* didn't find that part hard to believe."

Despite her best intentions not to let him charm her, a smile slipped out at his rueful tone.

Regret clouded the pure blue of his eyes as he looked at her holding the ice pack to her eye. "Jenny, I have to tell you again how sorry I am that all this happened. Cherry, the storm, all of it. I wanted today to be perfect for you, but as usual, I've only succeeded in making a mess of everything."

He looked so earnestly miserable that she could feel a little more of her resolve erode away like the sea nibbling at the sand.

"Why did you want everything to be perfect?" she asked.

He said nothing for several moments, then he sighed. "I didn't want you to break things off with me. That's what you planned to do last night, wasn't it?"

She stared. How had he figured it out? "You are entirely too good at reading women."

"No. Just you."

His words seemed to hang in the air between them. She wanted to protest that he didn't know her at all, but she knew it would be an outright lie. He just might know her better than anybody else ever had, something she found terrifying.

"Why, though? That's what I can't quite figure out," he went on. "Why were you all set to push me away? I could understand if you never wanted to see me again after the disaster of today. Any woman would probably feel the same. But before this, I thought things were going well. You seemed happy. I know I was happy. Did I completely misread things?"

He looked so bewildered she had to fight the urge to reach across the space between them and grab his hand.

Physical contact between them right now was not a good idea. In fact, if she were smart, she would probably lock herself in the bathroom all night until the snow cleared and she could be safely back in Pine Gulch.

How could she tell him that all the reasons she'd been compelled to end things with him had just crystallized into the form of that poor, misguided girl in the restaurant?

Cherry Mendenhall was *Jenny*, with a little more time and few more drinks under her belt. Oh, she wanted to think she would never throw a drunken scene in a restaurant over him but she would *want* to and that seemed just as demoralizing.

When he moved on to his next conquest—as she had absolutely no doubt he would—he would leave her heart scraped raw and she would be as devastated and lost as Cherry.

"They were going well," she finally said.

"So why were you putting on the brakes?"

She couldn't tell him the truth so she avoided the subject. "You can't honestly tell me your heart would have been broken if you didn't see me anymore, Seth."

"Oh, can't I?" he murmured, his eyes an intense blue in the dancing firelight.

She studied him for a long moment, her heart pounding, then reality intruded and she shook her head, forcing a smile. "Your reputation doesn't do you justice. You almost had me believing you."

"Screw my reputation!" He rose and towered over her suddenly, all the easy amiability gone from his posture, reminding her again that a big, dangerous man lurked beneath all the smiles and flirtation.

"Screw my reputation," he repeated. "Just for one second, forget everything you might have heard about me from mean-hearted people who ought to just keep their frigging mouths shut. If today hadn't happened with Cherry and you'd never heard any of the gossip—if you only had to judge me on the man you've come to know this last month—would you still be so damn cynical and judgmental? Or would you at least be open to the possibility that I might care about you?"

Her answer seemed important to him in a way she couldn't understand so she pondered it.

"I don't know," she finally had to admit. "I'm not the best judge of character when it comes to men."

"You don't think you can trust your own instincts, just because your ex was a bastard and messed around on you?"

She flushed. "Who told you that?"

The anger seemed to leave him as suddenly as it appeared and he slid back into the armchair, looking tired somehow.

"Cole. One day when we were working on the car, he told me his dad walked out on you for his twenty-year-old girlfriend. He abandoned all of you to move to Europe with her. Cole calls him Dick the Prick, by the way. Sounds pretty apt, from what he's told me."

A startled laugh escaped her. Oh, Richard would hate that. "It's apt. Believe me."

She had never heard Cole say anything derogatory about his father and she couldn't quite fathom him telling Seth all that. From the way Cole had treated her since Richard had moved to France, she had been certain he blamed her for his father's defection. What was it about Seth that made Cole trust him with the truth? Her son had opened up to this man in a way he hadn't to the family therapist they'd seen after the divorce, or to her, or to his grandfather.

She didn't understand it, but she could only be grateful for the comfort it gave her to know that perhaps her son didn't hate her after all.

"Until the day Richard told me he was leaving, I had no idea he was cheating on me. I was completely oblivious. I thought I had the perfect life, the perfect marriage. You wouldn't believe how smug and self-righteous I was. I even used to give relationship advice to my friends! And all the time, my husband was sleeping with another woman."

"You think that automatically makes you a lousy judge

of character? Because you made one mistake? Because you didn't know your husband was cheating? Maybe he was just a master manipulator."

She definitely could see that now, but at the time she'd been completely oblivious to it. What if Seth was doing the same thing to her and she was too blind to see it?

"Maybe you are, too. How do I know you're not cut from the same cloth, that you won't say anything, do anything, to charm your way into a woman's bed?"

She regretted her words as soon as she said them, especially when his eyes darkened with some emotion that looked suspiciously like hurt. "Is that really what you think?"

"I don't want to think that," she whispered. "When I'm with you, I want to believe every word you tell me. It's when I step back that all the doubts crowd in and I can't understand what we're doing here. Why would a man like you even want to be with me?"

His laugh sounded raspy and rough. "You have no idea what you do to me, do you?"

She blinked, then her heart seemed to flutter when he stood up and pulled her to her feet as well.

"Fine," he growled. "I'll show you."

He kissed her and the heat in it scorched her right to her bare toes. She curled them into the carpet and just held on, swept into the firestorm he stirred inside her.

After those first fiery moments that left her nerve endings ablaze, he gentled the kiss and his mouth was achingly tender.

"I want you, Jenny," he said softly against her mouth, sending tiny ripples of need through her. "But if this was only about sex, I could have done something about it weeks ago."

Though she felt boneless and weak from his kiss, some-how she marshaled enough strength to give him a skeptical look. "You're so sure about that?"

In answer, he kissed her again, until her hands wrapped around his neck and she had to hold on tight to keep from melting onto the carpet.

"Pretty sure, yeah," he murmured, with a supreme confidence she couldn't deny, given the evidence she had just provided him.

"You tremble every time I touch you. Did you know that? Even if I just happen to brush up against you when we're walking somewhere. That's an incredibly arousing thing for a man, to know he has that kind of effect on a woman."

Her face burned. She thought she had hid her reaction so well. It was the height of humiliation to learn he'd known all along.

But his eyes were anything but gloating. "You have no idea how hard it's been for me to keep my hands off you these last few weeks. If this had just been about getting you into bed, we would have been there a long time ago. But if nothing else, that alone should tell you that you mean more to me than that. I haven't pushed you. I've been patient and low-key and noble, while I've been burning up from the inside out."

"Seth—"

Whatever she wanted to say was lost against his mouth when he kissed her again, this time with a slow and gentle tenderness that made her eyes burn with emotion.

"I care about you, Jenny. Not just you but Morgan and Cole, too. There's something between us. Something I've never known before, something I don't quite know what to do with. You scare the hell out of me and that alone ought to tell you this is different than anything I've ever experienced. I've never been afraid of any woman. Well, not since Agnes Arbuckle, my junior-high English teacher."

She smiled, trying to imagine him sitting in a classroom giving book reports and learning to diagram sentences.

"You scare me, too," she murmured, but she defied her own words by tugging him closer and kissing him.

Despite everything, in his arms she felt safe from the storms outside, from the howling wind of her own uncertainties and the lashing, pounding ice crystals of self-doubt.

They stood for a long time wrapped around each other while the fire sparked and hissed. All those tender, frightening emotions of that night in her garage came rushing back and she was helpless against them.

She wasn't sure how—everything seemed a blur but his mouth and his hands and his strength—but somehow they ended up in the bedroom of their suite.

He lowered her to the mattress of the canopy bed, and she shivered as his big, powerful body pressed her into the thick, fluffy comforter. Next to all his hard muscles, she felt small and feminine and wanted.

He gazed at her in the glow from the firelight, his eyes glittering, then he kissed her again and she surrendered to the magic.

He trailed kisses down her neck and she moaned, writhing as he unerringly found every one of her most sensitive spots—and a few she'd never realized were there.

"You smell so good." His voice was rough and aroused. "There's this meadow up in the high country where we take our cattle. In early summer it explodes with wildflowers. Lupine, columbine, Queen Anne's lace. A hundred different colors. There's nothing I love more than riding a horse across it just after a rainstorm, when everything smells fresh and sweet and gorgeous."

He trailed kisses to the V-neck of her sweater, then up the other side again. "Every time I'm near you, I feel like it's June and I'm standing in the middle of that meadow with the sun warm on my face."

Oh, he was good. Everything inside her seemed to stretch and purr and she finally had to slide her mouth to his, just to stop the unbearably seductive flow of his words.

For long moments, they touched and kissed and explored, until she was breathless, trembling with need.

Finally, when she wasn't sure she could bear any more, Seth rolled onto his back, breathing hard.

"We're going to have to stop here, sweetheart. After a month of foreplay, I'm just about at the limit of my self-control where you're concerned."

She shifted her head on the pillow and studied him, those gorgeous eyes hazy with need, those sculpted, masculine features that made her ache just looking at him.

"Stop it," he ordered darkly.

"What?"

"Looking at me like that. You're not making this easier. Sometimes it's hell trying to do the right thing."

He was right. They should stop teasing each other before they passed the point of no return.

She knew making love would be a mistake right now, that she would have to face a mountain of regrets in the morning.

But this might be her only chance with him. Despite his tender words, she knew she couldn't hang on to him for long. Soon enough, she would return to real life. To parent-teacher conferences and doctor appointments and the responsibilities that sometimes seemed more than she could bear.

But for now they were here alone together, sheltered from the storm in this romantic room.

She wanted to live. For once, she wanted to throw caution into the teeth of that blizzard and grab hold of her dreams.

She smiled and reached to touch his face, her fingers curving along his jaw. "Why don't we just stop trying, then?"

He gazed at her for a long, charged heartbeat and she thought for a moment he would be noble and walk away. Then he made a low, aroused sound and kissed her with a ferocity that took her breath away.

He'd been holding all this back, she realized, stunned to her soul as he nipped and tasted.

The hunger rose inside her and she needed closer contact between them. With fingers that trembled, she worked the buttons of his shirt, until all those hard muscles were bared to her hot gaze and her exploring fingers. She smoothed a hand over his chest and was stunned by the rapid pulse of his heart.

He let her touch and explore him for a long time. Finally, his eyes heavy-lidded, he pushed her back against the pillows and pulled off her sweater in one smooth motion, leaving her only in her bra and slacks.

She had to wonder if some subconscious yearning for just this had compelled her to wear something besides her usual no-nonsense white underclothes. Instead, she had picked a pair of black tap pants and a matching lacy bra. She could only be glad for the instinct when his eyes darkened.

"Well, well," he said, his voice low, rough. "Who would have guessed the elementary school principal likes naughty underwear? I think there are hidden depths to you, Ms. Boyer."

She could feel herself blush and cursed her redhead's skin, especially when so much was exposed.

He didn't seem to mind. "You have the most incredible skin I've ever seen," he murmured, then his mouth dipped to the V of her bra. "Pale and creamy, like fresh, warm milk. Except when you blush, then it makes me think of strawberries. Plump, juicy strawberries melting in my mouth."

"I get sunburned just walking to the mailbox. It's a redhead's curse."

She completely forgot her train of thought—why she could possibly think her complexion woes might be of interest to anyone—when his hands reached the front clasp of her bra and he slid the lingerie away from her body.

Suddenly she wasn't convinced this was such a good idea.

Why hadn't she thought this through a little better? Sexy lingerie could only take her so far in situations like this.

She was thirty-six years old and had given birth to two children, one now a teenager. Her stomach hadn't been flat for fourteen years and right about the time she hit thirty, she'd started needing underwires in her bras.

That blasted self-doubt suddenly came rushing back and she wanted to yank the comforter over her. She couldn't compare very favorably to all the sweet young things he was used to.

She braced herself to meet his gaze, suddenly afraid of what she would see there.

She wasn't prepared for the blazing tenderness in his eyes, for the heat and the hunger that seared her.

For a moment, something stunned, almost overwhelmed, flickered in his eyes and she would have given anything to know what he was thinking. He didn't say anything to assuage her curiosity, just continued to gaze at her until she couldn't bear it anymore.

She pulled him to her and lost herself in the storm.

A long time later, after he had divested them both of the rest of their clothing and they had teased and tasted until they were both trembling with need, he framed her face in his hands and kissed her with more of that aching tenderness.

She wrapped her arms around him and held on, their gazes locked, as he entered her. Her entire body seemed to sigh a welcome and she arched to meet him.

"You scare the hell out of me," he repeated softly.

"What?" she teased on a moan, feeling more powerful than she ever had in her life. "A big strong man like you afraid of a little thing like me?"

He repaid her by thrusting deeper until she felt every muscle inside her contract. With one more arch of his body, she climaxed suddenly and wildly, gasping his name as wave after wave of sensation poured over her.

His mouth found hers and his kiss was fierce and possessive as he swallowed the rest of her cries. He gave her only seconds to recover before he thrust into her again. To her astonishment, her body rose instantly to meet him again.

His breathing was ragged as he reached between their bodies and touched her. She exploded again in a hot fireburst of sparks and this time he followed her, his mouth hard on hers as he found release.

He awoke in the night to find himself in a strange bed with a warm woman in his arms and the smell of rainwashed wildflowers surrounding him.

Jenny.

They were snuggled together like spoons, her sweet little derriere pressed against him and his arm resting across a very convenient portion of her anatomy.

He shifted on the pillow so he could see her, that wispy

red-gold hair, the delicate line of her jaw, her creamy skin that tasted every bit as delicious as it looked.

A strange tenderness welled up in his chest like the hot springs in the high country above the Cold Creek.

He wasn't used to this complete sense of rightness he experienced with her in his arms.

It was odd for him. He'd always been a little uncomfortable spending the entire night with a woman and was usually pretty good at finding excuses to go home before this particular stage in the game.

But he couldn't imagine a single place on earth he would rather be at this moment than right here with the snow still drifting down outside and Jenny warm and soft in his arms.

She was still asleep. He could feel her breasts rise and fall in an even rhythm against his arm, and he tightened his hold, astonished at the contentment pouring through him.

Was this what his brothers woke to every morning? If so, he wondered how the hell either of them managed to climb out of bed at all.

He'd been with his share of women. More than his share, probably, if truth be told. Right now, he saw all those other encounters for what they were. A desperate, pathetic search for exactly this kind of tenderness, for the close connection he and Jenny had shared.

Everything that had come before seemed suddenly tawdry and cheap and he was ashamed of himself for thinking those quick encounters could ever make him happy.

They might have offered momentary pleasure—he couldn't deny that—but it was like the tiny glow from a birthday candle compared to the million-watt floodlights of joy burning in him with Jenny in his arms.

He didn't have a name for all the emotions pouring

through him. He suspected what they might be, but he wasn't sure he was quite ready to admit to them yet.

His arms tightened around her again, and at the movement, she stirred.

"Sorry," he murmured in her ear. "I didn't mean to wake you."

"Is everything okay?" she asked, her voice rough from sleep.

He kissed the long, slender column of her neck and felt that slow, astonishing tremble.

"Oh, much better than okay. Everything is perfect."

Chapter 14

Jenny wasn't sure how many times they made love in the night. She couldn't seem to get enough of this wild heat between them.

This was probably number four. Or maybe five. She wasn't sure, she just knew she had awakened some time before to find sunlight streaming through the window and Seth beside her, his face shadowed with stubble and a certain warmth in his eyes she'd come to know well in the night.

"Looks like the storm's stopped," he said.

They would have to leave soon, she knew, but for now the man she loved with a fierceness that shocked her was here in her arms, and she wasn't ready to let him go.

She kissed him, her hands tracing the hard planes of chest then heading south. She was enjoying the anticipation curling through her—the way his stomach muscles contracted as she touched him—when suddenly her cell phone went off.

During a bored moment a few weeks ago, Morgan had programmed it to play a vocal version of Jingle Bells for the ringtone and they both stared at it as the merry little tune chirped through the room.

"I should get that," she finally said when the singers had sung the first verse and started jingling all the way.

"Do you have to?" He kissed the spot just below her ear he had somehow discovered drove her crazy and she groaned.

She had a wild urge to abandon good sense and let the thing ring, but already that world she feared so much was intruding on their haven. She was a woman with responsibilities and she couldn't just throw them out the window—no matter how much she might want to.

With a deep, regretful sigh, she reached for her phone on the bedside table. "It might be Dad or one of the kids. I have to see."

He sighed and slid away slightly, though he stayed far too close for her to keep a coherent thought.

She didn't recognize the incoming number but she answered it anyway, hoping the caller couldn't hear that ragged edge to her voice.

"Hello?"

There was a pause for three or four seconds. "Jen? Is that you?" she finally heard and her heart sank as she recognized Marcy Weller's voice.

She sat up, pulling the sheets around her.

"Hi Marcy. How are you?"

Her assistant gave a crazed-sounding laugh. "Oh, just dandy. I'm only in charge of planning a dinner party for fifty people in ten hours and the caterer has to pick today of all days to go flaky on me."

The faculty party. She hadn't given it a thought since

the day before. How much power did Seth hold over her if he could make her completely forget something she'd been obsessing about for weeks?

In an effort to shore up the sagging morale at the school and to try yet again to make a connection with her staff—some of whom were still resentful the school board had brought in an outsider—she'd decided to dig into her own savings to throw a party for the faculty and staff at the school. Marcy had offered her parents' large, elegant house as the venue since they were traveling during the holidays.

Her vivacious assistant had taken over the party planning, handling all the details and leaving Jenny only to worry.

Which she'd forgotten to do for the last twenty-four hours.

She gathered her thoughts and tried to sound professional and composed. "What do you mean? What's wrong with Allen?"

"Not him. His stupid wife," Marcy exclaimed. "Candy went into labor three weeks early, can you believe it? How can she do this to us? Where are we supposed to come up with a caterer at the last minute?"

Jenny gave a startled laugh, but Marcy went on before she could comment.

"This is just like Candy," Marcy said darkly. "She always hated me. She hasn't changed a bit since she was head cheerleader at high school—she can't stand not being the center of attention."

"I really doubt she planned going into labor just to inconvenience you and ruin our faculty party."

"You don't know her like I do. I wouldn't put anything past her."

Jenny didn't know her at all, she just knew Allen was

a great caterer she'd already used twice since she came to Pine Gulch.

"What are we going to do?" Marcy wailed. "Oh, this is a nightmare! Between yesterday's blizzard and now Candy's selfishness, this party is going to be a total bomb."

"Calm down. We'll figure something out. I can't imagine Allen didn't have at least some of the prep work done for the party, since it's only in a few hours."

Marcy drew a breath and Jenny could picture her moving into one of the calming yoga moves from the class she took from Marjorie Dalton that she practiced in times of stress. When she spoke, some of the hysteria seemed to be gone from her voice.

"He tried to tell me everything that was ready for the party but I could hear Candy yelling at him to hurry up in the background and he was so flustered I couldn't make sense of half of it. He did tell me where the spare key is to his kitchen, though."

Jenny rose and started pacing the room, lost in administrative problem-solver mode.

"Okay. Here's what we're going to do. You've got the key and the menu we agreed on. You can run over to Allen's place right now and see if you can figure out how much prep he's finished and how much we still have left to do."

"I can do that. It's only a few blocks away. Better yet, why don't you meet me there? We could do this faster with two of us."

She turned around and saw Seth lounging against the pillows watching her with that light in his eyes again. She abruptly realized she'd left the sheets behind on the bed and was pacing the room dressed in nothing but her cell phone.

She cleared her throat, knowing she would look more foolish if she scrambled back under the blanket, as she wanted to do. Instead she reached for the closest article of clothing—his shirt—and slipped into it.

"Well, there's a bit of a hitch there. I was, um, stranded in Jackson last night by the storm."

"You're in Jackson?" All the panic—and more—returned to Marcy's voice and she spoke the last word about three octaves higher and several decibels louder than the first two. "When I called your house and your dad said to call you on your cell, he didn't say anything about you being out of town!"

"I'm out of town for now," Jenny said, hurrying to calm her. "But I'm sure the roads are clear now and I'll be heading back to Pine Gulch as soon as I can, I promise. I can be back in…"

She gave Seth a questioning look and almost dropped the phone at the expression in his eyes, something murky and unreadable that sent her stomach twirling and had her pulling his shirt more tightly around her.

Those gorgeous shoulders rippled as he shrugged and held up three fingers.

"Three hours," she told Marcy. "Though I'll do everything I can to make it in two and a half."

"That's still not enough time for us to get everything ready!"

"It will all be okay, I promise. Try to call Allen at the hospital to figure out where things stand and see if he can walk us through whatever recipes are left."

Marcy was only slightly mollified to have a plan of action. "Ten hours, Jen. That's all we've got."

"I know. We'll figure it out, I promise."

"We'd better. You know how important this is."

She thought of her faculty and how hard she had worked to earn their trust and acceptance. A good school administrator could accomplish nothing without the support of her teachers and she still had a long way to go for that. She hoped this party might melt some of their reserve.

"I know."

"I hope so. This is my one big chance with Lance and I can't afford to blow it!"

Okay, perhaps she and Marcy weren't quite on the same page here, she thought with a smile. She was desperate to build a team with her faculty while Marcy's motives had more to do with a certain physical education teacher she was interested in.

"You know how long it took me to work up the nerve to ask him to be my date tonight," Marcy went on. "I wanted so much to impress him by throwing this really terrific party and now it's all going to be ruined because of stupid Candy Grumley."

"We'll get through this, I swear. Lance won't know what hit him, okay? Just call me on my cell when you've had a chance to assess the situation in Allen's kitchen."

"I don't want to call you when you're driving, especially in these conditions. I'm sure the roads will still be slick."

She didn't want to tell Marcy not to worry about that since someone else would be at the wheel—especially when that someone was a presently naked and extremely gorgeous Seth Dalton.

She felt herself blush. "Don't worry about that. Just call me."

She wrapped up the call a few moments later and closed her phone to face Seth, who was still watching her with that lazy smile.

She wanted desperately to climb back into that bed with him but she knew it was impossible.

"I've got to get back. I'm… I'm sorry but it's an emergency."

"Sounded urgent."

"That faculty thing I was telling you about. We're having a holiday party tonight. Allen Grumley is catering it for us and his wife has apparently gone into labor three weeks later. Marcy thinks she did it on purpose."

"Candy always was a prima donna."

She picked up a pillow and smacked him with it. "Not you, too! For heaven's sake, can't a woman even go into labor without the world assigning ulterior motives?"

He laughed and fended off her attack, then grabbed her and pulled her to him.

She let out a sigh, regret a heavy ache inside her that she wouldn't share this magic with him again. "I'm sorry, but I really do have to get back to deal with the crisis."

He arched an eyebrow. "In that case, maybe we'd better save time and share the shower."

Sharing a shower turned out not to be the world's most efficient idea after all.

She hadn't really expected it to save any time, but she also hadn't been able to resist one more chance to kiss him and touch him. They made love with slow, almost unbearable tenderness, and she had to hope the shower spray hid her tears.

At last they were on their way. Seth drove his pickup through the snow with his usual competence even under the snowy conditions and she was grateful for his presence.

She spent most of the drive making lists and trying to figure out what they still needed to accomplish to pull off the party.

An hour or so from Pine Gulch, Marcy called again. "Is

this an okay time for you to talk on your cell? The roads aren't too slick?" she asked.

"It's fine," Jenny assured her. "I'm not driving."

In the pause that followed, she could almost hear the wheels in Marcy's head turn as she tried to figure out who Jenny might have gone to Jackson with, but to her relief, her assistant said nothing. She was grateful, since she didn't want to have to lie.

"Okay, things aren't quite the disaster I feared," Marcy said. "The desserts and the appetizers are done and so is the salad. Allen only had about half of the au gratin potatoes ready. Knowing how fast those go around here, I was thinking of having some baked potatoes set out when they're gone."

"Great idea."

"Even I can handle baked potatoes. My mom has two ovens in her kitchen and I can set them on a timer to be finished just as the party's starting. And I can cook the ham at my place, too. He's got those all ready to go."

"Wonderful. It sounds like you've got everything under control."

"Not everything. Here's the sticky part. Remember we were offering ham and Allen's famous coq au vin? He has all the stuff for the chicken but I've got no idea how to throw it together."

Jenny's mind raced. Her skills in the kitchen were not the greatest, though she figured she could follow a recipe if they had one. Coq au vin sounded more than a little challenging. Just the name was enough to make her break out in hives. "Is there something else we could substitute?"

"Any ideas?"

She thought through her poultry repertoire, which was pretty limited to roast chicken and a moderately good recipe for grilled lemon-herb chicken breasts.

"See if you can find a recipe somewhere in Allen's kitchen. I'll be there as soon as I can. Between the two of us, we can probably figure something out. Thanks so much for everything you've done so far. It's a lot of work and I owe you big-time."

"I won't let you down, I promise."

"Just make sure you leave enough time so you can get ready and put on all your sparkly stuff for Lance."

"Are you kidding? I'm not going to all this work to impress him, just to show up in an apron and a pair of jeans!"

Jenny laughed and hung up.

"If we pull this off, it's going to be a miracle," she said after she'd folded her cell phone.

"Anything I can do?" Seth asked. "I'm not a whiz in the kitchen, but I can take orders."

The Pine Gulch gossip mill would just about start spinning off its axis if she showed up at Marcy's house with Seth Dalton in tow as a sous chef.

She mustered a smile. "I think we'll be okay. But thanks."

A muscle tightened in his jaw, but he said nothing for several more miles. Finally when they were nearing the outskirts of town—near where Cole had crashed the GTO—he spoke in a deceptively casual voice.

"Why aren't you taking a date tonight?"

The unexpected question had her pen scratching across the list she had been making.

"How do you know I'm not?"

It was a stupid thing to say, but her only excuse was that he'd flustered her. Something dark and formidable leaped into his gaze and she swallowed, struck once more by how easy it was to forget his easygoing nature covered a hard, dangerous man.

"Are you?"

"No," she admitted. "I didn't…it didn't seem appropriate."

"Why not?"

"I don't know. I guess because I'm the principal." And because the only man she wanted to take was the last one she ever could.

He was silent for another block or so, then he cast her a long look across the cab of his truck. "Even if you *had* decided to ask a date, you would never in a million years have taken me, would you?"

She did *not* want to have this conversation right now, so close to home and all the things she had to deal with there.

"Seth…" she began, but had no idea where to go after that, so her voice trailed off.

In that single word, Seth heard the hesitation in her voice and knew his suspicion was true. Despite everything, despite these last few wonderful weeks and the incredible night they had just shared, she still was ashamed to be seen with him.

Hurt and anger poured through him in equal measures and his hands tightened on the steering wheel. He wanted to lash out at her, to attack and wound until she bled as he did.

Just then the truck slid on some slush and he had to concentrate to keep control in the slick driving conditions. By the time he did, the hurt had just about overwhelmed the anger.

"I get the picture now," he said quietly. "A guy like me is fine for a little romp in the sack but when it comes to anything deeper, you're not interested."

"That is not true."

"Isn't it?"

"You know things are complicated for me right now."

"Your precious reputation. Right."

She bristled at the scorn in his voice. "I have nothing

else *but* my reputation right now, as far as my faculty is concerned. It would be different if I'd been here a year or two and had some kind of track record with them—if they knew me and my capabilities. But right now I'm a wild card and my every move is endlessly dissected and analyzed in the faculty lounge."

"And of course we wouldn't want anybody to suspect you might have a pulse."

"It's more than that! I can't afford for my judgment to be questioned on anything."

"Being seen with me would certainly show lousy judgment on your part. I get it."

It was only a party. Why was he making such a big deal about it? Intellectually, he knew his reaction was out of proportion to the situation. But he couldn't seem to hold back the tide of hurt washing over him.

The whole thing had an oddly familiar feel to it. He tried to figure out why and was almost to her father's house when it hit him like a snowplow coming through the windshield.

It felt familiar because he'd been down this road before. Many times before. He had spent the first twelve years of his life trying to win the approval and acceptance of someone determined to reject him at every turn.

Hank Dalton had been a bastard who'd treated all three of his sons with varying degrees of cruelty.

He had tried—and failed—to mold Wade into a carbon copy of himself. He had disregarded all of Jake's dreams of being a doctor and completely dismissed his middle son's intellect and quest for knowledge. As for Seth, he might as well not have existed for all the notice Hank paid his sickly youngest son.

He remembered how he used to follow his father around, copying his every move—from his cocksure walk to the way he wore his hat to that hard-ass, screw-you stare his father had perfected.

All for nothing. His father hadn't noticed a damn thing except the asthma Seth had no control over.

His jaw tightened. He wasn't that weak, puny kid eager for any scrap a bastard like Hank Dalton might toss at him anymore. Long before the year he turned twelve, when Hank had died, he'd given up on his father ever seeing him as anything other than a worthless runt, always out of breath and clinging to his mother.

He'd come a long way since those days, so far he thought he had put all that behind him. So why did Jennifer Boyer's blunt rejection seem so painfully familiar?

He thought of the night they'd just shared, the heartbreaking intimacy of it and the connection he had never experienced with anyone else. He replayed again the pure, incomparable sweetness of holding her in his arms while she slept and he was astonished and terrified by the raw emotion welling up in his throat.

He swallowed it down, forcing it back by concentrating on the road.

"I see," he said when he trusted his voice again.

She sent him a searching look and he gave a casual shrug, determined not to let her see how she had eviscerated him. "No big deal. I've got plenty of things I could do tonight."

He must not have been completely successful at hiding his hurt because her eyes darkened.

"I'm sorry, Seth. But please try to see this from my perspective."

"Oh, I do," he assured her. "Nothing possibly could be worse than letting the faculty and staff at Pine Gulch Elementary see their new respectable principal hanging out with the town's biggest hellion. What a nightmare that would be for you."

"You don't need to use sarcasm."

"Yeah, I do." The tenuous rope he had on his emotions frayed abruptly. "Dammit, Jen. How can you even care what other people think, after what we've just shared?"

"What did we share? I slept with you, but that certainly doesn't make me unique among the female population of Pine Gulch."

Ah. Direct hit. He almost swayed from the force of it, but drew in a breath to steel himself against the pain. "It was more than that and you know it."

Her hands clenched in her lap and she was trembling as though she was standing out in the snow with bare feet.

"It was a mistake," she said quietly. "A lapse of judgment on my part brought on by the storm and the enforced intimacy of the situation. One that won't happen again. I can't see you anymore, Seth."

He should have expected it, but somehow he hadn't been prepared for the panic burning through him, raw and terrifying. He wanted to rage and yell and beg her not to cut him off from something that suddenly seemed as vital to him as breathing.

There was nothing he could say, though, nothing he could do to fix this and he could only be grateful they had reached her father's house.

He pulled into the driveway and sat there, his hands on the steering wheel.

"That's probably for the best," he finally said, though everything in him howled in protest at the outright lie. "I won't be your guilty secret, Jen. Some kind of stud you turn to when you're bored or lonely. I care about you. Hell, I think I might even be in love with you."

Her gaze flashed to his and he saw shock and disbelief there but he plowed forward.

"I don't know. This is all new to me." His laugh was rough and scored his throat as though he'd swallowed a dozen razor blades. "Can you believe that? The hellion of Pine Gulch has never been in love before."

He didn't give her a chance to respond. "But if that's what this is, I don't want it. At least not with you. I can't love a woman without the guts to take a chance on something that could be wonderful."

"Or miserable," she whispered.

"Or miserable," he agreed. "But we'll never know, will we? Because you've decided I'm not good enough for you."

"That is not true!"

"Isn't it?" He felt a hundred years old, suddenly. Old and tired and terribly, terribly sad.

On bones that seemed to creak and groan, he climbed out and walked around to her side of the truck, opening the door pointedly. "Goodbye, Jen. You've got a whole list of things to do before your big party so I'm sure you'll forgive me if I don't come in."

She didn't move for a long moment, the only color in her face the shiner Cherry had delivered. Finally she slid down, hesitated for just an instant—just long enough for him to pray she would fall into his arms, that she would kiss him and make all of this go away.

But she didn't. She didn't even look at him again. She just seemed to square her shoulders, then she walked away.

He waited just long enough for her to open the front door, then he climbed back into his truck and backed out of the driveway—heading toward the misery he knew was the rest of his life.

Chapter 15

It was tough to get a good drunk on at one in the afternoon. Oh, he tried, but all he had in the house was beer and he didn't feel like driving back into town for something harder.

After two Sam Adams, he decided it was pretty pathetic to sit there in his cold house with only Lucy for company, wasting perfectly good beer when he wasn't at all in the mood.

Driven by emotions he didn't know how to deal with, he finally decided to channel all this restless energy into trying to catch up on the work he'd neglected in order to take Jenny shopping. He grabbed his coat and hat, whistled for Lucy and headed out through the cold to the indoor arena.

It didn't help much, he decided an hour later atop a big, rawboned bay mare he was training for a client. A little but not much.

His chest still ached and he couldn't quite keep the knot out of his throat, but at least he wasn't sitting around feeling sorry for himself.

He was roping one of the iron calf heads they used for training when Lucy suddenly barked a happy greeting. The loop landed yards shy of the mark as he turned quickly in the saddle to see who had come in.

The hope in his chest died a quick and painful death when he saw his oldest brother leaning against the top rail of the arena gate.

He gave a mental groan. This was just what he needed. His brother tended to see far too much and was never shy about doling out advice, wanted or not.

As tempted as he was to ignore Wade and just keep on roping, he knew he would only be delaying the inevitable. He took his time coiling the rope, then nudged the horse toward the fence.

"She's looking good," Wade said when he neared.

He dismounted. "Yeah. I imagine Jimmy Harding will be pleased with her when I'm done."

"For what he's paying you to train her, she ought to be able to stand on her back legs and salute the flag as it goes by."

He bristled. Here was the fight he was itching for. How considerate of Wade to hand deliver it. Though the fence was between them, that didn't stop him from climbing in his brother's face. "Are you implying Harding's not going to get his money's worth?"

Wade sniffed, then raised an eyebrow at the half-empty beer bottle Seth had brought along and left on the railing a few yards away. "Not at all. I just wondered if your usual training method involves working with a horse when you're half plastered."

"I had exactly two and a half beers! What are you, working for the state alcohol commission?"

"Nope. Just a concerned brother."

"Who should learn to mind his own damn business," Seth snarled, yanking the saddle off the horse.

Wade just watched him for a long moment while Seth led the horse back to her stall.

"You want to talk about it?"

"What?" He grabbed a brush and started grooming the horse.

"Whatever has your boxers in a twist."

"Nothing."

"You sure?"

"Fairly, yeah," he drawled. "Contrary to popular belief, I think I know my own mind."

"I never said you didn't. But do you know your own strength? Because if you tug that brush much harder, Jimmy Harding is going to look mighty peculiar riding his bald horse."

He froze when he realized what he was doing. He let out a breath and eased up a little then pulled off the bridle and gave the horse one last pat before he let himself out of her stall to face his brother.

"You want me to talk about what's bothering me? Sure. I'll talk about it. How's this? I've got this brother with a beautiful wife and three great kids, one more on the way. His life is frigging perfect, which makes him annoying as hell to be around, especially since he thinks he knows every damn thing in the universe."

Wade seemed in a particularly jovial mood because even that direct attack didn't seem to get his goat, to Seth's frustration. He only gave a cheerful smile that made Seth want to take out a few teeth. "If I knew everything, I wouldn't need to ask what has you drinking two and a half beers in the middle of the afternoon, would I?"

Seth released a slow breath. None of this was Wade's

fault. Venting his hurt and rage at Jenny on his relatively innocent brother was unfair and slightly juvenile.

He was bigger than this. A few years ago he probably couldn't have said the same thing, but he'd come a long way in those few years, thanks in great measure to Wade's astonishing confidence in him.

If not for his brother's encouragement and support, Seth might never have found the courage to follow his dreams and build this horse arena, diverting Cold Creek resources in an effort to diversify and build up the equine operations of the ranch.

His brother had placed a great deal of faith in him the last two years. He deserved better than to be sacrificed to the sharp edge of Seth's temper.

"Don't worry about it," he managed after a minute. "I'm sure I'll be fine in a day or two."

He paused, feeling awkward as a brand-new boot. "Sorry to take my bad mood out on you."

Wade studied him and he had to wonder how much of his turmoil showed up on his features, especially at his brother's next words.

"Does your lousy mood have anything to do with the lovely new elementary school principal you took to Jackson yesterday?"

He could feel a muscle work in his jaw and he fought the urge to pound his fist into that support. With his luck, he would probably not only break his fist but send the whole barn tumbling down around his ears.

"You could say that."

"The great Seth Dalton having woman trouble? This has to be one for the record books."

"Yeah, yeah. Hilarious, isn't it?"

Something in his tone had Wade giving him an even

longer look. Whatever his brother saw had him straightening. "Whoa. I was joking about the woman trouble, but this is serious, isn't it? Trouble with a capital L-O-V-E."

Seth made a scornful, snorting kind of noise that didn't convince Wade for a second.

"Carrie said this one was different," his brother said, shaking his head. "She predicted after that day we went up the mountain for Christmas trees that you were going to fall hard, but I couldn't see it. I should have listened to her. That means I owe her dinner at the Spring Creek Ranch. Man, you know how much that place costs?"

He stared at his brother, appalled. "You and your wife bet on my love life?"

Wade grinned, looking worlds different from the surly widower he'd been until Caroline Montgomery blew into their lives. "Yeah, I should know better, shouldn't I? Carrie knows a mark when she sees one. I guess that's what comes from growing up with a con artist for a father."

Quinn Montgomery, Caroline's father and their mother's second husband, had enjoyed a fairly profitable career on the grift until the law had caught up with him a few years before he'd met Marjorie.

Despite his somewhat shady past, all the Dalton sons had come to have a deep affection for the man. How could they help it when he plainly adored their mother and had given her the joyous life she'd been deprived of in her first marriage?

"So what's going on with Jennifer Boyer?" Wade asked. "I'm assuming the shopping trip to Jackson and your unexpected stay didn't go well."

The understatement of the whole damn year.

"Why should I tell you? Remind me again when we became best girlfriends, here?"

"If you can't get advice from your brother with the frigging perfect life, where else can you turn?"

He had a point. Though his brother was only six years older than he was, Wade had been more of a father figure through most of his life than Hank had ever been. The Dalton patriarch had died of a heart attack on Wade's eighteenth birthday and from then on, Wade had stepped up to show Seth by example how a decent man should live his life.

He hadn't always followed his brother's lead but he had always respected him and at least listened to his advice. It couldn't hurt, he decided.

"All right. You want to know what's wrong? I'll tell you. You'll appreciate this, I'm sure. You know how you've spent the last twenty years telling me my wild, reckless ways were going to catch up to me some day? Guess what? Big surprise, you were right."

"Yeah?"

"Did you know my reputation is somewhat tarnished in Pine Gulch?"

"Don't know if I'd say tarnished. Maybe dented a little in spots."

"Well, Jenny Boyer is looking for a saint, apparently. And too bad for me, I lost my halo sometime around my sixteenth birthday."

He waited for some wisecrack from his brother, some "I-told-you-so" kind of gloat but Wade just looked at him, and the sudden compassion in his eyes turned the lump in his throat into a damn boulder. He worked to swallow it, fighting back the horrifying emotion burning his own eyes.

"I'm sorry, man."

"Yeah. It sucks."

"She's wrong about you," Wade said after a moment,

looking about as uncomfortable as Seth was with this conversation. "You might not be a saint but beneath all those dents, you're a good man."

"Uh, thanks. I think."

"You are. You're a hard worker, you're about the most honest man I know, you always dance with all the wallflowers at any party, and you're the first one I'd pick to back me up in a fight. I'm proud of you, Seth. I haven't said that nearly enough over the years, but I am."

He placed a hand on Seth's shoulder for just a moment then let it drop, to Seth's vast relief. Much more of this and he'd be bawling like a just-weaned calf.

"Come on down to the house for dinner, why don't you? Caroline's fixed a roast and some of those twice-baked potatoes you like so much. I think Nat might have even made a cake."

He mustered a smile, wondering if he'd always be the bachelor uncle his brothers would have to leave a place for at the table. "Thanks anyway, but I've got some things to do here. I'm not very good company anyway."

"You know the kitchen's always open if you change your mind."

"Right. Thanks."

Wade left and Seth leaned against the stall railing for a long time watching Jimmy Harding's mare munch her feed and wondering how long it took to heal a broken heart.

"Everything is perfect. I can't believe we pulled it off!"

Hundreds of twinkling lights reflected off the tiny sparkles of glitter in Marcy's upswept hair but they didn't hold a candle to the brilliant glow in her eyes.

From somewhere deep inside, Jenny forced a smile for

her giddy assistant. "You did all the work and you deserve every bit of the credit."

"Ha. I was a wreck. You're the one who came through with the coq au vin. Everyone's been raving about it and they can't believe you fixed it all by yourself! I don't know how you did it."

Jenny had to admit, she had no idea. She had been so numb after her fight with Seth that she could barely remember anything after he dropped her off and drove away.

I care about you. Hell, I think I might even be in love with you.

As they'd been doing for hours, his words seemed to ricochet through her mind, bouncing off every available surface.

It couldn't be true. He was only saying that because he was like a thwarted child, willing to say anything to get his way.

No. That was unfair and didn't mesh at all with the man she'd come to know these last weeks. He had never lied to her and she couldn't imagine he would start with such a whopper.

Did that mean he had been sincere?

Despite the room full of people she knew she should be working hard to impress with her warmth and wit, she couldn't seem to think about anything else but those stunning words.

"Is everything okay?" Marcy asked, jerking Jenny back to their conversation.

"Sorry. Everything is great. Look what a wonderful time everyone is having and it's all because of you."

It *was* a great party, one she was sure everyone would remember for years. The food had been delicious, the company entertaining and everyone but her seemed to be in a holiday mood.

"I mean it, Marcy, you saved my bacon on this one."

Her assistant looked pleased with the compliment but she continued to look at Jenny with concern.

"Too bad you're not enjoying it," she said.

Jenny started. Was she that transparent? "Of course I am!" she lied. "Why would you say that?"

"You've only been looking at the clock every five minutes and you haven't left the kitchen for long all night. Keep it up and your faculty is going to think you don't want to spend time with them."

"That's not it at all," she exclaimed, horrified she might have given that impression. "I just… It's been a rough day, that's all."

Marcy arched an eyebrow. "Does your rough day have anything to do with the shiner you got from one of Seth Dalton's ex-girlfriends?"

The platter of finger food she'd been replenishing at the buffet table nearly slipped out of her hands and she looked around frantically to be sure no one else overheard.

"You know?" she hissed

Marcy gave her a rueful look. "My cousin Darlene works at the Aspen during the ski season. She makes major cash in tips, let me tell you. One time Harrison Ford came in and left her fifty bucks! She said he's even better-looking in person than on-screen. Anyway, she said she saw you and Seth Dalton having dinner. She knew Seth, of course— who, by the way, she says is better-looking than even Harrison Ford. And she recognized you because she dropped her little brother off one day at school. He's in Mr. Nichols's fifth-grade class."

Marcy snagged a chicken roll from the plate and popped

it into her mouth before going on. "So, Amy says you were enjoying your meal when suddenly another waitress's roommate comes over and starts making this big scene about how Seth dumped her. Amy was in the kitchen and didn't see the whole thing but she said this girl tried to slug Seth but hit you instead."

Jenny couldn't seem to breathe and knew her cheeks must be ablaze with horrified color. "Does everyone know?"

Marcy shrugged. "I doubt it. Everyone's been asking me if I knew what happened to your eye and I just told them the same story you told, you know, about slipping on an icy step. I figure it's none of their business."

Before Jenny could thank her for that, at least, one of the third-grade teachers approached them.

Susan Smoot was a widow who had taught at the school for thirty years. Rumor had it the other woman had had her eye on the principal's office for a long time and Jenny knew she had been one of her most vocal critics when the school board opted to go outside the district to hire her.

She was a formidable enemy—though Jenny had a feeling she could be a powerful ally, as well.

"Thank you for the party, Ms. Boyer. Everything was delicious."

Though she was still rocked by Marcy's revelation, Jenny managed to put it away for now and smile. This was the warmest snippet of conversation she'd ever received from the woman and she didn't want to ruin it.

"Thank you, Susan. Please, I've been here for three months now. When do you think you might consider calling me Jennifer?"

The teacher's mouth twitched but Jenny couldn't really tell if it was a smile. "If you do this again next year, you might want to have it someplace where those of us who don't like the loud garbage that passes for music these days can find a place to hear ourselves think."

"Great idea," she said.

Susan's gaze fixed on the black eye that stood out no matter how she tried to camouflage it with makeup. "And you know, the best thing for icy steps is to sprinkle a little kitty litter on it, Jennifer. Works better than salt and won't kill your flowerbeds in the spring."

"I'll keep that in mind. Thank you."

As soon as the other woman left, Jenny turned quickly back to Marcy and dragged her into the kitchen for a little privacy. "Who else do you think knows I was in Jackson with Seth Dalton?" she asked.

Marcy looked taken aback by the frantic note in her voice. "I don't know. Why does it matter?"

"How can you ask that? Of course it matters! Do you think Susan Smoot would find it an amusing little anecdote that I was decked by one of Seth's jealous ex-lovers? Or even that I was in Jackson having dinner with him in the first place?"

Marcy made a scornful noise. "Let me tell you about Sue Smoot. Most of the time her husband, Carl, was a fine, upstanding citizen. President of the Lions Club, first tenor in the church choir, the whole thing. But every once in a while he'd go on a holy tear and get completely loaded. Before he retired, my dad was the police chief and he used to come home with all kinds of stories about that crazy Carl Smoot. One time he took a shotgun and sprayed every single stop sign in town. Every one! Sue stuck by him through it all. I figure she can't throw any stones at you just for having dinner in Jackson with Seth Dalton on the same night some woman decides to go mental."

"I shouldn't have been there with him. It was a mistake."

"Are you kidding? Any woman who finds herself on the receiving end of that man's undivided attention ought to get down on her knees and consider herself blessed."

She stared at her assistant. "He's a player! Everybody says so. He dates a different woman every day."

"Not true. Maybe he used to a few years ago but ever since the Cold Creek started their horse operation, he's been a different man. He still likes a good party, but he's settled down a lot now that he has some focus."

"I heard you talking to Ashley Barnes that day in the office when she was upset he didn't call her back. You told her about the Seth Dalton School of Broncbusting. You said he was a dog!"

"No, *Ashley* said he was a dog. If you remember, I said he was a good guy, just a little on the rowdy side. He is. His blood might run a bit hot, but that's not such a bad thing, if you ask me, as long as he finds the right woman to help him channel it."

"I'm not that woman!"

Marcy smiled, the sparkles in her hair reflecting the recessed lights in the kitchen. "I don't know. Darlene said he looked whipped in the restaurant before the big scene with the other girl. She said the two of you were holding hands and everything."

I care about you. Hell, I think I might even be in love with you.

She shivered but before she could say anything, Lance Tyler poked his head inside the kitchen. "Marcy, why are you hiding out in here? Are you going to make me dance with Mrs. Christopher all night?"

"Sorry. I'm coming."

She gave Jenny a quick hug and took one last parting shot.

"You know," she whispered in her ear so the P.E. teacher couldn't hear, "somewhere out there is a rider who can tame even the wildest bronc. You'll never know if you don't climb on."

After she left, Jenny leaned against the counter, her mind whirling.

I can't love a woman without the guts to take a chance on something that could be wonderful.

His words echoed in her ears, louder than the music from the other room, louder than the dishwasher busily churning away beside her.

The ache in her chest seemed unbearable and she pressed a hand to it, then felt something crack away under her fingers, something hard and brittle.

She was a fool. A scared, stupid fool.

She loved him. With all her heart she loved him, and she was throwing away any chance they might have together because she was too afraid to trust him—and more afraid to trust herself and her own instincts.

She was so worried about what other people thought that she refused to pay attention to those instincts. She didn't deserve the respect she was so desperate to earn from her faculty, not if she couldn't make up her own mind about what was good and right and couldn't stand up for those decisions, even if she faced criticism for them.

Seth was a good man. A kind, decent, *wonderful* man, who had done nothing but open his life and his heart to her and her family.

Sweet assurance flowed through her and she remembered the tenderness in his eyes the night before, how safe and warm and cherished he made her feel.

She straightened from the counter. She had to find him, right this moment, to see if she had completely ruined everything or if there might be any chance they could salvage something from the wreckage she had left behind with her stupidity.

She rushed out of the kitchen and blinked, a little disoriented to find the lights and the music and the people. The party was still going strong—her party, the one she had thought so vitally important.

How could she leave in the middle of it?

No, she was going to trust her instincts on this one. She had to find Seth now, tonight, before she lost her nerve.

Marcy and Lance danced by at that moment and she stepped forward and grabbed her before she could whirl away again.

"Marcy, I have to go. I… I'm sorry. I'll explain later."

Her friend gave her a careful look, then grinned with delight. "I don't think you need to explain."

She smiled back, the first genuine one she'd felt since she walked away from Seth.

"You were right. I want my eight seconds. No. More than that. I want forever."

Chapter 16

Seth stood just inside the doorway to the Bandito, wondering what the hell he was doing there.

For some crazy reason, he thought his favorite haunt would be just the thing to lift him out of his misery. Usually he loved walking inside the honky tonk—the clink of pool cues setting shots, the music, loud and raucous, the smell of barley and hops and people having a good time. Most of all, he loved the chorus of greetings he received every time he walked in.

This had always been his place, the one spot where he wasn't just Wade and Jake Dalton's wild and reckless kid brother.

But now as he looked at the string of blinking Christmas lights strung across the mirror behind the bar, the cheap foil garlands hanging from the tables and the same faces he'd been seeing here since he was old enough to drink, all he felt was the bitter sting of his own loneliness.

This wasn't what he wanted.

What do you want? he asked himself, but he knew the answer before the question even entered his mind.

Jenny.

He wanted Jenny Boyer, in his arms, in his heart, in his life.

He pushed that dead horse off him and was just about to walk back out into the cold when a buxom blonde wearing a skimpy Mrs. Santa Claus outfit approached him.

"Hey, Seth!" Twice divorced, Dawna McHenry was ten years his senior—and she'd been hitting on him since he turned sixteen. "Haven't seen you around in a while."

"Hey Dawna. It's been a busy few weeks."

"Well, you're here now. That's the important thing. What do you say to a dance?"

One of Alan Jackson's rollicking holiday songs was playing on the jukebox, but Seth couldn't manage to summon even the tiniest spark of enthusiasm to rip up the wooden dance floor right now.

"Sweetheart, you know how much I hate to disappoint a lady. It's nothing personal, I swear, but I'm not much in the mood for dancing tonight. Can I take a rain check, though?"

"You know my umbrella's always open for you, darlin'," she purred, but her smile had slipped a little.

Maybe his own miserable mood opened his eyes a little, but for the first time he saw through her bright cheer to the emptiness beneath. She was just looking for somebody to take away the pain for a while and he was sorry it could never be him.

He wanted to make it better for her, but he didn't know how until his gaze landed on the middle-aged man sitting at the bar. Roy Gentry was another of the Bandito regulars. A shy cowboy with a small plot of land and his own herd, he never said much to anybody—and became even more tongue-tied when Dawna was near.

"You know who I bet could use a little of that cheering up you're so good at? Roy over there."

Dawna cast a look at the bar. "You think?"

"Oh, yeah," Seth answered. "I bet he gets real lonely all by himself in that big house his folks left him, especially this time of year. Why don't you go see if he wants to dance?"

Dawna looked again and he hoped this time she saw beyond Roy's shy awkwardness to the man who never had a mean word to say about anybody and who always put a little extra in the bartender's tip jar.

She gave the cowboy another considering look. "I wouldn't want anybody feelin' bad this time of year. You know, I might just do that."

She flitted away from him and headed toward the bar. Seth lingered long enough to watch her lean in and say something with one of her bright smiles. He couldn't hear over the music but he saw Roy give a quick, forceful shake of his head, then Dawna tugged him off his bar stool anyway and dragged him over to the dance floor.

He wanted to think it was divine providence—or at least a gift from the King—but right at that moment, Elvis starting singing "Blue Christmas" on the jukebox. Dawna threw her arms around the cowboy for a slow dance, and poor Roy looked like he didn't know what hit him.

If he'd had a beer right then, he would have lifted it in a salute to the man. *I'm right there with you, brother,* he thought, hoping he and Elvis might have just planted the seeds of something.

Good deed accomplished, he turned to go when he heard a woman's voice calling his name in a question.

For about half a second, he thought about pretending

he didn't hear whoever she was and just continuing on his way. But she called his name again and he turned slowly with a sigh.

The ready excuse on his lips slipped away when he saw the tall brunette in slacks and a holiday sweater beaming at him.

"It is you! Hi, Seth. Remember me?"

"My word. Of course I do. Little Amy Roundy." He hugged her, stunned that this pretty, self-assured woman was the same girl he'd known since kindergarten.

"It's Amy Underwood now."

"That's right. Where is the lucky man?"

She made a face. "Pool table. I imagine my brothers are trying to hustle him out of our traveler's checks by now. They have no idea what they're up against. George plays the part of a mild-mannered, polite, slightly clumsy Brit but he'll rip them apart."

He smiled and knew he couldn't leave now, much as he might want to. Amy had been one of his best friends in elementary school and he hadn't seen her in years.

By tacit agreement he steered them both to the only empty booth, where he took the seat across from her. "I hadn't heard you'd crossed to this side of the pond and finally come back for a visit," he said when they were seated. "How's life in the British Isles?"

"Just ducky, love." She smiled and dropped the accent. "Seriously, I love it. I miss my family and the mountains sometimes, but George and I have made a home there."

"What about kids?"

"Three girls. I've got pictures and everything."

She pulled out her cell phone, punched a few buttons, then held it out to him. He spent a minute admiring the image on the screen of three gorgeous little girls with blond curls and their mother's smile.

"What about you? Is there a Mrs. Dalton?"

He summoned a smile from somewhere deep inside. "Two of them. Both married to my brothers."

"You haven't made the big leap?"

He started to make some flippant remark but Amy's stern look caught it before it could escape. He suddenly remembered he could never hide anything from her. She and Maggie Cruz, Jake's wife, had been his best friends in grade school. They were the only kids in his class who hadn't bullied the wheezy runt he'd been.

Hank had just about popped a vein when he found out his youngest son's two best friends were girls but that had only made Seth more determined to keep them.

"No. Not yet," he managed.

Marriage. Now there was something he hadn't given much thought to. His parents' marriage had been a nightmare, enough to sour anybody on the institution. But his brothers had managed to move on and build amazingly happy lives.

For the first time, he started to wonder if he could ever do the same. He thought again of how he'd felt waking up with Jenny in his arms that morning and he suddenly wanted that every day, with a fierce and terrible ache.

Only too bad for him, the woman in question wanted nothing to do with him anymore.

He shifted his attention back to Amy, wondering what she saw in his face to put that soft, sympathetic look in her eyes.

She touched his hand. "You would make a wonderful husband, Seth."

He forced a laugh at that outright hyperbole. "Right.

I'm willing to bet if you took a poll of all the women in this room, you would probably be the only one with that opinion."

She looked at him for a long moment then shook her head. "It doesn't matter what they think. If you find the right woman, her opinion is the only important one."

Didn't he just know it?

He must have made some sound because Amy sent him another sympathetic look. "Want to talk about it?"

No. He wanted to hop in the GTO and drive as far and as fast as he could to outrun this pain, this hollow fear that he would be spending the rest of his life alone.

No, he didn't want to talk about it. But something about his old friend's compassion made him want to confide in her.

"How long do you think it will take your Brit to clean up over there at the pool table?"

Jenny drove through the streets of Pine Gulch, a strange mix of anticipation and anxiety churning through her. Would he even be willing to see her when she reached the Cold Creek after the hideous way she had treated him?

She had to try. Even if he slammed the door in her face, at least she would not have to live the rest of her life with regrets, knowing she might have touched the stars.

On the outskirts of town, she drove past the bright lights of the town's single tavern. The Bandito was doing a brisk business tonight, she thought, then took a closer look and nearly drove off the road.

She knew that red car in the parking lot. Seth's brawny GTO hulked in the corner, shiny and sleek and so distinctive she couldn't possibly mistake it for anyone else's car.

So much for sitting at home pining over her.

He was inside the tavern probably having a wonderful time while she was out here dying inside.

She pulled her SUV into an empty space in the parking lot, trying to figure out what she should do. She had two choices. She could go back to the faculty party and get on with the business of forgetting about him, as he had obviously decided to do about her.

Or she could grab hold of the rigging and climb on.

She owed him an apology. By putting so much stock in gossip and rumor about him, she had treated him with terrible unfairness and she had to let him know she was sorry for it.

Even if he decided not to accept her apology, she would at least know she'd tried to offer it.

She turned off her vehicle and slid out, suddenly aware as she stepped onto packed snow of her holiday cocktail dress and high heels. She was going to look conspicuous, foolish, walking into the honky tonk like this.

People would wonder what she was doing there—and when the people in the packed tavern saw her with Seth, rumors would start flying before she would even have time to sit down.

She almost climbed back into her car, then she shook her head. No. She was strong enough to face a few rumors. She wasn't ashamed of her feelings for Seth. She loved him and she wouldn't hide it. Let the whole town see, she thought.

That defiant energy carried her to the front door of the Bandito and just inside, but there she stopped as the panic and self-doubt started to nip at her like an unruly puppy.

She scanned the crowd, already painfully aware of the stares. She didn't see him at first, then when she found him, that little yip of self-doubt turned into a pack of ravaging wolves.

He was sitting in a booth, cozying up to a brunette Jenny didn't recognize, someone tall and shapely and beautiful. Their heads were close together and the woman was laughing at something he said and Jenny felt like her heart had just been ripped out and thrown on the dance floor for everyone to stomp on.

This was stupid. Humiliating tears welled up in her eyes at her own idiocy and she wanted frantically to get out of there, but she felt frozen in place by this wild storm of emotions.

She was just trying to force herself to move when his gaze suddenly shifted from the woman beside him to the doorway where Jenny stood, exposed and heartsick.

Whatever he was saying to the other woman died as he stared at her.

Everything else in the bar—the laughter, the bright lights, the loud, pulsing music—faded away to nothing as their gazes caught and held.

Jenny couldn't breathe suddenly, stunned by the raw emotion in his eyes, pain and joy and something else she couldn't identify.

Her husband had never looked at her like that, she realized. Not once, in all their years of courtship and marriage, had he ever looked at her like she was his salvation, his entire world.

How could she turn away from this? She loved this man. She loved his strength, she loved his goodness, she loved the sweet and healing laughter he had brought into her life.

And she suddenly wanted everyone to know it.

Her pulse sounded louder than the music blaring from the jukebox as she forced herself to move forward on legs suddenly weak and jittery, until she stood at the edge of their booth.

Once she reached her destination, she didn't know where to start. She might have lost her nerve completely except that Seth hadn't looked away from her, even for a second.

They stared at each other for a long moment, until the brunette actually broke the silence.

"Hi. You must be Jennifer."

That had her blinking and she managed to wrench her gaze from Seth to look at the woman, who actually seemed very nice, with warm brown eyes and an approachable smile. Too bad Jenny might just have to take a page from Cherry Mendenhall's book and deck her.

"Seth has just been telling me all about you," the woman went on.

She thought she heard Seth make a groaning kind of sound but she couldn't be sure.

"Has he?" It was all she could manage to say.

The other woman gave a smile Jenny would only have called mischievous if had come from one of her students. "Oh, yes. I'm Amy Underwood, an old friend. Sit down, won't you? Here, you can have my seat. I was just leaving to find my husband."

Husband. Right. Husband was good.

"He's sexy and British and I'm crazy about him," the strange woman added with a laugh. "Just in case you were wondering."

"Amy," Seth said in the chiding voice one reserved for old friends.

She laughed again, getting to her feet. "What did I say?" She didn't wait for an answer, just blew him a kiss. "We're in town until after the day after New Year's. Come and meet George and my girls. I want to know how the story ends."

"Yeah," he muttered. "So do I."

She walked away but Jenny remained standing by the booth, unsure where to go from here.

"What are you doing here, Jen?" he said after a long moment. A note of cool reserve had entered his voice and she winced from it even as she knew she deserved it.

"I was wondering if you would like to dance."

He gazed at her and she saw a host of emotions sift through his eyes. "Here?" he finally asked, looking around the crowded tavern.

"Here. Or at the faculty party. Or wherever you would like."

He gazed at her, stunned by her words, by the offer he knew must have cost her dearly.

Already, he was aware of the curious stares in their direction. Tongues were certainly going to wag with tales of the elementary school principal showing up at the local tavern in party clothes and a black eye and immediately sidling up to his table.

She must have known the gossip would start up before she even walked into the place, yet she had come anyway. She had faced her fears, had all but begged for the very scrutiny she claimed to be so eager to avoid.

For him.

He had never been so humbled.

Joy and sweet relief exploded in him, washing away the hurt and bitterness and angry. She was here, coming to him despite her fears and her uncertainties. He had no choice but to take the precious gift she offered and hold it close to his heart.

He reached for her hand and almost yanked her into his arms right there in the Bandito in front of half the town but he knew that would be pushing things. Instead he uncoiled from the booth, threw some money on the table for his drink, and headed for the door, tugging her along behind him.

"Where are we going?" she asked a little breathlessly.

In answer, he pulled her out of the tavern. The cold December air blew through his jacket and he realized he hadn't given this a whole lot of thought, driven only by the need to be alone with her.

He had to kiss her in the next twenty seconds but he wasn't going to make her stand out in the cold for it, not in her skimpy cocktail dress. Thinking fast, he bundled her into the GTO, then slid into the driver's seat and started the engine.

The heater churned out blessed heat and at last he pulled her into his arms and kissed her as he'd been dreaming of doing since the moment they left the inn in Jackson.

She returned his kiss with a warmth and enthusiasm that took his breath away and they embraced there like a couple of hot-blooded high-school kids at an overlook. Much more of this, and they would be steaming up those windows, he thought.

"I've never made out in a muscle car before," she said after a long, heated moment. "It's kind of sexy."

"That's the whole idea," he managed, then lost his train of thought when she trailed kisses down his jawline to the curve of his neck, then back up.

"Can I just say, for your first time, honey, you're doing *great*," he drawled.

He felt her laughter against his skin and wanted to taste all of it. He dipped his mouth and caught hers again. Despite their playfulness, there was a poignant sweetness to her kiss, a gentle healing that seemed to wash away all the hurt of the afternoon and evening.

"I'm sorry about today," she murmured after a long moment, framing his face with her hands. "I'm so sorry I hurt you. It was never about you, Seth. It was me and my own insecurities. I was too afraid to rely on my judgment, to trust that the man I was falling in love with would be willing to catch me on the way down."

He almost couldn't speak, overwhelmed by her words. "What changed?" he finally asked, his voice hoarse.

She was quiet for several moments, the only sound the whirr of the heater and the distant bass throb from the music inside the bar. They would have to leave soon, he thought. They couldn't stay in the Bandito parking lot making out all night, but for now he didn't want to move, more content than he'd ever been in his life.

"Did I tell you about the nightmare I had after Morgan's bad asthma attack, the night my car wouldn't start and you drove us to the clinic to meet Jake?"

He shook his head, shifting so he was leaning into the corner of the seat and her cheek was resting against his chest. He held her close, his hand playing in her incredible hair. It wasn't the most comfortable position but he didn't mind as long as he could hold her.

"I dreamed I couldn't find Morgan," she went on. "She was sick and she needed me and no one would help me look for my child. It was a terrible, helpless feeling. I was just about to hit bottom when someone suddenly appeared out of nowhere and starting shoving away obstacles and pushing people back so I could reach my destination and find my child. I couldn't see his face but I knew even before he turned around who it was."

She touched his face, her eyes soft and a tender smile hovering around that lush mouth. Him? She dreamed of wild and rowdy Seth Dalton coming to her rescue like some kind of hero out of a movie?

"My subconscious has always known what I've been afraid to admit. I need you in my life. I need your strength and your kindness and your laughter."

He pressed his lips to her fingers, wondering if it was possible for a man to burst with joy.

"I love you, Seth. With everything in my heart I love

you and I want everyone in the world to know. I want to run ads in the newspaper and send up hot air balloons and climb to the top of a water tower somewhere so I can graffiti it on the side."

He laughed, completely charmed by this side of her.

"Then you would get arrested for vandalism and I'd have to come pay you conjugal visits—which would be hot and all at first but would probably get old after a while. How about you just settle for whispering it in my ear for the rest of your life?"

Jenny blinked at him. The rest of her life? That certainly sounded...permanent. Was the hellion of Pine Gulch actually proposing?

"I know it's early in the game here," he went on, and she could swear there was a hint of color on his cheekbones in the dim light, "but I just want you to know where I stand. I might just have to put my foot down on this one. I love you and I want everything. The house, the dog, the kids, two cars—three if you count the GTO, which we might have to lock up for a few years until Cole learns to drive a hell of a lot better."

He smiled again and kissed her and all her worries and insecurities seemed to curl up and float away. He loved her. This strong, wonderful man loved her, quiet, boring Jennifer Boyer.

She still didn't quite understand it but she wasn't going to waste any more time doubting it, not when his eyes promised a future of laughter and warmth and joy.

"I love you, Jenny," he repeated. "I want everything."

She smiled and touched his face again, those wild and gorgeous features she loved so dearly.

"You drive a hard bargain, cowboy," she murmured. "But I'll see what I can do."

Epilogue

"Call me crazy, but aren't you supposed to be enjoying yourself?"

Seth swallowed the miserly sip of beer he'd just taken, set his tankard down and aimed a cool look at his older brothers across the table at the Bandito.

"I *am* enjoying myself," he answered Wade. "Who says I'm not enjoying myself?"

If he sounded a trace defensive, he had to hope neither Wade nor Jake noticed. To his chagrin, his brothers didn't miss much. Wade raised an eyebrow at Jake and they both snickered.

"I'd say the evidence speaks for itself," Jake answered, "considering you've been nursing that same beer all night and by my count, that's the third woman you've turned down for a dance in about ten minutes."

It was the fourth, but he wasn't about to point that out.

"I guess I just don't feel like dancing tonight," he said,

wondering why the lights in the tavern seemed so harsh, the music uncomfortably loud. "Since when is that against the law?"

Jake and Wade looked at each other again, then both of them laughed.

"I wouldn't say it's against the law, exactly," Wade said with a particularly annoying smirk. "Just against the natural order of things where you're concerned. This is your last night to solidify your reputation. I can't believe you're not taking advantage of it. You're breaking all those poor girls' hearts."

Friday night at the Bandito was hopping. A live band from Sun Valley rocked the place and the battered dance floor teemed with locals and tourists looking for a good time.

Six months ago, he would have been one of them but it was amazing how a few months could change a man. It had changed this one enough that he suddenly decided he'd had enough of the stuffy tavern, especially when he knew the June night outside would be cool and sweet.

He slid out of the booth and stood up. "I appreciate the thought behind this little party but I think I'm going to head on home now. Thanks for the beer."

His brothers both stared at him like he'd stripped naked and started boot-scootin' across the tabletop.

Jake was the first one to speak. "This is your bachelor party and it's barely nine o'clock! I told Maggie not to expect me to roll in until after closing time."

He waited for some similar comment from Wade but his oldest brother was giving him a careful look. "Your feet feeling a little chill there?"

He raised an eyebrow. "Just because I don't feel much

like ripping up the town doesn't mean I've got cold feet about getting married tomorrow."

He'd be lying if he didn't say the whole idea of marriage still scared the heck out of him. But he was crazy-mad for Jenny Boyer—more than he'd ever believed it was possible to love someone—and he couldn't even bear the thought of any kind of future that didn't include her.

The last five months had been as close to paradise as he'd ever imagined and he knew things would only get better.

"I don't have cold feet," he repeated.

Before he could say more, his old friend Dawna McHenry approached their table with a big smile on her face.

"Hey there, Seth!"

"Hey, Dawna." He kissed her cheek, thinking how pretty she looked in her pink flowered sundress. Since Christmas, when she'd started dating Roy Gentry, Dawna seemed different. Her hair wasn't so brassy now and she wore it in a softer style.

"Is Roy with you tonight?" he asked.

"Of course. He's over at the bar," Dawna said. Seth followed her gaze and found the quiet cowboy smiling in a bemused, besotted kind of way in their direction. He smiled back, feeling a definite kinship to the man. If Jenny were here, he'd be looking at her with that same expression in his eyes.

Dawna tucked her hand through his arm. "So tomorrow's your big day. I'd ask you to dance but I saw all those other girls who came over here walk away with big old dejected looks on their face."

"Dawna—"

She shook her head and gave his arm a squeeze. "That's all right with me. I just wanted to tell you how happy I am for you and Ms. Boyer. She's one nice lady."

"Thank you. I'll tell her you said so."

"You do that. Good luck tomorrow." She gave his arm another squeeze then kissed him again and turned back to her quiet cowboy.

"Man, I hardly recognize Dawna McHenry these days. I wonder what's gotten into her lately," Wade said.

"She's in love," Jake said. "It changes a person."

He looked at his brothers and thought how those words certainly applied to the Dalton brothers. Wade wasn't the stressed, workaholic widower he'd been before Caroline Montgomery blew into their lives. Since marrying their neighbor Magdalena Cruz, Jake had learned not to be so serious all the time, to find a little enjoyment in life besides his patients.

Seth had probably changed more than either of them. He wanted far different things out of life than he had before Jenny Boyer and her children captured his heart. Where this would have been his idea of a good time six months ago, now he just wanted to go home and wait out the last few hours until their lives merged.

He smiled at his brothers. "Like I said, I do appreciate the effort you boys took to wrench yourself away from your women for the night but I don't think any of us are really enjoying this. I don't really need a bachelor party. Why don't we call it a night?"

He was a little annoyed to see neither brother was paying attention to him. Their gazes were both fixed on the door.

"Uh-oh," Jake said, his voice sounding oddly strangled. "Here comes trouble."

Seth turned around to see what they were both so fascinated by and just about tripped over his boots. Three women had just walked into the Bandito. Like plenty of other women in the tavern, they looked more than a little wild—heavy makeup, teased hair, tight jeans.

His heart seemed churn right out of his chest, especially when the redhead in the middle caught his gaze. She gave him a long, sultry look and sauntered over to their table, her partners in crime right behind her.

Seth suddenly discovered a pressing need to take a long sip of his neglected beer to soothe his parched throat.

"Well, aren't you three a sight?" Wade drawled and the woman on the right gave a pleased grin.

"Aren't we, though?" Caroline said, looking pleased as a little filly with a new fence post. She leaned forward a little and though Seth couldn't seem to wrench his eyes away from the little redhead who owned his heart, he thought he heard Wade swallow hard.

"We decided we were bored with our little bachelorette party, just us girls," Caroline went on. "We thought this might be the place to find us some rowdy cowboys."

"And you got all dressed up and everything," Jake murmured.

"You can blame Marjorie for that," Maggie said, sliding into the booth next to her husband. "We were just playing around with lipstick shades trying to find a good one for Jenny to wear tomorrow and Marjorie seemed to think it was a real hoot to lay it on thick and heavy. We all got a little out of control and before we knew it, here we were looking like we just stepped out of a bad country music video."

"For a pregnant woman, you're pretty hot," Jake said.

"I do what I can," Maggie purred.

Seth continued to stare at Jenny, falling in love with her all over again. It wasn't because she made one heck of a sexy party girl. It was that light in her eyes that hadn't been there five months ago, the joy and the happiness he saw in her face every time she looked at him.

"Hey, cowboy. Feel like dancing?"

The words were barely out of her mouth before he grabbed her arm and hauled her out onto the dance floor. The band obliged them by starting up a slow song—not that it mattered since he would have held her close no matter what they were playing.

He pulled her against him and suddenly he didn't mind the stuffy air or the loud music. With her here, with her soft and sweet in his arms, everything felt right again.

"Sorry we crashed your bachelor party," Jenny said into his ear, her voice pitched just loud enough to be heard over the music. "I thought we should leave you boys alone to-night but I was overruled. I hate to tell you this, but the women in your family are on the formidable side."

"Yeah, you're going to have a real tough time fitting in, aren't you?" he said drily.

She made a face. "Hey, I got all tarted up to come down here. I deserve points for that, at least."

"You can have all the points you want, sweetheart."

He leaned close and whispered in her ear, the way he knew drove her crazy. "I've got a muscle car parked out front. What do you say we drive up to the lake and make out all night?"

She gave that sexy sigh of hers and he was humbled all over again to know this smart, beautiful woman had some-how chosen him.

"That's a tempting offer, cowboy, but I'm afraid I'd bet-ter not. I'm getting married in the morning and I'm not sure I could look Father White in the eye with razor burns and love bites."

He grinned, only a little disappointed. They had the rest

of their lives and he intended to fill every day of it showing her how much he loved her. "Despite appearances to the contrary right now, I guess I just might make a respectable woman out of you after all, Jenny Boyer."

"Not too respectable, I hope."

He pulled her closer. "That's a promise."

* * * * *

Also by Michelle Major

HQN

The Magnolia Sisters

A Magnolia Reunion
The Magnolia Sisters
The Road to Magnolia
The Merriest Magnolia
A Carolina Valentine
The Last Carolina Sister

The Carolina Girls

A Carolina Promise
Wildflower Season
Mistletoe Season

Harlequin Special Edition

The Fortunes of Texas

The Taming of Delaney Fortune
Fortune's Special Delivery
A Fortune in Waiting
Her Soldier of Fortune
A Deal Made in Texas
Fortune's Fresh Start
Her Texas New Year's Wish

Visit her Author Profile page at Harlequin.com,
or michellemajor.com, for more titles!

A DEAL MADE IN TEXAS

Michelle Major

To the Fortunes of Texas team of editors—
thank you for helping me make this story shine.

Chapter 1

"I love weddings."

Gavin Fortunado glanced at his sister Schuyler, who stood next to him in the ballroom of the Driskill Hotel in downtown Austin, her long blond hair pulled into an elaborate braided updo. The understated opulence and elegant decor of the historic venue only made the starched collar of the tuxedo he wore feel even stuffier.

"I know you do." Gavin drained the glass of bubbly champagne he'd raised after his father's toast to another sister, Maddie, and her new husband, Zach McCarter. The fizzy liquid churned in his stomach, and he looked toward the crowded bar, mentally calculating how long it would take to get to the front of the line and order a whiskey neat. He had a feeling he'd need something more substantial than champagne to make it through this evening.

He placed his empty glass on a nearby table as Schuyler wrapped her elegant fingers around his arm. "Maddie is a beautiful bride," she said as she leaned against him, dabbing at the corner of one eye with her free hand.

"Yep." He patted his sister's hand. "You were, too." Schuyler had married Carlo Mendoza, vice president of Mendoza Winery, last spring in the sculpture garden at the winery in the Texas Hill Country outside the city. Just as he had this weekend, Gavin had flown in from Denver for Schuyler's big day. He loved his three sisters and appreciated that two of them, who were now married, had picked great guys. He liked and respected both of his brothers-in-law. Any guy who was man enough to take on Schuyler or Maddie was definitely ready to join the family.

Speaking of Schuyler's husband, where was Carlo now? Gavin could use a diversion before Schuyler started in on him.

Too late.

"I'm sure you'll find a beautiful bride, as well." Schuyler gave his arm a squeeze. The touch was gentle, but somehow Gavin felt like an animal caught in a steel trap. Sweat beaded between his shoulder blades and rolled down his back. He groaned inwardly as he noticed the line at the bar had gotten longer.

"You did a great job with all the wedding planning," he said, ignoring his sister's comment. "I know Maddie appreciated it since she's so wrapped up in the Fortunado Real Estate Austin office right now. I don't know how you convinced Mom to allow another wedding to take place here instead of in Houston. I thought she'd pressure Maddie and Zach to get married closer to home."

"It's only a couple hours' drive from Mom and Dad's house, but Maddie couldn't spare any extra time. She and Zach are burning the real estate candle at both ends these days."

Gavin loved all his sisters and brothers, but he and Maddie were only nine months apart in age, so they'd always been especially close. Her relationship with Zach had gotten off to a rocky start last year, as both of them had been vying to be named the new president of Fortunado Real Estate, the company Kenneth Fortunado had founded and devoted his life to for years.

Of the six Fortunado children, Maddie was the one most invested in the family business, although the baby of the family, Valene, was quickly coming into her own as a real estate agent. Their oldest brother, Everett, was a successful doctor. Connor worked as an executive at a corporate search firm in Denver so Gavin hung out with him on a regular basis. Ever since coming to Austin last year, Schuyler had joined the staff of the Mendoza Winery, heading up branding for the company. Gavin had spent his entire career with a corporate law firm headquartered in Denver. He knew his parents were proud of all of them, but Maddie had the same passion for real estate as Kenneth, and she'd gone toe-to-toe with Zach until they'd fallen in love.

It made Gavin smile to see his practical, pragmatic sister head over heels, especially since Zach was the perfect partner for her, as driven and dedicated to the business as Maddie.

"Maybe you'll be the one to tie the knot in Houston," Schuyler suggested cheerily. "I could see it at—"

"Stop." Gavin managed to extricate himself from his sister's grip without having to resort to chewing off his own arm. "I'm not getting married. What is it with everyone and this obsession with weddings? Mom and Dad have been dropping not-so-subtle hints since I stepped off the plane."

Schuyler sighed. "We want you to be happy."

"I *am* happy," Gavin insisted.

She arched one delicate brow in response. "You could be *really* happy."

Gavin rolled his eyes. He wasn't about to get into an argument about his level of contentment. Of course he was happy. Why wouldn't he be? He had a great job working with a prestigious law firm and was on track to be named partner within a year. He owned a fantastic loft in the bustling Lower Downtown neighborhood. The city was a perfect mix of urban and outdoorsy, with enough cowboy left to appeal to his Texas heart. Plus, Colorado offered almost limitless opportunities for the adrenaline-pumping adventures Gavin couldn't seem to get enough of during his downtime. He rock-climbed, mountain-biked and skied every weekend throughout the winter. Well, not this January weekend since he was at his sister's wedding, being subjected to the third degree by his well-intentioned family.

"Look at Everett," Schuyler continued, pointing across the room to where their brother stood talking to a friend of their parents'. His wife, Lila, was at his side, Everett's hand on her back. "He's happy."

As if on cue, Everett glanced down at Lila, and the tenderness in his gaze made Gavin's chest ache the tiniest bit. Lila smiled up at him, practically glowing, and he drew her in closer. Gavin studied the couple, high school sweethearts who'd reunited last spring after years apart. There was something different about them tonight, a new kind of energy to their already strong connection.

Schuyler nudged him, drawing his attention back to her. "Don't you want a woman to look at you like that?"

"What I want is a drink," he told her. "And for you to drop the subject of my love life."

"When was the last time you had a serious girlfriend?"

Never, Gavin thought to himself. He only dated women

who wanted the same things he did: fun, adventure and a good time. "Would you like a glass of wine?"

"You didn't answer my question." Schuyler placed her hands on her slim hips. As Maddie's matron of honor, she wore a burgundy-colored cocktail dress and matching heels that gave her a few extra inches of height. At six feet two inches tall, Gavin still towered over his petite sister. Her classic features and tiny frame made her look like any other beautiful young woman, but Gavin knew underneath the subtle makeup and coiffed hair beat the heart of a tenacious fighter. Once Schuyler latched on to a cause, she gave "dog with a bone" new meaning. It had been that determination that had led the Fortunados to the discovery that they were actually part of the famous Fortune family.

Schuyler loved a challenge and a quest, and Gavin didn't relish being her next one.

"Who says I don't have a serious girlfriend?" he countered, willing to say just about anything to make her drop the subject. "Maybe I just didn't want to subject her to my crazy family."

"I don't believe you."

"Doesn't make it less true. If you all weren't such true-love tyrants, I would have told you about it before." Gavin smiled to himself. That should be enough to keep her occupied for a while.

He realized his mistake as her eyes lit with excitement. "Who is she? How long have you been dating? Why didn't you bring her to the wedding?"

"I'm heading to the bar," he said, invoking his big-brother selective hearing. "I'll get you a glass of Chardonnay. Oh, and it looks like Maddie is having trouble with her train. You have work to do, sis."

"Gavin, I want to hear about your lady."

"Maddie needs you. Gotta go." He moved around her, dodging like he was back on the high school football team when she reached for him.

"Valene can help. Wait… Gavin."

He waved over his shoulder and called, "Back in a sec," having no intention of returning to his sister. She'd regroup soon enough, anyway. Another glance over his shoulder showed Schuyler following him.

He tugged at his collar and glanced around, catching the eye of the slim redhead standing near the corner of the bar. Not exactly catching her eye, as he got the impression that she'd been watching him approach. Either way, she was a friendly face and he'd take it.

"Christine," he called, not daring to check on Schuyler's approach. He wrapped an arm around Christine Briscoe's shoulders. "Great to see you. How have you been? You look lovely. Shall we dance?"

"Um…" Christine, who'd worked for his father's real estate agency in Houston for close to a decade, seemed at a loss for words. That was fine. Gavin didn't need her to speak. As long as she came with him.

The man standing next to her, average height with dark hair and the start of a paunch that indicated he'd done too many keg stands back in college, frowned and made to step forward. Gavin took an immediate dislike to the guy but flashed a grin and held up one finger. "You don't mind if I steal Christine for a dance, right?"

He didn't wait for an answer. He grabbed Christine's hand—soft skin and fine-boned, he noticed—and tugged her toward the dance floor, breathing a sigh of relief as he saw that Schuyler had been waylaid by a distant cousin on their mother's side of the family.

The music changed from an up-tempo dance number to

a slow ballad. Automatically, he wrapped his arms around Christine's waist, careful to be respectful of her personal space since he'd basically hijacked her for this dance.

She lifted her hands to his shoulders and glanced up at him.

"Hi, there," he said with his most charming smile.

"Hi," she breathed. "You, too. Well. Thanks. Yes."

He felt his mouth drop open and closed it again. "I think I missed part of the conversation."

She tugged her bottom lip between her teeth and his mouth went dry. He'd known Christine for years, but how had he never noticed the way her mouth was shaped like a perfect Cupid's bow, the lower lip slightly fuller and damned kissable, if he had the inclination?

Which he didn't. He couldn't. She was a cover to save him from his sister's meddling in his private life. Clearly, Schuyler had messed with his head because he'd never thought of Christine as anything more than a casual friend before this moment—never gave her much thought at all if he had to admit the truth.

"I'm responding to your comments," she answered, somewhat primly. "It's great to see you, too. I'm well. Thanks for the compliment. Yes, I'd like to dance."

"Ah." He felt one side of his mouth curve. This time the smile was natural. Why did it feel so unfamiliar? "You're precise."

She frowned. "Oh, you weren't looking for a response? The questions were rhetorical." Color flooded her cheeks and it fascinated him to watch the freckles that dotted her skin almost disappear against the blush. "I should have figured."

"No... I..." He shook his head. "I'm a little bit off my game tonight."

"Your game," she murmured.

"Not that this is a game," he amended quickly. "It's a wedding."

"Your *sister's* wedding," Christine agreed, sounding amused.

"The Fortunados are dropping like flies," he said, glancing around for Schuyler, whom he thankfully didn't see in the vicinity. "Schuyler seems to think I'm next. Can you keep a secret?"

Christine nodded solemnly.

"I told her I have a girlfriend."

"But you don't?"

"No, and that's how I like it." He pulled her closer to avoid a couple trying some sort of complicated spin and tried not to notice the feel of her soft curves pressing against the front of his tux. This dance was about avoiding Schuyler. Nothing more. "For some reason, my sister can't seem to accept that. It was easier to lie, although I'm not sure she believed me."

"I'm sure you could find a girlfriend if you wanted one."

He grimaced. "But I don't want one. Not even a little bit."

"Oh."

He had the strange sensation that he'd disappointed her and didn't like the feeling.

"How's Denver?" Christine asked quietly after a moment of awkward silence between them.

"Good," he answered and struggled to come up with something better to say. Something interesting. Charming. Gavin was well-known for his charm. He had an easy way with women that made him popular, even with his ex-girlfriends. Where was that legendary charm now?

He couldn't figure out what the hell was wrong with him. Had he allowed Schuyler to rattle him that much? Hell, he came from a family of six kids. Good-natured teasing was nothing new.

"Did you cut your ski trip short to come to the wedding?"

He blinked. "I did, actually. How did you know?"

"Your sisters talk about you a lot," she said. She stiffened in his arms, making him regret questioning her. He liked dancing with Christine. She was just the right height and her body fit against his perfectly. She smelled clean and fresh, like strawberries or springtime or sunshine. Okay, that was stupid. Sunshine didn't have a scent.

He needed to get a hold of himself, but all he could manage was hoping she'd relax into him again. The song ended and another ballad began. Gavin would have to tip the bandleader later for his sense of timing.

"Do you ski?" he asked, tightening his hold on her ever so slightly, splaying his hand across her lower back.

She laughed, low and husky, and his stomach flipped wildly. He hadn't expected that kind of laugh from strait-laced Christine Briscoe. "No skiing for me. I've never even been to Colorado."

"You'll have to visit," he told her. The way her eyes widened in shock was like he'd invited her to have wild monkey sex on the hood of his car. The image did crazy things to his breathing, and he pushed it out of his mind.

"Th-things are b-busy," she stammered, "at the office right now."

"That's right. You moved to Austin to manage the new branch. My dad mentioned that."

"I'm originally from Austin, and it was a great opportunity," she confirmed. "Of course, I loved working for your dad in Houston, too."

"Of course." He felt the sensation of someone staring

at him and glanced toward the bar. The man Christine had been standing next to was still there, shooting daggers in Gavin's direction.

"Did I steal you from your boyfriend?" Even though it was no business of his, he didn't like the idea of this woman belonging to another man.

She shook her head, her full mouth pursing into a thin line. "Maddie and Zach invited everyone from the Austin office to the wedding. Bobby and I work together, but that's all, despite his best efforts. He's a good real estate agent but can't seem to understand that I'm not interested in dating him. In fact, you kind of rescued me."

"So then I'm your hero?"

Christine blushed again, and Gavin couldn't help but wonder what it would take to make her whole body flush that lovely shade of pink.

"I don't know about that," she murmured, her gaze focused on the knot of his bow tie.

He forced a chuckle, ignoring the pang of disappointment that lanced his chest at her words. What was going on with him tonight? He didn't want or need to be anyone's hero. "Already you know me too well," he said as the song ended.

Her eyes darted to his like she'd been caught with her hand in the cookie jar. "I should get back to…um…the bar." She squeezed shut her eyes then opened them again and offered him a lopsided smile. The first strains of a popular country line dance song started. "I'm not much for this kind of dancing."

"We have that in common," he told her then led her through the crowd. "Thanks for helping me out," he said as they stopped at the end of the bar. At least the guy from earlier was nowhere to be seen. He waited for her to say something, oddly reluctant to have this strange interlude come to an end.

She crossed her arms over her chest and nodded, barely making eye contact. "Enjoy the rest of your night."

"You, too," he said and took a step away, to be almost immediately stopped by an old family friend.

He glanced over his shoulder to see that Christine had already turned toward the bar. She was well and truly done with him.

Gavin didn't have much experience with being blown off by a woman, but he recognized the signs just the same. Christine Briscoe obviously wasn't having the same reaction to him as he was to her. He was more disappointed than he would have imagined.

Chapter 2

Christine picked up the glass of wine the bartender placed in front of her and drained half of it in one long gulp.

She'd just had her heart's desire handed to her on a silver platter and she'd made a mess of the whole thing. Gavin Fortunado might not be a hero, but he'd been her secret crush since the moment she'd set eyes on him almost ten years ago.

For ten years she'd harbored fantasies about her boss's adventurous, drop-dead-gorgeous youngest son. Then tonight, out of nowhere, he'd taken her into his arms, like a scene from every Hallmark movie she'd ever watched. And she loved a good romance.

Unfortunately, Christine hadn't even been able to put together a decent sentence. He'd actually flirted with her. Of course, Gavin flirted with everyone. Not that she knew him well, other than adoring him from afar, but he'd come into the Fortunado Real Estate Agency office in Houston often enough over the years.

She'd watched his easy banter with his sisters as well as the women who worked in the office. He was always charming but respectful and had a knack for remembering names and details. Half the women she knew in Houston had a crush on him, and she imagined it was much the same in Denver.

At first, when his gaze had met hers as he strode toward the bar, she'd thought he might call her out for staring. She'd been trying to ignore Bobby, who seemed to think he was God's gift to women. He was harmless but annoying, and Christine wasn't sure why he wouldn't give up on her. Maybe because she had very little social life to speak of so he assumed she should be grateful for his attention.

Irritated was more like it.

He'd been blathering on about some property he couldn't close, and Christine had been watching Gavin talk to Schuyler. Or rather argue. She was used to seeing Gavin smiling and jovial and hadn't understood the tension that made his broad shoulders appear stiff. Unlike her own, the Fortunado family was tight-knit so it bothered her to see the brother and sister at odds.

She'd been shocked when Gavin had approached the bar and taken her hand. It might have been a simple dance to him. For Christine, having Gavin pull her close, her body pressed against his, was the culmination of all her secret desires come to life. Of all the single women at the reception, he'd picked her. Did that mean something?

Probably not, but a girl could dream. Sadly, all she'd be left with was her dreams since she'd been so discombobulated that she hadn't been able to truly enjoy the moment. Or relax. Or hold up her end of the conversation.

What was the point, anyway? Gavin lived life in the fast lane. She could barely get out of first gear. Normally, her boring routine didn't bother her. She was good at her job, had a cute apartment and a sweet rescue dog that adored her. She owned her own car and one designer purse she'd splurged on last year. The barista at her neighborhood coffee shop sometimes remembered her order, which never failed to make her feel special. She had a good life.

Only occasionally did she think about what it would be like to have more. To be fun and sporty like her sister, Aimee, or confident in the way of the Fortunado sisters. To be the kind of woman who could attract a man like Gavin.

She took another drink of wine and turned back toward the reception. The dance floor was filled with wedding guests, all of them laughing and swaying whether they had rhythm or not. Christine should join the crowd. Despite her two left feet, she loved to dance. But the thought of drawing attention to herself made her cheeks flame. Drat her pale Irish complexion. She had no ability to hide her feelings when her blush gave them away every time.

She had a travel-size powder compact in her purse. Maybe a little freshening of her makeup would help her feel more confident. Out of the corner of her eye, she saw Bobby heading in her direction. She grabbed the glass of wine and slipped into the hallway, turning the corner toward the bathroom, only to find her way blocked by Gavin and Schuyler. Immediately, she slipped behind a potted palm, curiosity about the Fortunados getting the best of her despite the fact that it was wrong to eavesdrop.

"Come on," Schuyler urged. "At least tell me her name. A name and then I'll leave you alone."

"You don't fool me for a second," Gavin said, amusement and irritation warring in his tone. "I'm not telling you anything."

Schuyler threw up her hands. "Because this mystery woman doesn't exist. Admit it, you aren't dating anyone."

Gavin opened his mouth, but Schuyler held up a finger. "At least not anyone serious."

"Oh, it's serious. It's also none of your business."

"Tell me something about her. One thing, Gavin."

"She has blue eyes," he answered without hesitation then added, "And fiery red hair."

"A ginger." Schuyler rubbed her hands together. "I need more details."

Gavin shook his head. "You said one thing. I gave you two."

"Where did you meet? Why didn't you bring her? How long have you been dating?"

"Schuyler, stop."

"I can't," she admitted with a laugh. "I need a new project now that Maddie's wedding is over. You're it."

"I'm not," Gavin insisted, running a hand through his thick hair.

He looked so uncomfortable and unaccustomedly vulnerable that Christine's heart stuttered. Tonight was the first time she'd seen this side of Gavin. He seemed almost human...not so picture-perfect, and it made her like him all the more. Which was dangerous, because she already liked him way more than was wise.

Without thinking, she took a step forward, away from her spot behind the fake plant. Gavin glanced up for one instant, and he looked so darn happy to see her. She wanted that look in his eyes to last. So instead of retreating, as her brain instructed, she moved toward them.

Schuyler glanced over her shoulder. "Hey, Christine. Are you having fun?"

Christine swallowed against the ball of nerves stuck in

her throat. "It was a beautiful wedding, and Maddie and Zach look really happy. You did an amazing job with the planning."

"Thanks." Schuyler's smile was so genuine, Christine almost let the conversation end there. She was an honest person who valued her job and the relationships she'd forged with each of the Fortunados. But dancing with Gavin had been like eating a bite of cake after dieting for years. One taste wasn't nearly enough. She wanted the whole piece. "Please don't be upset with Gavin," she said, working hard to ensure her voice didn't waver.

Schuyler frowned. "Do you mean our argument out here?" She laughed softly. "Don't worry. It's a friendly brother and sister thing. I have to convince him to give up the name of the woman—"

"I asked him not to say anything." Christine wrapped an arm around Gavin's waist and leaned in close. "I wasn't sure if your dad would approve of us." She glanced up at Gavin and smiled. He was staring at her like she'd just sprouted a second head. Not exactly catching on to her plan, which made sense because she didn't actually have one.

"Wait." Schuyler gasped, her gaze ricocheting between the two of them. "What?"

Christine looked at Schuyler once more. "I hope you can understand…we wanted to keep things private. It was never my intention to deceive you, but—"

"Are you saying that you're Gavin's ghost girlfriend?"

"I know it probably comes as a surprise."

"Understatement of the century," Schuyler muttered. "You can't expect me to believe—"

"It doesn't matter what you believe." Gavin looped an arm around Christine, dropping a kiss on the top of her head that she felt all the way to her toes. "Christine isn't a ghost, but think about how you were giving me the third degree. I didn't want her to have to deal with that, not when I wasn't here to protect her."

Christine resisted the urge to whimper. Maybe it was the wine, but the thought of Gavin protecting her made funny things happen to her insides.

Schuyler's mouth dropped open. She stared at them for several long seconds. Christine tried to act normal and not like she might spontaneously combust at any moment. She rested her head against Gavin's chest, and as great as dancing with him had been, this took things to a new level. Without having to concentrate on the steps, she could enjoy his warmth and the feel of his rock-solid muscle. Not to mention the way he smelled, a mix of expensive cologne and soap. Would it be weird if she reached up on tiptoe, buried her face against his neck and just sniffed? Yeah, definitely weird.

She waited for Schuyler to call them out on the lie. No way would anyone, let alone Gavin's perceptive sister, believe that they were a couple.

"Well…okay, then," Schuyler said slowly. "I'll admit I'm at a loss for words."

"Thank heavens for small favors," Gavin muttered.

"I still can't believe… I mean how long have you two been an item?"

"A while," Gavin said before Christine could answer. A good thing, too, because the reality of what she'd done was suddenly crashing over her.

"Don't tell your dad," she blurted, earning a frown from Schuyler and a gentle squeeze from Gavin.

"He loves you like you're part of the family," Schuyler told her. "You know that."

"He loves me *working* for the family," Christine clarified. "This is different."

"Gavin, tell her she has nothing to worry about from Dad or Mom."

"I have already, but you still need to honor Christine's feelings." He lifted a hand to Christine's chin, tipping it up until she was forced to meet his green eyes. This close she could see the gold flecks around the edges. She half expected to see anger or frustration for what she'd done, but he looked totally relaxed.

That made one of them.

"Christine makes the rules," he murmured and before she could react to that novel concept, he brushed his lips over hers.

The kiss started innocently enough. She had the mental wherewithal to register that his mouth was both soft and firm. He tasted of mint gum and whiskey, a combination that had her senses reeling.

She felt him begin to pull away and some small, brave, underused part of her rebelled at the thought. She wound her arms around his neck and deepened the kiss, sensation skittering down her spine when their tongues mingled. A low moan erupted from her...or did the sound come from Gavin? The sound jolted her out of her lust-filled stupor and she jerked back. She'd had a couple glasses of wine, but not enough to excuse her basically mauling this man in front of his sister.

"I guess you guys are the real thing," Schuyler said with a laugh. "No one can fake that kind of chemistry."

"Right," Gavin murmured.

Christine kept her gaze on Schuyler. She had no idea what Gavin was thinking at the moment and was almost afraid to find out.

Schuyler wagged a finger at her brother. "Take care, big brother. Christine isn't like your usual girlfriends. She's special. Dad will kill you if you hurt her."

"I'm not going to hurt her," he said tightly, and Christine felt the arm still holding her go taut.

"He won't," she confirmed. She didn't need Schuyler reminding Gavin that she had nothing in common with the gorgeous, sexy women he usually dated. "He's amazing."

Schuyler laughed again. "If you say so. Shall we head back inside? I need a drink after this little bombshell."

"We'll meet you in there," Gavin said, and Christine wanted to argue. She wasn't quite ready to face his reaction to what she'd just done.

"Don't take too long," Schuyler told them, grinning at Christine. "Maddie should be throwing the bouquet soon. We need to position you front and center."

Christine tried to laugh, but it came out more like a croak. "Sure," she managed and waved as Schuyler walked away.

When they were alone, she forced herself to turn to Gavin again. "I'm so—"

Her words were cut off as he fused his mouth to hers.

Gavin hadn't meant to kiss Christine again. He was still in shock from her announcement to Schuyler. He appreciated what she'd done. He'd been quickly running out of options when it came to distracting his sister from her obsession with his nonexistent girlfriend.

He owed her his thanks, but all he could think of was tasting her sweetness. His hands skimmed along the silky material of her dress, then over her hips, which held just the right amount of curve. And her reaction to him was a revelation. Straitlaced Christine Briscoe could kiss. She met him stroke for stroke, nipping at his bottom lip as if asking for more. Gavin lost himself in her, pulling her tight until her breasts pressed against his chest. As she had when they were dancing, she fit against him perfectly.

She was perfect.

How the hell had this happened?

Voices drifted from around the corner, and he took a step back, knowing the dazed look in her eyes probably mirrored the one in his.

"Hey, ladies," he called as a group of his mother's friends passed, several of them craning their necks to get a better look at Gavin and Christine.

He shifted so that he was shielding her from the curious gazes.

"We need to talk," he whispered when the women had passed.

Christine nodded, staring at the floor.

Gavin drew in a breath. Was she terrified of him now? She'd tried to save him from his sister, and he'd all but shoved his tongue down her throat. She'd seemed a willing participant at the time but now...

Another group of people turned the corner toward them, and Gavin automatically laced his fingers with Christine's and led her down the hall toward the hotel lobby. Her heels clicked against the pristine marble floors as they passed the stately columns that, along with the beautiful stained-glass dome, was the hallmark of the Driskill's famous lobby.

"Hey, Christine." The man she'd been standing with at the bar earlier, Bobby, waved from where he stood in front of the concierge desk. "A few of us are going to bail on the dancing and head to an Irish pub around the corner. Want to—"

"Oh, no," Christine whispered, her lips barely moving.

"She's busy," Gavin called and headed for the elevators along the far wall. She followed him in without protest but tugged her hand away as he hit the button for the fifth floor.

"Are you staying here, too?" he asked, not sure how to broach the subject of what had just happened between them. His wildly successful legal career had made Gavin believe he could talk his way out of any situation. Not so, apparently.

She shook her head, a lock of fiery hair falling forward to cover her cheek. Had he run his hands through her hair, loosening the elegant chignon? He couldn't remember but suddenly he wanted nothing more than to see the bright strands cascading over her shoulders. He'd told his sister he was dating a woman with blue eyes and auburn hair. Maybe he'd been unconsciously thinking of Christine after their dance.

"Gavin, I—"

The door opened, cutting off whatever she was going to say to him. An older couple got in.

"Going down?" the man asked.

Gavin shook his head. "Up."

"We'll ride along," the woman offered. "You two look fancy."

"Wedding reception," Christine said quietly.

"I love weddings." The woman sighed. "Always so romantic."

Her husband snorted. "Except when your brother got sloshed and threw up on the dance floor at ours."

"He had food poisoning," the wife said, her tone clipped.

"Forty years." The man lifted his hands. "She still can't admit that her no-good brother's a drunk."

"At least he still shows up for holidays," the woman shot back. "Unlike your rude sister and her—"

"Our floor," Gavin interrupted when the elevator dinged. The door slid open, and he placed a hand on Christine's back. "I'm at the end of the hall," he told her when the door closed behind them with a snick.

His hand stilled as he realized her shoulders were shaking. Oh, God. Not tears. He could handle an angry jury or a recalcitrant witness. But tears killed him, especially the thought that he'd caused them.

"Don't cry," he whispered. "It will be—"

A sob broke from her throat. No, not a sob. Laughter.

She lifted her face, and he realized her tears weren't from anxiety, but amusement. "I know our relationship is five minutes long and a complete lie," she said, wiping her cheeks as she laughed, "but promise we'll never fight about your drunk brother."

He grinned and looped an arm around her shoulder as they started down the hall. "Fortunados can handle their liquor," he promised. "Do you have a sibling? I don't even know."

"A sister. Aimee is a year younger than me and perfect in every way."

"Perfection must run in the family."

As lines went, Gavin thought it was a pretty good one. Both subtle and charming. Christine only burst into another round of laughter. He was definitely losing his touch, although it was somewhat refreshing to be with a woman who didn't melt in a puddle at his feet. Gavin liked a challenge.

He wouldn't have pegged Christine as one, but this woman surprised him at every turn.

"I'm sorry," she whispered, clasping a hand over her mouth when a snort escaped.

He unlocked the hotel room door and gestured for her to enter.

"I hate to be indelicate," he said when they were both inside, "but are you drunk?"

She shook her head and drew in a shuddery breath. "It's just been a crazy night, you know?"

"I do. Would you like a drink now? I have a bottle of Mendoza red that was left in the welcome bag for wedding guests. Or water?"

"No, thanks." Now that her laughter had stopped, Gavin could almost see the wheels turning in Christine's brain as she became aware that she was alone with him in his hotel room.

"Would you feel more comfortable if I propped open the door?" He shrugged out of his jacket, tossing it onto the edge of the bed.

"I trust you," she whispered.

He blew out a breath, surprised at how happy the simple statement made him. He loosened his bow tie then undid the top button of his tailored shirt.

"Christine, I want to—"

"I'm sorry," she blurted. All the amusement from minutes ago had vanished from her features. "I shouldn't have butted into your conversation with Schuyler. You don't need my help to handle your sister and—"

"On the contrary. I want to thank you. You rescued me."

She wrapped her arms around her waist, and he could see her knuckles turning white from pressing her fingers against her rib cage. "I'm not sure what possessed me to get involved," she admitted. "I guess because you helped me with Bobby earlier."

"Bobby is a putz."

One side of her mouth curved, not a true smile but a step in the right direction. "That's true, which makes our situations different. Schuyler is your sister and she cares about you."

"She's also relentless." He took a step toward her, slowly, like he was approaching an animal that might spook at any moment. He didn't want to spook her. "Would you like to sit down?" He inclined his head toward the couch positioned in front of the room's large window. "We can talk about next steps."

Her cornflower-blue eyes widened. "Next steps. Okay."

He grabbed two bottles of water from the mini-fridge and set them both on the coffee table before taking a seat next to her. "In case you get thirsty."

"You're really not mad?" She leaned forward and slipped off the heels she wore, revealing the most adorable painted pink toes Gavin had ever seen.

Hell, when was the last time he'd been with a woman? Granted, he'd been busy with work so his personal life had taken a back seat. But he was too far gone if a glimpse of toenail polish could mess with him like this.

"Christine, I'm grateful. I'd already made up a girlfriend. You made her a reality."

She tucked her legs underneath her. "And the kiss?"

"You'll never hear me complain about a beautiful woman kissing me."

She rolled her eyes. "I took it too far."

"You were convincing."

Color stained her cheeks. "Maybe I missed my calling. I should have been an actress."

"Hmm." Gavin didn't like the sound of that. It bothered him more than it should to think she'd been faking the kiss, even though that was what this whole thing was. A fake. He forced a smile, unwilling to let her see his reaction. Best to keep things light and casual, and he could do that better than almost anyone he knew. "I'm hoping you'll be interested in a repeat performance."

Christine made a sound that was somewhere between a yelp and whimper. "Of the kiss?"

Hell, yes.

"Actually, I was talking about you acting as my girlfriend." He ran a hand through his hair. "While I'm in Austin for the next few weeks."

"Weeks?" She uncurled her legs and dropped her feet to the thick carpet. For a moment he thought she was going to bolt. Then she placed her elbows on her legs and rested her head in her hands. "Weeks," she repeated on a slow exhalation.

"I'll make it worth your while."

Her head snapped up. "Like I'm a hooker?"

"Of course not." He shifted closer. "What I meant to say was it will be easy for you."

"You think I'm easy?"

"No. God, no." He leaned back, raised his gaze to the ceiling, hoping for some way to salvage this conversation. When he found no inspiration from above, he looked at Christine again, only to find her grinning at him. "That was a joke?"

She nodded. "You're different than I thought you'd be," she said quietly. "Not quite as perfect as you look at first glance."

"Is that a compliment or a criticism?"

She bit down on that full lower lip, and his insides clenched. "A compliment. It's good to know you're human."

"I don't usually like it when people tease me," he admitted.

"Oh."

"I like it with you."

"I'm glad." Another smile, this one almost shy. "I know you don't think I'm an easy hooker. You want me to pretend to be your girlfriend so your family leaves you alone. We'd have a fake relationship. That sounds simple."

Did it? Gavin wasn't sure what to make of his feelings for Christine, but they definitely weren't simple.

"Right," he agreed anyway. "One of the law firm's larger clients is based in Austin and we're finalizing a merger with another financial institution. Everything should be complete by the end of the month. It makes sense that we'd be together now, and then when I go back to Denver, you can break up with me."

"Like anyone is going to believe that," she said with a harsh laugh.

"Long distance relationships are tough. I don't think it will come as a huge surprise."

"The part where *I* break up with *you* is going to be the surprise." She sat back on the sofa, so close that he could feel the warmth of her body. "Your family knows you're a bit of a playboy."

"Am not."

She rolled her eyes. "How many women have you dated?"

He thought about that, grimaced. "Since when?"

"I rest my case," she told him.

"But this is different." He took her hand, laced their fingers together and looked directly into her eyes. "You've changed me."

Chapter 3

Christine felt her mouth go dry at his words. She'd changed him?

"At least that's what my family needs to believe," he clarified.

"Schuyler agreed not to tell anyone," Christine argued, although the thought of how she'd go about convincing people that she and Gavin were really a thing made goose bumps dance along her skin. Talk about the adventure of a lifetime.

"We *told* her not to tell anyone." He traced his thumb in circles against the sensitive skin on the inside of her wrist. "But there's no way she's going to be able to resist."

"So we'll need to convince your family this is real," she whispered. "Your parents will be upset they didn't know."

"They'll understand," he assured her. "I'll make sure they do."

"I hate lying to your father…to anyone in your family. They've been so good to me."

"This isn't going to change anything," he promised.

But Christine knew nothing would ever be the same. She should stop this charade right now, march downstairs and explain to Schuyler that it was all a big misunderstanding. Although she was sober, maybe she could pretend to be drunk. Blaming her crazy behavior on alcohol might give her a decent excuse.

Gavin's jacket began to ring. He stood and moved toward the bed, pulling his phone out of the pocket of the discarded tuxedo coat.

"Hey, sis," he said into the device. "No, I'm not coming back down." Pause. "Yes, she's with me." Pause. "I don't think she's going to care about the bouquet." Pause with an added eye roll. "Don't go there, Schuyler. I told you this is special. She's special. Let me enjoy it, okay?" Pause. "I understand and appreciate it. I love you, too." Pause. "Okay, I'll see you at the brunch in the morning."

He punched the screen to end the call then tossed the phone on the bed again.

"You missed the bouquet."

Christine stood. "I'm okay with that. You shouldn't be annoyed with Schuyler for calling. I don't want this to complicate things with you and your family."

He moved toward her. "My family is always complicated, especially now that the Fortunes are involved. My only concern is you. As much as I appreciate what you did earlier, if you aren't okay with this arrangement, we'll end it."

Here was her chance. A dance, a few kisses and she'd go back to her normal life before the clock struck midnight, like some sort of Fortune-inspired Cinderella.

But she couldn't force her mouth to form the words. Despite this whole thing being fake, she wasn't going to miss her chance at getting to know Gavin. Under what other circumstances would a man like him choose to date someone like her?

Not that she was down on herself. Christine liked her life and felt comfortable with who she was. Usually. But she wasn't the type of woman who could catch Gavin Fortunado's attention. Until now.

"I don't want it to end," she said, embarrassed that she sounded breathless.

Gavin didn't seem to notice. He cupped her cheeks in his hands. "Me neither," he whispered and kissed her. Once again it felt like fireworks exploding through her body. The kiss was sweet and passionate at the same time. He seemed in no hurry to speed things along, content to take his time as he explored her lips.

Then his mouth trailed over her jaw and along her throat, her skin igniting from the touch. He tugged on the strap of her dress, and it fell down her shoulder. He kissed his way from the base of her neck to her collarbone. Her body was all heat and need. She wanted so much from this moment that she couldn't even put it all into words.

"You're so beautiful," he whispered.

The compliment was like a bucket of ice water dumped over her head. She wrenched away, yanking her dress strap back into place.

"Don't say that," she told him, shaking her head. "You don't have to say that."

Confusion clouded his vivid green eyes. "In my experience, women like to hear those words."

She swallowed. How was she supposed to respond without sounding like she was fishing for something more? That wasn't the case at all. In fact, she felt the opposite.

She didn't want or need him to tell her she was beautiful because it simply wasn't true.

Christine prided herself on being pragmatic about her appearance. Growing up, she'd been a chubby girl with thick glasses and bright red hair that was more frizz than curls. Her mom had forced her to keep it in frizzy Annie-style curls that were anything but flattering. Christine had spent years enduring teasing, much of it led by her younger sister, until she'd become an expert at not being seen.

Aimee, with her larger-than-life personality and classic beauty, had been happy to step into the spotlight. She went to parties and on dates, while Christine spent most of her high school years in her room reading or listening to music. No one in her family seemed to notice or care as she slipped further into the periphery of their lives.

She'd decided to change things when she went away to college. She'd gotten contacts and started running, shedding the excess pounds that had plagued her for years. A bevy of expensive hair products helped her tame her wild mane, and the color had mellowed from the bright orange of her childhood. Her dad had called her "baby carrot" as a kid, and her sister had amended the nickname to "jumbo carrot" due to Christine's size. Even though she thankfully hadn't heard the nickname in years, it was how she still thought of herself.

She took pains with her appearance and she knew she wasn't ugly. She was decent-looking, in fact. But beautiful? No, not to someone like Gavin.

"This is not real," she said, both for his sake and to remind herself.

Gavin's thick brows furrowed. "That doesn't mean—"

"What's your favorite color?"

"Um…blue."

"Mine's purple." She crossed her arms over her chest, aware he was still staring at her like he couldn't quite follow the direction of her thoughts. Join the club. Her mind and heart felt like they'd survived an emotional tornado, hurricane and maybe a tsunami thrown in for good measure, all in one night. "Favorite food?"

"Pizza."

"I like burgers and fries."

His mouth quirked. "That's kind of cute."

"Burgers aren't cute."

"You're admitting you like them as opposed to giving me some line about loving salmon and kale. That's cute."

"I take yoga classes and run before work. What do you do to work out?"

One brow arched. "So you're flexible?"

With a groan, she stepped around him toward the hotel room desk. "Do you want me to write all this down?" She picked up a pen and the small pad of paper with the hotel's logo.

"The ways you're flexible?"

"Gavin, be serious. You were the one who said your family would find out about us. We need to have our stories straight." Christine clutched the pen and paper to her chest and fought the urge to whimper as Gavin ran a hand through his hair. She could see the muscles of his arm flexing under his white shirt. "When did we meet?"

"We've known each other for years."

"Right. I mean when did we—"

"It was Thanksgiving break my senior year of college. I was getting ready to retake the LSAT after my not-so-stellar performance the first time around."

Christine inclined her head, surprised and charmed he'd remember the very first time they met. "You were studying in the conference room at the Fortunado Real Estate office. It was quiet because of the holiday."

"And I was bitter because my buddies had flown to Aspen for the weekend." He started undoing the buttons of his shirt, casually, as if it wasn't a big deal for him to be undressing in front of her. Of course, he wore a white T-shirt under the formal shirt, so it wasn't a true striptease.

Christine's heart stammered just the same.

"You were the only one in the office," he continued. "You kept bringing me coffee and takeout."

She shrugged. "It was my first week working for your father and I wanted to be helpful in any way I could."

"Do you remember what you told me after I'd complained to you for the millionth time about life being unfair?"

She shook her head. She hadn't remembered speaking to him at all. She'd graduated college a semester early and had felt lucky to be hired by Kenneth right away. It had taken almost a year on the job before she believed her boss wouldn't walk into the office and tell her he'd made a horrible mistake taking a chance on her. Having Gavin in the office during the quiet lull of the Thanksgiving holiday had made her so nervous. All she'd been able to do was refill his mug and send out for sandwiches.

"You told me to channel my inner Elle Woods."

Christine gave a soft chuckle. "I loved *Legally Blonde*."

"Clearly. You gushed about the movie. I didn't know what you were talking about," Gavin said with a grin. "I went back to my parents' house and rented it."

"You watched *Legally Blonde*?"

"Oh, yeah. I not only watched it, I was also inspired. I mean, if Elle Woods could get into law school, what excuse did I have?"

She snorted a laugh then pressed her hand to her mouth. "Tell me you didn't use scented pink paper for your admissions application."

"Not exactly." Gavin draped the crisp white shirt over the back of the desk chair then held up his hands, palms out. "If you tell anyone I said I was inspired by that movie, I'll deny it. But I might have Reese Witherspoon to thank for my law career." His smile softened. "And you."

Christine felt her mouth drop open. "I...had no idea."

"It seemed like a stupid thing to admit at the time. But I've never forgotten. You helped me then, and now you're saving my bacon once again. I owe you, Christine."

"It's not a big deal," she said automatically. But it was. It was that time he'd spent in the office poring over law books that had given her an initial glimpse of who Gavin truly was on the inside. Through the years she'd remained convinced he was more than the rakish attorney who was always scaling mountains or hurling himself down ski slopes in his off time. Back then he'd been nervous, vulnerable, and she hadn't been able to resist him. Just like she couldn't now.

She lifted the paper and pen. "We should still go over some more details if we're going to make this relationship believable." Not that it would be difficult on her part. One look at her face and it would be clear to everyone that she was already half in love with Gavin.

"How about we watch a movie while we talk?" He winked. "Elle Woods for old times' sake?"

"Sure," she whispered.

He picked up his jacket then patted the bed. "Make yourself comfortable. I'm going to order something from late-night room service. Can I tempt you with a hamburger?"

Christine started to shake her head but her stomach rumbled. "No cheese and medium-well, please."

He nodded. "Got it."

She placed the paper and pen on the nightstand and climbed onto the bed, butterflies racing across her stomach. She was in Gavin's bed. Or *on* it. Close enough.

He used the room's landline to place the order then clicked the remote to turn on the TV, searching until he found *Legally Blonde*. "I haven't watched this movie in years," he told her.

"It holds up," she said, choosing not to share that the movie was on her regular rotation of Saturday night rom-coms. It struck her that tonight was Saturday and here she sat watching a movie, as had become her weekly routine. Only tonight instead of curling up with her black lab, Diana, she was in one of the most beautiful hotels in Austin with Gavin.

She loved her dog, but this was way better.

Her nerves disappeared as soon as the movie started. She and Gavin talked and laughed, and then ate when the food arrived. He cleared the empty plates when the movie ended, placing the tray outside the hotel room door.

"I think you should stay a bit longer," he said, checking his watch. "The reception isn't scheduled to end until midnight, and knowing my family, they'll be closing down the place."

"I don't want to keep you from going to sleep," she said, stifling a yawn.

"Apparently, I'm not the one who's tired."

"It's been a kind of crazy night for me," she admitted.

"If you want to go I can—"

"We could watch another movie?" She smiled. "Something with lots of action to keep us awake."

"Good idea." He returned to the bed and flipped through channels until he found an old James Bond flick.

"Who's your favorite Bond?" she asked.

"Sean Connery." He moved to the center of the mattress. "In case you're interested, I make a pretty good pillow."

Her girl parts went wild. She scooted closer, and he lifted one arm, tucking her against his chest.

"I bet you're a Daniel Craig fan," he said, resting his chin on the top of her head.

"Every woman with a pulse is a fan of Daniel Craig."

She felt his chuckle against her ear, and the rhythmic up and down of his chest. As bizarre as the night had been, it was the stuff of her fantasies to be cuddling with Gavin. If only the night never had to end.

Chapter 4

Christine blinked awake, disoriented for a moment at the unfamiliar surroundings. The something—someone—moved next to her and the previous night came flooding back.

She turned to find Gavin asleep next to her, lying chest down with his hair rumpled and a shadow of stubble covering his jaw. Somehow they'd both ended up under the covers. He still wore his white T-shirt, and she was in her dress. The last thing she remembered was James Bond being served a shaken-not-stirred martini.

Now pale light spilled in from the room's picture window. She glanced at the clock on the nightstand. Seven in the morning.

Well, she'd successfully missed the end of the reception, but if she didn't leave quickly, she might run into the Fortunado family heading to breakfast.

With as little movement as possible, she slipped out of

the bed. Gavin made a snuffling sound but didn't wake. Christine grabbed her shoes and purse. Without bothering to look in the mirror, she let herself out of the room.

She didn't need to see her reflection to know that she wasn't a pretty sight. She had no intention of allowing Gavin to see her this way, either.

The door closed with a soft snick, and she turned, only to come face-to-face with Valene, the baby of the Fortunado clan.

Her brown eyes widened. "Hey, Christine."

Christine smoothed a hand over her tumbling hair. "Hi, Val. Going to work out?"

Valene wore athletic shorts and a fitted tank top. Earbuds dangled from either side of her head. Her wavy blond hair was pulled back in a high ponytail. "Yeah. How about you?" One delicate brow rose. "That's Gavin's room, right?"

"Is it?" Christine's voice was a croak.

"And you're wearing the same dress from the wedding last night," Valene pointed out, none too helpfully as far as Christine was concerned. "Schuyler said Gavin left the reception early because he wasn't feeling well."

"I think he's okay now," Christine answered, purposely ignoring the question in the other woman's dark eyes. "Well, I should be going. Have a great day."

Without waiting for a response, she hurried down the hall, only taking a few steps before realizing that she'd be waiting for the elevator with Valene. Why did decisions made late at night rarely hold up to the light of day?

She breathed a sigh of relief when she noticed the sign for the stairs, pushing open the door and racing down four flights. The stairwell led out to the parking garage. She shoved her feet back into the heels and made it to her

Subaru hatchback and then away from the hotel without seeing anyone else she knew.

Thank heaven for small favors.

Quite small since she understood that although Valene had been shocked enough to allow Christine to escape this morning, there would be no avoiding the Fortunado sisters for long. Valene worked out of the real estate agency's Houston office but visited Austin regularly to help with establishing a new client base. Even if she didn't see Valene right away, the sisters would talk. Gavin seemed sure they didn't have anything to worry about, but Christine remained unconvinced.

Walking into her condo, she was greeted with an enthusiastic bark. Diana trotted toward her, tail wagging and ears pricked up. Christine smiled despite her tumbling emotions. Nothing like unconditional love to work as a distraction.

"Hey, girl." Christine crouched down to love on the dog. "Did Jackson take good care of you last night?" At ten years old, Diana was fairly mellow and low maintenance. As she did on nights when she worked late, Christine had asked her neighbor's preteen son to dog-sit Diana.

The dog pressed her head against Christine and gave a soft snort, making the tension in her shoulders lessen slightly. "Let me shower and change, and we'll go for a walk."

The dog turned in a happy circle at the mention of her favorite word.

"You would not believe the night I had," Christine said as she placed her purse on the counter and headed for the bathroom, Diana following close on her heels. The dog had been her roommate and companion for so long, she thought nothing of carrying on a one-sided conversation.

She told Diana about Gavin and their arrangement. The

dog inclined her head, as if truly listening. Christine was grateful for the sympathetic canine ear. Most of her girl-friends were in the real estate industry or knew the Fortunados, so she couldn't share the arrangement with any of them.

Her sister would have a field day giving Christine grief about only being able to find a fake boyfriend. Even as adults, their relationship was fraught with teasing, all one-sided. Christine had never allowed herself to think much of it, although it was strange that they couldn't seem to shake their childhood roles.

Aimee was beautiful, popular and funny. She worked as a hairdresser in a busy salon in one of Austin's tonier suburbs. She had tons of friends, a steady stream of rich boyfriends and remained the apple of their father's eye. Yet she never seemed to tire of pointing out Christine's shortcomings.

It had been easier when Christine lived in Houston. She'd come up with plenty of excuses over the years as to why she could only return to Austin once or twice a year for family functions.

But now that she'd moved back to her hometown, her mother made it clear she expected to see more of her.

After her shower, she dressed in a sweatshirt and loose jeans, laced up her sneakers and headed out the door with Diana. As always, the dog was thrilled to check out the scents along the walking trail situated about a block from the condo.

Christine waved to neighbors and tried to keep her thoughts from straying to Gavin. Why had she agreed to be his pretend girlfriend?

She had no answer, other than the fact that it was her best—and possibly only—chance of ever spending time with him.

Maybe that was a good enough reason.

Diana whined softly as they got to the open meadow that bordered the trail. Christine unclipped the dog's leash, and Diana sped off to investigate the nearby trees.

Christine's phone dinged, and she pulled it out of her pocket, drawing in a quick breath at the text message.

I missed you this morning. Talk soon?

She and Gavin had exchanged numbers in his hotel room, but it still shocked her to see his name on the screen.

How to respond?

Last night had been one of the best of her life, even though nothing had happened between them. Okay, she was disappointed nothing had happened. She'd spent the night in a man's bed and all he'd done was snuggle her. Did that say more about Gavin or her? She was afraid the answer was the latter.

Yes, she knew he respected her and she'd heard him tell his sister that Christine was special. Now, that felt like an excuse for keeping things basically platonic between them.

But he missed her.

That was a good sign, right?

She tapped in the start of several responses and almost immediately deleted each of them. Too sweet. Too trite. Trying too hard.

Finally, she sent a smiley-face emoji.

And immediately regretted it. Her mother sent smiley-face emojis about everything. All Christine needed was to add an "LOL" along with several exclamation points and she'd officially become the fuddy-duddy she was afraid might be her destiny.

Diana barked at a squirrel, and Christine pocketed the

phone with a sigh. She wasn't sure what she'd gotten herself into with Gavin Fortunado, but there was no doubt she was in over her head.

"Where's Christine?"

Gavin made a show of checking his watch as Schuyler dropped into the chair next to him. For the morning-after brunch she'd traded her bridesmaid dress for a pair of slim trousers and a pale pink sweater, her blond hair in a low ponytail. He had the sudden urge to tug on it, as he had to annoy her when they were kids. "It's ten o'clock. Isn't that too early for an interrogation?"

"One question does not an interrogation make," she countered, forking up a piece of pineapple and popping it into her mouth.

"Hey, you two." His youngest sister, Valene, slipped into the chair on his other side. She wore a gray sheath dress and an understated pendant necklace around her neck. When had the baby of the family grown up so much? "What's the deal with you and Christine?" she asked Gavin.

He glared at Schuyler. "So much for keeping things on the down low."

"I didn't say anything," she told him, arching a brow at Valene.

"She didn't need to." Val sipped her glass of orange juice. "I caught Christine doing the walk of shame from your room this morning on my way to work out."

"Seriously?" Schuyler demanded, eyes narrowing. But to Gavin's utter shock, her stare was focused on Valene and not him. "You worked out already? Stop making me feel like a slacker, Val."

Val rolled her eyes and winked at Gavin. "So..."

"She wasn't doing the walk of shame," Gavin said

through clenched teeth, wishing for something stronger than coffee in his china cup.

"Don't get me wrong," Valene told him, ignoring Schuyler's continued glare. "I approve. She's a definite improvement over that bimbo you were dating when I came to Denver last year."

"She's probably too good for you," Schuyler added absently. "How did you get her to take you on in the first place?"

"Feels like an interrogation," Gavin muttered under his breath.

Schuyler chuckled. "You know I'm joking. You're a catch, Gavin."

"It's just a surprise that you've let yourself be caught." Valene bit into a slice of bagel slathered with cream cheese.

"I don't want to talk about this with either of you." He inclined his head toward the rest of the family, who were gathered around Maddie and Zach on the other side of the room. "Especially not here."

"You need our expertise," Schuyler told him. "Christine is amazing. She's the kind of woman…"

"I'd want at my side for always," Gavin whispered, unaware that he'd spoken aloud until both of his sisters gasped.

Schuyler grabbed his arm. "Are you saying…"

"Did you ask her to marry you?" Valene leaned closer. "Are you and Christine engaged?"

Gavin felt his Adam's apple bob in his throat as he swallowed hard. "I didn't say that."

"It's true, though. I can tell by the look in your eyes." Valene let out a little squeal of delight then lifted her bagel and smiled blandly at the group sitting at the next table. "Try the blueberry cream cheese. It's amazing."

"Can you two be more obvious?" Gavin tugged his arm out of Schuyler's grasp.

"You're getting *married*," Schuyler told him, and he didn't dare contradict her. "You can't keep it a secret."

Fake dating to fake engaged in twenty-four hours. His stomach pitched as he thought about Christine's reaction to this new development.

"And there's no reason to." Valene dabbed at the corner of her mouth with a napkin. "Everyone loves Christine."

"She's a private person," he said, realizing the excuse sounded lame.

Schuyler nodded just the same. "I get that, but she's like one of the family to us. She's going to be one of the family soon. How soon? Have you set a date?"

He shook his head, trying to reel in his thoughts. What was he doing here? "Not yet. We didn't want to take any attention from Maddie and Zach."

Both of his sisters nodded in agreement.

"I'm sure that was Christine's idea," Valene said. "She's so thoughtful. We'll make sure she knows how welcome she is." She looked past him, her eyes widening. "Oh, they brought out a fresh tray of pastries. I need to get to them before Everett and Connor snag the best ones." She pushed back from the table. "I'll be right back. Who wants a donut?"

"Me." Schuyler raised her hand. "Bring one for Gavin, too. He's probably hangry and hungover."

"I'm neither," he said, although his head was starting to ache. Was it too early for a shot? "But I'll take a Bloody Mary, please."

Valene laughed as she walked away.

Schuyler wasted no time. She turned to Gavin and started in on him again. "Christine is going to get the wrong impression if you try to keep her a secret much longer, especially since you're in Austin for the rest of the month. She needs to start wedding planning, and I can help. Think about it, Gavin. She's going to be your wife. I get the business about being private, but if you make her feel like everything's okay, she'll believe it."

"Do you think I haven't?"

"I think you don't have much experience with a woman who you can be proud to bring home to Mom and Dad."

"That's not—" Gavin stopped, ran a hand through his hair. It was exactly the truth. Even though his relationship with Christine was a complete fake, he hadn't dated anyone with her amount of class and elegance in years. Christine was the kind of woman a man thought of spending his life with, and Gavin's stomach pitched at the realization.

"Bring her to the family reunion," Schuyler told him, breaking into his tumbling thoughts.

"What family reunion?"

"The one I'm planning to introduce everyone to the new Fortunes."

He shook his head. "I thought *we* were the new Fortunes."

She leaned forward, her eyes dancing with excitement. "There are more, Gavin. Dad has a half brother, Miles. He lives in New Orleans and has seven kids. Ben and Keaton put me in touch with the youngest son, Nolan. He's recently moved to Austin."

Ben Fortune Robinson had spearheaded the search for his illegitimate siblings after discovering that his tech mogul father was really Jerome Fortune, who'd faked his death years earlier. Jerome reinvented himself as Gerald Robinson and built his tech empire, but in recent years the family's focus had been on their new siblings. Keaton

Whitfield, a British architect who was now living in Austin, had been the first of the secret illegitimate Fortunes Ben had tracked down. Together, the two of them had worked to uncover Gerald's other grown children and bring them into the fold.

Schuyler was the Fortune expert as far as Gavin was concerned, so he knew from her that Gerald's estranged wife, Charlotte, had actually known about his other children for the duration of their marriage and hidden the information from everyone. To learn there were even more previously unknown Fortunes out there… Gavin didn't know what to think.

"Schuyler, last year you were the one who wasn't sure if the Fortunes could be trusted. That was the whole basis for you infiltrating the family through the Mendozas."

She smiled wistfully. "Thank heavens for that brilliant idea. Otherwise, I never would have met Carlo."

"Can we keep on topic?" Gavin asked. Once again he wondered what it would have felt like to grow up an only child.

"We have to welcome the New Orleans Fortunes into the family, just like the Robinsons did for us. They're as innocent in all the family intrigue as we were, but we can't deny the connection. I'm going to make sure it goes well." She rubbed her hands together. "The reunion is going to be held at the Mendoza Winery. Nolan seems like a good guy. He promised he'd get his brothers and sisters to attend. I'm not sure about his parents yet, but I'm still hopeful."

"You never give up," Gavin murmured with a smile.

"It's one of my best traits," she answered. "I think the Fortune Robinson siblings are going to come, as well. I talked to Ben last week and he seemed amenable to the idea."

"What does Dad think of all this?"

Schuyler shrugged. "He's going back to enjoying his retirement after Maddie and Zach return from their mini-honeymoon, but I know he's curious about our new extended family. He and Mom have agreed to drive up and meet everyone. We'll all be here. Except maybe Connor. I'm not sure about his schedule and you know how dedicated he is to the search firm. He promised to try. Either way, the rest of the Fortunados will show a united front in welcome."

"It looks like you've worked out all the details."

"I'm doing my best. Now that Maddie's happily married, I can turn even more of my attention to the reunion." She wiggled her eyebrows. "And to making sure you don't mess things up with Christine before your big day."

I can't mess up something that doesn't really exist, Gavin thought to himself. Although he wasn't sure that rationale actually held water. It felt as if he'd already made a huge misstep by asking her to enter into a fake relationship.

He actually liked Christine quite a bit. More than he'd expected and definitely more than he had any other woman he'd recently dated. But it would complicate things if he tried to turn their pretend love into something real. Plus, despite what his sisters now believed, he still barely knew her. There was no explaining the connection he felt between them, yet he couldn't deny it.

"Don't tell me you've already done something stupid," Schuyler said, studying his face.

"No," he answered automatically then schooled his features. His sister was far too perceptive for his own good.

"You'll bring her to the reunion?" she asked again.

"You know she wants to keep our relationship private," Gavin argued weakly. "A Fortune reunion is the least private activity I can imagine."

Schuyler waved away his concern. "Valene saw her leaving your room, so someone else might have, as well. Besides, she'll want to start planning the wedding. Does she have a dress yet?"

"Um… I don't think so."

"Val and I will take her shopping. We have to plan the perfect bridal shower, too."

"Slow down, Schuyler." Gavin held up a hand like he was giving a command to an eager puppy. "All of this is going to overwhelm her. I don't want that. Even though we're engaged, Christine and I are going to take things at our own pace. If she wants—"

"You're in Austin until the end of the month, right?" his sister interrupted.

"Yes."

"Then it's no longer a long-distance romance where you can sweep her off to Colorado and have her all to yourself." She speared a piece of melon from her plate. "I assume that's what you've been doing. Unless you've been secretly coming to Austin for clandestine dates? Where did you get engaged, anyway?"

Gavin's heart started to leap in his chest. There were so many moving parts in this situation. He needed to talk to Christine to make sure they both kept them all straight. Hell, he wanted to talk to Christine again just to hear her voice.

"Colorado," he told his sister, deciding it was best to stay away from any pesky details. "Everything has been in Colorado."

"That makes sense," she agreed.

Good thing it did to someone.

"Austin is different than a lot of places. It's a big small town in some ways. You know that. It would be silly for you to try to keep things a secret, and I doubt it would work anyway. If you talk to Mom and Dad, they'll understand, but you can't keep trying to hide it. Mom will drive you crazy with attempts to nose into your love life, anyway."

Gavin pointed his fork at Schuyler. "I guess you get it honestly."

"Does that mean you'll bring Christine to the reunion?"

Out of the corner of his eye, Gavin saw Everett and Lila approaching the table. He might have to take his sister's advice and go public with his relationship with Christine, but he didn't intend to reveal it this morning. "I'll invite her," he promised, "but the decision whether to attend will be hers."

"Oh, we can convince her," Schuyler assured him with a smile.

"No pressure," he said, pushing back from the table. "I mean it. I don't want you or Maddie or Valene to make her feel like she has to accept."

"Gavin, you have a protective side when it comes to your future bride." Schuyler grinned. "It's adorable."

He shook his head. "I'm going to talk to Mom and Dad. Let me tell them about Christine and the engagement, okay?"

"Sure," Schuyler agreed. "But I've already told you, the family loves her as much as you obviously do. There's nothing to worry about."

Gavin's stomach pitched at the mention of the *L* word. Those four letters were definitely cause for concern. Fearing that Schuyler would be able to read his emotions, he turned to greet Everett and Lila then made his way toward the rest of the family at the other side of the room.

He knew he needed to talk to his parents about Christine but didn't relish the thought of lying to them outright about his relationship. He told himself it would be better if he waited to speak to his dad in private. Although guilt sat heavy in his gut, he made it through the rest of the brunch then retreated back to his room, changed into a T-shirt and sweatpants and headed out for a run.

He expected to miss the bright sunshine and crisp air in Colorado but it felt good to be back in Texas. After a four-mile loop around downtown Austin, he showered, changed and then texted Christine to see if she could have dinner.

The challenge was knowing what to call the invitation. A fake date? A business meeting? In the end, he left it at "Want to grab dinner?"

His chest constricted when her return text lit up his screen. She had plans for the evening. Should he read more into the terse message? Was she angry that he'd texted instead of phoning? Could she be regretting their agreement enough to call off their arrangement?

Disappointment crashed through him, both because she wasn't available and due to the thought of her possibly backing out of the pretend relationship.

This discontent was new for him. Gavin didn't usually allow himself much time for reflection or self-analysis. Deep thoughts weren't really his deal. As a middle child in a big family, he'd learned early on that the best way to get noticed was action as opposed to introspection, which suited his restless nature just fine.

He'd climbed trees, raced his bike along dirt paths and generally careened through his childhood with an abandon that seemed to both amuse and terrify his parents. He knew they'd been happy when he finally settled on law school, and the constant challenges in his professional life kept his adrenaline moving just like the extreme sports he loved. But lately mastering even the most technical ski slopes hadn't been taxing enough to help him feel settled at the end of the day. Not like he had spending the night with Christine curled next to him.

He had friends in Austin who would be up for a night out, but the idea of going out with anyone but his fake girlfriend held no appeal. In the end, he pulled out his laptop and got to work preparing for the meeting he had scheduled with the firm's client next week.

His fingers itched to call Christine, but she hadn't given him any indication in her text that she wanted to talk to him. Not even a smiley-face emoji like the one she'd sent earlier. The simple plan for getting his family to stay out of his love life was already far more complicated than he'd expected.

Chapter 5

When the knock sounded on her office door Monday morning, Christine was already on pins and needles. She hadn't talked to Gavin other than a simple text about dinner the previous night. When she'd texted back that she had plans, he hadn't responded and she'd been too nervous to suggest an alternate time to get together.

She imagined him having second, third and fourth thoughts about their arrangement, especially after spending what to him must have been a boring night in his hotel room. Falling asleep after watching movies together—talk about a wasted moment. She figured she'd never get the chance for a do-over.

Maddie and Zach had flown to Cabo for a short mini-honeymoon. Neither of them was willing to leave the Austin branch for too long when business was picking up so much. Christine had no doubt they trusted her to run the internal side of things at the office, and Valene had postponed her return to Houston until they got back. Even Kenneth was pitching in despite his recent retirement. But she still appreciated their commitment and understood their mutual dedication to Fortunado Real Estate was part of what made them such a perfect couple.

Christine might have had a crush on Gavin for years, but what did they really have in common? She loved her work and knew he enjoyed his law career, but that was where the similarities ended. He was a high-powered corporate attorney who worked with big-name clients, and she was more comfortable behind the scenes, keeping everyone in the office organized and on track. She led a quiet life, and he was always off on some new adventure during his downtime.

It had pained her to say no to his dinner invitation last night, even if she was sure he was offering because they needed to confirm their stories before revealing their relationship to his family. But since she'd moved back to Austin, her mother had insisted she come to dinner every Sunday, sitting down to a meal with her parents and sister. And if she needed a physical reminder of why she and Gavin weren't a great match, her sister, Aimee, was more than happy to provide it.

Aimee was a talented hairstylist but had trouble holding down a job, bouncing from salon to salon so often that only her most loyal clients stayed with her. Still, she always made wherever she landed sound like the most exciting place on the planet to work. Her sister relished every opportunity to point out what a boring life Christine led and how old-fashioned it was to stick with the same company for a decade. Last night had been no exception. The owner of Aimee's most recent salon had invited her to go to the Bahamas for a weekend. Although the guy sounded like a total creep to Christine, her sister insisted Christine was just too much of a stick-in-the-mud to appreciate an opportunity for adventure.

Someone knocked again, more insistently this time, and Christine realized she'd been lost in her own thoughts.

"Come in," she called, pasting the polite smile on her face she knew any of her coworkers would expect to see.

Her jaw dropped when Gavin walked into her small office, and it felt like all the air in the room had been sucked out the moment he entered.

She shut her mouth and attempted to draw a breath but ended up choking and sputtering, reaching for the glass of water next to her computer. Her hand tipped it and water spilled across her desk.

With a yelp-cough, she jumped up, at least having enough sense to pluck the stack of contracts she'd been inputting before they were soaked through. She rushed to the utility closet in the corner of the office and grabbed a roll of paper towels, turning back to find Gavin lifting her wireless keyboard and phone out of the water.

"What a mess," she muttered then quickly cleaned up the spilled water, still coughing every few seconds.

She could feel her face flaming with embarrassment. Only when she'd dumped the last of the wet paper towels in the trash can next to her desk did she look up at Gavin.

"You're cute when you're flustered," he said, tossing the paper towels he'd used to dry the bottom of the keyboard and her cell phone case into the trash.

She gave a small laugh, which turned into a cough.

"Going to make it?" he asked, arching one thick brow.

"I'm fine," she whispered and took the phone and keyboard from him. "Mortified, but fine. Coordination isn't always my thing."

He winked, and her stomach felt like it had taken the first plunge on a roller-coaster ride. "Good to know."

"I didn't expect to see you here." She busied herself with rearranging the items on her desk, trying to ignore how close Gavin stood and how her body reacted to him.

"I'm meeting with my dad in—" he checked his watch "—five minutes."

"Oh." Disappointment washed through her at the knowledge that he hadn't stopped by to see her. Of course, why would he stop by for her when he could easily—

"Are you free for lunch after?"

Her mouth dropped open again and she pressed it shut. "Mmmhrmrh."

One side of his mouth quirked. "Is that a yes?"

"Yes," she breathed and was rewarded with a full grin.

It was like being struck with a two-by-four. She felt dazed, like she'd held her breath too long and was getting light-headed from the sensation.

Okay, maybe she was light-headed. *Breathe. Remember to breathe.*

"I'd like to speak to my dad about us," Gavin continued like she wasn't having an internal freak-out inches away from him. "If that's okay with you?"

"Us?" she squeaked.

"Our relationship."

"Our *fake* relationship," she clarified.

"Yes, well…" He massaged a hand along the back of his neck, and she wondered if she wasn't the only one trying to hide her nerves. "What would you think about a pretend engagement?"

Christine choked out shocked laugh. "Excuse me?"

"I…uh…my sisters… There was a little…uh…misunderstanding at breakfast the morning after the wedding."

"A misunderstanding that ended up with us engaged?" she asked, pressing her palms to her cheeks, which felt like they were on fire.

"It's not much different than dating."

The sound that came from her throat sounded like the creaking of the old screen door at her parents' house.

"I'm sorry, Christine." He started to reach for her then rubbed his neck again. "I should have said something, but they were so happy about it. I thought an engagement might be...uh...fun."

"Fun," she repeated. She started to shake her head, but Gavin was looking at her with so much hope that she couldn't stand to disappoint him. It was what she told herself but only part of the truth. She also didn't want her time with Gavin—pretend or not—to end. "Sure. It could be fun."

"Really?"

She smiled when Gavin's voice cracked on the word like a teenage boy.

"Yes," she confirmed and when he grinned, she had to believe she'd made the right decision. "So you're going to tell your dad we're engaged?"

He nodded. "Before I speak with him, I wanted to make sure you hadn't changed your mind about the arrangement and now the engagement. When you blew me off last night, I wondered if—"

"I have Sunday dinner at my parents' every week," she interrupted. "The only thing that could get me out of it is a trip to the emergency room, and there's a good chance my mom would pack up the food and bring it to the hospital. She has this notion that eating a meal together will suddenly make the four of us into a happy family after almost three decades."

"That's great," Gavin murmured then shook his head at her frown. "I'm sorry. I don't mean it's great for you. It's not great that you have to deal with that, but I thought you were blowing me off."

She inclined her head as soft pink tinged his cheeks. Was Gavin Fortunado blushing?

"I wouldn't blow you off," she whispered, her voice sounding husky to her own ears. "Ever."

He drew in a breath like her words meant something to him. As if she meant something to him, which was impossible because before Saturday night they hadn't done much more than speak in passing throughout the past ten years.

Except he remembered the first time they'd met. He'd told her she'd helped convince him he could make it to law school.

Something tiny and tentative unfurled in Christine's heart. It felt a lot like hope. Possibility. Her chance for something more.

The same unfamiliar streak of boldness that had prompted her to act at the reception flashed through her again. She stepped forward, placed her hands on his broad shoulders, rose up on her tiptoes and then kissed him.

Their mouths melded together for a few seconds. She wouldn't allow it to go any further, not in her office. Even though the door was closed, several of her coworkers would feel no hesitation about knocking and walking right in.

When she started to pull away, Gavin gripped her hips with his big hands and squeezed. The touch reverberated through her body, sending shock waves of desire pulsing through her.

She moaned and then felt him smile against her lips. "I can't wait for lunch," he said, the rough timbre of his voice tickling her senses. "Suddenly, I'm starving."

Then he let her go, and she had to place a hand on the corner of her desk to steady herself.

Good gravy, the man could kiss.

"I'll meet you at the reception desk in twenty minutes?" he asked over his shoulder.

"Sure." She held up a hand to wave then pulled it to her side. What kind of a ninny would she be to wave to him like he was a knight heading to battle? He was going to talk to his father, and Kenneth Fortunado loved each of his six children and wanted their happiness above anything.

She only hoped Gavin's happiness wouldn't come at the expense of her heart.

"You look chipper today."

Gavin tried to wipe the grin off his face as he entered Maddie's office, which was currently occupied by their father. Kenneth sat behind the computer, a pair of wire-framed reading glasses perched on his nose. Although he'd officially retired last year, Kenneth was still in his prime and Gavin knew his dad was plenty capable of holding down the fort until Maddie and Zach returned.

One of the things Gavin missed most about living in Texas was spending time with his family. Despite occasionally wishing he were an only child, he truly loved being part of the Fortunado brood. His childhood had been idyllic, tons of love and laughter provided by the close bond his mother had fostered among all the siblings.

"It was nice to have everyone together for the wedding." He dropped into the chair across from the desk. "I also like seeing you in your natural habitat. Do you miss the daily grind of the agency?"

Kenneth smiled and shook his head. "I'm having a great time cheering on Maddie and Zach from the sidelines. It was one of my more genius moves to arrange for them to work together last year."

"Among a lifetime of genius moves," Gavin murmured with an exaggerated eye roll.

"Smart boy." His father steepled his fingers. "The smartest one remains marrying your mother. We're thrilled that Maddie's found so much happiness with Zach. It's what we want for each of our children." He raised a brow. "If you know what I mean?"

"As a matter of fact..." Gavin's stomach knotted even though his father had given him the perfect opening to discuss his relationship with Christine. He hadn't felt this nervous since he'd sat before his dad and explained that he was taking a position with a firm in Denver instead of the offer from one of his father's friends at a prominent Houston law firm. "I'm dating someone and thought—"

"That's wonderful, son." Kenneth's wide smile made guilt seep through Gavin's veins like poison. "Is it serious? Why didn't you bring her to the wedding?"

"Actually, it's serious and she was at the wedding." Gavin cleared his throat. "We've been keeping things private because she was worried about—"

"Worried?" Kenneth interrupted.

"About you," Gavin said softly. "What you'd think of our relationship."

"Why would I have a problem if she makes you happy?" He leaned forward, resting his elbows on the desk, the gold band on the third finger of his left hand shining. "Does she make you happy?"

Gavin thought about Christine's sweet smile and the way she looked at him like he was the only man in the world. "Yes," he murmured, almost more to himself than his father. "Christine makes me happy."

"Christine?" His father's expression went blank. "You're not talking about our Christine?"

"I am." Gavin drew in a deep breath as Kenneth frowned. "Although I wouldn't exactly say she belongs to the family."

"Would you say she belongs to you?"

Gavin thought about that then shook his head. "She's her own person. I like that about her." He held up a hand when his dad opened his mouth to speak. "But she's dedicated to you and to Fortunado Real Estate in general. Your approval of our relationship is important to her."

Kenneth inclined his head. "And you?"

"She's important to me," Gavin said immediately, surprised to find how much the statement resonated in his chest.

"Why haven't I heard about the two of you dating before now?"

"As I said, she wanted to keep things private at first to ensure it didn't impact her working relationship with anyone here."

"What's changed?"

Gavin fought the urge to grimace. It felt vaguely like facing a stiff cross-examination. "It's more than just dating, Dad. Christine and I are engaged."

"To be married?" his father asked, thick brows rising.

"That's the plan, and I'd like your support. You know I'm going to be spending the next few weeks in Austin. I don't want to have to hide anything or skulk around playing cloak and dagger if I want to see her. Plus, Schuyler is insisting Christine come to the reunion she's planning."

"I'm glad you talked to me," Kenneth said with a nod. "I don't like secrets."

Gavin chuckled. "Like discovering we're part of the famous Fortune family?"

"Some things even I can't control," his father admitted,

almost reluctantly. "But you don't have to hide a relationship from us, son. I've told you we want your happiness above all."

Gavin didn't bother to explain how unhappy it made him that his family took such an interest in his love life. That feeling as though he were under the microscope had forced him into this arrangement with Christine in the first place.

But that wouldn't do any good at this point. Besides, he wasn't ready to end things before they even really got started. Pretending to be in love with and engaged to Christine might be a farce, but he liked her and knew they'd have a great time together over the next few weeks until he returned to Denver.

"Does that mean you approve?"

"You don't need my approval." His father smiled. "But of course I'm happy for you. Your mother will be, as well. You know how much we like Christine. Frankly, she's quite a step up in quality from the women you normally date."

Gavin rolled his eyes. "Schuyler said almost the same thing. I date decent women."

"Not in the same league as Christine."

"My girlfriends have been in Colorado," Gavin protested. "You haven't met most of them."

"Connor keeps us updated. He's ridiculously good with details."

"Connor should learn to keep his mouth shut. I'm not even sure he knows many of the women I've dated, so I'm not sure what makes him such an expert."

"He cares about you. We all do."

"I know."

"We care about Christine, too. Take care of her, Gavin. You aren't known for your staying power in relationships."

Ouch.

"Well, I'm committed to Christine now." Gavin smiled

even as another wave of guilt crested inside him. His dad was right. Gavin didn't do long-term. It hadn't been a conscious decision, but he certainly had a habit of dating women who felt the same way about no-strings-attached as he did.

Christine was different. He knew that, even though their relationship was pretend. It was crucial he make sure they both remained on the same page so that she didn't get hurt.

"I'm glad to see it," his dad told him with a wide smile. "Your mom and I want you to be happy."

"Thanks, Dad. I *am* happy." He made a show of checking the Rolex that encircled his wrist. "I also need to get going. Christine and I are going to lunch."

"Enjoy," his dad answered, sounding pleased. "Let's plan a dinner with the two of you and your mom and me. I'm sure she'd be happy to come up from Houston to celebrate your engagement."

"Sure." Gavin walked toward the door. "I'll talk to Christine and we'll figure out a night that works."

"I'm really happy for you," Kenneth said, and Gavin left the office, trying to ignore the acid that felt like it was burning a hole in his stomach.

Chapter 6

Christine felt her smile falter as Gavin approached the reception area. He'd been sweet and flirty in her office earlier but now looked like a black cloud was following him. Had the conversation with his father gone badly? Was Kenneth angry that she and Gavin were supposedly dating?

"Lord, he's hot," came the appreciative whisper from behind Christine.

She looked over her shoulder toward Megan, the agency's young receptionist, who was staring at Gavin like he was the best thing on the menu at an all-you-can-eat buffet. "Um...yeah."

"Ready?"

She turned back to Gavin. "Sure. Is everything okay?"

"Fine," he snapped then closed his eyes for a moment. When he opened them again, the cloud had disappeared and a smile played at the corner of his mouth. He leaned in and kissed her cheek. "Don't mind me."

She heard Megan's gasp and felt color flood her cheeks. With a simple buss to the cheek, Gavin had effectively outed them to the entire agency. She knew that by the time they got back from lunch, everyone would know.

Maybe she'd order a drink with her meal. If only it was that easy.

"Be back in an hour," she said to the receptionist, purposely avoiding eye contact with the pretty brunette.

"I'll be waiting," came the reply. "We'll have a lot to talk about."

A drink couldn't hurt.

She and Gavin walked out into the hazy sun of the January afternoon, and she tightened the belt on her Burberry knockoff trench coat. She earned a decent salary with the agency but most of it went toward the monthly mortgage on her condo. She liked having a place to call her own more than she needed designer clothes.

"There's a new barbecue place a couple of blocks from here," she offered.

He stopped, inclined his head as if studying her. "I love barbecue."

Christine willed herself not to blush again. She wasn't about to admit she knew his taste in food from his sisters and from listening to stories of their family vacations over the years. That would make her seem like a total creeper.

"Me, too," she answered and started down the sidewalk in the direction of the popular restaurant.

Gavin fell into step beside her but didn't say anything more. When they stopped at a crosswalk, the silence became too much.

"Is your dad angry?" she asked, crossing her arms over her chest. "Does he hate the idea of the two of us? We don't have to do this. I mean, if it's—"

He reached out a finger and pressed it to her lips, effectively silencing her. She could barely remember to breathe when he touched her, let alone speak. "I'm sorry I've been quiet," he told her. "My dad is happy about our relationship."

The light changed and they began walking again. "Is there another problem?" she asked, glancing at him out of the corner of her eye.

"Everything's fine." He flashed a smile that didn't come anywhere near to his eyes.

Christine sighed. What now? Did she push him for the truth or let it slide? As much as she'd admired Gavin from afar for so many years, she didn't truly know him well. For all she knew, he had a toothache or had argued with his father about the Texans' chances in the playoffs this year.

They arrived at the restaurant, and he held the door open for her. She walked to the hostess stand and tried not to grimace as the woman looked between Christine and Gavin then did a double-take when he placed a hand on Christine's back, as though she couldn't imagine a man like him would be out with someone like her.

Sadly, Christine didn't blame the woman.

They followed the hostess to a table near the back of the crowded restaurant. Austin had plenty of barbecue joints but this was her favorite.

Christine made a show of studying the menu, almost disappointed when the waitress quickly took their orders.

She slipped the paper wrapper from her straw and tied it in a knot. As usual with this little ritual, the knot held when she made it but tore as she tightened it, and she sighed as the paper ripped.

When she glanced up, Gavin was smiling at her. "What's that about?"

She scrunched up her nose. "You never played the straw wrapper game?" She laughed when he frowned. "If the knot rips, someone is thinking about you. If not, you're out of luck."

"Yours tore off center," he pointed out.

"It always does."

"I'm thinking about you."

"You're sitting across from me," she said with a laugh.

"I thought about you all day yesterday," he continued. "About how much fun I had on Saturday night, especially the part where you curled against me in your sleep."

Her breath caught in her throat. "I don't remember that."

"You were asleep," he whispered and his voice took on a sexy edge.

"What exactly happened with your dad?" she blurted, somehow unable to let the subject go. "You haven't done a great job of convincing me he approves." Gavin's expression went from flirty to subdued in an instant. Way to ruin a moment, she chided herself.

At that moment the waitress brought their food. Gavin picked up his glass of iced tea, gripping it so hard his knuckles turned white. "He doesn't want me to hurt you."

"Oh," Christine breathed, knowing if she said anything more her voice would reveal that she shared the same fear.

"I don't want to hurt you," Gavin said, and somehow the words sounded like a promise. "I'm not going to hurt you," he added, almost like he was reassuring himself as much as her.

"Gavin." She reached across the table and placed a hand over his. He released his death grip on the glass and she saw his shoulders relax slightly. "We both know what this is," she said, even though it already meant so much more to her. "You aren't going to hurt me."

He nodded as if bolstered by her confidence. "I like you, Christine."

Warmth spread through her body at the simple pronouncement. "I like you, too."

"Do you think we could focus on that part?" He curled his big hand around her fingers. "We're friends who are getting to know each other better over these next few weeks. It doesn't have to be forced. I'm excited to hang out with you."

She swallowed. "You are?"

"Don't look so surprised," he said with a smile. "You're way more fun than you realize."

She laughed. "That might be the nicest thing anyone has ever said to me. I have a reputation for being organized, not fun."

"Then we'll work on your reputation."

She liked the sound of that.

"Is there anything else you need?"

Christine yanked away her hand and glanced up at the hostess, who'd returned to the table in place of the waitress who had taken their order.

The raven-haired beauty was looking directly at Gavin as if he was the only one sitting at the table. "We're fine," he answered with a polite smile.

"Are you new to Austin?" the woman asked. "I haven't seen you in here before and I would have noticed."

Christine frowned as she picked up her chicken sandwich and took a bite. She couldn't believe the woman was flirting with Gavin right in front of her. Not that she could blame her. It was still almost difficult to look him in the eye some of the time. His gaze on her made her feel like her skin was on fire.

The hostess hooked two fingers in the waistband of her low-slung jeans, revealing the top edge of some kind of tattoo on her hip. She looked like she knew plenty about adventure and probably would have been friends with Christine's sister during high school. Certainly a woman who wouldn't have noticed Christine, unless she'd needed tutoring.

"I'm here for work," Gavin said, letting a bit of Texas drawl seep into his voice. "Originally from Houston."

"I could show you around," the woman offered with a sexy little half smile.

Christine figured if she tried that move she'd look like she was trying to hide something in her teeth.

Gavin returned the smile but gestured toward Christine. "I think we've got it covered."

The hostess's eyes widened. "You two are together?" She wagged one perfectly manicured nail between the two of them. "I thought she was your secretary."

"My fiancée," Gavin clarified without hesitation.

Christine drained her iced tea and held the glass out to the woman. "Could I get a refill?"

"Uh…sure." The woman took the glass and turned from the table.

"That was unexpected," Gavin murmured, digging into his own lunch.

Christine snorted. "You don't fool me. I bet women hit on you *all* the time."

"Not all the time."

She rolled her eyes. "Just on days that end in *y*?"

He grinned. "Something like that."

The hostess returned with the iced tea, placing the glass and a fresh straw on the table without a word and then walked away again.

Christine picked up the straw and pointed it at Gavin. "Why don't you have a girlfriend?"

"I was waiting for you," he said, making her laugh again.

"That's a bad line, even coming from your pretty lips."

He dabbed at one corner of his mouth with the napkin. "I've never been called pretty before. It suits me, I think."

"It's no wonder you became an attorney. You're such a smooth talker."

"I can't tell if that's a compliment or a criticism."

"An observation." She leaned in and repeated, "So why don't you have a girlfriend?"

He sighed. "You sound like one of my sisters."

"Which is not an answer to the question," she pointed out.

He studied her for a few long moments. "You do understand that I'm used to using my pretty mouth and fancy words to deflect questions I don't want to answer."

"I do."

"You're not going to let me get away with that?"

"I'm not," she said quietly. It might be the wrong thing to say. For all of Gavin's ease with people, she could tell he was a private man at heart. But she wanted to know that side of him, the part behind the handsome mask. Christine might not be the most adventurous or exciting person, but she knew how to be a good friend. She wanted to be Gavin's friend.

The waitress came to clear their plates, and Gavin gave her his credit card.

"Thank you for lunch," Christine said when the woman left again.

"My pleasure."

"Tell me about you and the lack of a girlfriend. Are you having trouble finding someone you connect with in Denver?"

He tapped a finger on his leather wallet. "I'm thirty years old," he said after a moment.

"Yes," she agreed. "Me, too. What does that have to do with dating?"

"At some point in the past couple of years, it changed. Expectations changed."

"Women got serious?"

"You could say that," he admitted. "Most of my friends got married. They settled down and bought real houses. Houses with yards in neighborhoods where you string up Christmas lights and build swing sets. Adult houses."

There was a thin note of panic in his voice, and she wasn't sure whether to smile or roll her eyes again. "You're not exactly a 'failure to launch' type of guy."

"Being good at my job versus good as a husband and possibly a father are different things."

The waitress brought the bill, and after Gavin signed the receipt, they headed back toward the agency. A few clouds hung in the sky, and she was glad for her jacket to protect her against the brisk breeze blowing through downtown. Gavin didn't seem to notice the cool air, although that could be because he was used to winter in Colorado.

"You come from an amazing family," she told him.

He looked down and flashed a lopsided smile. "That's kind of the point. My dad is fantastic and my parents' marriage is as strong as ever. He always found time for each of his kids as well as my mom, despite how hard he worked. I know how to be an attorney, but that's nothing compared to being a husband or father. I don't know that I'm ready. I'm not sure I'll ever be ready. How could I compare to my father?" She noticed his hand clenched and unclenched at his side, a nervous gesture that was out of character for him.

This was it, Christine realized. This was Gavin behind the mask.

She reached out and took his hand in hers. "It's not a competition. Your parents want you to be happy, however that looks for you."

"I *am* happy," he insisted, squeezing her fingers. "I keep trying to tell them. I think maybe I wasn't cut out for more than what my life is now. I don't know how to admit that to anyone in my family. What if I don't have it in me to give more?"

At that moment a man burst from the crowd walking toward them, on his phone and clearly in a hurry, jostling people on either side. Before Christine could react, Gavin put an arm around her shoulder, tucked her to his side and shifted so that the man bumped into him instead of her.

Gavin didn't break stride or make an issue of it. He simply ensured that she wasn't bothered as he maneuvered them through the groups of working folks headed for lunch.

"You have plenty to give," she said, tipping up her head to look at the strong line of his jaw. She wanted to add that he just needed to meet the right woman. And maybe she could be that woman, but she didn't say those things because she couldn't bear to let herself believe they might be true. Despite his assurance, Christine understood that the only way to ensure Gavin wouldn't hurt her would be to not open her heart to him. A challenge, given how much she already felt.

They were almost to the agency office, so she started to pull away. Gavin didn't release his hold on her. He drew her into a quiet alcove between the buildings, turning to face her.

"When you say that, I almost believe it," he whispered. "I *want* to believe it."

"It's true."

She rose up on tiptoe to kiss his cheek, but he captured her mouth with his, his lips firm and smooth as they grazed over hers.

Her insides danced, electric sparks erupting along her spine. His tongue traced the seam of her lips and she opened for him, winding her hands around his neck and pressing closer.

Everything around her melted away as he deepened the kiss. He made it too easy to forget that the only reason they were together was to appease his family. Christine hated that he had any question as to whether he could handle a real commitment. Even if their time together was temporary, at least she could spend the next few weeks proving that he was capable of opening himself to someone.

But right now all she wanted was to lose herself in this moment. And when he groaned softly, it was everything. She'd done that to him. A low whistle from the street had her pulling away.

"I can't... We shouldn't... This isn't the place."

He drew in an unsteady breath. "I'm sorry. You're right, of course. I just can't seem to control myself around you."

Now, *that* was definitely the nicest thing anyone had ever said to her. "I'm glad," she told him honestly, earning another smile. "But I do need to get back to work."

"Me, too." Then he leaned in and kissed her again. "When can I see you?"

"You're seeing me right now."

"A date," he clarified. "I want to spend time with you. We're friends. Remember?"

"Oh." She blinked. The way he was looking at her made her forget this was fake. "We could have dinner this week?"

"Perfect." He took her hand and led her back out into

the street, stopping at the door of the agency. "Tomorrow night?"

"Okay." She swallowed. He wanted to see her again so soon, and not just because it was part of the charade.

She took a step away. "I'll see you tomorrow, then."

He kissed her one more time then walked toward the black SUV parked at the curb.

Christine straightened the collar of her jacket and then entered the office, shocked to find Megan along with two of the female agents staring at her from the waiting area.

"Gavin Fortunado?" Molly, one of the agents, practically hissed. "You've been holding out on us, girl. We want all the details of how you landed a fine man like that."

"He is so not your type," Megan said, shaking her head.

"How do you know my type?" Christine couldn't help but ask.

"I heard you were into Bobby."

Christine shook her head. "Only in his dreams."

"I told you so," Jenna, the other agent, said.

"Seriously." Molly took a step forward. "How long has this been going on with Gavin?"

Oh, no. Once again, she'd been so caught up in enjoying Gavin's company that she'd forgotten to clarify the details of their supposed relationship.

"A while. We're actually…" She cleared her throat. "Engaged."

"Are you joking?" Molly demanded. "How did you pull it off?"

Jenna swatted her on the arm. "You can't ask someone that."

"Come on, that man should be with a supermodel." She gestured toward Christine. "No offense. You're pretty but he's ah-may-zing."

"I know," Christine agreed immediately. She took a step forward. "I'll let you in on a little secret."

All three women leaned forward slightly.

"The way he looks isn't even the best part about him."

"Whatever," Megan said. "I'm not sure I'd be able to notice anything else."

Christine shrugged. "Then you'd be missing out."

There was a deep throat-clear, and all four of them turned to see Kenneth standing at the edge of the hallway. "Megan, could you pull our files on the Rosedale neighborhood? I want to compare comps for one of Maddie's clients looking at a house on Oakmont Blvd."

"Right away, Mr. Fortunado." The young woman scurried around to her computer.

"I'm meeting a client out in East Oak Hill," Jenna said quickly.

"I'm heading to an association meeting," Molly offered.

Christine noticed that none of them made eye contact with Kenneth. "Will you send me the listing information for the Hyde Park property when you get back?" she asked Jenna.

"Sure thing," the woman answered, her voice a nervous squeak.

Christine smiled as she approached Gavin's father and they walked toward her office together. "They're terrified of you," she said, patting his arm. "No one in Austin realizes you're just a big teddy bear on the inside."

He let out a low laugh. "Don't tell them."

"It's our secret," she agreed, turning into her office across the hall from the one Kenneth occupied this week.

"Speaking of secrets," he said in his deep baritone.

She schooled her features then turned. "Gavin spoke to you."

"You know you're already like one of my own daughters. Both Barbara and I feel that way. I'm thrilled that you'll be officially joining the family."

Emotion clogged Christine's throat as she nodded. Over the past decade working for Kenneth, she'd come to feel almost closer to him than she did her own dad. He never judged her for the things she wasn't but appreciated her for who she was.

"You never have to hide anything from me. I want you to be happy."

"Gavin makes me happy," she said, appreciating that she could give him a response that wasn't a lie. She suddenly had a clearer understanding of Gavin's mood earlier. It felt wrong to deceive Kenneth and the rest of the Fortunados.

At the wedding she'd acted impulsively, wanting to live out one of her secret fantasies and save Gavin from Schuyler's matchmaking in the process. But these weren't strangers whom she'd walk away from when Gavin returned to Denver and their relationship ended.

"I'm glad," Kenneth told her. "Barbara will be, too."

"I want you to know I'm still committed to the agency," she said quickly. "That won't change."

"I know." Kenneth frowned, his thick brows lowering over eyes that reminded her of Gavin. "I trust you implicitly, Christine. You just concentrate on staying happy, and I sure hope my son continues to be a part of that."

"He will," she whispered, somehow knowing Gavin would be the key to both her happiness and her heartbreak.

Chapter 7

Gavin lifted his hand to knock on the door of Christine's condo the following evening, only to have it swing open.

"I can't go out with you," she whispered, her face pale and eyes wide.

He tightened his grip on the bouquet of roses he held. "Why? What's wrong?"

"It's Diana. She's sick." She took a step back, and he stepped into the condo. It was decorated in neutral colors but with colorful posters and pillows that gave it a homey look. Quite a bit different from the contemporary furnishings and unadorned walls of his loft in downtown Denver.

"Is Diana your daughter?" How had he missed the fact that Christine had a kid?

She gave him a funny look. "She's my dog."

He heard a low whine from the back of the condo, and Christine turned and started down the hall. She glanced over her shoulder at him. "I'm sorry. I'll call you tomorrow, okay? I've got to get her to the vet. They're staying open for me."

It was clearly a dismissal but Gavin wasn't about to walk away when she was so upset. He shut the front door and followed her into the kitchen, finding her kneeling next to a medium-size black lab that was on its side on the hardwood floor.

The dog looked up when he entered, gave a halfhearted bark then lowered her head to the floor again.

"What happened?"

"I'm not sure," Christine said, trying unsuccessfully to coax the dog to her feet. "Come on, Di. You can do it."

"I'll lift her," Gavin offered.

"She sheds," Christine told him, her voice hollow.

"It's fine. What kind of car do you have?"

"A Prius." She ran a trembling hand over the dog's head. "Normally, Di rides shotgun."

"We'll take mine. She'll be more comfortable in the cargo area. Do you have an extra blanket?" Gavin moved forward and knelt on the other side of the animal. "Hey, girl. Wanna go for a ride?" The dog's tail thumped as he pet her soft fur.

"You don't have to do this," Christine protested.

"I'm not leaving you."

He met her worried gaze, hating the panic in her eyes. "She's going to be okay," he said quietly, even though it was a promise he had no business making. But he would have told Christine anything at the moment to make her feel better.

She nodded and talked softly to the dog as Gavin scooped the lab into his arms. He straightened and started for the front door as Christine grabbed a blanket from the back of the sofa.

They got the dog into the back of his Audi SUV, and Christine told him which way to drive to get to the vet's office. Other than giving directions, she didn't speak, and he wasn't sure what else to say. He liked dogs well enough but couldn't begin to guess what had made hers sick. He reached across the console and took Christine's hand, wanting to offer whatever reassurance he could.

The vet's office was only a ten-minute drive from her place, and as she'd mentioned, the staff was waiting for the dog. The doctor, a gray-haired man in his midfifties, greeted both Christine and Diana by name as he instructed Gavin to follow him to the back of the clinic. Gavin placed Diana on one of the exam tables then returned to the waiting room and sat down next to Christine.

"I'm sorry," she whispered when they were alone. "This isn't your problem and—"

"I want to be here," he told her, lacing their fingers together. "I want to know you're okay. Tell me about Diana."

A hint of a smile curled her lips. "I adopted her from a shelter in Houston when she was only four months old. It was right after I started working for your dad. I'd graduated college and moved into my first apartment on my own so I wanted a dog for protection."

"How did she get the name Diana?"

"The shelter called her Princess. She'd been found as a stray. They don't know what happened to her mom or any other puppies from the litter. So I changed her name to Princess Diana."

He chuckled. "That's a funny name for a dog."

"Yeah," she agreed. "I might have entertained some girlish fantasies about my own Prince Charming back in the day. But despite the name, Di is so special. She was a holy terror when she was younger. Chewed everything she could get her teeth on. But it was love at first sight. We went for a walk tonight after work and she seemed fine. When I got out of the shower, she was on the floor." Her voice broke and she swiped at her cheeks. "I can't lose her. I don't understand what happened. I took her to the dog park after work, and she was acting a little out of it when we got home, almost like she was drunk. Then she settled down so I thought she was fine. Why didn't I realize something was wrong?"

"They'll figure it out," he assured her, wrapping an arm around her shoulder and pulling her close.

Normally, Gavin didn't do well with tears from women. Growing up in a house with three sisters, he'd seen plenty of crying in his day, but as an adult he steered clear of emotional scenes. Yet he couldn't imagine a place he'd rather be at the moment than at Christine's side.

She rested her head on his shoulder and they waited. Trying to distract her, he kept up a litany of questions about the dog, prompting her to share many of Princess Di's adventures over the years. Her love for the dog was evident as she spoke, and he hoped with everything inside him that the dog would recover.

The vet came out into the waiting room a few minutes later, studying a chart as he entered.

"How is she?" Christine leaned forward, clutching her hands tight in front of her.

"She's showing signs of poisoning, although I can't narrow down what could have caused it at this point. We've given her activated charcoal and IV fluids. You said on the phone she hadn't gotten into anything hazardous?"

Christine shook her head. "Unless it was something at the dog park that I didn't see. I've heard stories of dogs getting sick there recently but I didn't pay much attention."

The vet frowned. "It's possible, I suppose. Keep her on a leash for a while."

"So she'll be okay?"

The older man nodded. "We'd like to keep her here overnight. She should be ready to go home in the morning, assuming there are no complications."

"Can I see her?" Christine asked, her voice shaky.

"She's resting," the doctor answered gently. "It might be better if you wait until the morning. It's a good thing you got her here as quickly as you did."

Gavin frowned as Christine nodded. He could tell she was fighting back another round of tears.

They left the office, Christine's features a mask of pain. "I let this happen," she whispered as she climbed into the Audi.

"It's not your fault," Gavin assured her, squeezing her hands. "If some idiot put poisoned food at the dog park, there's nothing you could have done to prevent it."

"I was visiting with people while she ran around with the other dogs. I wasn't watching closely enough."

Gavin pulled the seat belt across her and fastened it. She was in no shape to take care of anything at the moment. It was painful to see Christine, who was always so quietly competent and capable, at a loss in this way.

"She's a dog at the park," he said, brushing the hair out of her face. "The whole point is to run around with other animals. The vet said she's going to be okay. It was smart that you brought her in for treatment right away."

She gave a small nod and leaned back against the seat, closing her eyes.

He got into the car and started back toward her house. They didn't speak during the short drive, but her breathing returned to normal and she seemed slightly calmer by the time he parked at the curb.

"Thank you," she said quietly, unbuckling her seat belt then turning to face him. "I'm sorry about the date." She shrugged. "Maybe we can take a rain check for later this week?"

"You aren't getting rid of me that easily." He turned off the SUV. "We can order pizza or whatever you want as takeout."

By the time he came around the front of the Audi, Christine was on the sidewalk. "I'm not great company tonight."

"Okay."

She threw up her hands. "Seriously, Gavin. You were such a huge help, but I'll be fine."

"*Seriously*, Christine." He reached out and brushed his thumb along the track of a tear that had dried on her cheek. "I wanted to hang out with you tonight. I still do. At least let me keep you company, since you're having a rough time. We don't even have to talk. Let's just eat and watch a movie."

"This isn't the night you planned."

"I planned to be with you," he answered simply and saw her draw in a sharp breath. "Let me stay."

She studied him for so long he felt himself wanting to fidget, but she finally nodded. "There's a pizza place around the corner. I have a menu inside."

"Pizza sounds great," he said, and taking her hand, they walked toward her condo.

By the time Christine finished her third piece of pizza, she felt almost human again. Maybe she should be embarrassed about her attachment to Princess Diana, but the dog had been a faithful companion and friend for ten years.

She'd been a source of unconditional love and had seen Christine through several lousy boyfriends and always made her feel better about the strained relationship she had with her family. Everyone loved Di, even her unemotional father.

"She's going to be fine." Gavin repeated his words from earlier, as if reading her mind. She still couldn't believe how readily he'd pitched in to help with her dog and then comfort her. Sure, she could have managed, but it had been nice for once to feel like she wasn't alone.

"I know," she answered. "I just miss her. Other than when I'm away she's always with me at night." She thunked her palm against her forehead. "That sounds pathetically like my dog and I are codependent."

He flashed a grin. "Dogs are great. My roommate in college had a husky, and I loved hanging on the couch with that furry beast."

"You don't have any pets?" she asked, taking a sip from her second beer of the night.

"Nah. I like animals but I travel a decent amount. It doesn't seem fair."

"You could get a goldfish."

"I'll keep that in mind," he told her with a chuckle.

They cleaned up the dishes, empty beer bottles and the pizza box, and then moved to the sofa in her family room. "Are you sure you're okay with a boring night of television?"

"Being with you isn't boring," Gavin answered and the sincerity in his tone made her heart skip a beat. He sat close to her on the couch, and it felt natural to cuddle into him as they watched an action flick playing on one of the cable channels.

"Can I ask you a question?" His voice was a soft rumble against the top of her head.

"Sure."

"Why don't you have a boyfriend?"

She tried to stay relaxed but felt her body stiffen. Lifting her head from where it had been resting on his shoulder, she scooted away. "I haven't met the right guy," she answered, hoping that would be enough.

"I remember saying the exact same thing to you," he told her, raising a brow. "You didn't let me get away with it."

"But you're much kinder than me," she said hopefully.

He laughed. "Try again. When was the last time you were in a serious relationship?"

"I dated a guy in Houston for about two years, but we broke up before I moved back to Austin."

He whistled softly. "Two years is a long time."

She shrugged.

"What went wrong?"

"Well…" She took a deep breath and thought about how to answer that question. "He wanted a schedule for…um… when we'd be together."

"When you'd go out?"

"When we'd *be* together." Color rushed to her cheeks. "In the biblical sense."

Gavin's eyes widened, and Christine wished for the ground to open up and swallow her whole. Why hadn't she just stuck to a vague version of the truth? They'd grown apart or wanted different things in life.

"He was a math teacher at a local community college, so logic and order were important to him. He created algorithms for our relationship and part of that was a schedule for the optimal timing of…you know."

"I know." Gavin nodded then quickly shook his head. "But I'm having trouble believing you."

"Maybe I shouldn't have made such a big deal about it," she said, echoing what her mother had said when Christine admitted to her the reason for the breakup. "I'm not exactly known to be adventurous. I've eaten the same type of cereal every day for breakfast for as long as I can remember. I'm not like you. My adventurous spirit is almost nonexistent. But that was too structured, even for me."

"Who says you aren't adventurous?" Gavin demanded softly.

She huffed out a harsh laugh. "No one needs to say it. Everyone knows it."

"I don't."

"You will," she countered. "You go heli-skiing and rock climbing and scuba diving." She held up a hand and ticked off their differences. "I'm scared of heights and speed and I can barely doggy paddle."

"There are other adventures you could have."

She wrapped her arms around her stomach and turned toward the television, hating the direction this conversation had taken. "At the end of the day, I'm a coward."

"I don't believe that."

"You're watching a boring movie with me and have dog fur stuck to your sweater." She rolled her eyes. "What's a typical date like for you in Denver?"

"Pretty similar," he said, deadpan. "Although sometimes I go for a crazy cat lady."

"I wish I knew how to let go and be wild."

Gavin leaned closer. "Do you have any memory of planting a mega kiss on me in front of my sister Saturday night?"

"Yes," she breathed.

He tipped up her chin and brushed his lips across hers. "That was not the work of a coward."

"It was different. I got swept away in the moment…in you."

"What's stopping you from doing that again? Every day, even?"

"Fear," she whispered, her eyes drifting closed.

She felt him smile against her mouth. "I love your honesty. There's no pretense with you."

"Too much talking," she told him, and deepened the kiss.

He let her take control, driving the intensity and pace. She pressed closer, and he lifted her into his arms. She ended up straddling him on the couch, loving the feel of his warmth beneath her. This was why it was a bad idea to schedule intimacy. The spontaneity of her connection with Gavin was one of the things that made it so special.

Well, that and the fact that it was Gavin under her. His big hands moved up her hips then under the hem of her sweatshirt, and she moaned when he skimmed his fingers along her spine.

"Lift your arms," he told her, and she automatically obeyed, too filled with need to bother being self-conscious. Her breasts were okay, she figured, and she'd at least had the forethought to wear a pretty bra tonight, preparing for all the possibilities before discovering Diana.

After tossing her shirt to the floor, he cupped her breasts in his hands then sighed with contentment. His thumbs grazed across her pebbled nipples, making heat pool low in her belly, but she wasn't going to be the only one half-undressed.

She pulled away from him and started undoing the buttons of his tailored shirt. He sat back against the couch cushions, seeming content to wait for her to finish.

When she did, he leaned forward so she could push the fabric off his shoulders. He shrugged out of the shirt then yanked the T-shirt he wore underneath over his head.

Christine thought for a moment that she'd died and gone to heaven. His body was absolute perfection. His shoulders were broad and his chest a wall of hard muscle. A smattering of golden hair covered his chest, and she splayed her hands over his bare skin, gratified when she felt his heart leap under her palm, and he groaned low in his throat.

He didn't try to hide that she affected him, even though she still had a hard time understanding why.

But now wasn't the time for second-guessing, not with his touch driving her crazy with need. He leaned in and trailed kisses against the base of her throat, his hands snaking around her waist, pulling her up so that she was lifted to her knees. His hot mouth covered her breast and she moaned, threading her fingers through his hair as his tongue circled her nipple through the thin fabric of her bra.

It was too much and not enough at the same time. Christine wanted more, and as she had the other night, she forgot about being afraid or judged. All that filled her mind and heart was this man and how much he made her feel. How much she wanted to experience with him.

Then her phone rang, the sound like a bucket of icy water splashed over her head. She scrambled off his lap and reached for the device, which sat on the end table next to the sofa.

"Hello," she answered and then cleared her throat.

The overnight vet tech was on the other end of the line. As Christine listened, tears pricked the backs of her eyes.

"That's great news. Thanks for calling."

She disconnected the call and turned to Gavin. "Di just

ate a bit of food and went out to do her business. She seems much better."

"She's definitely on the road to recovery."

"It sounds like it."

"I never doubted."

She nodded, then reached for her sweatshirt, suddenly self-conscious of sitting there in her bra.

"I should probably let you get some sleep tonight," Gavin told her, grabbing his T-shirt from the floor and shrugging into it.

Christine wanted to whimper in protest, both at him covering that amazing body and the thought of him leaving.

Of course, he was right. As much as she wanted to throw caution to the wind and rip all his clothes off, that would be the worst idea ever. The *best* worst idea ever.

"Thank you for tonight," she told him, standing and crossing her arms over her chest. "For dinner and your help and staying and…" Oh, Lord, she was babbling. She couldn't actually thank him for kissing her, could she?

"You aren't boring," he said as he buttoned his collared shirt. "Or a coward."

"Okay," she agreed, not wanting to talk about this. Hating that she'd admitted her fears to him. She had to remember to hold a piece of herself back; a lot of pieces, if she was smart. Because if she let Gavin all the way in, it would kill her when their time together ended.

"I had a great time being spontaneous with you," he said, his full lips curving at the corners.

That made her laugh. "Me, too."

"Will you text me tomorrow when you pick up Princess Di? I'd like to know how she's doing."

"I will," she said, and the fact that he cared about her sweet dog made her heart melt even more.

He took a step toward her, bent his head and kissed her. It felt like a promise of more, and Christine wanted all of it.

"Good night," he whispered. "Sweet dreams."

"Ya think?" she murmured without thinking, then blushed again as Gavin chuckled.

She locked the front door behind him, then straightened the condo and got ready for bed, missing Diana but comforted knowing the dog would be home tomorrow.

The happy glow Gavin had given her also gave a huge amount of comfort. And not just the crazy-good make-out session, although that had been...well...crazy-good. But his steady presence had made such a difference. Christine was used to doing things for herself. Even with past boyfriends, she'd remained steadfastly independent.

Her competence was her one inherent gift; at least that was how it felt growing up. She'd taken care of her family because that was the one way she knew to show love that they wouldn't refuse. It was unfamiliar to rely on someone else, and she would never have expected Gavin to be so easy to lean on for support. It made her goal of keeping her heart out of their arrangement even trickier.

But tonight she focused on how happy he made her. Wasn't she due for a little happiness?

Chapter 8

By Friday Gavin's mood was as dark as the clouds that billowed across the sky above Austin, a harbinger of an impending thunderstorm. As much as he appreciated the predominantly sunny days in Colorado, sometimes he missed a good soaking rainfall.

Although not when the skies opened up as he parked two blocks from the restaurant where he was meeting Schuyler and Everett for lunch.

He dashed from his car toward the diner situated across from the Austin Commons complex, trying to stay under the awnings of the buildings he passed. Still, he was more than a little wet when he burst through the door. Schuyler waved to him from a table near the front, and both she and Everett grinned as he slipped into his seat.

"Where's your umbrella?" Schulyer asked, making a show of dabbing her napkin on the lapel of his suit coat.

"I don't own one," he admitted, making a mental note to find a store that sold umbrellas after lunch today.

"You've lived in Denver too long," Everett told him.

Gavin rolled his eyes. "I have an ice scraper."

His brother chuckled. "Not going to do you much good around here."

"I'll dry off eventually." Now that he was seated, he glanced around the diner's homey interior, appreciating the retro vibe of the decor. "What made you choose this place for lunch?"

"Best pie in town," Schuyler told him.

Everett nodded. "Lila wants me to bring her home a piece of lemon meringue. And cherry. And pecan."

"Wow." Schuyler glanced up from her menu. "I don't remember Lila having such a huge appetite."

"She's…uh…" Everett threw a look to Gavin then drew in a deep breath. "I'll share them with her."

"You could probably eat a whole pie on your own," Schuyler answered absently.

As he had at Maddie's wedding, Gavin wondered again if Lila and Everett might be expecting. But if his brother wanted to keep the news private for a while longer, he'd respect that.

"How's Christine?" Schuyler asked after the waitress had taken their orders.

"Fine." The truth was he hadn't spoken to Christine since he'd left her house earlier in the week. She'd texted him an update and photos of Princess Di, who seemed to be recovering nicely. While the dog was undeniably cute, Gavin had hoped for a little more. It was strange to find himself in this role reversal. Normally with women, he was the one trying to take things slow.

He'd learned early on in his dating life that if he didn't

stay cognizant of managing expectations, he'd end up hurting women he cared about. So he'd established guidelines for himself around dating—how many times a week he could see a woman, the amount of phone calls or texts. Maybe it was cold, but he liked to think it had prevented heartache for his girlfriends and guilt for him.

Christine was different in so many ways. The romance might be pretend, despite their off-the-charts chemistry, but he liked spending time with her. An evening of a vet emergency, carryout pizza and an old movie had been the most fun he'd had in ages. He could be himself with her and wanted to make her see how much she underestimated herself. Gavin hoped their friendship would continue even after he returned to Denver, although the thought of moving into the "friend zone" and never kissing her again held no appeal whatsoever.

He'd expected her to call or reach out to him to let him know she wanted to see him again. That was how things usually went with women. He couldn't decide if Christine was playing it safe because of their arrangement or if she truly wasn't that interested in him outside of what was expected to maintain the ruse of being in love.

"Have you two thought any more about wedding plans now that you're in Austin?" Schuyler asked.

Gavin shrugged. "We're both busy."

"That's silly," she insisted. "Let me help."

"Schuyler could take care of everything," Everett added, none too helpfully in Gavin's opinion.

"Don't the two of you have enough of your own marital bliss to keep you occupied? How come everyone has so much time to worry about my love life?"

"We don't want you to mess it up," Schuyler said gently. "No one likes seeing you lonely."

Gavin felt the simple pronouncement like a sharp right to the jaw. "I'm not lonely. I have plenty of friends."

She shook her head then sipped at her water. "You have buddies to hang with and work colleagues. It's not the same."

Gavin darted a pleading glance at Everett. "Can you throw me a line here?"

"You have seemed at loose ends," Everett answered.

"Loose ends? How can you say that? I'm about to make partner."

Everett shrugged. "Having a good job isn't the same thing as having a good life."

"Coming from the man who was solely dedicated to his job until recently."

"Lila changed everything."

The waitress brought their food—a club sandwich for Schuyler and himself and a burger for Everett. As she placed the food in front of them, Gavin felt his frustration mount. This fake engagement with Christine was supposed to alleviate the pressure from his parents and siblings, not add to it. What would it take for them to get out of his business?

"I think it's great that the two of you are so happy," he said, forcing his tone to remain neutral. "Christine and I will start wedding plans when we're ready, but you have to trust that I can manage my own life. I'm not a kid who's going to make a stupid decision."

"Fair enough," Everett conceded, then took a big bite of his burger.

Schuyler looked less convinced. Despite the fact that she was one of the middle Fortunado siblings, she'd always been a caregiver for her brothers and sisters. Their mom found it amusing to watch Schuyler fuss like a mother hen, and Gavin knew she did it because she cared so much.

"You said you wanted to talk about the reunion," he told her.

She pointed a fry in his direction. "I'm going to let you change the subject because I love you. But know that we're all sticking our noses where they probably don't belong for the same reason. If you ever want to actually talk about your relationship with more than one-syllable answers to my questions, I'm here for you."

Gavin blew out a breath. Irritating as they could be, he loved his sisters and brothers with his whole heart. "I'll remember that. Thank you."

She smiled then popped the fry into her mouth. After she'd swallowed, she pulled out a pen and a small notebook from her purse. "I've confirmed with Nolan that his brothers and sisters will be there. They're flying in just for the party, so it will be a quick trip."

She flipped open the notebook. "The Paseo Fortunes aren't going to be able to make it because Grayson has some kind of rodeo award ceremony they're attending in Dallas. Nate promised they'd find another time to come to Austin to meet everyone."

"Lila heard that Gerald and the triplets' mom have rekindled their romance now that he's separated from Charlotte," Everett said between bites. "Obviously, it's a pretty big deal since Gerald and Charlotte were married for so many years. She can't be happy about losing him to his first love."

"Especially when she went to such great lengths to keep him from knowing about the triplets."

Gavin shook his head. When Schuyler first realized their connection to the famous Fortune clan, she'd traveled to the tiny town of Paseo, Texas, to talk to Nathan Fortune. Nate, along with his brothers Grayson and Jayden, were three of the illegitimate children of Gerald Fortune, who'd had a brief affair with their mother, Deborah, back when he'd been Jerome Fortune.

It was crazy to think that Jerome Fortune had been desperate enough to fake his own death and reemerge as Gerald Robinson as a way to escape his domineering father, Julius. And just as shocking to discover that their dad, Kenneth, was one of Julius's illegitimate sons, making them all Fortunes.

"Could you imagine Mom and Dad getting divorced at this point?" he asked his siblings, confident in his parents' love for each other.

"No," Schuyler answered immediately. "But I also couldn't imagine Mom trying to keep Dad from knowing he had three sons out in the world."

"Not just three sons," Gavin corrected. "Aren't there a bunch more illegitimate Fortune children out there?"

Everett nodded. "As far as the family knows, they've all been uncovered at this point. Apparently, Charlotte kept a secret dossier on each of them without Gerald's knowledge."

"It sounds like Gerald and Charlotte's marriage wasn't exactly perfect," Gavin said.

"Not at all," Schuyler agreed. "It still amazes me how open most of his legitimate kids have been about getting to know these half siblings. It's part of why I have such high hopes for the reunion. I really want all of us to feel like a family."

"Why is it important to you?" Gavin asked.

Schuyler was quiet for a moment before answering, "When I decided to infiltrate the Mendozas to get the goods on the Fortunes, I expected to be disappointed. Not only did I meet Carlo and fall in love, I also learned that the Fortune family is filled with a lot of decent people trying to make the best of difficult situations. I can't help but think that we have more in common with them than we might realize. Strength in numbers and all that."

Everett frowned. "As usual, it sounds like you've got everything figured out. Why do you need our help?"

"I'd like you to reach out to Gerald's sons. I know Ben and Keaton are willing to meet and I'm sure I can convince the sisters to attend, but I have a feeling the other brothers will respond better to a little 'mano a mano' talk."

"Don't you think Gerald's kids have enough to deal with right now?" Gavin took a long drink of iced tea. "First, all the illegitimate siblings showing up and then their parents separating? It's a lot to handle."

"But this is something positive," Schuyler insisted. "We're not a threat to them and neither are the New Orleans Fortunes. But we agree the Robinson siblings have handled all of the changes in their lives exceptionally well. I'm hoping they can help the rest of us."

"I'm willing to call Wes," Everett offered, mentioning Ben's twin.

Schuyler beamed at their eldest brother then turned her laser-focused gaze to Gavin. "What about you?"

"Big family parties make me itchy," he said, pretending to scratch at his arms and earning a fry in the face from his sister. "I'm more a lone-wolf type."

Everett let out a bark of laughter. "Not exactly spoken like a man who's ready for a trip down the aisle."

"I didn't mean it like that," Gavin amended, realizing he needed to watch what he said if he was going to make this fake engagement believable.

Schuyler seemed to take his comment in stride. "You can't spout that lone-wolf nonsense now that you're engaged to Christine. She's…" A wide smile split her lips as she glanced toward the door. "Speaking of your better half..." she said, wagging her brows at Gavin.

He turned to see Christine placing an umbrella in the stand next to the diner's entrance. She was with a woman he'd seen the other day at the agency office and the man who'd been hitting on her at Maddie's wedding.

His gaze narrowed as the guy leaned in to speak into Christine's ear. She laughed softly but shifted away, placing the other woman between her and her would-be suitor. Had the guy not heard she was dating Gavin? Was it possible he just didn't care?

As if sensing the weight of Gavin's gaze, Christine glanced toward him. His heart stuttered when she smiled as if the surprise of seeing him made her happy. Then her gaze flicked to Everett and Schuyler and he saw her draw in a sharp breath. She was nervous. He didn't want anything about their arrangement to make her nervous. She knew how much everyone in his family liked her. Although maybe that was part of it. She was afraid of what would happen when their time together ended.

He rose from the table at the same time she excused herself from her coworkers. The man—Bobby, if Gavin remembered correctly—gave Gavin a slow once-over then followed the other woman toward a table.

Christine walked toward Gavin and there was nothing fake or forced about taking her hand and brushing a lingering kiss across her mouth.

"Hi," he whispered against her lips.

"Hi," she breathed.

"Hey, Christine," Schuyler called from behind him. "Great to see you."

Gavin kept Christine's hand in his as he shifted so that she could speak to his sister and brother. It wasn't what he wanted. He wanted to pull her out of the restaurant and find a quiet place to reconnect with her, and if he was being totally honest, to kiss her senseless.

"Hey, Schuyler." Christine smiled. "Hi, Everett."

"How's the old man doing at the new office?" Everett asked with a wink. "Is he driving everyone crazy with his type-A personality?"

Gavin felt Christine stiffen next to him even though her smile remained fixed in place. "He's great, as usual."

Schuyler rolled her eyes. "Everyone probably feels like they're getting a break with him compared to Maddie and Zach. Those two are intense when it comes to real estate."

"We miss them, too," Christine said.

"Chris, we're ready to order. You coming over?"

Gavin felt his eyes narrow as Bobby called to Christine. "Who calls you Chris?" he muttered with a frown.

"Only my family and Bobby," she said. "I don't like the nickname."

"I don't like that guy," he said, dropping a quick kiss on the top of her head. "You can sit with us if you want."

"We're talking about the reunion I'm planning," Schuyler told her. "I'm so excited you'll be there, too. You're already like one of the family."

"Oh…uh…thanks." A blush rose to Christine's cheeks.

"Where's your ring?" Schuyler's gaze had zeroed in on Christine's left hand. "I thought you'd be wearing it now that everyone knows about the two of you."

Gavin's stomach pitched. He hadn't thought about—

"It's at the jeweler being sized," Christine answered, squeezing his hand.

Schuyler nodded. "I can't wait to see it."

"It's beautiful," Christine said with a smile only he seemed to realize was fake. "I should go. Great to see you all."

Reluctantly, he let go of her hand. "I'll call you later?"

"Sure."

He leaned in to whisper in her ear, "And you'll answer?"

She nodded. "Of course."

"Great. I'm planning something for Sunday, so I hope you're free."

Her face went suddenly pale. "Sure. I guess."

Okay, that wasn't the response he'd expected, but he didn't want to push her for an explanation in front of his siblings.

He kissed her again, somewhat placated when she sighed and relaxed into him. That was more like it.

"Chris, come on."

"Can I punch that guy?" he asked in a tone low enough only she could hear.

"I don't think your dad would approve," she told him with a teasing smile before walking away.

"You've got it bad," Everett said when he sat down again.

"I'm ready for the wedding bells," Schuyler added in a singsong voice, then hummed a few bars of "Chapel of Love."

"You know Valene's still single?" Gavin grabbed a fry from Schuyler's plate. "And Connor. I'm off the market so why don't you focus on one of them for a while?"

Everett chuckled. "You're such an easy target."

"Plus, you're only in Texas for a few weeks." Schuyler grinned at him. "Now that she's said yes, we've got to make sure you don't mess things up."

"I'm not going to mess up," Gavin said, pulling out his wallet when the waitress returned with the check. "Anything more we need to know about your reunion? I've got to get back to the office for a meeting."

As Schuyler went over details for the event, Gavin

glanced behind him to the table where Christine sat with her coworkers. His gut clenched when she smiled at something the woman said. He didn't want to mess things up with her, but already their arrangement was more complicated than he'd ever imagined.

Mostly because of his feelings for her. She'd done him a favor as a friend by distracting Schuyler at the wedding and then agreeing to pose as his fiancée for his time in Austin.

It wasn't supposed to be more than that. He'd dated plenty of women and managed to keep his heart out of the mix with all of them. Why was Christine different?

She'd told him that she wasn't his type, and on the surface that might be true. But the connection he felt to her was undeniable. This crazy need to be near her made him both excited and anxious. He'd been joking when he made the crack about being a lone wolf, but it wasn't too far from the truth.

With her sweet smile and gentle spirit, it somehow felt like Christine was changing everything.

Chapter 9

Either Gavin Fortunado had missed his calling as an actor or he was actually interested in her. Christine touched her fingertips to her lips when she was back in her office after lunch, imagining she could still feel the warmth of his mouth on hers.

Although she'd been a bundle of nerves running into him at the diner with Schuyler and Everett, he'd seemed relaxed and happy to see her. The way he'd taken her hand and then kissed her had made her feel like she was really his fiancée. But the rush of excitement brought on by that thought was followed almost immediately by a clenching in her heart.

If she let herself believe that, it could only end in heartache. When this started, she'd expected to put on a show when they were around his family. She would never have guessed she'd be going on actual dates with Gavin. And while she knew she should keep her walls up because of the risk to her heart, there was no way to deny how much she wanted to be with him.

She pulled her phone from her purse and dialed the familiar number.

"Christine?" Her mother picked up on the first ring. "What's wrong?"

"Nothing, Mom." Christine swallowed against the tension that accompanied every conversation with her mother. "I'm calling to say hi and see how you're doing."

"It's the middle of the day," Stephanie Briscoe pointed out as if she might not realize it. "Did you get fired?"

"No," Christine answered through clenched teeth.

"You said you were running the real estate agency those Fortunados own in Austin."

"I still am. It was a promotion."

"It sounds like a lot of work," her mother said drily. "I wasn't sure you'd be able to handle it."

"Mom." Christine sighed. How many times did she have to have some version of the "you can't handle your own life" conversation with her mother? "I've been working for Kenneth for ten years. I'm good at my job. They trust me. They rely on me."

"I worry," her mother whispered, indignation lacing her tone. "I'm your mother. That's *my* job."

"Okay," Christine agreed although her mother's concern had always felt more like judgment. "But I'm doing fine." She didn't mention the recent fall-off in business since the beginning of the year. In a meeting with Kenneth yesterday, they'd chalked it up to a normal post-holiday lull, but he hadn't seemed convinced and neither was she. Things had gotten off to a great start when Maddie and Zach had first taken over. She hated the fact that they'd be returning to trouble, even though it had nothing to do with Christine's role at the agency.

She wished she could mention the issues to her mother. It would be nice to have the kind of relationship where she went to her mom—or her dad, for that matter—for support and advice. But that wasn't the way of things and she didn't expect their family dynamic to change anytime soon.

"I'm glad," her mother answered. "I just want you to be okay."

"I know, Mom." She didn't bother to mention that it was the other Briscoe daughter who needed her mother's concern. Her sister, Aimee, had recently been fired from her job, and while she'd quickly been picked up by another salon, her spotty employment record was becoming a problem.

Christine had successfully graduated college and had a career she loved, but Aimee had floundered since high school, despite being a talented hairstylist. Their parents couldn't admit that the favorite daughter was the failure of the family, and Christine, whom no one had ever expected to amount to much, was thriving. She certainly wasn't going to point it out.

She decided instead to get to the real reason she'd phoned. "I'm calling about Sunday. I might not be able to make dinner."

"Christine, no. You promised when you moved back to Austin that you'd make an effort."

"I have," Christine insisted, hating being put on the defensive. "I've come for dinner every week."

"It's important to your father and me that the four of us spend more time together. Your sister is going through a rough time, and she needs our support."

Christine didn't want to hear about Aimee's rough time,

which most likely stemmed from too many nights of partying with her friends and the monumental hangovers that seemed to prevent her from showing up to work on time.

"I understand, Mom. It's just one Sunday. I promise."

"Why can't you come?" her mother demanded. "Are you behind at work and need to catch up?"

"I have a date," Christine blurted.

Silence from the other end of the line.

"Since when?" Stephanie asked. "Who is this guy who wants to keep you from seeing your family? I don't like the sound of it."

Christine had to work not to growl into the phone. She loved her mother, but for some reason the love she received in return always manifested in criticism. It had been that way since she could remember. Her mother had constantly commented on Christine's weight or lack of friends, comparing her to Aimee with Christine always falling short.

"He's not trying to keep me from seeing you. I didn't mention it to him."

"Bring him to dinner," her mother answered simply.

"What?"

"You heard me. Unless it's some casual fling or you're worried we won't approve. I want to know more about your life, Christine. Let us meet your boyfriend. I want us to be closer. After the incident with my heart last year, you know I've been reevaluating things and focusing on what's important. You're important to me, sweetie."

Christine sighed. Just like that, all the fight went out of her. In addition to the position in Austin being a promotion, she'd taken the job to be closer to her family, and particularly her mother. Stephanie had a heart attack in March of last year, spending four days in the hospital then successfully completing months of cardiac rehab. Christine appreciated everything her mom was doing to make better choices in her life. She might not feel like she belonged in her adventurous, outgoing family, but she loved them.

In the hospital, her mother had told her she regretted that they hadn't been closer. She'd said she wanted another chance to repair her relationship with Christine. Wasn't that what every nonfavorite child wanted to hear from a parent, even as an adult?

"I'm not sure what time we're going out," she admitted. "But if it works, I'll bring Gavin to dinner."

"Gavin," her mother repeated, her tone gentler now. "I like that name. Does he make you happy?"

"Yes," Christine answered without hesitation. "So happy."

"Then I can't wait to meet him."

Christine said goodbye and disconnected the call. She'd purposely not mentioned Gavin's last name or that he was supposedly her fiancé. It was bad enough her mom would share with her dad and sister that Christine had a boyfriend. Christine still wasn't certain she'd have the nerve to take Gavin to Sunday dinner with her family, although the truth was he'd fit in better with them than she ever had.

She turned her attention back to her computer. Kenneth had tasked her with reviewing the agency's historical contract data to find a pattern to help determine why many of their deals were suddenly going south. It was worrisome but the task was something she could manage, unlike her feelings for Gavin.

Right now she needed to feel like she had control over something and it certainly wasn't going to be her wayward heart.

* * *

"We're doing what?" Christine felt her mouth go dry as she stared at Gavin.

"Ziplining," he repeated softly. "If you're up for it."

She concentrated on pulling air in and out of her lungs without hyperventilating. "Did you miss the part where I said I'm afraid of heights?"

He smiled.

"Deathly afraid," she added.

He took her hand and drew her closer. They stood in the area between her kitchen and family room on Sunday morning, light spilling in from the window above the sink. Gavin had arrived minutes earlier and looked even more handsome in a casual cotton button-down shirt and jeans than he did in his normal workweek uniform of a suit and tie. His hair was slightly rumpled and a thick shadow of stubble covered his jaw, like he hadn't bothered to shave for the entire weekend.

She was a big fan of this outdoorsy side of him.

Although not a fan of his plan for the day.

As if sensing her unease, Diana rose from her dog bed in the corner and trotted over for a gentle head butt.

"She can sense your fear," Gavin said, bending to scratch Di behind the ears just the way she liked. The animal promptly forgot about comforting Christine and melted into a puddle on the hardwood floor, exposing her belly for Gavin's attention.

"Traitor," Christine muttered.

"If you don't want to try it, we can do something else." Gavin glanced up as he rubbed the blissed-out dog's belly. "But you mentioned that you'd like to become more adventurous. The guy who runs the outfitter is a friend of mine from high school. I trust him implicitly so I figured this would be a safe way for you to face one of your fears."

"Safe," she repeated, testing the word on her tongue. How could she possibly be safe while harnessed to a cable and soaring through the air?

"I'll keep you safe," he said, straightening and looking into her eyes with so much sincerity that it took her breath away for an entirely different reason. A reason that made her knees go weak. "Do you trust me?"

She nodded, not convinced she could manage actual words at the moment.

One side of his mouth curved as if her answer made him happy.

"Are you ready for an adventure?" he asked.

She nodded again.

His smile widened. "I promise you'll be okay."

She said goodbye to Princess Di and followed Gavin out of the house, locking the door behind them.

When they'd gotten into his vehicle and turned onto the ramp for the interstate, he smiled at her. "How was your week?"

"Long," she admitted. "And busy."

"Maddie and Zach return later tonight, right?"

She nodded. "I'm glad they got away but it's too bad it was such a short honeymoon and they're coming back to—" She broke off, not sure how much to reveal about the drop in business at the agency.

"What's going on at the office? Is everything okay with Dad?"

"He's amazing as usual," she answered immediately. "Why do you ask?"

"You had a strange reaction when Everett asked about him in the diner the other day."

She shook her head. "It's not your dad. I'm not sure whether it's supposed to be a secret or not, but there have been some strange things happening with some of our deals lately."

"What kind of strange?"

"We're losing clients and having trouble with existing contracts. It doesn't make sense based on how strong business was right out of the gate. I'm not sure what's going on, but your dad's upset about it."

"Does Maddie know?"

"Not yet. It came to light this week, but there's definitely a pattern. Your dad didn't want to bother them while they were on their honeymoon. We're scheduled to meet to go over reports and trends tomorrow morning."

"She and Zach will figure it out," Gavin said, smoothing his thumb across the back of her hand. "There has to be an explanation."

"I hope so. We all had such high hopes for the Austin office." She stared out the window as the scenery changed from urban to more rural. It was one of the things she loved about Texas—the wide-open spaces. Even in the middle of the city, there was a sense of the cowboy spirit that made the state so special. Austin had a different vibe than Houston had, a more eclectic atmosphere with most folks taking the local slogan Keep Austin Weird quite seriously.

"Do you miss Denver?" she asked, glancing toward Gavin.

His fingers tightened slightly on the steering wheel. "I miss heading up to the mountains to ski on the weekends," he admitted. "Denver still has a bit of the cowboy feel to it, so it's not that different from Austin. A lot sunnier and less humid, I guess."

"My hair would love it." She tugged on the ends of her long locks. "Some days I'm a massive frizz ball no matter how much product I use."

"Your hair is amazing," he said. "The color is so bright."

She groaned softly. "They used to call me carrot top in school. I hated having red hair."

"It makes you special," he told her.

You make me special, she wanted to say but managed to keep her mouth shut. She'd told herself she would stay in the moment today and not worry about what might happen with Gavin or how much being with him made her heart happy.

Nope. She was keeping her heart out of the mix.

He exited the highway onto a two-lane road that led into the rolling hills north of the city.

"You doing okay?" Gavin squeezed her hand, and she hoped he didn't notice her sweaty palm.

"I can't believe I agreed to this." She leaned forward when the first zipline tower came into view, the seat belt stretching across her chest. "It's so high."

"You've got this," he assured her.

If only she had his confidence.

He parked in front of a cabin that seemed to be the outdoor company's office. Austin Zips read the sign above the covered porch.

Gavin got out of the Audi and walked around to her side. Her body felt weighted with lead, but she forced herself to climb out and pasted a smile on her face. "Looks like fun," she said, shading her eyes as she gazed up at the ropes course that had been built behind the office.

"Liar," Gavin whispered.

She laughed. "It's the stuff of my worst nightmares," she admitted. "But I'm going to face my fears."

Gavin leaned in to kiss her. "That's my girl."

"Fortunado!" A man's deep voice rang out from the door to the office.

"Hey, Marc," Gavin called. "Thanks for letting us come out on such short notice."

"It's our slow season," the man said as he walked forward. "But I'd always make time for you, buddy. I hear you're now one of the big-wig Fortunes."

Gavin's expression didn't change, but Christine felt a wave of tension roll through him. "You know how things go," he said casually. "It just means an even larger family."

"Sure," the man agreed affably. As he came down the steps, Christine couldn't help but smile. Gavin's friend could have been the Keep Austin Weird poster child. His sandy-blond hair was long enough to be held back in a man bun. Despite the temperatures hovering in the low fifties, he wore a pair of board shorts and a floral-print silk shirt like he should be hanging on a tropical beach instead of in the middle of nowhere outside Austin.

He shook Gavin's hand and did a couple of friendly back slaps then turned to Christine. "Gavin mentioned you have a bit of a fear of heights?"

She licked her lips and nodded.

"I want to reassure you," Marc said, leaning closer, "that you're in good hands with me. I've only had—" he tapped a tanned finger on his chin "—I guess that would be a half dozen equipment failures this year, but only one of them was fatal."

Christine took a step back. "Um…"

Marc threw back his head and laughed. "Joking with you, darlin'. We have a perfect safety record at Austin Zips."

"Right." Christine tried to laugh, but it sounded more like a croak. "Of course you do."

Gavin shook his head. "Not funny, Marc."

"Sorry." The man held up his hands, palms out. "We're

going to make this easy and fun. By the time you're finished, you'll be shouting, 'More, Marc. Give me more.'"

Christine felt her eyes go wide.

"You seriously need to grow up," Gavin said, and his tone held a vague warning.

Marc seemed to get the message because he launched into an in-depth overview of the zip lines, the safety procedures and inspections that occurred each day and the standards his company followed to ensure a safe and fun experience for its customers.

Christine appreciated the information, and it gave her more confidence in Marc's level of professionalism.

"We're going to take the Mule out to the first platform. I have helmets and water already packed." He pointed to a four-seater utility terrain vehicle parked at the far side of the building. "You two load up while I grab my sunglasses and I'll be right out."

He jogged up the steps and into the building.

"You're going to be fine," Gavin said, wrapping an arm around her shoulder.

"Famous last words," she whispered, earning a chuckle from him.

"It's not too late to turn around. We can bag this whole idea and go see a movie or take Di for a walk. I'm just happy to have a day off and to spend it with you."

Christine appreciated the out, but she wasn't going to take it. "This is my chance to have an adventure." She flashed what she hoped was a confident smile as they got into the Mule with Gavin following. "Even if it's a mini-adventure."

"The first of many," he told her.

The sun had warmed things enough to turn it into a perfect January day in Texas. She kept her focus on the blue sky and how nice it felt to be sitting so close to Gavin as Marc joined them and they headed across the rolling hills.

The zip line course was situated about a quarter mile from the building, traversing along the perimeter of the woods that bordered the property. As they got closer she realized the cables not only ran next to the woods but also through the trees, so that she'd actually have the sensation of soaring through the forest, if she could manage to keep her eyes open.

Marc parked then led them to the first platform. He gave another safety talk and explained how the two points of contact system with the safety lines worked. She and Gavin put on helmets and then the harnesses while Marc used his walkie-talkie to radio someone. A minute later an ATV sped toward them through the forest.

"This is Chip." Marc introduced an older man, who was well over six feet tall and skinny as a rail. "He's going to be leading the two of you today and I'll follow."

Chip winked at Christine. "I'm going to go first down each run so you'll know it's safe."

She nodded then felt Gavin massage her shoulder. "You look a little pale," he said gently.

"Has anyone ever thrown up mid-zip line?" she asked Marc.

He laughed. "You'd be the first, darlin'. But don't worry about that. Do whatever's gonna make you feel better in the end."

"You've got this, Adventure Girl," Gavin told her as she clipped into the safety line then climbed onto the platform. Marc snapped Chip into the harness and with a playful wave, he took off across the huge open space between where they stood and the next platform.

"Wow," Christine whispered when Chip landed on the other side.

"Easy enough, right?" Marc asked.

Despite her racing heart and sweaty palms, she nodded.

He crooked a finger at her. "Do you want to go next?"

She shook her head. "Gavin will go."

"Are you sure?" Gavin asked.

"You need to be on the other end to catch me," she told him.

"I'll definitely catch you." He allowed Marc to connect his harness to the cable then took off, giving an enthusiastic whoop of delight as he sped from one platform to the next.

"I'd like to go home now," Christine whispered, earning a belly laugh from Marc. "Gavin made it look so easy. He's going to think I'm the biggest wuss in the world when I puke or pee myself on this harness. Could you imagine a worse way to end a date? I'm going to ruin everything."

"Darlin', I've known Gavin since we were stealing hootch from his daddy's liquor cabinet. I've seen lots of ladies on his arm over the years but never has he looked at one the way he looks at you. Don't worry about ruining anything. If you climbed down this platform and said all you want to do is go shopping at the nearest mall, that man would gladly hold your bags."

Christine smiled despite her fear. "I doubt that, but I appreciate you saying it."

"It's the truth."

"No shopping malls," she said, stepping forward. "I'm going to conquer my fear today."

"That's what we like to hear." Marc snapped her harness to the cable, explaining once again how to use the active brake if she felt she needed it.

Her knees trembled as she inched to the edge of the platform, and sweat beaded between her shoulder blades.

Gavin shouted words of encouragement, but she could barely make them out over the pounding in her head. She drew in a breath and took off, screaming first from terror and then with excitement as she sailed across the air toward the trees. She hit the brake lever the way Marc had shown her as she approached the next platform and a moment later Gavin's arms were around her. Good thing, too, because she wasn't sure she could stand on her own at the moment.

Chip unfastened her harness and she wrapped her shaking arms around Gavin's neck. "I did it," she whispered. "And I didn't pee myself."

Both men laughed and Chip patted her helmet. "Way to hold it together."

"You were amazing," Gavin said, kissing her cheek. "Are you ready to go again?"

She drew in a deep breath, most of her nervous butterflies replaced by exhilaration. "I am. Thank you for this day. It's the best ever."

He grinned and kissed her.

Marc joined them on the platform. "Okay, lovebirds. Let's hold off on the spit swapping until we're back to solid ground." He pointed at Christine. "Nice work. Next, we're going to show you how to curl into a ball to go faster."

The nerves returned, but Christine quickly tamped them down. She was going to try whatever Marc threw at her. The idea that she wasn't a total wimp made her feel braver than she ever could have imagined.

"I'm ready," she said, tightening the strap on her helmet. "For anything."

Gavin stood below the final platform, smiling as Christine rappelled down toward him, marveling at the change in her. As beautiful as she'd been at the start of their zip line adventure, there was something even more appealing about her now, a sense of abandonment that made her breathtaking. She was windblown with flushed cheeks and a smudge of dirt down the front of her shirt.

She hopped down the last few feet, grinning widely and doing a funny little dance with her upper body as Chip unstrapped the rock-climbing gear from her waist.

"She's a helluva sport," Marc said, handing Gavin a bottle of cold water. "I can't imagine bringing a woman who's deathly afraid of heights out here and having her handle it like a champ."

"She did great," Gavin agreed.

"You like her."

"She's extremely likable."

"Nah." Marc nudged his arm. "I mean, you really *like* her."

Gavin paused in the act of opening his water bottle. He hadn't mentioned the engagement to Marc. It was one thing with his family, but he figured it would be better to keep his story simple where he could. The pretend engagement definitely complicated things.

But he did really like Christine. Way more than he ever would have guessed at the beginning of their arrangement. Was that only a week ago?

How had his feelings changed so quickly?

"Where did the two of you meet?" Marc asked.

"She worked for my dad for years and now runs the Austin branch of the agency."

"So you thinking of moving back?"

Gavin felt himself frown. "My life's in Denver," he said quietly, suddenly understanding the point his siblings had been trying to make when they said a job was not the same thing as a life.

Marc slapped him gently on the back. "Not that I'm trying to skim your milk, but if the long-distance thing doesn't work out, I may have to swoop in to comfort her."

Gavin thought about the expiration date on their arrangement and his gut tightened. "No one's swooping in with Christine," he told his old friend.

Marc only laughed. "You've got it bad," he said, then walked forward to help Chip put away the equipment.

Christine grinned as she approached, pumping her fists in the air. "Did you see me?"

He smiled, pushing aside his discontent over the boundaries and timeline that defined their relationship.

"You were amazing." He wrapped his arms around her waist and lifted her off the ground. She smelled like a tantalizing mix of shampoo and the outdoors, fresh and clean. "Skydiving next?"

She laughed and kissed him. "Let's not get crazy."

When he lowered her to the ground, she cupped his cheeks in her palms. "Thank you, Gavin. I would never have done something like this on my own."

"I had no doubt you could."

Marc and Chip joined them and they rode back to the office. Christine laced her fingers with his like it was the most natural thing in the world, and damn, he wanted it to be.

"How about the ropes course?" Marc asked Christine with a wink. "It should be a piece of cake now that you're a master of heights."

Gavin expected her to decline, but she nodded and grinned at him. "Sounds great to me. What do you think?"

"Let's go," he told her and for the next hour they traversed the suspended ropes course, crossing bridges and climbing through obstacles. He could tell she was scared but never let that fear slow her down.

The sky was beginning to turn shades of pink and orange by the time they headed back toward Austin. Christine pulled out a pen and a small notebook from her purse and ticked off a list of other activities she wanted to try now that she knew she could overcome her fear of heights. Gavin's chest constricted as he listened to her plans.

He could see himself with her on every adventure, from bungee jumping to riding the roller coasters at the state fair. At the same time, he'd never imagined himself in a long-term relationship. Part of what allowed him to be so open with Christine was, ironically, knowing their time together had a built-in expiration date.

He could give himself fully because it was safe. But wanting more felt dangerous, both to him and to her. He didn't want to hurt her but his past had shown him that he wasn't the type of man who had more to give a woman like her.

"When did your fear of heights start?" he asked, needing to get out of his own head and the doubts swirling there. "You managed today like a pro."

Her grip tightened on the notebook. "My family went on a vacation when I was younger to a waterpark near Galveston. We were all supposed to go on this super-high slide, but I didn't want to."

"Because of your fear?"

She tugged her bottom lip between her teeth. "Not exactly," she admitted after a moment. "I was overweight as a girl. It was a pretty big issue for my dad. He'd been a marine, and physical fitness was important to him. My younger sister was always into sports, and I never felt like I fit in. We're a year apart and as we got older, my dad started taking us on extreme vacations. I could never keep up so I think maybe I developed all my fears—heights, water and speed—as a way to have an excuse not to participate."

"So if you didn't participate, what happened?"

Her smile was sad. "The first couple of trips were difficult because he'd try to force me to do things. Eventually, I just stayed behind with my grandma."

"While your family went on vacation without you?"

"It wasn't a big deal," she insisted. "In fact, I had a much better time with my grammy than I would have if I'd tried to keep up with the rest of them."

"Christine—"

"Anyway, that's how it started." She gave him a smile that was as bright and brittle as a piece of cut glass. "But today changed everything. Thank you."

"You don't have to thank me. I'm glad I could be there with you. Now, what are you thinking for dinner?"

She sucked in a breath and glanced at the clock on the Audi's dashboard. "Oh, no. Is it really after five?"

He nodded. "Time flies and all that."

"I'm supposed to be at my parents' for dinner by six. It felt like we zip-lined for thirty minutes."

"More like three hours plus time for the ropes course. Where do your parents live?"

"On the west side of Austin, near West Lake Hills."

"I could—"

"They want you to come, too," she blurted then covered her face with her hands. "I'm sorry. I should have said something earlier. I tried to get out of the dinner, but I told you my mom thinks that Sunday dinners with the four of us will somehow bring us closer."

"I don't—"

"I'm sure it sounds horrible," she continued, shifting her

hands to glance at him from the corner of her eye. "I don't blame you for not wanting to go. But it's out of the way to go all the way back to my place. If you just drop me off at my parents' now, after dinner I can call an Ub—"

"I don't mind going," he interrupted, reaching out to tug her hands away from her face. "I'd like to meet your family."

She wrinkled her nose. "Why?"

"Because I want to know you better," he said with a laugh. "You know my family, and they all love you."

"My family is different from yours, and not in a good way."

"It doesn't matter."

"There's nothing to learn about me from meeting them."

"If your mom wants me there, I don't want to rebuff the invitation."

"Are you sure?" She sounded even more nervous than she'd been before the zip line tour. "I can make an excuse. This definitely wasn't part of our arrangement."

"I'd like to join you for dinner with your parents and sister," he said gently. "But only if you're okay with it. If not, I'll drop you off around the corner then come back and pick you up when you're ready to leave."

"Seriously?" she couldn't help but ask. "You'd do that for me?"

Gavin was quickly coming to realize he'd do just about anything for this woman, but he wasn't about to admit it out loud.

"That's what friends are for," he answered instead.

Chapter 10

Christine tried not to look like she was about to throw up as she opened the door to her parents' house and led Gavin inside.

At this point she would have taken skydiving, maybe even without a parachute, over introducing him to her family. The prospect of it had seemed manageable during the drive, thanks to Gavin's quiet confidence, but the reality of it was a different story.

"Chris?" her mom called from the kitchen, and she grimaced. She hated the nickname her family still insisted on using. It brought back memories of being a chubby kid with an unfortunate bowl haircut that made her look like a boy. She'd tried her hardest to fit in but ended up feeling lousy about herself most of the time.

She wanted to believe she'd shed her self-doubts the way she had her extra weight, but it was easier when she was away from this house and her family.

"Hi, Mom," she said with a forced smile as she entered the kitchen.

Her mother looked up from where she was cutting tomatoes for a salad, her eyes widening at the sight of Gavin. Christine might not be the fat, awkward girl she once was, but she knew her mom wouldn't expect her to be dating someone who looked like Gavin.

Christine's dad walked into the kitchen from the family room. "Hey, kid," he said, taking in Christine's tousled hair and dusty clothes. "Looks like you need a shower."

"We went zip lining and didn't have time to change before coming here," she reported. "Mom and Dad, this is Gavin Fortunado. My...um...boyfriend." Cursing her fair complexion, she willed away the color she could feel flooding her cheeks. She hoped Gavin was okay that she didn't mention their pretend engagement to her family. She understood why it helped with the Fortunados, but the shock of her having an actual boyfriend would be plenty for her parents and sister.

"Fortunado? Like the family who owns the agency where Christine works?"

Gavin nodded. "Kenneth is my dad. Christine and I met at the office in Houston."

"I'm Stephanie and this is Dave," her mother told him, her tone almost dazed. "Are you a real estate agent?"

"Nice to meet you," Gavin said smoothly, walking forward and shaking first her father's hand and then her mother's. "I'm actually an attorney, and I'm sorry Christine and I are a bit of a mess. She just had to do the ropes course after we finished the zip line tour, and time got away from us."

Dave Briscoe gave a disbelieving laugh. "Chris on a ropes course? You've got to be kidding."

"I'm not." Gavin pulled out his phone. "She did fantastic. Would you like to see the photos?"

Her mother put down the knife. "I would."

"Did they have a harness big enough for her?"

The comment came from behind her and Christine turned, her chest tightening as her sister, Aimee, sauntered into the room. She wore a black tank top and tight jeans that hugged her trim hips. Aimee placed an empty beer bottle on the counter and gave a bubbly laugh, like this was all a big joke. "Oh, wait. She's not fat anymore. I always forget."

"I lost the weight years ago," Christine said through clenched teeth.

Gavin gave her sister the barest hint of a smile then took out his phone and pulled up the photos for her mother.

"Good for you, Christine," her mom said, taking the phone from Gavin and scrolling through the photos. "You don't look scared at all. Dave, look at these pictures."

"It was fun," Christine said quietly, darting a glance at her sister. Historically, Aimee did not respond well to Christine getting attention from their mother.

"Do you live in Austin, Gavin?" She moved around the counter, tugging on the hem of her tank top, revealing more of her world-class cleavage.

Christine glanced at Gavin, but he didn't seem to notice. How was that even possible?

"Denver," he answered. "I'm in Austin for a few weeks because of work."

"Do you ski?"

"Whenever I get the chance."

"I'm road-tripping up to Vail with some friends next month. I just ordered a new set of twin tips."

"Sounds great," he said, but shifted closer to Christine.

She tried to take comfort in his presence but couldn't seem to settle her nerves. "Aimee, Mom said you lost your job."

"I got another one," Aimee snapped. "A better one." She

turned to Gavin. "We're looking to do the back bowls. Expert terrain only. You should meet us up there. It's an awesome group."

"Thanks for the invite," he said.

"Chris doesn't ski," Aimee announced as if Christine had tried to make Gavin believe that she did. "There's no way she'd be able to handle even the bunny hill." She laughed again. "Don't even get me started on a chairlift. With her fear of heights—"

"You should take a look at the photos," Gavin told Aimee as Christine's father handed back his phone. "She's got that fear of heights under control."

Christine glanced toward her father, who was studying her like he'd never seen her before. It had been so easy to believe she'd conquered the worst of her fears when they'd been in the middle of their date. Now she felt as awkward and bumbling as she always had with her family.

"It's nice to see you smiling," Dave said finally, inclining his head toward Gavin's phone.

Not exactly a ringing show of support but it felt like a huge endorsement from her normally recalcitrant father. Aimee must have noticed it, too, because her eyes turned hard.

"Let me show you my workshop while the women finish up dinner," Dave told Gavin. "Got a beer cooler out there stocked with cold ones."

Gavin nodded but looked at Christine's mom. "Do you need help with anything?"

Christine watched her mother's face soften. Her parents loved each other, but theirs was a traditional marriage with the bulk of the household duties falling to Stephanie. She could tell it meant a lot to her mom that Gavin offered to help. Once again Christine reminded herself that today was merely a detour on the trajectory of their relationship, which couldn't end in anything but heartache for her. How much of her heart she gave him was the only question.

"Thank you for the offer," her mom said, blushing slightly. "But I've got things under control. Dave is so proud of his workshop. You go with him."

"I'd love a beer, then," Gavin said to her dad and followed Dave toward the garage that housed his workshop.

"He's so handsome," her mom said when the door closed behind the two men. She fanned a hand in front of her face. "Makes me feel like I'm having a hot flash."

Christine knew exactly how her mother felt.

"It's difficult to believe you landed someone like him," Aimee said, opening the refrigerator to pull out another beer. The workshop was their father's man cave and a space where Christine's mother rarely ventured. Instead, she kept a few beers stocked in the kitchen fridge for when friends or her daughters stopped by. Of course, Aimee didn't bother to offer one to Christine now.

"He's great," Christine murmured, hoping to avoid an in-depth conversation about Gavin. The Briscoe women might not be close, but she feared that her mom and sister would be able to read the lie of their relationship on her face nonetheless.

"What's he doing with you?" Aimee asked as she popped the top on the beer bottle.

"Be nice," their mother chided.

"We have a lot in common," Christine said, automatically going to the cabinet to begin setting the table. It was the second Sunday of the month, so that meant meat loaf. She could smell it baking, and the scent brought back both good and bad memories from childhood. Her mother had always been a great cook, although it still embarrassed Christine to remember herself as a girl, trying to take an extra portion at mealtimes or sneaking into the kitchen late at night to munch on leftovers.

Aimee took the napkins out of the drawer and followed Christine to the table. "Like what?"

How was she supposed to explain her connection to Gavin? On the surface, they were a mismatched pair, but he seemed to like her just the way she was. She saw beyond his polished playboy facade to the kindhearted man he didn't reveal to many people. That sort of connection would be lost on her abrasive sister, most likely chalked up to wishful thinking on Christine's part.

"Well, we both like zip lining." She grinned when Aimee snorted. "I'm also going to learn to water-ski this summer." Gavin gave her the confidence to conquer her fears. She'd never been a strong swimmer, mostly because as a kid she hadn't wanted to be seen in a bathing suit. But she could start doing laps in the pool at the gym where she belonged. By summer, certainly she'd be ready for waterskiing.

"Is Prince Fortunado going to teach you?" Aimee asked, her tone at once bitter and teasing.

"Maybe." Christine bit down on her lip. On second thought, Gavin probably wouldn't be around to see her water-ski, if she even managed it. Aimee didn't need to know that. She placed a plate at the head of the table and glanced up to meet her sister's gaze. "Or you could help me. I remember how great you were when we'd go out to Aunt Celia's place in the summer."

"That's a lovely idea," their mother said, clapping her hands together. "I'd love to see you girls doing something together."

Aimee looked torn between shooting down Christine and placating their mother. "If I have time," she agreed eventually. "We'll see."

Christine smiled even as her stomach pinched. She wished she understood where the animosity between the two of them had originated. Their parents loved them both, although Dave Briscoe had made it clear that he wished he'd had a son. Aimee had done her best to fill that void by being a rough-and-tumble tomboy growing up, interested in sports and cars and whatever else she thought would bring her closer to their father.

Christine had been the odd one out, so Aimee's constant resentment didn't make sense, but it had persisted just the same.

Maybe it was silly that she still wanted a relationship with her sister, but she couldn't help it.

"It's obvious Gavin really likes you," Stephanie said, ignoring her younger daughter. "I like seeing you this happy."

"Thanks, Mom."

Aimee grumbled a bit more but they managed to get dinner on the table without an outright argument. Christine's father was more animated than she'd seen him in years during the meal. It was clear he liked Gavin, and Christine felt the all-too-familiar guilt that she was exposing her family to their fake relationship. Obviously, her parents would be sorely disappointed when she and Gavin parted ways. But she consoled herself with the knowledge that at least now they saw her as more than just their boring, awkward daughter.

Thanks to Gavin, she felt like so much more.

She made an excuse about needing to prepare for a Monday meeting, and they said their goodbyes soon after dinner. The sun had fully set while they were at her parents' and she was grateful for the cover of darkness so she had a bit of time to regain control of her emotions.

The ride back to her house was quiet, and she wasn't sure what to make of Gavin's silence. Her family and her role in it were the polar opposite of the tight-knit Fortunado clan. Even discovering the connection to the famous Fortunes had only seemed to bring them closer. She couldn't imagine anything that would truly bridge the distance in her family.

When he pulled up in front of her condo, she pasted on a smile and turned to say good-night, only to have him lean across the front seat and fuse his mouth to hers.

Her breath caught in her lungs, and she immediately relaxed into the kiss even though the intensity of it shocked her.

"That was fun," he whispered against her lips.

She pulled back with a soft laugh. "You must be talking about the kiss because dinner with my family was about as much fun as a root canal."

"They don't give you enough credit," he said, his tone serious.

She shrugged. "It's hard to break old patterns. You wouldn't understand because your family is perfect."

"Hardly," he answered with a snort. "I don't think any family is perfect."

They both looked out the front window as headlights turned down the street, illuminating the front of the Audi. "I need to take Princess Di for a walk," she said, her heart suddenly beginning to pound in her chest. "Any chance you want to join me?" It was such a simple question, yet it felt funny requesting something from Gavin. He had initiated most of the time they'd spent together, and it felt strange to be so nervous—like somehow she was imposing on his evening.

He flashed a small, almost grateful smile. "I'd love to."

They walked to her condo hand in hand, and she unlocked the door, immediately greeted by the dog. While Gavin got busy loving up Diana, Christine pulled on a heavier jacket and took the dog's leash from its hook in the laundry room. She grabbed a flashlight, as well, and they headed out to the street.

"My family sometimes feels larger than life," Gavin said as they walked, Princess Di happily sniffing the edge of the sidewalk as she trotted along. "We all have big personalities."

"It's one of the things I liked best when I first started with Fortunado Real Estate," Christine admitted. "Your dad is great and it was fun when any of the kids or your mom stopped by the office."

"Yeah. We're a ton of fun." Gavin scrubbed a hand across his jaw, the scratchy sound reverberating in the quiet of the evening and doing funny things to Christine's insides. "But growing up it was hard to get noticed—there were so many of us doing different activities. Honestly, my mom is a saint for handling all of it. But that's part of how I became an adrenaline junkie. All of my antics were a way to get attention."

"Really?" Christine was shocked by the admission. "The adventurous side of you seems so natural."

He shrugged. "I guess it is by this point, but sometimes it feels like a compulsion rather than something I do because I love it. Don't get me wrong, I like to have fun, but I wonder if there's more to me than working and taking off on the weekend for more thrill-seeking."

"I think there is," she said softly.

"I don't even own a houseplant," he told her out of nowhere.

She frowned. "Um…okay."

"I know that sounds random." He shook his head. "But I'm not exactly known for my skills at adulting. I have a great job, but even at the firm I'm the guy who woos the prospective clients. I move too fast to be able to stay with one for the long haul, so much that it's a shock I'm in Austin for so long. I admire your dedication and how steady you are."

"Thank you," she whispered.

"And your sweetness and loyalty," he continued. As the dog blissfully investigated a nearby shrub, Gavin turned and cupped her cheeks between his palms. "Your family doesn't have any idea how lucky they are to have you."

She swallowed the emotion that threatened to clog her throat. She wanted to believe that. It didn't matter that she was a grown woman and had made a wonderful life for herself. The fact that she'd never fit in with her parents and sister was like an itch that she couldn't seem to scratch, always distracting her from allowing herself to be truly happy.

"I'm lucky to have you," he continued, and her heart soared. "Even if it's only for a few weeks, I'm grateful for our time together."

Right. Like a balloon that had been stuck with a pin, her happiness deflated, thanks to the reminder that their arrangement was temporary. Gavin might enjoy being with her, but he wasn't looking to make this into something real. He had no problem remembering the parameters of their relationship. Why did she?

"We should head back," she said, pulling away and tugging on Di's leash. "I actually do have a meeting first thing tomorrow with Maddie and Zach."

He frowned but dropped his hands. The cool night air swirled around her, making her body miss the warmth of his touch.

She purposely kept a greater distance between them as they returned to her condo. What was the point of letting him close when he was just going to walk away? She might not be the most confident woman in the world, but she had enough self-respect to not allow herself to turn into a blathering idiot begging him to want more. At least not to his face.

"Can I see you this week?" he asked, placing a hand on her back as she unlocked her door.

Whenever you want, her heart shouted. It felt like her emotions were rattling her insides like bars on a prison window. What would happen if she threw her self-respect to the wind and invited him in? Would he take her up on the invitation?

Instead, she smiled and shook her head. Physical distance was the only way she could think of to keep her feelings for him from spiraling out of control. "It's going to be crazy around the agency with your sister and Zach returning. I think it would be better if we waited until the reunion next weekend."

"Oh." Gavin's thick brows drew together over his gorgeous green eyes. "Is everything okay?"

I'm falling for you, she wanted to tell him. *I don't know how to stop it or protect my heart.*

But she did know and, unfortunately, it involved keeping her distance unless they had to be together for the ruse. She hated pushing him away, but what choice did she have?

"Everything's fine, but I'm busy and I'm sure you are, too. I mean, the sooner you close the new client, the sooner you'll be able to head home. Right?"

"I guess," he said slowly. "I'm in no hurry."

"Me neither," she admitted before she could stop herself. Princess Di gave a soft whine, ready to be in bed for the night. "Let's talk in a few days," she told Gavin with fake cheer. "Thanks again for the adventure, and for joining my family for Sunday dinner—an adventure unto itself."

He stepped back, studying her face as if trying to figure out why she was acting so remote. She couldn't explain it to him, couldn't bear for him to deny that he would hurt her.

Already her heart ached more than she could have imagined.

"Good night," she said and slipped into her quiet house.

Chapter 11

Gavin tugged on the collar of his crisp white shirt as he approached Christine's front door Saturday night. He hadn't been this nervous about a date since...well, he'd never been this nervous.

Other than a couple of awkward phone conversations and a few random texts, he hadn't spoken to her since the previous Sunday evening. He wasn't sure what went wrong. They'd had a perfect day, even if the visit to her parents' had been a tad uncomfortable.

Actually, the new understanding of the role Christine played in her family made him furious. Beyond her dedication to his father and the family business, Christine was an amazing person in her own right. Maybe he hadn't noticed her understated beauty and charm at first—or in the ten years he'd known her. But now that he'd spent time with her he couldn't envision his life without her sweetness and light in it.

Except that was exactly what was going to happen at the end of the month. He'd mentioned the predetermined finish to their arrangement, hoping to coax some sort of reaction from her, but she hadn't batted an eye. Not that he blamed her. He'd all but told her he was a bad bet for a relationship. Why wouldn't he expect her to take him at his word?

In fact, her mood seemed to change after he revealed his feelings about his own childhood, the ones that left him riddled with guilt for being an ungrateful schmuck. His family was fantastic and what did it matter if he had to work to be noticed in the midst of so much love? But he'd gotten so used to pushing himself for the rush of adrenaline that he didn't know any other way to live.

Yet with Christine it was easy to slow down and enjoy the moment, whether walking her dog or watching her conquer her fears. She made everything a little brighter, helped him breathe easier than he could ever remember.

He'd gotten himself onto a crazy treadmill of working hard and playing hard, a cliché overachiever in every area except the one that counted the most—his personal life. He'd always doubted he had the capacity for the kind of love his parents had, the kind Everett, Schuyler and Maddie had found. As crazy as it was and despite the unexpected way their connection had come about, he saw that potential with Christine. And now he doubted she'd give him a chance to prove it.

He knocked, smiling as Princess Di gave a loud *woof* on the other side of the door.

"I'm ready," Christine said as she opened it.

Gavin started to smile then felt his jaw go slack.

"Wow," he murmured as he took her in.

"Is this dress okay?" She smoothed a hand over the front of the soft fabric. The dress was black and strapless with a thin sash around the waist and fell to just above her knees. She'd paired it with a delicate gold necklace, dangling earrings and a pair of the sexiest heels he'd ever seen. This was a Christine he hadn't seen before. Her hair was swept to one side and fell in soft waves over her bare shoulder. His fingers itched to touch it, to touch her. He wanted to pull her close and hold on all night. "Schuyler said cocktail attire, but I don't want to seem overdressed."

"You're perfect." He shook his head, his brain jumbled as if he were the ball in an arcade pinball machine. "So damn beautiful."

She laughed and a blush stained her cheeks. He'd missed seeing that rosy glow. He'd missed her so much it made him feel like a fool. It had been six days. Barely any time at all and yet...

He leaned closer, breathing in the delicate scent of her.

"What are you doing?" she asked with a laugh, taking a step back into her condo.

"Making sure you hadn't changed shampoos since I saw you last."

"You're crazy," she told him.

"For you," he confirmed.

Di nudged Christine's legs, trying to reach Gavin. "Hey, girl," he said, bending to scratch behind the dog's furry ears. "I missed you, too."

"Gavin." Christine's tone was serious. He frowned as he straightened, wondering what he'd done wrong now.

"Yes?"

"You look nice, too," she said, almost shyly.

He swayed closer, ready to meld his mouth to hers, but she turned away, grabbing her purse from the entry table. "We don't want to be late. Schuyler wants the family there before the New Orleans Fortunes are scheduled to arrive at four."

"There's plenty of Fortunados to handle the welcome." He moved closer, crowding her a little. Her breath hitched and it gave him so much satisfaction to know she wasn't as unaffected by him as she acted.

"It's important," she insisted.

He sighed. "You're right, of course."

"Of course."

"First, I have something for you." He pulled a small velvet pouch from the inside pocket of his suit jacket.

Her mouth formed a small O as she watched him take a six-prong diamond solitaire engagement ring from the pouch. "I think you need to be wearing a ring when we get to the reunion."

"Yes," she breathed then pressed two fingers to her lips. "I mean, you're right. You didn't actually ask me anything." She stared at the ring. "But, yes, just the same."

It made him ridiculously happy to hear her say yes. He slipped the ring onto her finger. "It's on loan from one of the firm's clients who owns a chain of jewelry stores throughout Texas."

"A loan," she whispered, seemingly unable to pull her gaze from the sparkling diamond. "You have some darn good connections."

"Thank you again for doing this, Christine."

"Of course." Her gaze lifted to his as she closed her left hand into a tight fist. "We should really get going."

He stepped back so she had room to close the door and resisted the urge to take her hand as they walked toward the Audi. Clearly, he'd spooked her last week with something he'd said or done. Now he'd given her an engagement ring. Not exactly taking things slow, even when it was all pretend. He appreciated that she was still willing to uphold their arrangement, but he worried that one wrong move on his part would send her running.

Which was the last thing he wanted.

He opened the passenger-side door then walked around the front of the Audi, wishing he'd thought to bring her flowers or something—anything—that would have given him an excuse to linger at her place and have her all to himself.

The drive to the winery was only thirty minutes from Christine's place, and she spent most of it asking him about his week.

His shoulders relaxed as he shared progress on negotiating the merger of one of his firm's larger manufacturing clients with another company. He'd been focusing on cultivating the client relationship and on making sure they were abiding by all the local, state and federal laws that governed the industry. In turn, he asked her for her take on the continuing saga of Fortunado Real Estate's Austin branch. He'd talked to Maddie after she'd been back a few days, and his sister had seemed both frustrated and confused by the falloff in business.

Christine didn't have any more answers than his sister had but was clearly just as upset by the issues.

They arrived at the Mendoza Winery, situated in the picturesque landscape of the Texas hill country, and Gavin took Christine's hand as they approached the entrance.

"It's Schuyler's big show," she whispered, and her words made him stop in his tracks. "What's wrong?" she asked as she turned to face him.

"I'm glad you're here with me tonight." He reached out and trailed a fingertip along her jaw. "Not because of our arrangement. It's more than that. You make me happy, Christine."

She hitched in a breath, and he could almost see the struggle as she tried to remain distant. He inwardly cheered when she went up on tiptoe to give him a quick kiss. "You make me happy, too," she said with an almost reluctant smile.

At this point he'd take reluctant. He'd take anything she was willing to give.

He glanced up as Schuyler called his name.

"Here we go," he whispered, and they continued toward the rustic yet modern lodge surrounded by acres of weathered grapevines. He hadn't been there since Schuyler's wedding and, once again, appreciated the beauty of what the Mendoza family had created.

Schuyler greeted Christine with a warm hug and a friendly chuck on the shoulder for Gavin. "You're late."

"I'm here now."

She rolled her eyes. "I bet the only reason is Christine."

"Maybe," he admitted.

"You would have skipped my reunion?" She glared at him, but he could see the sisterly amusement in her eyes.

"I would have made it eventually."

"Go on in." She waved them past her. "Our family's already here, along with Olivia and Alejandro." She glanced at Christine. "I wish I had a cheat sheet to give you for keeping all of the Fortunes straight. Olivia is one of Gerald Robinson's daughters. She and Alejandro Mendoza first met when he came to Austin from Miami for a wedding. They're pretty cute together." She checked her phone. "Nolan just texted. He and his brothers and sisters are on their way."

"Are his parents coming?" Gavin asked, thinking of his father.

Schuyler's mouth pinched into a thin line. "Their names are Miles and Sarah," she said quietly. "They didn't make the trip from New Orleans. Some kind of prior commitment, according to Nolan." She shook her head. "I don't think that's the truth."

"How did Dad respond?"

"He's taking it in stride. I think he's disappointed, but hopefully the Robinson siblings will show. That would help take his mind off Miles as well as the trouble with the agency. Apparently, Fortunado Real Estate isn't the only company having problems. Olivia told me her dad is stressed out because of some glitch with a processor manufactured by Robinson Tech. There's talk about a giant recall. It's as out of the blue as the trouble at the agency. I'm hoping this night will help everyone focus on more positive things."

"It's so nice that you put all of this together," Christine said. "Family is important, no matter how different the members of it might be."

"I couldn't agree more." Schuyler beamed. "I'm so glad you're here. We all are."

Gavin saw Christine's shoulders stiffen slightly, although not so much that Schuyler would notice. He knew what it meant and quickly ushered her into the winery.

"We're going to be okay," he told her in a hushed tone. "No one is going to get hurt in all of this."

She smiled but her eyes remained strained. "I know." Glancing around the interior of the winery, her features softened again. "It's gorgeous."

"Weren't you here for Schuyler's wedding last year?" It embarrassed him that he didn't remember, but surely she would have been invited? Christine was important to his family. She'd been a constant in their lives for a decade. The thought made guilt wash over him once again. Why hadn't he noticed her before now?

She shook her head. "I was invited but couldn't attend.

My mom had a heart attack last spring so I spent a lot of time with her."

He stopped and stared down at her. "I didn't realize. She seems healthy now."

"She is," Christine said with a nod. "It's part of why she's so intent on the family dinners and all of us getting close. She's gotten a new lease on life."

"You have some explaining to do, son of mine."

At the sound of his mother's voice, he turned to see her approach, her arms held wide. "Hi, Mom." He bent to hug her, breathing in the familiar scent of the perfume she'd worn since he was a kid. "You look lovely."

"You look like you've been keeping secrets." She pulled away and wagged a finger at him. "I'll deal with that in a minute," she said, then turned to Christine. "First, let me say hello and congratulations to this beautiful girl."

"Hi, Barbara." Christine leaned in to hug his mother. "It's nice to see you."

"You, too, dear." Barbara took her hand. "Kenneth tells me you're doing great things in Austin. He had such fun working with you last week."

"It seemed like old times," Christine admitted. "I'm surprised he was willing to hand the reins back over to Maddie and Zach without a fight."

Barbara laughed. "Don't let him fool you. He's loving every minute of retirement."

"Probably because he gets to spend more time with you," Christine said, and his mother looked pleased at the compliment.

Seriously, how was it that Christine hadn't been snatched up before now? Beautiful, sweet, smart and possessing one of the kindest hearts he'd ever met. Some man was going to be lucky to have her as his wife.

The thought that it wouldn't be him made Gavin's stomach turn like he'd just eaten food that had gone bad. But he knew she deserved someone better. Someone who could give her the kind of devotion she deserved.

"Speaking of spending time with people…" His mother turned her knowing gaze back to him. "Why was this relationship kept a secret?"

Gavin opened his mouth to answer, but Christine placed a hand on his. "It was my decision," she told his mother. "I wanted a chance for us to get to know each other—just the two of us—before we shared it with the family."

His mom smiled. "We can be a bit much."

"In the best way possible," Christine said, and Barbara gave her another hug.

"We're thrilled for both of you," his mom said. She held up Christine's hand. "It's a beautiful ring, lovely and classic just like the woman wearing it. I hope this means—"

"Mom." Gavin grimaced. "Please don't give us pressure about planning a quick wedding like Schuyler and Maddie have been. We're taking our time."

She took Gavin's hand and squeezed. "I was about to say I hope this means you'll be spending more time in Texas. And not that we're going to lose Christine to Colorado."

"I'm in Austin until the end of the month," he said, choosing not to directly answer the question. Of course, his mother already knew his plans for the next couple of weeks. But he wasn't about to address his future with Christine, not when his hold on her at the moment felt tenuous at best.

His mom inclined her head to study him before her attention was drawn to the front of the room. "Our New Orleans guests have arrived. I'm going to collect your father and go say hello."

Christine moved to his side as his mother crossed the

room. "What is it about the Fortunes, legitimate or not, being so darn attractive? You have some mighty gorgeous genes in your family."

He chuckled despite the tension running through him. Each new leaf uncovered in the mess of a family tree Julius Fortune had planted added additional complications to all their lives. Of course, last year the Fortunado branch had been the ones complicating everything.

As Gavin watched his parents greet the new arrivals to this odd family reunion, he had to agree with Christine. Seven of the eight newcomers to the party were clearly related, he assumed, based on how they resembled each other, much the way he and his siblings looked alike.

He'd done a bit of research on Miles Fortune and his New Orleans family. Nolan, who was the youngest son and a recent transplant to Austin, looked the most comfortable. Gavin guessed that had something to do with the woman on his arm, a brunette with long hair and a sweet smile. The rest of the group seemed hesitant to join the party, and Gavin didn't blame them. They were all making the best of a difficult situation.

"None of us got to meet Julius Fortune," he said tightly, "but by all accounts he was a sorry excuse for a man."

"Yes," Christine agreed, shifting closer so that the length of her body was pressed against him. Was it an unconscious move on her part or could she possibly know how much comfort he took in her nearness? "Despite that, his sons have good lives and from the looks of it, amazing families. I think that says something about all of you. If nothing else, remember you have that in common with your new relatives."

"Thank you," he whispered, placing an arm around her shoulder. "You make everything better."

She tipped up her chin to stare at him as if his words surprised her. He couldn't resist kissing her soft lips and didn't care that they might have an audience of his family, both new and old.

"Ah, young love," his brother Connor drawled as he gave Gavin a hearty slap on the back. "You two are damn adorable."

Gavin threw an elbow, but Connor dodged it with no problem. "And you're a pain in the—"

"Hi, Connor," Christine said, breaking apart from him.

His brother leaned in for a quick hug. "Hey, lovely lady. It's great to see you." He hitched a thumb in Gavin's direction. "How did you get mixed up with this clown?"

"Just lucky, I guess," Christine answered, taking Connor's teasing in stride.

He winked. "Well, let me know if he gets out of line. I'd be honored to step in as your overprotective brother."

Gavin snorted. "You realize the two of us are actually related? What happened to you being too busy to come down for this?"

"Blood relations can't be helped," Connor answered. "And I wouldn't have missed this reunion. What do you think of the new crew?"

"I think we can all appreciate what they're going through, dealing with the knowledge of our shared family history." He shrugged. "I also think it's interesting that Dad's half brother isn't making an appearance tonight."

"I don't see any of the Robinsons here tonight, other than Olivia," Connor added. "I'm a little surprised at that. They've all seemed fairly open to this bizarre turn of events."

"I'm sure it's been tough with Gerald and Charlotte separating. Maybe that changes things for some of them? I couldn't imagine Mom and Dad ever breaking up."

"Thank heavens for that," Connor agreed. "I've heard that Charlotte hasn't taken the separation well."

"Can you blame her?" Christine asked, and Gavin realized there were things she didn't understand about the situation.

He shrugged. "Apparently, she knew about her husband's infidelities and kept some kind of a dossier on the illegitimate kids he'd sired."

Christine's big eyes widened. "That's awful."

"No doubt. I'm going to grab a drink then head over to introduce myself to the newcomers," Connor told them. "Can I get either of you something?"

"I'm fine for now," Christine responded.

Gavin shook his head. "Me, too."

When Connor walked away, she took Gavin's hand. "It means a lot to Schuyler that all of you are here." She glanced to where his sister and Carlo were talking to Nolan Fortune, tall and lean with dark brown hair. He held tightly to the hand of the woman at his side. "I think we should join them."

He nodded, unsure of why he felt so out of sorts or how to explain the way having Christine at his side soothed him. They approached the foursome, and Schuyler smiled gratefully.

"Let me introduce you both to my brother," she said. "This is Gavin and his fiancée, Christine Briscoe." She inclined her head toward the other couple. "Gavin, meet Nolan Fortune and *his* fiancée, Lizzie Sullivan."

"Thanks for coming tonight. I heard you've moved from New Orleans to Austin recently."

The man nodded, his brown eyes warm. "I'll always love NOLA, but my heart's in Texas so this is where I belong." He leaned in and dropped a gentle kiss on the top of Lizzie's head. "It's good that we all get together."

"I couldn't agree more," Gavin answered.

"Carlo and I are going to check on the food," Schuyler said. "If you or any of your siblings need anything, Nolan, just let me know."

"Will do." The man glanced around as Schuyler and Carlo walked away. "I think I could use a glass of the Mendoza wine I've heard so much about."

Gavin motioned to one of the servers holding a tray of wineglasses. "I can help with that."

Each of them took a glass of wine, and after thanking the server, Gavin lifted his glass. "A toast to new family and friendships. Sometimes the best endings come from the strangest starts."

Nolan and Lizzie shared a long look.

"I feel like we should ask how you two met," Christine said. "There's a story there."

Lizzie smiled. "It is a strange start," she admitted. "I saw Nolan playing in a jazz band in Austin the holiday season before last and we struck up a conversation from there."

Nolan draped an arm over his fiancée's shoulder. "But we didn't reconnect until this past December. I tried my best to mess things up, but she gave me another chance. Best moment of my life."

Gavin watched Christine's eyes light as she listened to the other couple. For all of her practicality, he realized she was a romantic at heart. And how had he honored that? With deals and arrangements, boundaries and timelines. What a fool he'd been.

"How about the two of you?" Lizzie took a slow sip of wine. "How did you meet?"

Gavin's stomach dipped as Christine's face fell for an instant before she flashed a too-bright smile. "We've known each other for years," she said airily. "It's the classic friends-first scenario."

"Friendship is key," Lizzie said, obviously sensing Christine's discomfort at being put on the spot.

"Actually…" Gavin leaned in, as if he was sharing a deep secret. "I'd had a crush on her for years."

"Who could blame you?" Nolan asked gamely.

"Exactly," Gavin agreed. "But I didn't think she'd ever go for a guy like me."

"He has a bit of a reputation," Christine offered, then added in a stage whisper, "As a *player*."

"No." Lizzie patted a hand on her chest, feigning shock.

"But I knew I'd have to be a better man to earn my place at Christine's side." Gavin twirled the stem of the wineglass between two fingers, the truth of that statement hitting him like a Louisville Slugger to the chest. "So I…"

"You became one," Lizzie finished.

"Working on it," Gavin clarified.

"Most of us are a work in progress." Nolan lifted his glass to study the burgundy liquid inside. "This wine is fantastic."

Gavin was grateful his new relative was giving him an out on a subject that cut a little too close to home. "It's a private vintage. They only bring it out for special occasions."

"I'm sorry my dad wouldn't—" Nolan cleared his throat "—couldn't be here for this."

"I know my parents would love to meet him."

"What about the other brothers?"

Gavin felt his mouth drop open. "What other brothers?"

"You don't know about Gary and David?"

He shook his head.

Nolan ran a hand over his jaw. "Our fathers weren't Julius Fortune's only illegitimate sons. He had two more."

"I wondered about that," Schuyler said, rejoining the group. "I heard Ariana Lamonte—or I guess Fortune now—the reporter who married Jayden of the Paseo triplets, made a reference to there being 'others.'"

"Why didn't you say anything?" Gavin asked, his gut tightening once again.

"From what I could tell, the Paseo Fortunes were ambivalent about all of this. It was before Gerald and Deborah had reconciled so Jayden seemed to care more about protecting his mom from being hurt again than uncovering any more Fortunes. I think Ariana dropped it out of respect for Jayden's wishes."

"Our dad has known about his birth father for a while," Nolan revealed, leaning in closer to his fiancée. "He's done some research on his own over the years."

"Julius Fortune was a real piece of work," Gavin muttered.

"Quite true," Nolan agreed.

Schuyler shook her head. "We've got to stick together in all this. There's too much stressful stuff going on already and we can't let Julius's mistakes continue to haunt us. I only wish the rest of the Robinsons had been able to make it. They—"

As if on cue, Olivia hurried over to them. She held her cell phone in front of her like it was a poisonous snake. Glancing around wildly, her gaze settled on Schuyler.

"What's wrong?" Schuyler asked as Olivia took a shuddery breath.

Conversation in the lodge fell silent as everyone's attention focused on Olivia.

She swiped her hands across her cheeks. "A fire," she whispered. "Someone set fire to our family home. The Robinson estate has been destroyed."

Chapter 12

Christine registered the collective gasp that went up in the room at Olivia's words.

Schuyler wrapped her arms around the other woman's slim shoulders as the Fortunados and New Orleans Fortunes moved to surround them.

"What happened?" Kenneth asked, making his way through to the two women.

Olivia blinked several times as Schuyler released her. Alejandro Mendoza took his wife's hand, and Olivia leaned into him, clearly needing the support. Christine knew Olivia's courtship with Alejandro had been a whirlwind, and she'd even heard whispers that the engagement had been a sham at the beginning. Clearly, the two were soul mates and she couldn't help but wonder if she and Gavin might also have a happy ending to their strange beginning.

Olivia shook her head as Alejandro pulled her closer. "We don't know exactly how it got started, but my brother

Wes overheard the fire chief talking about suspected arson. Dad's the only one living at the estate at the moment, although Deborah is there quite a bit and each of us stops by when we can." She glanced at Schuyler. "We were all getting ready to come here. I think if someone did this purposefully, they must have known the estate would be empty tonight. In fact, things would have been worse except..." Her voice broke off as a sob escaped her lips.

"What is it?" Schuyler demanded. "Is everyone okay?"

Olivia shook her head. "I asked Ben to stop by the house and pick up a couple of photo albums. Apparently, he got there when the fire was really raging. He called 911 but tried to fight it on his own before the firefighters arrived. He—" She paused again, placing a hand over her mouth as she shook her head.

Christine automatically reached for Gavin's hand.

Kenneth placed a gentle hand on Olivia's arm. "Tell us," he whispered. "Is your brother okay?"

She gave a small shrug. "We don't know. He's on his way to the hospital. The EMTs tell us it's severe smoke inhalation." She dragged in a shuddering breath. "Alejandro and I need to leave. I have to get to the hospital—everyone's planning to stay there until we hear more about Ben. But I wanted you to understand..." She placed a hand to her cheek and shook her head. "I don't know what since none of this makes sense. The Fortune Robinsons would have been here, Schuyler. I promise."

"Of course. What do you need us to do?" Gavin's sister asked. "Please, Olivia. Let us help. We're your family, no matter how crazy the circumstances."

Olivia flashed a watery smile. "Would you go out to the estate? It kills me that there's no one from the family there, but our priority is Ben. It's the house we all grew up in, and no matter what kind of problems Mom and Dad have been having recently, there are so many memories."

Although her parents' house didn't exactly fill Christine with sentimental thoughts, she thought about the Fortunados' stately home in Houston. She'd been to Kenneth and Barbara's home a number of times through the years and it had always struck her as such a happy place, as if the walls held on to the memories of children growing up there and of the bond among the Fortunado children. If the Robinson estate was anything like that, the loss of it would be far greater than simply physical property.

"Of course," Schuyler said and the entire room seemed to nod in unison.

"I've got to go," Olivia whispered.

"Do you need someone to drive the two of you?" Gavin asked, stepping forward. "With the shock and upset—"

"Thank you," Alejandro interrupted. "But we'll be fine."

Olivia nodded. "My family and I appreciate your willingness to help. We're grateful for each of you."

With that, she and Alejandro turned and walked out of the winery. There was a moment of heavy silence before the room exploded in shocked murmurs and muted conversations.

Gavin quickly grabbed a chair from a nearby table and climbed up. He shot Christine a grateful smile when she lifted two fingers to her mouth for a sharp whistle that drew everyone's attention to him.

"The fire at the Robinson estate is a tragic turn of events," he began, "especially if the cause of the blaze turns out to be arson." He drew in a breath as if he felt the shocking possibility like a blow. "But the Fortune Robinsons need us now. All of us. We may not know each other well yet, but this is the time when we become one family."

Pride bloomed in Christine's chest as she glanced around to see all eyes riveted on Gavin as he spoke about the importance of solidarity and support. Even though most of his work was done in boardrooms with company leadership, she could imagine him in a courtroom, commanding the attention of judge and jury.

He tasked Valene and two of the New Orleans Fortunes—the oldest brother, Austin, and the baby of the family, Belle—with rounding up blankets, snack baskets, clean clothes and toiletry kits to take to the hospital for the Robinsons during the time they were keeping vigil for Ben. He asked Everett, his doctor brother, to head directly to the hospital to use his connections to facilitate whatever he could for the family. Schuyler volunteered to coordinate meals, and Maddie offered to secure a furnished rental house for Gerald Robinson and stock it with groceries and other household items before he got there.

Christine smiled and nodded as Gavin met her gaze across the sea of Fortunes. How was she supposed to do anything but fall in love with this man?

Oh. She placed a hand on her chest as panic washed through her. She was in love with Gavin. It was more than a crush or infatuation. So much for guarding her heart so she wouldn't be hurt at the end of this.

The knowledge that the end was inevitable did nothing to stem the tide of emotions she felt for him. The week of keeping her distance was forgotten like yesterday's news. After easing herself away from the group as Gavin mobilized everyone who was left to head to the estate, she hurried to the bathroom and splashed cold water on her face.

Nothing had changed about her outward appearance. She saw the same blue eyes and red hair holding its style thanks to a truckload of product, pale skin that looked a bit pastier than normal thanks to her panic-inducing revelation.

But inside her was a tumbling avalanche of doubt and fear. It was difficult to believe that her heart, which was so sure and full at the moment, could be in grave danger of shattering at the end of the month.

She took a few steadying breaths then headed back out.

Gavin waited in the dimly lit hallway.

"You don't have to do this," he said quietly, his face a stark mask.

Had he somehow read her mind? As if she had a choice on what her heart wanted—*who* her heart wanted. It had always been him.

She swallowed and tried to figure out how to explain her emotions to him without sending him running in the other direction. "I—"

He moved forward, taking her hands in his. "You've been great tonight. The best. But I know that it's overwhelming, all these Fortunes, and now the fire. It goes way beyond what you signed up for with us."

Did it ever, she thought.

"I can drop you at home before heading to the estate. I totally understand that you might not want to be a part of this mess. We're not your problem so—"

"Stop." She shook her head. He'd completely misread her reaction, but she couldn't blame him. She'd *tried* to pull away this week. Look where that had gotten her. "I'm going with you to the estate if you want me there."

"Of course," he answered without hesitation. The intensity of his gaze made her breath catch. "You've been the most amazing sport about all of this."

She choked out a laugh. So much for his devotion. A good sport? It was as if she could feel her heart splintering into a thousand pieces. She swallowed and tried not to let her emotions show. This was her chance. He'd given her an out. She should be smart and take it.

"It's all part of our deal," she answered with forced cheer.

His brows drew together, and he opened his mouth as if he wanted to argue with her assessment then snapped it shut again. "Are you ready?"

She nodded and followed him out of the winery. The only people left were servers, cleaning up the deserted party.

"You did an amazing job of rallying everyone," she told Gavin as they pulled away from the curb.

"We attorneys like to hear ourselves talk," he said with a wink.

"You do that too much."

He chuckled. "Talk?"

"Downplay the good things you do," she clarified and saw his knuckles tighten on the steering wheel. "Maddie told me you do pro-bono work with low-income families in the court system in Colorado."

"I've had a lot of success in my career. It's easy to give back in some small way."

"According to her, you devote a ton of hours to the cause."

"I have time on my hands when ski season ends."

"Gavin." She adjusted the seat belt strap so she could turn toward him. "This is what I'm talking about. I'm not sure why you want everyone to see you as this cavalier party guy, but it's a mask."

"Hiding my insightful thoughts and hidden depths."

"Yes," she answered simply. "You're a good man. I wish you could see yourself the way I do."

A muscle worked in his jaw as he accelerated onto the

interstate. "I wish I could be the man you see," he said after several long minutes.

They drove the rest of the way to the Robinson estate in silence, although it was more comfortable than awkward. At some point Gavin reached across the front seat and laced her fingers with his. She was coming to expect the way he seemed to need to touch her as if she grounded him in the midst of the chaos swirling around them.

They exited the highway and drove through an upscale neighborhood of mansions. Christine gasped when the estate came into view. She hadn't seen the house in person before today, but given Gerald's success in the tech industry, she'd imagined it as spectacular.

It probably had been prior to today. But now she could only describe the scene in front of her as horrific. Fire trucks still lined the driveway, although the fire had been out long enough that the remains of the building were no longer smoking. The west section of the mansion, which clearly housed the garage, was still intact for the most part. As for the rest of the building, the walls that were left were no more than a blackened shell. Most of the structure was rubble and ash.

"Do you really think it was arson?" Christine asked as they parked behind Kenneth's Mercedes.

Gavin seemed as stunned by the scene as she felt. "I can't imagine who would do something like this. I've never heard rumblings that Gerald has any sworn enemies. If a person set a fire intent on doing this much damage, they must really hate him."

"It's unbelievable."

They got out of the SUV and joined the rest of the family who had assembled on the driveway in front of what should have been the front door.

"Has someone talked to the fire chief?" Gavin asked his dad.

"Not yet." Kenneth shook his head. "I think we're all paralyzed in the face of this much destruction. They're lucky Ben was the only one injured in the blaze. The level of damage blows my mind."

"I'll find him," Gavin said and jogged off in the direction of the row of fire trucks.

Barbara rested her head on her husband's shoulder. "It's awful but we both know home is where the heart is. Gerald and his family will survive this. He can rebuild and make new memories while holding on to the old."

Christine agreed, but that fact didn't make the devastation more palatable.

"I wonder if Charlotte knows," Connor murmured.

"I'm sure someone called her," Kenneth said. "Although I imagine she has everything of either sentimental or monetary value that belongs to her out of the house. I know Gerald wanted to make a clean break, especially after reconnecting with Deborah."

Gavin returned at that moment. "Normally they wouldn't allow access to the house so soon after firefighters got things under control. Apparently, Olivia told her dad we were coming out here. Gerald made some calls to ensure we'd be good. He has friends in high places. The chief says we can go in the areas they've deemed safe but to be careful of debris."

They each nodded.

"Let's split into groups," Gavin told them. "Connor and Savannah, you take some of us and start at the far end of the house nearest what's left of the garage. Mom and Dad, you take a group and start in the center and spread out. Chris-

tine and I will lead a crew to the far end of the rubble. I'm
guessing that's where we'll find the master suite."

He gazed at what used to be the estate's main structure.
"Look for clues as to what the room might have been used
as and base your search for salvageable items there. As an
example, you might find an appliance or two that tells you
that room is the kitchen."

"What are we looking for?" Savannah asked, glancing
over her shoulder toward the house.

"Anything of value, either financial or sentimental. Don't
worry too much about pedigree or authenticity on any of
the pieces we collect. This day is going to haunt the Robinson family, and I'd like them to know we were able to
save something."

As his family and the Fortunes from New Orleans split
up to tackle the first step in helping to heal their Robinson
relatives, Gavin returned to Christine's side. She could see
the tension around his mouth and eyes, feel the tension radiating from him.

"What if someone did this to my parents' house?" he
asked softly. "It's unimaginable."

Once again she tamped down her doubts and wrapped
her arms around his waist. "We're going to get them through
this," she promised. "You're one family now. That matters."

He blew out a breath and kissed the top of her head.
"You have no idea how glad I am that you're here with me."

"There's no place I'd rather be," she assured him, and
together they followed his family into the wreckage.

Chapter 13

It was almost midnight before Gavin walked Christine to the door of her condo.

"This was not the night I'd planned," he told her, rubbing a hand over his eyes.

They'd stayed at the Robinson estate until darkness made it dangerous to pick through the destruction. Although the house had been effectively torched, they'd managed to find a number of personal mementos that remained undamaged. They'd put the items into boxes and driven them to the rental house Maddie had secured.

It had seemed a sorry collection pushed into one corner of the empty garage, but Gavin hoped they'd bring some comfort to Gerald and the rest of the family.

They'd gone to grab dinner with Maddie, Zach, Schuyler, Carlo and Connor. Somehow Gavin needed the tangible reminder of his connection with his siblings. With everything going on from new Fortune revelations to the trouble with the family business to the fire, being able to laugh with his family was a balm to his soul. Had he been wishing for life as an only child just a couple of weeks ago? What a fool he'd been.

His family was a gift, just like this time with Christine. He'd taken both for granted. That was his problem and why he knew he had to let Christine go at the end of all this. He didn't have enough inside him to give her what she deserved.

"No one can plan for tragedy," she said, pulling a key ring out of her purse. "It's how a person handles it that shows what they're made of." She turned to him. "You were strong, articulate and compassionate tonight. It says so much about you as a person."

Damn. He wished he were a better man because walking away from Christine was going to hurt like hell.

"Right back at you," he said, then did a mental eye roll. He must have used up all his decent words earlier because he couldn't seem to form a coherent thought at the moment.

She unlocked the door and opened it to allow Princess Di onto the small porch. The dog's tail wagged enthusiastically as she greeted first Christine then Gavin with a head butt to the legs before trotting down the steps to do her business in the bushes.

"Do you need to walk her?" he asked, smiling at the dog. He really needed a pet. Maybe having something to come home to would help his outwardly exciting life feel not so lonely on the inside. "I could—"

"One of my neighbors took her out earlier." Christine leaned inside and flipped on a light. "She'll be ready to hunker down for the night after her potty break."

"Right." Gavin rubbed a hand along the back of his neck. "I guess I should—"

"Would you like to come in for a bit?" she asked, almost hesitantly.

"Yes," he breathed, thanking the heavens for her invitation. It was ridiculous, this constant need to be with her. Reckless to allow himself to depend on her in any way. But he couldn't help himself. She was like a cool drink, and he'd been in the emotional desert of his own making for far too long.

She whistled for the dog, and Diana came loping back up the steps and into the house.

"Let's talk about your mad whistling skills," Gavin said as he closed the door behind them.

She grinned. "What can I say?" His insides tightened as a blush stained her cheeks when she added, "I'm good with my mouth."

If she'd smacked him over the head with a sledgehammer, he couldn't have been more shocked. He felt his mouth drop open, and desire pounded through him, flooding his veins with a sharp yearning.

Before he could get his muddled brain to form a response, she turned away. "Would you like a drink?" she asked over her shoulder. "A glass of water?"

"Sure." She toed out of her strappy heels and just that innocuous movement made another wave of need crash through him. Once again her pink-painted toes were the sexiest thing he'd ever seen.

She continued to the kitchen, hanging her purse over a chair. She took a dog biscuit from the cookie jar on the counter and then tossed it to Princess Di, who expertly caught it. The dog padded over to her bed while Christine pulled two glasses from an upper cabinet and filled them.

All the while he stood rooted in place, every cell in his

body tingling with awareness and—Lord help them both—unbridled lust.

"Gavin?" She stared at him with wide eyes from the kitchen as if he were a hungry lion and she was the proverbial lamb invited to his feast. "I was joking about the mouth comment," she said with a hesitant laugh. "I went too far. I'm sorry."

Her apology jarred him from his lust-filled stupor. He ate up the distance between them in three long strides. "You never need to apologize," he said, cupping her face in his hands. "Yours is the most tantalizing mouth in the universe." He kissed her, nipping at the corner of her lips. "I thank my lucky stars each time you kiss me."

She moaned in the back of her throat as he ran his tongue along the seam of her lips. "Open for me," he whispered, and she did, her tongue mingling with his until his mind was swimming once more.

He ran his fingers through her hair, the way he'd been longing to all night, plucking out the thin pins that held the style in place.

At this moment he didn't give a damn that she was too good for him. He couldn't find it in himself to care about anything except the feel of her pressing into his chest. Her curves, her scent, the sweetness of her very essence.

Then she pulled away, and Gavin wanted to growl his protest. Was she going to send him away? Close herself off the way she had in the past week? He wasn't sure he could take that distance again.

"Why haven't we had sex?" she blurted, her eyes a little hazy but otherwise focused intently on his.

Just when he thought she couldn't surprise him anymore, another inadvertent blow sent him reeling.

"Um... I'm trying to respect you," he said, the words ringing false even to his own ears.

Her delicate brows drew together until she wasn't so much frowning as glaring at him. "You only sleep with women you don't respect?"

"No," he answered quickly. "I didn't mean that. What I'm trying to say is..." Oh, hell. What was he trying to say?

"You don't want me like that," she supplied and it took a moment for her words to register in his muddled mind. Right now the majority of his brain cells had gone on hiatus, allowing the lower half of him to take over the controls. That half wasn't exactly known for its good judgment.

"I want you in every way possible." He moved forward, and she stepped back as if putting distance between them was an unconscious response. No. He couldn't let her put up a wall between them. Not tonight.

He softened his tone and let his need for her flood his gaze. His career and the choices he'd made to keep himself closed off in his personal life had made him a master of the poker face.

He wondered if he'd ever been like Christine, whose beautiful emotions were written on her face.

"You agreed to help me because of the pressure from my family," he said slowly, needing the words to come out right. Knowing this moment mattered. "I don't want to take advantage of that...of you."

One side of her mouth kicked up. "What if I want to be taken advantage of?"

"Christine."

She studied him for a moment, and he could almost see the emotional war going on inside her. Which side would win out?

"I want you, Gavin."

He could have dropped to his knees in thanks. At the same time he didn't want her to have any doubts or regrets so he asked, "Are you sure?"

She took a step closer and wrapped her arms around his neck. "Never more sure," she promised and kissed him.

He let her set the pace and gave himself over to her slow, seductive torture. He couldn't remember the last time he'd been this happy, and it was all because of the beautiful woman in his arms.

More.

That was the refrain echoing in Christine's mind as she kissed Gavin. His hands reached up to stroke her bare shoulders, thumbs grazing over her collarbones. The feather-light touch made goose bumps break out along her skin, and all she could think was *more*.

She broke off the kiss, gratified when it took a few seconds for Gavin's gaze to focus on her. He'd given her the choice tonight, and she loved him for it. For so many reasons. Despite her doubts and the understanding that heartbreak was inevitable, she wanted this moment. This man.

Hitching in a breath, she pushed the suit coat off his shoulders and tossed it onto the counter. Gavin's nostrils flared as she moved closer and tugged on his tie, loosening the silk and sliding it from the collar.

"You can probably do this with more efficiency," she said, her voice husky as she started at the buttons of his shirt with shaky fingers.

"I like you undressing me," he whispered.

With every button, another inch of his muscled body was revealed. The shirtless Gavin she'd seen in photos from Fortunado beach vacations over the years didn't do justice to Gavin in the flesh. Heat radiated from him, and his skin felt soft yet firm under her touch.

When he'd shrugged out of the shirt, she took a moment to admire his body in a way she hadn't been able to the night of Diana's trip to the vet. Her girlie parts screamed to get on with things but she hushed them. This was every one of her fantasies come to life, and she had every intention of savoring the experience.

He gave her a sexy half smile. "I had no idea I could be so turned on just by how you look at me."

She reached out a hand and smoothed it up the hard planes of his chest. "How about when I do this?" she asked, wondering where in the world this confident seductress had been hiding.

Or perhaps not hiding. Maybe she'd simply been waiting for the right man to unlock her passion.

No doubt that Gavin held the key to everything.

"I love it."

She took her other hand and skimmed it across the front of his trousers, and she knew without a doubt he wanted her. He let out a soft groan as she cupped him then he encircled her wrist with one hand. "You're making me crazy, and I love it."

"It's an adventure," she told him, earning a low laugh.

"The best kind," he agreed, lifting her hand to his shoulder. Then he reached around and unzipped the back of her dress. The silky fabric slid down her body and over her hips with ease, pooling at her feet.

Although inwardly cringing at standing in front of this perfect man in nothing but a black strapless bra and pair of lacy panties, Christine forced herself not to squirm. As she had minutes earlier with him, Gavin took his sweet time studying her, his chest rising and falling sharply as his gaze wandered along her body.

The need and desire she saw there gave her confidence, and for the first time she tried to see herself through Gavin's eyes. Clearly, he liked what he saw. Although she hadn't been overweight for over a decade, Christine still viewed herself through the lens of the chubby girl she'd once been. The misfit. The loser.

But she was a different woman now, and it was past time she start embracing who she'd become. She refused to allow herself to be stuck in her old insecurities.

Biting down on her lower lip, she reached around her back and unclasped the bra strap, tossing the thin piece of fabric to one side. Then she hooked her thumbs into the waistband of her panties and slid them down her hips.

All the while, Gavin's gaze remained on hers as his breathing grew more ragged.

"You have too many clothes on," she whispered.

"Damn straight," he agreed, his voice shaky.

He made quick work of his shoes and socks then unfastened his belt buckle and took off his pants, pushing them down his hips along with his boxers.

Suddenly, Christine had the realization that they were standing at the edge of her kitchen. Now what? She'd only been intimate with her previous boyfriend, and that had strictly been a lights out in the bedroom type of affair. Spontaneity was new for her, and while her body was a big fan, her brain wasn't quite sure how to deal with the reality of her new adventure. "Oh, my gosh."

Gavin chuckled. "I've gotten a lot of reactions in my day, but that's a new one."

"We're in the kitchen," she told him.

His grin widened, and he stepped forward. "You've never christened your kitchen?" he asked with a wink.

She shook her head.

He moved closer, reaching for her. "I like watching you try new things, and I have lots of them planned for tonight."

"You have a plan?" Her voice came out in a squeak.

"Do you trust me?" he whispered against her mouth, licking across the seam of her lips.

"Yes," she breathed.

"Good," he said and lifted her into his arms.

She gasped. The feel of his body was even more amazing than she could have imagined. Then she gasped again when her backside hit the smooth wood of the kitchen table.

Gavin trailed kisses along her jaw then down her neck and lower. He cupped her breasts in his big hands. When he took the tip of one, and then the other, into his mouth, she moaned from the pleasure of his mouth on her body. One hand moved lower, grazing her hips before gently pushing apart her legs and inching closer to her center.

She thought the attention to her breasts was enough to drive her mad with desire, but this was something else entirely. His fingers found a rhythm that had her craving more, the pressure in her body building with excruciating sweetness until she finally cried out. It felt as though a thousand stars were crashing over her, bathing her in a bright light that was like nothing she could have imagined.

Gavin kissed her, deep and slow, as the pulsing release subsided.

"I'll never look at this table the same way again," she whispered when he pulled away.

"I'm going to take that as a compliment," he answered with a husky chuckle.

"But you didn't…" Christine cleared her throat. "We aren't finished?"

"Not by a long shot." He gave her a sexy half smile that made her toes curl. Then he bent and took a wallet from his pants' pocket, pulling out a condom wrapper. "The next part of my master plan is moving to the bedroom."

"I like that plan."

She went to stand but before she could get to her feet, Gavin picked her up, one arm under her knees and the other cradling her back.

"Down the hall?"

She nodded. "You're pretty good with your hands," she told him, placing a hand on his bare chest. "But you haven't turned me into so much contented jelly that I can't walk."

"Pretty good?" He made a sound low in his throat. "That sounds like a challenge. And I could carry you for miles."

She bit down on the inside of her cheek when a denial popped to her lips. She might not feel confident about her body, thanks to years of being overweight, but she knew enough not to point out her flaws to Gavin.

He seemed as enthralled with her as she was with him, and that thought only served to open her heart to him even more.

"I can hear you thinking," he told her as he entered her bedroom.

She laughed softly as he tugged down the comforter and sheet and placed her on the mattress. "Then you'd better distract me."

"Exactly what I had in mind."

He opened the condom wrapper and, a moment later, skimmed his hands up her body until he was leveraging himself over her. She could feel him between her legs, but he held still as he smoothed his thumbs along the sides of her face, gazing into her eyes with an intensity that stole her breath.

"You're amazing," he whispered.

She automatically shook her head. Christine knew she was many things. Smart. Loyal. Dependable. Okay, that sounded more like she was describing her dog, but it was difficult to argue with the truth.

Gavin gripped her head and said again, "You. Are Amazing."

Oh, no. She blinked several times. There was no way she was going to cry in front of him because he'd said something nice and she wanted desperately to believe him. She lifted her head and kissed him. Then he was inside her, moving in a rhythm that she knew was unique to the two of them. It was everything, and she still wanted more. Pressure built again, consuming her, but this time she wasn't alone in giving in to the pleasure. Gavin stayed with her, in her, until they lost themselves in the moment and all the things she felt but couldn't put into words.

And Christine knew the emotion…this night…this man…would change her life forever.

Chapter 14

The next morning Gavin blinked awake, disoriented for a moment by his surroundings. The bedrooms at both his loft in Denver and the Driskill, where he was staying in downtown Austin, were decorated in a neutral color palette and dark wood furniture, so the pale blue walls and creamy white furniture he woke up to weren't what he expected.

The woman curled against him, still fast asleep, was another unexpected occurrence. Well, not exactly unexpected. He'd spent most of the night making love to Christine, which had been better than he ever could have imagined.

But Gavin didn't typically spend the night with the women he dated. More than typically. He didn't ever stay over an entire night. He also hadn't had a woman stay overnight with him since… Well, Christine's sleepover in his hotel room after Maddie's wedding had been the first.

It was part of his unwritten list of relationship rules not to complicate things. Simple was easier when it came to

women, but Christine and their unorthodox arrangeme.
were changing everything, especially his self-control.

He thought about sneaking out quietly but couldn't quite
force himself to move. Her bright auburn hair was messy—
thanks to him, most likely—and he loved how relaxed and
unguarded she appeared in sleep.

Scratch that last bit. He liked it very much. Not loved.
He wasn't a man who threw around the word *love* in any
capacity with the women he dated. Dangerous territory that
led to expectations he couldn't possibly meet.

Maybe that was why it was so easy to let down his guard
with Christine. Their built-in end date was a safety net for
his heart. So why did it feel like he was walking on an emotional tightrope with nothing but cold, hard ground beneath
him as a landing?

He shifted away as a reality he wasn't willing to accept
pummeled at his defenses, a tornado of doubts and long-
held beliefs tearing at his walls.

Christine sighed then opened her eyes, her gaze soft
and sleepy. Damn if he didn't want to pull her close, bury
himself inside her and try to give her everything he'd never
thought himself capable of offering a woman.

The mental reminder of his own shortcomings was
enough to have him jerking away and climbing out of bed
as if she'd just tried to bite him.

He was a damn coward.

She sat up, lifting the sheet to cover her beautiful breasts.
Now that he knew firsthand the sweet taste of her skin and
the way she fit with him, he had to force himself not to
crawl under the covers again.

"Good morning," she said, and he hated himself for the
doubt that clouded her eyes.

"Hi. I've got to go."

"Oh." The smile she gave him was shaky at best. "I un-
lerstand."

She couldn't possibly because he was fumbling around
with no playbook for this moment. Clearly, since he was
making a complete mess of it. "I had fun last night," he
said, even as he pulled on his trousers.

At some point during the night, he'd brought his clothes
into the bedroom and put on boxers to sleep. Now he fastened his pants and reached for his shirt even as he shoved
his feet into his loafers.

"Me, too," she said, tucking a loose strand of hair behind one ear. "Have you heard anything more about Ben
or confirmation on the cause of the fire?"

Gavin glanced at his phone sitting on the nightstand.
He hadn't even thought to touch the thing since she'd invited him in, so caught up in Christine as he was. He shook
his head. "That's why I need to leave. I want to check on
Ben."

She nodded, although the doubt remained in her gaze.
"Let me know how he's doing. Maybe later we could—"

"I have a meeting tomorrow morning with a client and
a presentation I need to finish. It's going to be a late Sunday in the office for me."

This time she didn't nod in agreement, and when her
eyes narrowed as she studied him, a bead of sweat rolled
down between his shoulder blades.

"Is there anything we need to talk about?" she asked,
and he could tell how hard she was working to keep her
composure. He couldn't admire her or hate himself any
more than he did at this moment.

"Nope," he lied.

"Right." She shifted to the edge of the bed, still holding the sheet up to cover her body. "I need to get dressed

and take Di for a walk." When he didn't move, one delica
eyebrow arched. "Which means you should leave now."

Bam.

He thought he couldn't admire her more, until she went
and gave attitude right back to him. Good for her. His
Christine was stronger than she believed herself to be.

No. Not his. He was in the process of messing it up, because that was how he handled real intimacy.

He wasn't sure if it helped or made things worse to know
he was an idiot.

With a sigh, he bent to kiss her goodbye. She turned her
face at the last moment so his lips landed on her cheek.

"Have a nice rest of your day," she told him, refusing to
make eye contact.

"I'll call you later," he promised.

"You can text me," she advised. "It's simpler that way."

Simple. Right. His new least favorite word in the English language.

"Have a good day," he said quietly. "And thank you again
for last night…for everything. I—"

"It's fine, Gavin. We have an agreement. I get that. I
hope you get positive news about Ben." With those polite
words, she showed him that he was—without a doubt—the
biggest jerk on the planet.

He didn't want to be. He didn't want this arrangement
or the way she made him feel more than anyone ever had.
But he couldn't find the words to make it better. Not when
the hollowness inside his chest was a gaping pit that he
couldn't seem to escape.

So he gave her a charming smile, even knowing she saw
through that tired mask, and walked away.

"You look like hell."

As Gavin climbed in the passenger side of his brother's

.r, Everett studied him over the lenses of his mirrored .unglasses.

"Just drive," Gavin muttered, buckling the seat belt.

Everett chuckled and pulled away from the hotel's entrance. They were heading to the hospital to check in with the Robinson branch of the family. Gavin had spoken to Wes Fortune Robinson earlier. Ben's twin had reported that his brother was in stable condition but they were still monitoring him to ensure there was no additional injury to his lungs.

Gavin's sisters had taken care of the rental house for Gerald, as well as baskets of snacks at the hospital and a meal service for each of the Robinson siblings for the next week while they were still in the early days of processing the tragedy of their family home being burned to the ground.

Gavin couldn't imagine what they were going through, losing so many precious memories and family heirlooms. And all that on top of the troubles at Robinson Tech.

He still had trouble processing that the fire had been ruled arson, as Wes had confirmed earlier. The tech industry might be cutthroat but who would have it in for Gerald so much that he or she would be willing to burn down the man's house? Couple that with the recall of one of their processors, and Gavin couldn't imagine things getting much worse for the tech company tycoon.

There was no doubt that Gerald had a crack legal team in-house or on retainer, but Gavin wanted to offer his help in whatever capacity was needed. Everett had offered to pick him up so they could drive over together. His brother had a friend on staff so he was monitoring Ben's recovery.

"Don't tell me you've already messed up things with Christine?" His brother gave a low chuckle even though Gavin didn't find any humor in the question.

"She's fine," he said through clenched teeth.

Everett shook his head and turned onto the boulevard that led to the hospital. "You messed it up. Did she dump you and give back that pretty rock she was wearing?"

"It's not like that."

"What's it like?"

How was he supposed to answer without lying? He'd been lying from the start, but his feelings for Christine didn't feel fake. Spending the night with her hadn't been part of their arrangement. The relationship was real and not real. And yes, he'd messed it up.

"I still don't get why everyone cares so much about my love life," he muttered.

"We want you to be happy." Everett gave him an annoyingly perceptive big-brother glance. "We love you, man."

Gavin pressed two fingers to his suddenly pounding head. Christine made him happy. Could all his doubts and fears be wiped away by something so simple?

"I *am* happy." He felt like a broken record. "I've got a great life. My life is the envy of everyone around me."

"Are you trying to convince me or yourself?"

Gavin sucked in a breath but didn't respond.

"No one would have guessed you and Christine would be such a perfect match. On paper, you're two very different people."

"I don't care what other people think." Which wasn't true since the whole reason this had started was to appease his family.

"She's good for you," Everett said, ignoring Gavin's opinion.

"Yeah," he murmured. "She's amazing, which means she should be with someone who can appreciate and take care of her the way she deserves. I'm not a great bet when it comes to long-term."

"That doesn't have to be true."

"But it is," Gavin countered. "We both know it. Since I've been in Austin, I think every single member of this family has warned me about hurting her. There's a reason for that."

"We're not used to seeing you like this, but we believe you can make it work."

"Right."

"You can make it work, Gavin. Just stop being an idiot."

Gavin laughed softly. "Easier said than done."

"Maybe," Everett agreed. "The right woman makes it worth it. I can't imagine my life without Lila."

"Speaking of you and Lila…" Gavin arched a brow. "Are you ready to talk about the new adventure you two are embarking on?"

Everett slanted him a look that answered the question without words. "You're more perceptive than you look. She wants to wait a few more weeks before announcing the pregnancy."

"I won't say a word." Gavin reached out a hand and squeezed his brother's shoulder. "But congratulations."

"Thanks." The smile Everett flashed was so full of love and happiness, it made Gavin's chest pinch. Would he ever feel that way? It was suddenly so easy to imagine a daughter with Christine's bright hair and sunny smile. But not if their relationship stayed in the pretend realm.

Everett pulled into the hospital parking lot a few minutes later. They weren't able to see Ben but they talked to Wes and Gerald. The police still had no suspects but the fire investigator had determined that the blaze originated in the master bedroom. It was strange, especially since Gerald hadn't been home at the time.

Although he didn't know the Robinsons well, Gavin still felt an overwhelming anger on their behalf toward whoever did this. It felt vindictive and personal. They needed to discover who was behind it. If an enemy was targeting Gerald Robinson, would they try something else or was destroying the family's home an isolated incident?

Gavin also had some things to work out in his own life. Namely his not-at-all-simple feelings for Christine. Was it as easy as Everett made it seem? Surely not. But he could manage it. All he had to do was talk to Christine and explain...

Explain what?

That he was terrified of hurting her. That he didn't believe he could make her happy. Neither would give her a reason to make their fake relationship real.

Scratch that. It was already real. Last night proved it. He could manage the rest. After all, it wasn't like he needed to drop to one knee.

He'd be going back to Denver at the end of next week. Why couldn't they have a long-distance relationship? He wasn't necessarily looking to have his cake and eat it, too, but why not?

Weekends and holidays together but enough separation that she wouldn't get the wrong idea about what he was able to give. They didn't have to be engaged. He might feel more for her than he had for a woman since...well, since ever. But that didn't change who he was at the core.

Why should it? He liked her. He had fun with her. Yet he didn't have to commit more than he could. At some point his family would give up with their insistence on seeing him settled. They'd understand he didn't have it in him. Surely, Christine would understand, as well.

He was an attorney, after all. He just needed to make his case to her.

Chapter 15

Christine transferred a call to Maddie's office then continued entering data into the spreadsheet pulled up on the computer in front of her. Megan had called in sick, which was a bad habit the receptionist had on Monday mornings. They'd have to discuss expectations of the job, but for now Christine was filling in at the agency's front desk.

Two new clients, both looking for large family homes, had everyone feeling a bit more positive about the future. Maddie and Zach were both talented, dedicated Realtors, and Christine knew they'd find a way to overcome the recent setbacks.

She'd do everything she could to support them, even if it meant long hours and little rest. Staying busy was a good distraction from the tightness that had gripped her chest ever since Gavin's abrupt departure yesterday morning. As promised, he'd texted her last night, but she'd been too emotionally drained to respond with more than a few quick keystrokes.

They'd spent an amazing night together, but now
felt as unsure about his feelings as she had weeks ago. [
he still see her as a friend doing him a favor? The phra:
"friends with benefits" came to mind, causing pain to slice
across her stomach. That wasn't what she wanted from
Gavin…from any man. Christine wasn't built for a casual
fling and mentally kicked herself for believing it was more.

Needing a short break to clear her head, she popped over
to Facebook. A sidebar advertisement for a popular Hill
Country wedding venue on the screen, and she couldn't
help but click on the link.

A moment later she sighed as she looked through the
slideshow of charming, rustic wedding snapshots. The cou-
ples looked so happy, and she could clearly imagine fu-
tures of babies, family holidays and years filled with both
laughter and tears. Not that her biological clock was exactly
ticking at the moment, but she wanted to marry and have a
family one day. It wasn't difficult to picture children with
blond hair running through a backyard or cuddling up with
a mini version of Gavin to read a bedtime story.

"Oh. My. God."

She started as Molly hovered over her shoulder.

Christine clicked the mouse, wanting to navigate away
from the jeweler's website, but the young Realtor swatted
at her hand.

"You're making plans," she said, excitement clear in her
tone. "You and Gavin are really getting married. April is
the perfect month for a wedding. It's not hot as an oven yet,
and the bluebonnets will be blooming."

Christine shook her head. "I told you we want a long
engagement not—"

"Did you say an April wedding?" Jenna joined them,
leaning over the reception desk with wide eyes. "I bet Gavin
will have a whole bunch of hot groomsmen."

Gavin's friends are half as hot as him, it's going to ␣e best weekend ever," Molly said with a laugh. "Chris-␣e, you are the luckiest woman on the planet."

"Why is Christine lucky?"

Jenna whirled around and Molly straightened as Gavin approached the desk. Christine lifted a hand to her cheek, knowing she must be blushing tomato-red. How much had he heard of her coworkers' ridiculous conversation?

"No reason," she told him, rising from the chair and straightening the hem of her silk blouse. "What are you doing here?"

"Come on, now." Molly grabbed Christine's arms and pushed her around the side of the desk. "Is that any way to greet your future bride? We were just talking about your April wedding. How many groomsmen are you planning to have? I'm just curious, you know?"

Christine squeezed shut her eyes for a quick moment and prayed for the floor to open up and swallow her whole. When everything remained the same, she glanced at Gavin with a shake of her head, mouthing "sorry."

To her utter shock, he seemed to take the whole situation in stride. He flashed his charming grin at first Molly and then Jenna. "Christine will make a beautiful spring bride."

The two women practically melted to the carpet even as Christine felt her normally nonexistent temper rise to the surface.

"Molly," she said with a calm she didn't feel, "could you watch the phones for a minute? I'd like to talk to Gavin in private."

"Private," Molly repeated in a singsong voice. "I know what that's code for."

Christine gave her a withering stare. "No. You. Don't."

The woman's smile faded, and she slid into the recep-

tionist's chair as if a teacher had just reprimanded h
"Take all the time you need," she said.

Jenna nodded. "I can help, too."

"Thank you. We'll be in my office." She raised an eyebrow in Gavin's direction, and when he winked, she thought she might feel steam coming out of her ears. She turned and stalked down the hall to her office.

"I like the sound of *private*," he said as he closed the door behind them.

"Are you out of your mind?" she demanded through clenched teeth. She wanted to scream the words, but the last thing she needed was Maddie or Valene, who was still in town from the weekend, running in to check on them.

"I don't think so." He took a step toward her, but she held up a hand, palm out.

"You let them believe we were getting married in three months."

Gavin was staring at her left hand, and she quickly pulled it to her side when she realized she was shaking.

"They seemed to be under that impression before I arrived on the scene."

"It was a mistake," she whispered, her cheeks growing hot again. "I was trying to correct it. We're supposed to be having a long engagement. Long enough that it will seem natural when it ends."

He shrugged. "What does the timing matter? It doesn't hurt anyone."

Me, she wanted to shout. *This whole thing is hurting me. Killing me.*

She drew in a deep breath. She would not break down in front of him. "What's going on between us?" she asked quietly.

He blinked then said, "We're friends."

Oh, gah. The friend zone. Was there anything worse?

"You're scheduled to return to Denver next week. What ~ppens then?"

She held up her hand, the diamond flashing under the office's fluorescent lights. "What about this?"

"I've been thinking about that." He shoved his hands into his pockets and stared at a spot beyond her shoulder. "I know this thing started as a favor. You helping me out to distract my family."

She nodded and wished she'd never agreed to any of it.

"But we've had a ton of fun these past few weeks. It's been a blast."

A blast. A blast right through her heart.

"What are you saying, Gavin?"

He met her gaze then, but she couldn't read the expression in his eyes. He smiled, all easy charm, and it was like looking at a stranger.

"Austin's a quick flight to Denver. We can still hang out. Long weekends. Holidays. I come down to Texas often enough."

"So we'd keep dating?" Christine pressed a hand to her chest. Somehow she thought she'd be overjoyed at his words. He didn't want their time together to end. But the ache in her heart grew deeper with every passing second.

"That's the plan. Of course we'd have to deal with the pretend engagement but—"

"You'd be my boyfriend?"

He lifted one hand and massaged the back of his neck. "If you want to put a label on it."

Her eyes narrowed, and he must have realized that was the wrong answer, because he flashed a sheepish smile. A "getting out of the dog house" smile.

"We spent the night together," she told him.

"It was wonderful," he agreed. "When I think about y
in my arms, it makes me want—"

"Then you left," she interrupted, needing to keep this
conversation on track. Even if she felt like the two of them
were stuck on a runaway train heading for certain disaster.
"You rushed out of there like I'd done something wrong."

"Not you, Christine. Never you." He shook his head.
"But this arrangement started with me asking you to live
a lie. I feel like I've taken advantage of you, and the fact
that we slept together only makes it worse."

Ouch. Just when she thought the pain couldn't cut any
deeper, Gavin managed it.

"I've got my life in Denver," he continued, running a
hand through his hair. "You're here."

"A quick flight away," she muttered, repeating his words.

"I never imagined things would go this way. I care about
you, more than I ever thought possible."

It was difficult to focus on his words over the roaring in
her own ears. Christine had spent most of her life feeling
like she wasn't enough. That she shouldn't expect too much.
That scraps of affection or love with conditions placed on
them were her lot in life.

Being with Gavin had changed that. She'd changed, and
even if it meant losing him, she wasn't willing to go back
to being the doormat she'd been before.

"I love you," she said quietly and the words felt right on
her tongue. Based on the stricken look that crossed Gavin's
face before he schooled his features, he hadn't been expecting her to say them. She tried for a smile, but it felt as if
her cheeks were made of ice. "I didn't mean for it to happen. I didn't even want it to happen." She managed a hoarse
laugh. "You're kind of irresistible."

"I'm not," he immediately countered.

I wish that were the case," she told him. "Do you know
ve had a crush on you forever?"

He shook his head, his jaw going slack.

"Yeah," she breathed. "So when you asked me to pose
as your girlfriend—and then fiancée—for a few weeks, it
was a no-brainer." She made a fist and gently knocked on
the side of her head. "Turns out I should have thought it
through a little more. I thought it would be a fun lark, you
know? My chance with a guy so far out of my league it's
like we aren't even playing the same sport."

"That's not true," he whispered.

"Which is exactly my problem," she admitted, crossing
her arms over her chest. "Because you made me believe
we had a chance. I lost sight of the lark part of things and
began to believe what was happening between us was real."

"Christine, you have to understand—"

"Let me finish, Gavin. I need to say this, and you need to
understand it." She pressed a hand to her hammering heart.
"I'm more than I ever believed, and you helped me see that. I
wish I could have gotten there on my own, but I'll be forever
grateful for the gift you've given me. I know now that I deserve
all my hopes and dreams coming true when it comes to love."

"You do."

"You deserve to believe in yourself, too."

He took a step back as if she'd hit him, then gave a
startled laugh. "I don't think my self-esteem was ever in
question."

"There's more to you than your career and your pen-
chant for hurtling yourself down treacherous mountains
or climbing sheer rock faces or any of the other extreme
activities you do."

"I don't think so," he said with another hollow laugh.
"All that extreme business keeps me pretty busy."

"You're a good man." She ignored his attempt t
levity to their conversation. "You have a big heart a
protective streak a mile long. You're dedicated and kind-

"Tell that to the companies that I've managed to put o
of business for the firm's clients."

"You have so much to give if you'd allow yourself to see
it. I can imagine you as a husband and a father—"

He held up his hands. "Whoa, there."

But she wasn't finished. "I can imagine growing old
with you and being at your side for whatever life brings.
I don't want a casual, long-distance...whatever with you,
Gavin. I want it all." She swiped at her cheeks when tears
clouded her vision. "I *deserve* it all."

"Yes," he whispered then closed his eyes. When he
opened them again, the emotion she'd seen there moments
earlier had vanished, and she had to wonder if she'd imagined it in the first place. "But what if I'm not the man to
give it to you?"

She drew in a breath and said the words that she'd never
expected to utter. The words that broke her heart. "Then
I'll find it with someone else."

Gavin stared at her as if he couldn't believe she'd be
able to dismiss him so easily. But it wasn't easy. It felt as
though she'd reached into her own chest to squeeze her
heart until she could barely tolerate the pain. At the same
time there was no doubt in her mind that she'd walk away
if he couldn't give her what she wanted.

As hard as she'd fallen for him over these past few
weeks, she'd also learned to value herself. She wanted to
be with a man who could do the same, and while it might
destroy her to have to accept Gavin wasn't that man, it was
a chance she had to take.

"I don't know what to say," he admitted.

That simple statement made her shoulders sag. It seemed

ous. She'd laid her heart out bare to him. He could
it in his arms or walk away and ignore her feelings
orse, stomp all over her love for him. She hoped beyond
pe that he'd choose her, that she hadn't misread or created
n her own mind the deep emotion she saw in his green eyes.

"I think," she whispered, slipping the diamond ring from
her finger and holding out to him, "that tells us both everything we need to know."

He stared at her for several long moments and then took
the ring from her, shoving it into his pocket. She hated to
see the pain in his gaze. Even though her own heart was
breaking, it didn't give her any relief to know that Gavin
was just as unhappy with this turn of events.

Still, she wouldn't compromise on what she knew she
deserved. Not for him or anyone.

"You should probably go," she whispered, gesturing to
her desk crowded with files. "I have a lot to get through
this afternoon."

He gave a jerky nod but didn't leave. It was as if he was
rooted in place, unable to move forward or back.

"Gavin, please. Don't make this harder on either of us."

"So it's the end?" he asked as if he couldn't quite believe it.

And she wasn't willing to cut him off entirely. It would
be like chopping off her own arm. "For now. We'll still be
friends...of a sort. Unless..."

He swayed toward her, pulled by an invisible thread.
"Unless what?"

Her mouth felt like it was filled with sawdust. How was
she supposed to answer? She'd told him she loved him, and
he'd given her nothing in return. "I'm not sure," she admitted. "Maybe one of us will figure it out."

"Okay, then," he said, his tone hollow. "Goodbye, Christine. For now."

Then he turned and walked away.

Chapter 16

Gavin drove around for hours after leaving Christine's office and eventually ended up on the highway, heading east toward Houston. He'd turned off his phone after five calls in a row from Maddie, four from Schuyler and one last call from Valene.

Obviously, word had gotten out that he and Christine were over. He still couldn't quite believe she'd…what? Broken up with him? Yes, they'd spent the past several weeks together but could it really be considered dating given how their relationship started?

His heart stuttered at the thought of losing her, offering a clear answer that his brain was trying to ignore.

She said she believed in him, told him she loved him, and somehow that honest admission had made every doubt and fear he'd ever had buzz through his veins like a swarm of angry bees.

It was one thing to be a part of her life within the con-

of their arrangement. Quite another to truly open
elf up to her. He might be a success at plenty in his
, but he'd never been able to handle personal relation-
ips for more than a short time.

His belief that he wasn't built for lasting love now felt
like a cop-out. He could be fearless on the slopes or in his
job but he was a coward when it counted.

The pain in her beautiful blue eyes had been like a knife
to the chest. He wanted to be angry with her. They'd had
a deal, and she'd gone and changed everything with her
sweet honesty.

He turned up the radio, trying to drown out the voices
in his head telling him he was an idiot. Two hours later
he pulled into the long, winding driveway that led to his
childhood home.

Once again he thought about the charred shell of the
Robinson house. He couldn't imagine that kind of tragedy
befalling his parents' home.

He parked and started up the walk to the front door,
which opened before he'd made it to the top step.

"What a wonderful surprise," his mother said, opening her arms.

He enfolded her in a tight hug, probably taking more
comfort from his mom's embrace than a grown man should.
He was too emotionally spent to care.

"I wanted to see you before I head back to Denver."

She pulled away, patting his arms. "I thought you were
in Austin until the end of next week?"

"I… Yeah…looks like I'm going to be leaving earlier
than planned."

He followed her into the house as she glanced over her
shoulder. "Any special reason?" she asked and something
in her tone made him stop in his tracks.

"They got to you," he muttered.

"Who?"

"The trifecta of terror." When she didn't stop walking toward the kitchen, he trailed after her. "Otherwise known as my three sisters."

"Would you like a glass of tea?"

"Sure. Thanks."

"I made banana muffins this morning."

"Okay." He took a seat at the island, drumming his fingers against the cool marble countertop. "Which one of them called?"

"I spoke with Maddie about an hour ago," his mother admitted. "She was worried about you and wanted to know if you'd contacted your father or me."

"Does she know I'm here?"

Barbara pulled a glass from the cabinet then took a pitcher of iced tea out of the refrigerator. "I texted her when I saw you coming up the drive. All three of them were worried."

He snorted. "Doubtful. More likely they all wanted to lecture me on how badly I messed things up with Christine."

She set the glass of tea in front of him then took a glass container of muffins from the pantry and opened the lid. "From the look on your face, I don't think you need that lecture."

"Which wouldn't have stopped Maddie."

His mother inclined her head as if considering that. "You're right."

He plucked a muffin from the container and popped the whole thing into his mouth.

"Those are made for biting," his mother gently admonished.

e finished chewing and then swallowed. His mom was excellent baker. "Gets to the same place either way."

She smiled. "Just like there are many paths to love."

"Wow," he murmured.

"Not the smoothest transition, I'll admit. But I assume you've driven all this way because you want to talk about your troubles."

He shook his head. "I want to eat muffins, drink iced tea and find a stupid action movie to watch on TV. I don't want to talk."

When Barbara said nothing in response, Gavin sighed. "Can I have another muffin first?"

"Bring it into the family room. We'll be more comfortable there."

He grabbed a muffin and his tea and then followed her into the wood-paneled family room. Dropping down on the overstuffed couch, he placed the glass on the coffee table and ate the muffin, again in one bite.

"It was all fake," he blurted, rubbing a hand across his eyes.

His mother's gentle gaze didn't waver. "Your relationship with Christine?"

"The engagement, the ring…everything." He nodded. "Schuyler was pushing me about my love life at Maddie's wedding, trying to set me up with every single woman she knew. It's been like that for a while. I'm not sure why everyone cares so much about me settling down, but I got sick of having people in my personal business. Who cares if I don't date seriously or stay single forever?"

"Your sisters want you to be happy," Barbara said.

Gavin leveled a look at her. "It's not just them. You and Dad are the same way. No one believes I can manage my own happiness. I know you mean well, but it makes me crazy. Did you ever think that I'm just not cut out for a committed relationship?"

"Not once."

His chest constricted at her quiet confidence.

"You're wrong," he whispered. "Clearly. Just ask Christine."

"It doesn't sound as if your feelings for her are fake."

"Not now," he admitted. "I guess not even at the beginning. I always liked her..." He closed his eyes for a moment. "I'm embarrassed to admit I never really noticed her before Maddie's wedding. She was the nice girl who worked for Dad."

"She was more than that."

"Yes...well..." Condensation pooled around the lip of the iced tea glass, and he ran a finger across it before taking a long drink.

"Tell me how this fake yet not-so-fake relationship started."

"I lied to Schuyler at Maddie's reception. Told her I had a girlfriend so she'd stop with the matchmaking business."

"Did she stop?"

"She didn't believe me," he said, shaking his head.

"Your sister knows you well."

"Lucky me."

"True."

He felt the wisp of a smile curve his mouth. Neither his sisters nor his mother would let him get away with much, and he loved them for it. Mostly.

"She was pushing me on the identity of my mystery woman and why I hadn't brought her as my plus one. I'd been dancing with Christine earlier in the night and told her how annoyed I was with the pressure to settle down. I'm not sure why, although I was grateful at the time, but she stepped in with Schuyler and claimed that *she* was my girlfriend."

"Schuyler believed that?"

His smile grew as he thought about Christine coming to his rescue that night. It had been refreshing, spontaneous and sexy as hell. "Christine is a great office manager, but she might have missed her calling with acting. She convinced Schuyler. She convinced *me*."

"Do you know she's always had a bit of a crush on you?"

"Not at the time." He frowned. "How did you?"

"Oh, sweetie. It's a mother's job to understand those kinds of things. That's part of the reason it made me happy to hear you two were together. She's got such a good heart, and you deserve someone like that."

"I don't," he whispered. "I hurt her, Mom."

"Because your feelings weren't the same as hers? I saw the two of you together. It didn't look fake." She leaned forward on her elbows. "No offense, son, but you aren't an actor."

"I cared…" He paused then said, "I *care* about her. I didn't expect it and things would have been so much easier if we'd stuck to the plan of having fun while I was in Austin. The engagement raised the stakes even more. Then it became more. I even suggested that we keep seeing each other after I go back to Denver."

"Where's the problem?"

"She told me she loved me." His body went tight as he waited for his mom's response.

"How dare she," Barbara murmured.

"Exactly."

His mother reached over and gave him a soft swat to the side of the head.

"What was that for?"

"Maybe I'm hoping to knock some sense into you amazing woman said she loves you and that's bad?"

"It means she has expectations," he said, then cringe

"And?"

"I've never been great with that. I don't date seriously. I'm not built for it. Why can't anyone understand that?"

She held up her hand and ticked off responses on her fingers. "One, because it's not true. Two, because it's a weak excuse. Three, because you love her, too."

He automatically shook his head. "I don't. I can't."

"Gavin."

"Mom, every woman I've ever dated has told me I'm not husband material. I'm perfect for a good time, a few laughs and fun weekends away. I don't stick."

"They were wrong."

"I've dated a *lot* of women," he said quietly, embarrassed at having this conversation with the woman who raised him but needing someone to understand just the same.

"I'm aware," she answered.

"I've messed up with plenty of them. Not on purpose but in the same way I ruined things with Christine."

"You only have to get it right once."

He shook his head. "I don't…" He closed his eyes and let the truth wash over him. "I love her," he whispered.

"Yes," his mother answered simply.

"But what if I hurt her and—" His lungs burned as he drew air in. "What if I'm not enough? What if I can't be the man she deserves? What if I end up with my heart broken?"

"My sweet boy," his mother whispered as if she was comforting a toddler with a skinned knee. "You are so brave and adventurous."

"No. I'm a spineless coward. When things got serious, I turned tail. She has no reason to give me another chance."

ne loves you."

s if that was reason enough.

"But—"

"Are you going to try to make it work? No one can force you. Not your sisters or me. The choice is yours, Gavin. How much do you love her?"

"With more of my heart than I even realized existed."

"What's the worst thing that could happen?"

He blinked as understanding dawned. "Giving up on this chance at happiness. I have to fight for her to take me back. If she doesn't, I'll respect her decision. But if I don't try, then I'm going to live the rest of my life regretting it."

"Can I give you a piece of advice?"

He laughed softly. "Isn't that what you've been doing this whole time in your subtle way?"

Barbara patted his hand. "Make it count. You're all about taking risks, and the stakes don't get any higher than when you're putting your heart on the line. Go big or go home."

"Really?"

"Would you ski down a bunny hill when the double black is there for the taking?"

He laughed. "You're comparing Christine to a ski slope?"

"I'm telling you not to hold back."

Okay. He could do that. His mother was right. He'd hurt Christine and now he had to convince her to try again. She deserved to have him risk everything.

He stood abruptly. "I've got to go."

"Back to Austin?"

"To Denver," he clarified, then held up a hand when his mother frowned. "Trust me. I'm going to make this count."

"I do trust you."

"Thanks, Mom. For everything." He gave her a quick

hug, then headed for his car. His dad walked into the ⎽
just as Gavin was exiting.

"Gavin." His father's expression was stony. "We ne
to talk about—"

"I'm fixing it," he answered without breaking stride.

"Good luck, then," his dad called.

Gavin would definitely need it.

Christine checked her makeup in the compact mirror
she kept in her desk drawer Thursday morning. Not bad,
she thought, given that she'd spent most of the previous
night in tears.

She hadn't heard from Gavin after he'd left her office
on Monday, not that she'd expected to. Hoped, but not expected. The news of their breakup—if she could call it
that—had spread like wildfire through the office. If she
had to guess, she would have said that several curious ears
had been pressed to the door of Christine's office to overhear the heartbreaking conversation.

She'd tried to play it off and had managed to hold herself
together when Maddie came in and threatened revenge on
her brother for being an idiot.

Christine had claimed ending the engagement was a mutual decision, and in a way it had been. She simply hadn't
been willing to take the scraps of affection Gavin offered.
Not when she loved him so deeply. It was his own fault.
He'd been the one to help her see that she deserved more
than she normally expected. Unfortunately, that newfound
understanding made it impossible for her to accept anything less from him.

It was only when she'd gotten home and curled up on
her couch in private that the heartbreak had truly washed
over her. Princess Di had joined her on the sofa, shoving

 out into Christine and then climbing onto her lap.
wrapped her arms around the sweet dog and cried
far too long.

So for the past two days, her routine had been the same.
Game face at the office then allowing her mask to crumble
once she returned home.

Today she'd woken up with the equivalent of a broken
heart hangover. It would have been nice to call in sick and
curl in a ball on the couch with a carton of Häagen-Dazs
and the TV tuned to some reality-television marathon. But
she had to pull herself together. So she'd applied makeup,
slipped into her favorite dress and then headed for the office. She'd stopped to buy a dozen donuts on the way in,
hoping the offering of dough and sugar would somehow
prove to her coworkers that she was moving on.

As if.

She shoved the mirror into a desk drawer and headed for
the conference room. Maddie had called an all-staff meeting in order to go over the latest sales figures and strate-
gies for salvaging their declining business.

All eyes turned to Christine as she entered the room.

"Am I late?" she asked, tucking her hair behind one ear.

"Right on time," Zach answered from his place near the
projection screen at the front of the room.

When Christine went to slip into a chair near the door,
Maddie, who stood next to Zach, gestured to her. "We've
got a place for you up here."

"Okay," Christine agreed, hoping no one expected her
to speak at the meeting. When she was seated, Maddie
clasped her hands in front of her chest.

"Now that we're all here," she announced, "we've got a
special presentation today. Could someone dim the lights?"

Christine frowned as she glanced around. No one seemed surprised at how oddly the meeting was startir

Maddie took the seat across from Christine and hit button on the laptop that sat in front of her on the conference table.

A background of a tropical scene with the words, "Love is the Adventure" superimposed on top of it displayed on the wide screen.

"It doesn't matter to me where I am..."

Christine froze as Gavin spoke into the silence of the room.

"As long as I'm with you."

She darted a quick glance at Maddie, who grinned broadly as she hit the computer's keyboard. A digitally edited photo of Gavin and Christine appeared on the screen. She recognized the original photo—it had been taken at the Fortune family reunion. Gavin had an arm slung over Christine's shoulder, pulling her tight to his side. She was leaning in, her head resting on his shoulder, and they both were smiling broadly.

The happiness radiating from her in the photo was undeniable, and a fresh wave of pain stabbed at her heart. But what surprised her was that Gavin looked just as happy, at peace and content in a way she thought she'd imagined during their time together.

Instead of the background of the Mendoza Winery, it looked like they were standing in front of the Eiffel Tower.

"Whether we're traveling to the great cities of the world," he said, his tone both tender and deliberate, "or to a tropical beach..."

Maddie winked at Christine as she clicked a button on the keyboard. Christine couldn't help but smile as her face, along with Gavin's, appeared superimposed onto the bodies ople lounging on the beach. The next photo showed n skiing, and in the following one they were traversing e Great Wall of China. She laughed, as did many of her oworkers, as the photos became an unofficial "where in the world are Gavin and Christine" montage.

Gavin continued to narrate all the adventures they could have together, and hope bloomed in her chest like the first crocuses of spring pushing through hard ground. That was the life she wanted, filled with fun and adventure, and most of all with Gavin at her side for every moment of it.

When the original photo popped up on the screen once again, someone in the back of the room flipped on the lights. Christine's breath caught as Gavin came forward.

"But in the end," he said, pinning her with his gaze, "I don't care where we are or what we do as long as we're together. I thought I had things all figured out but you changed everything for me. You changed me."

She shook her head automatically. She was the one who'd changed over these past few weeks. How could he—

"I love you, Christine," he said softly as he came to stand in front of her chair. "I can't imagine my life without you. I don't want to be half in or to put any limits on us. I want it all. I want to be the man you deserve." He reached out a hand, and she placed her fingers in his, the warmth of his touch sending sparks shooting along her skin. It had only been a couple of days since she'd seen him, but she'd missed this like he'd been gone for months. When she'd heard through the office grapevine that he'd returned to Denver, she figured it was the end.

But now he was offering her a new beginning.

He pulled her to her feet and lifted her hand to his mouth, brushing a soft kiss across her knuckles. "You deserve to be loved for exactly who you are. You're beautiful inside

and out, kind and generous, and you make everythin
my life better." He squeezed her fingers. "You are my li.

"Oh," she breathed. She wasn't sure she could put to
gether any actual words without bursting into tears.

"If you give me another chance," he continued, and she
felt her eyes widen as he dropped to one knee, "I'll spend
the rest of my life showing you how much you mean to me."

There was a collective gasp in the room as he took out a
small black box, opening it to reveal the sparkling diamond
solitaire she'd already come to think of as hers.

"I don't want to wait," he told her with a hopeful smile.
"I can't imagine losing you and I promise I'll never give
you a reason to doubt me again. I love you so damn much,
Christine. Will you marry me?"

Words. She needed words. Around the galloping beat
of her heart and the blood hammering through her brain,
she managed to nod.

"Yes," she finally whispered, and Gavin let out a pent-up
breath that told her he hadn't been confident in her answer.
But she had no doubt she'd love this man forever.

"I love you," she said as he slipped the ring onto her finger. "I'll love you for all of my life, Gavin."

As he stood and kissed her, a cheer went up throughout
the room. Christine only had eyes for Gavin. She knew
her life would never be the same and she wouldn't have it
any other way.

In the past month she'd discovered a strength in herself
she hadn't known she possessed and a love with a man who
made her happy in ways she could never have imagined.
She planned to hold on tight for whatever adventure life
brought her way.

Epilogue

"I touched a fish," Christine said with a wide smile. "You must be sick of hearing me say that, but I still can't quite believe it." She giggled. "I swam with fish in the ocean and I didn't drown. It was like I was the Little Mermaid. Everything was beautiful. I can't believe I missed out on that for so long."

Gavin leaned in for a quick kiss, tucking a loose strand of hair behind her ear. They sat on two lounge chairs at an exclusive resort outside Cancún, watching shades of pink and gold streak across the evening sky.

"I'm glad you enjoyed snorkeling," he said. "Are you ready for parasailing tomorrow?"

"I'm ready for anything with you," she confirmed, then placed a hand on her stomach. "But let's not talk about it or I might lose my nerve."

"You can do it," he told her, taking her hand as he leaned back in his chair. "I believe you can do anything."

She bit down on her lower lip as tears pricked the ba▌ her eyes. Would she ever get used to his unwavering sup▌

She watched the waves curling against the shoreline several minutes, letting the sound of the surf relax her. still feel a little guilty leaving Austin when things are so tumultuous with the agency and the Fortunes."

Gavin squeezed her fingers. "We're here for the weekend, sweetheart. Maddie and Zach totally support you taking a couple of days off."

Christine nodded. Gavin had suggested the spontaneous trip to the beach over dinner with his family the evening after he'd proposed to her. Her first instinct had been to say no, but both Maddie and Kenneth, who'd driven over from Houston with Barbara for the impromptu celebration, had agreed it was a fantastic idea.

Schuyler had taken her on a quick tropical-vacation shopping spree since Christine's only bathing suit was one she'd owned since college.

Her new life would take some getting used to, but she wouldn't change a thing. Every day with Gavin would be an adventure, whether he was at her side as she conquered her fears or they were settling into a normal routine in Austin. Gavin seemed to enjoy being back in Texas, opening his law firm's Austin branch.

They'd already talked about finding a house together, and Christine had agreed to sublet her condo to her sister when they did. Her parents had been supportive and surprisingly excited for her when she'd shared the news of her engagement with them. Aimee hadn't said much but she'd shoved a wedding magazine toward Christine and mumbled that she'd marked the pages with "not hideous" bridesmaid dresses.

She hadn't bothered to reveal the details of how her relationship with Gavin had actually started. No one seemed

ot his feelings for her. After years of feeling like she
t fit, Christine had discovered that believing she was
thy of being treated with love and respect made all the
fference. They had a long way to go to become the close-
knit family her mother hoped for, but Christine actually
believed they had a chance of getting there.

So much of that had to do with how she'd changed and
grown in the past few weeks. She was becoming exactly who
she was meant to be and felt more confident than ever. She
credited Gavin for helping her to see herself in a different way.

"I don't think I've ever enjoyed the ocean like this," Gavin
said, his thumb tracing small circles on the center of her palm.

"Come on," she chided. "You don't have to pretend
like this is something new for you. I know you've been to
beaches all over the world."

"Yes," he agreed slowly, "but I was always moving, looking for the next thrill. Now I'm content. You're the best
adventure I can imagine, and I don't need anything else."

He tugged on her hand and scooted to one side of the
cushioned chair. She moved next to him, resting her head
on his chest as he wrapped his arms around her.

"Thank you," he said against the top of her head, "for
seeing something in me that I couldn't see in myself. I love
you, Christine."

"I love you, too," she whispered. The connection they
shared meant everything to her, and she was excited for
a lifetime of both big adventures and tiny moments with
Gavin. Her heart overflowed with happiness as they
watched the sun dip below the horizon. Each day would
be a new beginning and she'd cherish every single one.

* * * * *

WE HOPE YOU ENJOYED THIS BOOK FROM

HARLEQUIN
SPECIAL
EDITION

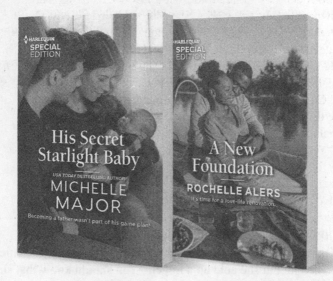

Believe in love. Overcome obstacles. Find happiness.

Relate to finding comfort and strength in the
support of loved ones and enjoy the journey
no matter what life throws your way.

6 NEW BOOKS AVAILABLE EVERY MONTH!

HSEHALO2021MAX

SPECIAL EXCERPT FROM

H HARLEQUIN

SPECIAL EDITION

Brian Fortune doesn't think he will ever find the woman he kissed at his brother's New Year's wedding. So when the search for the provenance of a mysterious gift leads him into a local antique store a few days later, he's stunned to find Emmaline Lewis, proprietor—and mystery kisser! Brian has never been the type to commit—but suddenly he knows he'll do anything to stay at Emmaline's side—for good...

*Read on for a sneak peek at
the first book in
The Fortunes of Texas: The Wedding Gift continuity,
Their New Year's Beginning,
by USA TODAY bestselling author Michelle Major!*

"I'd like to take you out on a proper date then."

"Okay." Color bloomed in her cheeks. "That would be nice." He leaned in, but she held up a finger. "You should know that since Kirby and the gang outed my pregnancy at the coffee shop, I'm not going to hide it anymore." She pressed a hand to her belly. "I'm wearing a baggy shirt tonight because it seemed easier than fielding questions from the boys, but if we go out, there will be questions. And comments."

"I don't care about what anyone else thinks," he assured her and then kissed her gently. "This is about you and me."

Those must have been the right words, because Emmaline wound her arms around his neck and drew closer. "I'm glad," she said, but before he could kiss her again, she yawned once more.

"I'll walk you to your car."

She mock pouted but didn't argue. "I'm definitely not as fun as I used to be," she told him as he picked up the bags with the leftover supplies to carry for her. "Actually I'm not sure I was ever that fun."

"As far as I'm concerned, you're the best."

After another lingering kiss, Emmaline climbed into her car and drove away. Brian watched her taillights until they disappeared around a bend. The night sky overhead was once again filled with stars, and he breathed in the fresh Texas air. He needed to stay in the moment and remember his reason for being in town and how long he planned to stay. He knew better than to examine the feeling of contentment coursing through him.

One thing he knew for certain was that it couldn't last.

Don't miss
Their New Year's Beginning
by Michelle Major,
available January 2022 wherever
Harlequin Special Edition books and ebooks are sold.

Harlequin.com

Copyright © 2021 by Harlequin Books S.A.

Get 4 FREE REWARDS!

We'll send you 2 FREE Books plus 2 FREE Mystery Gifts.

FREE
Value Over
$20

Both the **Romance** and **Suspense** collections feature compelling novels written by many of today's bestselling authors.

YES! Please send me 2 FREE novels from the Essential Romance or Essential Suspense Collection and my 2 FREE gifts (gifts are worth about $10 retail). After receiving them, if I don't wish to receive any more books, I can return the shipping statement marked "cancel." If I don't cancel, I will receive 4 brand-new novels every month and be billed just $7.24 each in the U.S. or $7.49 each in Canada. That's a savings of up to 28% off the cover price. It's quite a bargain! Shipping and handling is just 50¢ per book in the U.S. and $1.25 per book in Canada.* I understand that accepting the 2 free books and gifts places me under no obligation to buy anything. I can always return a shipment and cancel at any time. The free books and gifts are mine to keep no matter what I decide.

Choose one: ☐ **Essential Romance**
(194/394 MDN GQ6M)

☐ **Essential Suspense**
(191/391 MDN GQ6M)

Name (please print)

Address   Apt. #

City   State/Province   Zip/Postal Code

Email: Please check this box ☐ if you would like to receive newsletters and promotional emails from Harlequin Enterprises ULC and its affiliates. You can unsubscribe anytime.

Mail to the **Harlequin Reader Service:**
IN U.S.A.: P.O. Box 1341, Buffalo, NY 14240-8531
IN CANADA: P.O. Box 603, Fort Erie, Ontario L2A 5X3

Want to try 2 free books from another series? Call 1-800-873-8635 or visit www.ReaderService.com.

*Terms and prices subject to change without notice. Prices do not include sales taxes, which will be charged (if applicable) based on your state or country of residence. Canadian residents will be charged applicable taxes. Offer not valid in Quebec. This offer is limited to one order per household. Books received may not be as shown. Not valid for current subscribers to the Essential Romance or Essential Suspense Collection. All orders subject to approval. Credit or debit balances in a customer's account(s) may be offset by any other outstanding balance owed by or to the customer. Please allow 4 to 6 weeks for delivery. Offer available while quantities last.

Your Privacy—Your information is being collected by Harlequin Enterprises ULC, operating as Harlequin Reader Service. For a complete summary of the information we collect, how we use this information and to whom it is disclosed, please visit our privacy notice located at corporate.harlequin.com/privacy-notice. From time to time we may also exchange your personal information with reputable third parties. If you wish to opt out of this sharing of your personal information, please visit readerservice.com/consumerschoice or call 1-800-873-8635. **Notice to California Residents**—Under California law, you have specific rights to control and access your data. For more information on these rights and how to exercise them, visit corporate.harlequin.com/california-privacy.

STRS21MAXR2

Love Harlequin romance?

DISCOVER.

Be the first to find out about promotions, news and exclusive content!

 Facebook.com/HarlequinBooks

Twitter.com/HarlequinBooks

Instagram.com/HarlequinBooks

Pinterest.com/HarlequinBooks

You Tube YouTube.com/HarlequinBooks

ReaderService.com

EXPLORE.

Sign up for the Harlequin e-newsletter and download a free book from any series at **TryHarlequin.com**

CONNECT.

Join our Harlequin community to share your thoughts and connect with other romance readers!
Facebook.com/groups/HarlequinConnection

HSOCIAL2021MAX

HARLEQUIN

Heartfelt or thrilling, passionate or uplifting—Harlequin is more than just happily-ever-after.

With twelve different series to choose from and new books available every month, you are sure to find stories that will move you, uplift you, inspire and delight you.

SIGN UP FOR THE HARLEQUIN NEWSLETTER

Be the first to hear about great new reads and exciting offers!

Harlequin.com/newsletters

HNEWS2021MAX